Legends and Liars

Julia Knight

www.orbitbooks.net

ORBIT

First published in Great Britain in 2015 by Orbit

1 3 5 7 9 10 8 6 4 2

A CIP catalogue record for this book is available from the British Library.

ISBN 978-0-356-50409-4

Typeset in Apollo MT by Palimpsest Book Production Limited,
Falkirk, Stirlingshire
Printed and bound in Great Britain by CPI Group (UK) Ltd, Croydon CR0 4YY

Papers used by Orbit are from well-managed forests
and other responsible sources.

MIX
Paper from
responsible sources
FSC
www.fsc.org   FSC® C104740

Orbit
An imprint of
Little, Brown Book Group
Carmelite House
50 Victoria Embankment
London, EC4Y 0DZ

An Hachette UK Company
www.hachette.co.uk

www.orbitbooks.net

Chapter One

Vocho threw the dice and loudly cursed himself for a fool. Treble cat's eye, of course it was, and now he was down a hundred Ikaran bushels, or about ten bulls in Reyes money.

Kacha stood the other side of the gaming table, clothed, after something of an argument, in an Ikaran dress in the latest fashion. A silky green sheath with a split up to the thigh – Vocho had been surprised to discover his sister actually had legs – and precarious heels that made her wobble and look far more fragile than her solid frame would usually suggest. The puffed sleeves covered the fact she wasn't a soft noblewoman and that her wrists and forearms were laced with muscles and striped with old scars. Her hair had been carefully coiffed, with much swearing, to hide the scar under her eye. No sword, which had irked her the most. She'd sulked in the shadows behind the avid-eyed men and women who'd just won on betting Vocho would lose, but now Kacha raised an eyebrow and smirked.

The dice were, naturally, rigged. Not that he'd tampered with them, oh no. Conduct unbecoming to a master of the duelling guild and all that, although not being a member of the guild any longer he tended to forget that bit. It was just no fun cheating people out of their hard-earned – or as was the case in this particular den of iniquity, hard-inherited – cash. So he hadn't rigged the dice, but someone certainly had. At least they were dry in here, as opposed to highway robbery which had mostly involved him being wet and cold. They had to do something for money – supplies were dangerously low. Besides, he had a plan.

A slight dark-haired man with small sharp eyes and a nose that looked like it had been thumped one too many times swept Vocho's money off the table and into his purse, which was already heavy. "Not lucky with the dice tonight, are you?" he said in Ikaran, a language Vocho could just about communicate in if he concentrated. "Perhaps you'd care to try something else?"

Vocho feigned nonchalance with an airy wave of his hand, as though the money hadn't been most of what they had left. "Such as?"

The dark-haired man – his name had never been offered, though mostly he was called Bear for some unmentioned reason – cocked his head on one side and looked Vocho up and down. Took in the slightly worn finery, the hat on the table with its jaunty if tattered feather, the mud-stained boots that had once been polished to a high shine but were now dull and cracked with constant use. Finally his gaze rested on the one thing Vocho knew he was really interested in – his sword.

It was, Vocho had to admit, a damned fine sword. Not too heavy, though heavy enough, perfectly balanced and with a devilishly handsome basket hilt that had been the envy of many a master in the guild – it had certainly saved Vocho's fingers a time or two. The hilt was a giveaway. It was a guild duellist's sword and no mistake, and very, very illegal to be walking around with here in Ikaras. And Bear was a collector, something of a connoisseur. Vocho was banking on it.

"A duel," Bear said now, and then added, as Vocho had suspected he would, "with a twist."

"Isn't that illegal?" Vocho asked.

"No more so than gambling with dice or wearing that sword in public. Anyone doing any of those things faces the galleys or perhaps even the gallows. Well? Are you a gambling man or not?"

"What sort of twist?" Vocho was fairly sure he knew the answer because Cospel had done his research well.

"Not you or I fighting," Bear said. "You're a man who knows how to use that sword, that's clear, and as a true Ikaran I know nothing about fighting with a blade like a common mercenary. The fight would be unequal."

Common mercenary? Vocho fought hard to keep the indignation from his voice. "I could tie one hand behind my back?"

A disturbance behind him made him turn for a second – Kacha had fallen off her heels and was being helped back to her feet by an amused bystander.

"Oh no," Bear said. "I value my skin far too highly."

"Who then?"

Vocho was pretty sure he knew the answer to this as well. Bear would pick someone who looked like they didn't know one end of a sword from the other but who was actually not too shabby.

From behind him came the unmistakable sound of metal hitting flagstones.

"I'm sorry, is this your knife?" Kacha said. "What? Oh, I see. That's the sharp end, is it? How exciting."

"We each pick someone to fight for us." Bear's sly grin made Vocho struggle to keep his own face straight. "You can pick first."

Vocho made a show of weighing it all up before he nodded slowly. "All right. What's the bet?"

Bear hefted his purse in his hands — there was enough money in there to keep Vocho and Kacha fed and housed for a month, and maybe enough to see about other things besides. "This against, well, what do you have left?"

Vocho pretended to think about it and then put his sword very deliberately on the table. "This. If your man can take it off mine, it's yours. If not, if my man takes the sword from yours then the money is mine."

"You have yourself a bet," Bear said as though he knew something Vocho didn't, giving Vocho palpitations, but there wasn't much choice by this point. They shook, and Bear's grin swelled into a full-blown smirk. "You choose first."

Vocho eyed the small crowd around the tables. Unlike Reyes, which had done away with titles and replaced its nobility with clockers who'd turned out just as feckless if not as inbred, Ikaras still had a full complement of blue-blooded young men and women with lofty titles and nothing much better to do than fritter away their time and money. Duelling had been popular for a time at least. Until too many ended up with serious holes in them or worse, and the Ikaran king had declared duels, along with the gambling that seemed to be the spur for most of them, illegal. That hadn't stopped events like this, only driven them from grand palaces to dingy little backrooms where the nobles' finery seemed incongruous in the smoke that leaked through from the rank bars that fronted them.

This particular lot didn't seem out of the ordinary, from

what Vocho had gathered since they'd arrived here a few weeks previously. Ikarans were less foppish and more direct than Reyens, perhaps, but no less vicious, or devious, when it came to it. But of course he and his sister had an advantage – a duelling guild education. Not to mention that in Ikaras ladies did not duel, ever. Ladies did not pick up anything with a sharp edge, or not in public at any rate. Vocho's surprise for Bear.

"My sister, I think, could take any one of you."

Bear grinned as though that was exactly the answer he'd been expecting. He pointed to a pigeon-chested young man in the corner, wheezing over a water pipe almost as big as he was. Bear waved him over and whispered in his ear. The young man nodded as though this was no surprise and started making himself ready. This seemed to include copious draughts of what was presumably something to sober him up – the water pipes' more insidious ingredients made all sorts of things dance in front of the smoker's eyes.

"Whoops," Kacha said, and metal rang on stone again.

A few muttered about ladies not duelling, but Bear sliced a glare around the room and they all shut up.

"You're on." Vocho picked up his sword and threw it to Kacha, who caught it neatly, unsheathed it and kicked off the heels she'd sworn about so much earlier.

To Vocho's consternation, Bear didn't look the slightest bit surprised. He nodded to one of his cronies while the rest made some room, and after a few moments Bear's duellist stepped forward looking far too at home with his sword.

The duellers sized each other up, before Kacha gave a brief salute and went for the other. The pokey backroom was soon drowned in the noise of swords clashing, the feet of the crowd stamping, a flurry of side bets between Bear's cronies. Bear's man was better than he looked – the pigeon chest disappeared, the shoulders came back. He was nifty on his feet too and had a style that seemed to confound Kacha at every turn. She was fighting in the Icthian style, a time-honoured method that was loose, fast flowing and devious, using not just the sword but everything else in range too – feet, elbows, handy bits of furniture. Above all it was elegant, which was not a description you could apply to Bear's man.

His sword was of a style Vocho hadn't seen before but had heard about. A *palla* they called it, a brutal-looking thing with a thick curved blade and not much of a guard, made for quick killing via brute strength not stylish swordplay. He used it far better than his looks had led Vocho to believe too, in a style Vocho had never seen before, a series of savage chops that appeared to give no thought to defence, yet somehow Kacha never got a touch on him. The man wasn't quick as such, but he was good.

Still, Vocho had every confidence in his sister. She hadn't been the guild master's assassin all that time for nothing. She didn't like using other people's blades, but as hers were still tucked up safe at the guild where they couldn't get at them, she didn't have much choice. She looked like she was missing the dagger she often kept in her off hand though, and was hard pressed to keep her guard up. She was quick enough, but if this went on too long she'd tire against the heavier blade and then he'd have her.

Naturally, Kacha being the bloody perfect person she was, she had a plan. She grabbed a bottle of something from a low table with her off hand on the way past, smashed it so she held the neck and used the jagged end to harry her opponent even as she thrust and parried with her sword. A slash to the face, a vicious thrust to the stomach, which the man only just avoided more by luck than judgement. She got in a few kicks as well, when she had the chance, but this was no easy opponent. For every thrust he had his *palla* in the way, for every feint he was ready, for every kick to somewhere soft he just wasn't there, and all the time that heavy blade was swirling, chopping, slashing, coming a shade too close for Vocho's liking.

The crowd catcalled and jeered, telling the man – Haval they called him, an odd name – to get on with it and beat her. All in all, this was taking a lot longer than Vocho had hoped. Kass must be off form, he thought, because despite the strangeness of the man's style she should have had the bugger by now.

Then she almost did have him – a vicious slash across where his face had been a second ago with the broken bottle while her sword arrowed towards his torso ready to winkle out his liver. It probably would have gone quite badly for him if the crowd hadn't erupted in displeasure, pelting Kass with bottles and other less savoury missiles from all sides. They could have coped even with that – Kass ignored them or batted them away and Voch was ready to step in, for Kass's sake not his own glory, of course – if not for the sudden prick of a blade at Vocho's waist.

"Even if she wins, you lose," Bear said into his ear. "I mean to have that sword. The sword that once belonged to the renowned, and disgraced, Vocho of the guild, the sword that killed a priest and started a war. Correct? Thought so. Now, tell your lovely sister to stop. Haval will have no hesitation killing her, and he can, believe me. Even Kacha the noted duellist can't stop him."

Vocho looked down at the whisper-thin stiletto that had pierced his tunic, his shirt, and threatened to do the same to his navel. Just as he was about to say screw it and give it a go, two of Bear's cronies came up beside him. The rest were crowded around Haval and Kacha, and other daggers were being drawn, flickering in the dim and smoky light. Sharp blades might be illegal in Ikaras, but money bought a lot of leeway.

"It's all about the sword in Reyes, yes? Or at least it was until they got those clockwork guns. Not here though. No duelling. No swords, no guns or not many, not yet. Lots of magicians though, enforcing the laws. So here we do things secretly. Subtle, not like you Reyes pigs. No chance for Vocho the Great to show off."

"You seem to have the advantage of me," Vocho managed, trying to move without seeming to. Didn't help because the blade point followed his belly button, and Bear's cronies had theirs join in. If he wasn't careful he might lose a nipple.

"As I should, seeing how much I paid to find out," Bear said. "Although you two stick out like barbarians here. Now, your sister or your innards. Your choice."

Not much of a choice then, really.

"Er, Kass? I think we're all done here," he shouted. "Hand the nice man the sword, would you?"

A sudden stillness at the other end of the room. Vocho could feel the outraged question even if he couldn't see her face behind all the onlookers. Silence followed, and Vocho didn't need to see to know she was assessing the situation, the number of people ranged against them. Luckily for his insides, she wasn't quite as rash as he was.

Finally a clang followed by a tinkling crash as she dropped his sword and the bottle.

"Excellent," Bear said. "Now, I wonder how much we'll get for turning in two Reyes spies in this time of coming war? Get moving."

A more insistent prick of a dagger into Vocho's back.

He moved but being Vocho couldn't keep his mouth shut. "I don't suppose you'll get much for us, considering we aren't spies."

Bear laughed in his ear. "Reyens in Ikaras, with all the trouble lately? What else would you be? I have to say the king was very upset with that business between you and Licio. He stood to make a great deal of money, and our king does not like losing that kind of opportunity. I'm sure he'd be most pleased to meet you, even if you aren't actually spying. I shall certainly be most pleased to spend the reward money, which I'm sure will be very generous."

Kacha stumbled in front of Vocho as someone pushed her from behind. The carefully coiffed fair hair had come unbound and now flopped against her forehead in its more usual manner. "Nice one, Voch."

As Bear shoved him on towards the door, Vocho took stock. It looked like they were in seriously big trouble here. The room only had one door, which had several of Bear's cronies loitering by it, supposedly blunted ceremonial daggers drawn. The single window was firmly shuttered, and with a half dozen men in front of it in any case. They might have more luck when they got out of there and into the inn beyond, where Cospel was waiting for them, hopefully still both sober and incognito. Vocho wasn't prepared to bet on it though.

A figure appeared in the doorway, silhouetted against the glare from the inn's lamps behind him. Vocho had the strangest feeling he should know who it was, but even when the figure stepped forward he couldn't place the man for some seconds.

He was tall and slender, older than Vocho by a decade or more, and he moved like he was on oiled springs. One hand was on a duelling sword even finer than Vocho's. He cocked an eyebrow at Bear, and his smile was as sharp as daggers. It was only when Vocho noticed all the gewgaws and trinkets adorning the man's very fine clothes – clothes with not a speck of dust or the ghost of a crease – that he realised who he was looking at.

Bear got there first. "Domenech?"

"The very same." Dom gave Vocho the sort of look that said, "Shut up and let me do the talking." He was glad to leave him to it. Sort of. The Dom he knew hadn't been that smart, but this Dom looked like he might be. It was a distraction, at least, one that he and Kacha might take advantage of. They shared a look, and he knew she was as ready as he was, if the opportunity should arise.

Then it was too late for any of the talking that Dom had in mind. Three of Bear's men lunged at him, and the room became a whirl of men and knives, one flashing duellist's sword and one heavy, chopping sort of sword as Haval decided that Dom was his for the taking.

The blade was still pricking Vocho around his kidneys and Bear had his arm twisted up behind his back as well. He obviously hadn't been paying attention elsewhere though because a sudden "Oof!" sounded by Vocho's ear, Bear's grip loosened, the blade fell away, and when Vocho turned, Kacha was standing like some sort of vengeful goddess with a high-heeled shoe in each hand. The end of one heel had blood on it, as did Bear's head down on the floor. His two cronies were too stunned to move for a second – a second too long, as Kacha aimed a vicious balls-high kick at one and Vocho used his elbows and fists to good effect on the other.

Finally they seemed unencumbered by anyone trying to kill them. Kill them right this second, at least. Vocho cocked an eyebrow at Kass and her unorthodox weapons.

"Someone had to bloody well pay for me getting dressed up like this. Be thankful it wasn't you." Kass took a swipe at a passing man with one heel, getting him a cracking shot in the stomach and bending him over, breathless. "Now stop pissing about and let's get out of here."

"That's a plan I can get behind. Where's Dom?"

Dom was by the shuttered window, having seemingly attracted the attention of just about every man with a weapon in the place. Even as they watched, Haval took out a chunk of shutter at Dom's back, missing him by a scant hair as Dom twisted away, skewering another man as he went. Another chop from that brutal blade, another chunk out of the shutter, and Vocho could see what Dom was about even if Haval was too caught up in trying to hack off his head to notice. Kass saw it at the same time.

Cospel appeared at the doorway, semaphoring desperately with his eyebrows. Vocho had been studying those eyebrows for a long time now, and was fairly sure that Cospel used them to articulate things he dare not say out loud to his employers. This time they seemed to say, "Over here, you stupid bastards."

Vocho went, though Kass hesitated. "But Dom?"

He grabbed her arm and yanked her over to the doorway and Cospel.

"Said he'd provide a distraction for you, miss." Cospel had a heavy pewter tankard in one hand and looked about ready to brain anyone who came too close. "And not to let you be stupid and stay in here."

A thundering crack came from across the room. Haval seemed to have realised what Dom was about, but too late. His heavy sword had burst open the shutter, and with a wink and a wave Dom flipped through the opening and out into the night. Haval roared after him, but the others seemed less keen to follow. Given that four of them were bleeding out onto the floor, Vocho couldn't blame them.

That said, there were eight Ikarans left upright and only three of them, armed with a tankard and some shoes, and the Ikarans seemed to like the odds of that much better. Two of the bolder ones began to advance, and the others fell in behind. Where in hells was his sword? There, half obscured by bleeding bodies where Bear had dropped it. Well, he wasn't leaving without it. Vocho gave Kass a shove through the doorway, spun and dropped, grabbed the sword and bounced back up – just in time for the lead two Ikarans to slash at his face. The rest came round, trying to flank him.

He flashed them a bright grin, saluted with his sword as though about to launch himself at them, then stepped back through the doorway. As soon as he was through Kacha slammed it shut and turned the key in the lock. Which just left them with a bar full of curious and not especially friendly-looking drunks. When the barman pulled out a thick slab of wood with some nails driven through it, followed by some of his patrons whipping out some impromptu but serious-looking weapons, Vocho made a snap decision.

"I say we run."

Kass winced – shying from a fight didn't come naturally – but said, "I don't think I ever heard you say that before, but you could be right. You've got the sword. You keep them busy while we clear a path. Make it quick, OK?"

"Thanks, I think."

"You're welcome." She was still smarting about the dress, he could tell.

Then there was no more time for talk. Two hulking great bruisers, the worse for wear but still steady enough on their feet, lumbered in front of Vocho.

"Here, ain't you that Vocho bloke?" one asked, and Vocho couldn't help but preen a little that they knew him.

"Nah, he's too little," the second one said.

"'T's him. I seen the pictures in the paper, and besides Bear said so. This here bloke caused all that ruckus in Reyes. Vocho the *Imbècil*, Bear said – that was it."

Vocho the *what*? His Ikaran wasn't up to much, but that certainly didn't sound like Vocho the Great, because he'd learned that word almost first of all. He swished the sword in front of their stupid eyes and prepared to show them that whatever *imbècil* meant, he wasn't one. Nothing like a good—

Kass yanked the back of his shirt. "God's cogs, will you come on? The guards'll be here any second, and you've got a ruddy great sword in your hand."

The two lumberers came for him brandishing a wicked set of brass knuckles and a foot-long metal spike, but a swipe of his sword kept them back. A *clonk* behind him – Cospel using the tankard to good effect – a muffled scream as Kass's shoe caught a man somewhere painful, and the doorway to the street was free. Lumberer number one looked like he'd just worked out that being a good foot taller than Vocho was probably all the advantage he needed, so Vocho didn't need any encouragement to throw himself through the door after Kass and Cospel.

Then they were running down the street as fast as they could, with a swiftly dwindling crowd after them. A few twists and turns, and they were on their own and out of breath. They stopped. Cospel bent over his knees, gasping. The multicoloured lights that shone from every building, leaked from all the stored sunlight of the glass that covered the city, made his face look like that of a demented clown.

"I could have taken them, no problem," Vocho said,

leaning against the cool throbbing blue glass of an upmarket tailor's. "What does *imbècil* mean?"

Cospel hesitated, and his eyebrows didn't know where to look. "Sort of . . . renowned. Infamous? Yes, that's it." His Ikaran was far better than either Vocho's or Kass's, though none of them was fluent yet.

"Renowned? Are you sure?" The way the lumberers had said it, Vocho wasn't so certain.

"Er, yes. Pretty sure. Anyway, look what I got." Cospel held up a clinking bag. "Once Dom got started, it was easy to pick up all the winnings."

Vocho took a look in the bag. Not bad for a night's work. "Cospel, have I ever told you that you're a marvel?"

"No, but you can say it again if you like, preferably in cold hard cash."

They made their way through the pulsing lights of the foreign city to the cramped rooms above a cobbler's that were their current home. Kass was unnaturally quiet all the way, and Vocho got the feeling it wasn't just because she was wearing a dress and sulking about it.

"Two things," she said when they got home and Vocho broached the subject. "One, how did Dom know where we were? Two, if he knows, who else does, and do they want to kill us?"

Chapter Two

Alicia laid her hands on the table, where Orgull, king of Ikaras, could see the markings that swirled over them. His eyes glazed as she showed him wealth and power falling into his lap, if only he listened to her.

"Reyes is weak," she murmured, a view echoed by the men and women around the king – his advisers, hangers-on and a few relatives. "And I – we – can help you make it weaker, so that you could just breathe on it and Reyes will fall. All that it has can be yours."

Orgull blinked hard and shook his head. Alicia smiled and the markings changed, faded away. Subtle, that was the way. Don't let him think he's being manipulated. She glanced at the life-warriors who stood, implacable as mountains, behind him, ready to die for him, trained from birth to know that he was the god of their world.

Orgull sat up straighter, his ceremonial knife glittering with every kind of jewel known to man, the folds of his opulent silks stretching over his pudgy form. He thought the silks made him look kingly, that the knife, even blunted, showed how much power he had. Instead they merely reinforced Alicia's impression of a soft and weak-willed fool, who valued surface appearances over substance. A man easily swayed by appeals to his vanity.

"Licio will be coming to negotiate. He's naïve at best, a pawn for you to play with," she said. "He wants your help to take back Reyes and make himself king. But if we do this right, Reyes and Ikaras will have one king. You. No less than your eminence deserves. Maybe not a king any more; with two countries you'll be an emperor for an empire."

The tang of blood tainted the air, and she could see the idea take root in his head. An Ikaran empire with him at its head. Control over whole mountain ranges rich in coal and iron, which other states would clamour to buy. And the city of Reyes – a harbour that could withstand any storm, the technology and resources to make things Ikaras could only dream of, and the guild. With the duelling guild within his borders, in his pocket, together with the life-warriors and a source of good steel, expansion towards the rest of the nearby states would be only a matter of time.

Orgull narrowed his eyes, but she didn't mistake the wistful look at her hands, the king maybe hoping that the markings would show him an even grander future.

"What are you suggesting? And does Sabates know that you're here?"

"It was Sabates who sent me," she said truthfully enough. She hadn't yet gathered enough power to topple the bastard from his position as head magician. Soon, though. Very soon, and then she'd show everyone. "He offers you our full support. The prelate of Reyes will fall, leaving Reyes even weaker. The guild will have a master of our choosing – Licio – who will do as we ask. All you then need to do is wait for the proper moment and leave everything else to us."

Orgull glanced at his advisers, but their answer was a foregone conclusion. She let a few markings writhe across her hands: Reyes in flames, Ikaras ascendant, Orgull triumphant. A nod from Orgull was all she needed.

"And our previous matter?"

"Ikaras has responded with commendable patriotism to your request," Orgull said and waved forward one of his advisers. "I suspect we have every Reyen in the city in custody. They're costing me a fortune to feed. Here's a full list, as requested, though none appear to match your descriptions." A sly look. "Might I ask why you want these two in particular?"

"All the better to help you, of course."

Alicia pulled on her gloves and made her way out of the audience chamber past starry-eyed guards and blindly grinning advisers. It was really all so easy if you had magic at your fingertips. A drop of blood here, a moving mark on her hand there to mesmerise the target, and then they would do precisely as you asked. Not for long, not unless you had some serious blood to play with, but long enough, especially if you were experienced, and Alicia was very experienced. She'd made it her business to be, her life's work with only two purposes in mind.

The king's palace was a fine one, a relic of the Castan empire, which had fallen centuries ago. It was full of golden sunlight, which streamed in the huge windows, lying in fat yellow stripes across ochre floors inlaid with all sorts of coloured stone. Fans powered by, she was given to understand, the sun-filled glass that covered every building, moved the air around in lazy swirls but managed to dull the molten-copper heat of an Ikaran summer.

It hadn't taken much persuading to hammer out the few last details. A nudge here, a prod there at an ambition the man already held dear, so the king would have no idea that he hadn't proposed everything himself. Sabates would be very pleased – a previous audience had paved the way, led to an edict that all Reyens in the city were to be turned over for a hefty reward. Vocho and Kacha couldn't help but be found. Neither could speak Ikaran worth a damn, and Kacha with her blonde southerner hair, Vocho and his big mouth, they'd stick out like plums in cream.

Sabates would be pleased with this further agreement too, but Alicia was content for reasons of her own, the same reasons that had led a distraught and penniless girl to the renowned Ikaras University nearly two decades ago. She stopped for a moment by one of the vast windows and looked through glass that tinted the world a deep blue.

The spires of the university sat atop the tallest building in Ikaras, peaks covered with silver-white glass that shattered the sunlight and drew it in, absorbed it, reused it to power lights and fans and kitchens. No one knew quite how, or if they did they were keeping quiet about it. A prosperous suburb had sprung up in the shadow of the university, making the most of the protection from the glare of the summer sun, and making the most, too, of the employment the university brought.

Ikaras was home to the single remaining university in the thirteen provinces, the only one that had survived the Great Fall when the Castans had left their spires and glass, their whirring Reyen clockwork. They'd left for no one knew where and, in every other province at least, had taken all their knowledge, all their engineers and artisans, with them, leaving those behind in ignorance and darkness.

All except the custodians of the university, who jealously guarded their knowledge, the papers they kept that were said to go back a thousand years. And jealously kept the other part of the university secret, or at least more secret.

Behind the twisting spires of glass lay a darker scholarship, one hidden away among dour, dim buildings beyond the velvet lawns and regimented hedges. Alicia couldn't see it from where she stood, but out there, behind the dreaming face of the university, was where she'd nursed her hate, where she'd found another with as much as she had and hitched her star to his. Sabates had taught her much, taught her how to be a magician, how to use blood and manipulate people to her will.

Almost two decades she'd studied for this. It would be worth it. Both her dreams could come true in one great manipulation. Subtlety, that was the key.

She made her way along the corridors of the king, the man who traditionally held the keys to the archives that held the secrets of the Castan — if only they could decipher them all. It was only this latest king who'd shown much interest or even allowed the opening of the archives, and they were finding new things every day, it seemed. Orgull was a man obsessed — he had to know how and why the glass worked, how it took in the sun and kept it, giving off heat when wanted, light when it was dark. The puzzle of it worried at his mind, wore it down like the constant movement of sand will wear down a rock, and he'd got as many scholars as he could find working on the problem, almost to the exclusion of all other study. It made it all the easier to nudge his mind towards where she wanted.

Alicia passed down mellow ochre steps to the plaza, then through a leaping arch of dazzling glass and into the quadrangle of the university. The centre was a geometrically designed and stringently kept pattern of many-coloured bushes, logs and gravel that, while pleasing enough to the eye, could only be truly appreciated from the highest towers. It was said, though Alicia refused to believe it, that if one were to get high enough to see straight down, the answer to Ikaras's glass, to everything in fact, would be revealed in its structure. More than one person had fallen to their death trying to reach the very pinnacle of the highest spire, up among the sacred magpies, in order to discover the secret.

Students strolled along the pathways or dashed, robes flying, to lectures. Alicia drew a few glances but not many, and everyone averted their eyes when they noted her gloves.

The buildings where the mages trained were dark and covered in creeping vines and poisonous shrubs, which sprouted, unchecked, from gaps in the stonework. Little light made it into these recesses or lit the half-hidden windows. The magicians weren't a secret, but not many came to their doors, and that suited them just fine. Alicia didn't even have to knock before one of the doors opened to admit her, and a shadowy figure greeted her with the words, "Everything is just as you asked in the bone room."

She nodded her answer and made her way there, sure-footed in the dark of one place a lamp would not stay lit in this city, not Ikaran glass lamps anyway. The bone room was instead lit with more traditional methods – oil lamps in holders around the wall, whose flickering bars of light and shadow, unlike the strident Ikaran lamps, seemed to hide as much as they showed. Alicia had always preferred them.

The bone room wasn't named idly, and it wasn't for the faint-hearted either. Magicians studied years to be allowed in here. Table legs, window frames, shelves, everything was made from bones, either as they came or carved, polished, slotted together to make surfaces – the inevitable by-products of using blood to power their magic. Contrary to popular belief, the bones weren't all human either. A handy subterfuge, that had been, from long ago. Tell everyone that only human blood would do, make them fear, make them beg, make them respect. For many magicians, and Sabates especially, manipulation of people was the key to magic.

A table was set in the centre of the room, a shining circle of blood on its top. She peeled off her gloves and threw them onto a chair, then breathed gently on the circle.

He must have been waiting for her, impatient as always. No sooner had she breathed on the blood than Sabates appeared, reflected in it.

"Well?" he demanded.

"Well, he'll do as we ask, of course. Did you doubt me?"

"Never."

Alicia raised an eyebrow but said no more. She'd cultivated Sabates for years now, leeched knowledge and power and prestige from him. Even murdered to keep her place as his favourite. No sense ruining it when her true goals were so close. "He'll do as we ask. In fact he's already started – I have a list of every Reyen arrested. Too many perhaps, and none that I think might be Kacha and Vocho. But his cells are bursting with Reyens, and who knows who's been missed? For all Ikaras and Reyes look to be about to go to war, there's many men and women looking to take advantage of it. Prices are up everywhere, and Reyens are doing a good trade in guns, among other things. What's two more among all those?"

A frown from Sabates. "I'm too far away; I can't find them at this distance. That tattoo on Vocho's back—"

"If you could just tune me in to it, I could try. I'm here, and so is Vocho, somewhere. If I could track him, then I can make sure he and his sister aren't around to bother you."

For some seconds she wasn't sure whether he'd do it, but in the end she got a measured nod. "Very well. Come closer."

She held in a smile and bent her head closer to the blood.

Petri Egimont stood in the prelate's receiving room with a drink in one hand, feeling like a spare part from one of Bakar's beloved clocks.

At least the clockwork of the city was finally working again, after weeks of hammering, forging and the Clockwork God knew what else. That had cheered Bakar, but not the news that he was no longer the only one who knew how it all worked. "Knowledge is power, Novatonas used to say," Bakar had said to Petri one morning. "And now what power do I have? None. Every damned clocker in the city has seen the workings now and is probably turning dreams of better ones in their head."

Petri had no answer to that. He'd always been a man who thought more than he spoke, but he found he had no answer to many things since Licio's plot to assassinate Bakar and wrest the rule of Reyes from him had been foiled. A plan Petri had, half unwittingly, been involved in.

The plan had disappeared in smoke, but many of the reasons for Petri joining with Licio remained. Some of those reasons had got worse in the meantime. Bakar had seemed to come to his senses a little – no more odd edicts or erratic behaviour, at least not openly – but his madness had burrowed under his skin. In private he was as obsessed and paranoid as ever, and was perhaps getting worse. Once a week or more Petri was summoned in the middle of the night to Bakar's rooms to find him wide-eyed and sweating, seeking reassurances that Petri was still there, that the Clockwork God still stood, that he was a good man, that no one plotted against him. Oh, he was paranoid all right, and perhaps not without cause, but how this manifested itself was almost beyond Petri's endurance, who'd not left this building in almost two months. No one was allowed in or out except with Bakar's explicit written permission. Bakar's own wife had been kept in her rooms for almost as long. No food but bread and cold meats – Bakar believed them difficult to poison, and fed a piece of everything to his cat before he tasted them in any case – and not much of those. "The Clockwork God says a little abstinence is good for the soul," Bakar had said.

And the clocks, clocks everywhere. His little spies, Bakar called them, saying he could see past, present and future in their workings. Ticking and fucking tocking in the background, blind faces watching, pendulums swinging until Petri wanted to scream. And yet no one else seemed to notice anything untoward about Bakar. Outwardly, as today, he seemed normal, his rational, genial self. The council said nothing, even if they noticed, because Bakar was letting them get away with murder, in at least one case literally. They said nothing, and behind closed doors Bakar consulted his clocks to see which of them would betray him. Whatever the clocks told him, it wasn't the truth.

Bakar appeared at his elbow, his hand too tight on Petri's arm. He stank of fear and stale sweat and the lavender he used because he knew he stank of fear.

"What do the clocks tell you?" he asked in a whisper.

"Do they tell you and not me? Hmm? Someone is plotting something – I know that – they always are. I see it in the twisting of the clockwork under the Shrive, in the way the escapements move, how the wheels falter in their turning. Only one person I trust, Petri, and that's you. The clocks tell me so. Who is it?"

A shaft of guilt. He was the only person Bakar trusted and the one person he shouldn't. Bakar had been a father to him for longer than his own father. Had taken him in, taught him, sheltered him. Brainwashed him. And how to answer his last question? A thing Petri had wrestled with each time it was asked, because the truth would see him dead.

"No one," he said now, as he said every time. "No one plots; that's what the clocks tell me." *Oh but they do plot, and I don't blame them. I want them to succeed because until they do I'm trapped here with you.*

Bakar clapped a hand on his shoulder. "Ah, Petri, always so trusting. One of your better qualities, I've always thought, but not one I can share. Everyone plots, even me. The trick is knowing which I can ignore and which I can't. Ah, here's Licio. As slippery as all the rest but useful perhaps."

Bakar left Petri to welcome the ex-king of Reyes, now a councillor and a conspirator.

After his failed assassination plot against Bakar with Sabates, Licio had retired to his country seat to "convalesce" after he'd supposedly been burned in a fire at his house, and his magician was . . . nowhere. Was it only coincidence that Sabates' disappearance corresponded with Bakar's outward return to normality? Once, Petri would have said yes, but having seen first hand Sabates' ability to coerce Vocho into trying to kill his own sister, now he wasn't so sure.

He wasn't so sure of a lot of things just lately. Petri stared at the clocks that lined the wall — brass, porcelain, silver and gilt, as well as a truly hideous affair from before the revolt that had brought Bakar to power, made of the bones and skin of men and women who'd died in the Shrive. At the top of the hour the time was struck on a skull that seemed to stare at Petri, mocking him.

Clocks slicing his life into well managed pieces with every tick and tock. A life lived on rails, everything happening as the clockwork predicted. He stared at the bone monstrosity and wished every single clock would fall and shatter into a thousand pieces. His life didn't run on rails; it couldn't. Yet Bakar lived and breathed when he should be dead, as though he'd known of the attempt on his life and had taken steps to avoid it, and Petri was still tied to him, still tangled in the clockwork with no way out except dying or running, but Bakar kept him locked up tight and wanted him to stay that way.

A commotion at the other end of the room broke into his thoughts. Licio, back from his convalescence, protesting undying devotion to the prelate. Ready to negotiate peace with Ikaras over the long-running border dispute, or at least that's what Bakar believed. Licio, who Petri had once been prepared to follow anywhere if it meant an end to his orderly, clockwork life.

The trouble was, Licio looked every inch a king. He strode across the room wreathed in smiles, graciously accepting a handshake here, dispensing a word there, glad-handing the prelate like he hadn't plotted his death not two months ago. Dispensing a sly look Petri's way, as though saying "You were in it as deep as me." As if Petri needed reminding.

A figure lurked behind Licio, and Petri was startled to

realise that he hadn't recognised Sabates to begin with. The magician seemed very different, it had to be said. The scars on his face were much softened and blurred and he wasn't wearing his usual midnight robes but the same as all the other men – breeches and shirt and tunic in bright colours, powdered hair curled into a coil over one shoulder. Gloves covered the writhing images on his hands that marked him as a magician. He inclined his head to Petri, cast a glance at Licio and Bakar, who were telling each other lies about how much they admired each other, and came over.

He didn't speak at first, making Petri fidget, but finally he relented and said in his softly spoken and slightly menacing accent, "Still trapped by your fate then, Lord Egimont?"

Petri hesitated to answer. Not just his fate trapped him now; he was caught between Bakar on the one hand and Licio and Sabates on the other. He'd betrayed them all in one way or another. A word from Sabates or Licio about what he'd done, and Petri's life would unravel in the tick of a clock.

Sabates knew it too. It was too much to hope that he'd leave Petri out of any new machinations. Petri had received several notes from Licio and had ignored them all, but he couldn't afford to ignore the two of them now Sabates was back.

The magician turned so his back was to the room and took off one glove. Petri looked up at the clocks in an effort not to see the markings that writhed over the man's hand but it was no good. He had to look, just as before he'd had to do as Sabates had said. The markings twisted like snakes as Sabates' voice slipped into his ear.

"See now, I can't trust you with much, not after before.

But Licio has persuaded me to give you one last chance. Just a little favour, and I'll be sure not to mention to Bakar how you plotted to relieve him of his position. A tiny little favour and you can be free, like you always wanted to be."

Petri strained to resist but he was bound by the markings – now a bird flying free, now a whispered word, now a clockwork cage – perhaps as hopelessly as Vocho had been bound by the magical tattoo on his back. He tried not to look, but the markings caught him anyway. Noose to ticking clock to flying bird. Sweat popped up on his brow, not just from the power Sabates was exerting on him but the thought of being cast adrift by a wrong word. He'd wanted to escape Bakar, true, but he had never wanted to kill him. Now he was trapped here because he had nowhere else. No one else. Maybe just a small favour if it meant he lived.

"Very small," Sabates said. "Tiny. You see that clock, the one with the bones? I will send you word, and on that day you will make it stop. Not by destroying it or anything obvious. You will unwind it, you will make it run down. And then you will be both safe from Bakar's wrath and free of his pernicious clockwork. Safe and free."

If only, if only. Could it really be that simple?

"Of course it could." Sabates had always seemed able to read his mind. "One small thing. I know I can trust you on this." The hand shot out and gripped Petri by the wrist. Sabates didn't look a strong man, too stooped and thin, but his grip was anything but weak, and a hotness flowed from his fingers, seemed to bring steam from Petri's skin. "You will do this. Call it payment for the other, for not doing exactly as your king commanded, for disobeying me. That will only happen once, do you understand? Don't fuck this up and you'll live to see the end of the Clockwork God. Disobey and . . ."

The markings were very clear and brought a terrible dryness to Petri's mouth. He'd betrayed Bakar and then Licio in turn, and he needed to pay for that. A risky game he played, but play he must if he ever wanted to break free of the clockwork that bound him.

Sabates cocked his head at Petri's hesitation. "Of course, the guild will still be in need of a master when the time comes. One who does as he's told, one who is loyal to Licio. More importantly, loyal to me."

Every man has his price. Petri had only lately realised how low his was. One moment of betrayal then, and afterwards he could pick up the threads of what honour he had left. "I don't want Bakar to die."

"I promise," Sabates said. "Not a drop of his blood will be spilled on my account, provided you do as instructed. Once that happens, the guild is yours. Always your aim, eh?"

"But Eneko—"

"Is a self-serving fool if he thinks he can deceive me. He pays lip service to Licio in secret, but I can see into his mind. Do you doubt that? No, of course you don't; you know I can. For now Eneko is useful, but he'll be a liability once Licio regains power. The guild is yours once Bakar is deposed." Sabates smiled, a nasty little thing. "Then you can invite your lovely Kacha back, and I will even try my best not to kill her for her impertinence."

A fleeting thought of her at the mention of her name, and Petri immediately knew it for the mistake it was.

"Yes, she and her brother are in Ikaras. I see you keep yourself informed even though you're tied to this building. As long as you do your part, and she keeps to herself, then no harm will come to her from me. Do tell her that in your next little love note."

"I haven't—"

"Haven't you? That surprises me. But you will. Petri Egimont, so predictable, will send his lady love a little note, warning her of what's to come."

Sabates looked up at the hideous bone clock, let one hand play across its grisly face. "You will, like clockwork. Don't forget to tell her if she interferes this time, there will be no doubt of her death, and her brother's. I'm sure you can fit that in around all your protestations of how you've come to your senses now. I know that's not entirely true, even if you don't. You still ache to be free, hmm?"

Sabates' smile softened, and the markings on his hands grew softer with it. Petri didn't believe either of those would save him, but he knew the truth when he heard it.

"I know what you want, Petri, and you know that I'm the only man who can give it to you. Freedom from all the chains of your life. In return, just that small favour."

Chapter Three

Kacha sat and watched out of the window, at least in part to check that no one had followed or found them, but also to think. Whatever they did, they had to do it quick. Rumours were rife in the city – of war with Reyes, of a delegation, Licio and others, coming to negotiate. Coming to make plans was Kacha's more informed guess. If Licio came, so would Sabates, and the closer he got the more likely he was to trace Vocho through that sodding tattoo on his back.

She rested her head against the window frame. Wind chimes, their tinklings endless prayers to the Ikaran gods, twisted and jangled in the breeze. Worst of all, she knew she was thinking those things to stop thinking on Petri. Was he thinking of her? She looked down at the ring on her finger. Was Petri thinking of her, and did she want him to? She twisted the ring, torn between throwing it into the street and keeping it for ever.

Her thoughts were interrupted by a disturbance in a bar over the street. Vocho, who couldn't seem to sit still lately and had never counted prudence among his virtues at the best of times, was grandstanding again. At least he hadn't challenged anyone to a duel – yet. Though that was probably more because his Ikaran wasn't up to it. Cospel was lurking in the background, his hand firmly gripping a solid-looking tankard. Always prepared for anything was Cospel, and most likely he'd have his ears wide open, ready to suck up all the information he could. He caught her eye and waggled his eyebrows in Vocho's direction, which she took to mean, "Not to worry, miss. I'm sober even if he ain't."

Another figure drew her eye in the deepening twilight – he was dressed in Reyen clothes, breeches and shirt and fancy tunic, though he'd foregone the cloak in the heat. His hat was at a jaunty angle, and there was something familiar about the way he walked, like his legs were oiled springs. He sauntered down the street not seeming to pay much attention until he was level with Vocho. Then he turned his face up to Kacha, and she could see who it was. Who she'd been hoping for, if she was honest.

"Dom?"

He grinned up at her, a smile as sharp as daggers, took a quick look about and was up the outside of the building in a flash, sitting on the sill and kissing her hand in another.

"My dearest Kacha, we really must stop meeting like this."

Kacha tried to ignore the door opening and Vocho peering around it like a naughty child. Dom was pacing up and down, glaring around the room and using some very choice words. "Why the hells did you come to Ikaras?" he finished.

"Where else were we supposed to go?" Kacha said. "We tried to find you, get you out of the Shrive, but you were already gone. Too many people know us in Reyes, and too

many of those people wanted us dead." She looked sideways at Vocho as he stood in the doorway. "Besides, we
needed a magician, and not that bastard Sabates either."

"What do you need a magician for?" Dom asked. "I'd
have thought you'd had enough of them."

Vocho stepped in before Kacha could answer. "Never
mind that. What are you doing here?"

Dom flashed his new sharp smile. "For the warm welcome,
obviously. It seemed sporting to tell you, as I was here.
You're not safe in Ikaras. You're not safe anywhere in the
provinces right now."

"Tell me something I don't know," Kass said.

"All right," Dom said levelly. "Licio has told the prelate
how you both tried to murder him – he's got witnesses
that put you at his house at the time – not to mention how
you were responsible for the jamming of the prelate's
beloved clockworks. He was most distressed, which might
be the understatement of the era. So we've got the murder
of the prelate's favourite priest for starters, and now the
attempted assassination of Licio. Oh yes, and the king told
them how he heroically foiled your attempt at assassinating
the prelate. Boys and girls, you are in deep, deep shit. All
of which has led to more pressure on Eneko to tell all he
knows about you. It'd help him a lot to be able to hand
you two over."

"Which is why you're here, no doubt," Vocho said. "So
you can take us back, and he can hand us over to Bakar?"

"Not exactly." Dom arranged himself in a chair by the
fire, and despite his news Kacha had to suppress a grin at
the way Vocho looked at him and his pristine clothes like
he'd happily throttle him and steal everything he was
wearing.

"Why are you here then?" Kacha asked.

"Oh, lots of reasons. Someone I'd like to see very much again is here. And besides, you two were quite fun and not too mean to an idiot, so I thought I'd help out. It was so very boring being my father's dutiful son, and you two helped me recall why I became a duellist in the first place. Going back to being the dutiful son would be torment, even if my father wouldn't have me arrested on sight. And I know things. Eneko's got people here; he's looking for you two, and he's not working on his own any more."

"Very informative," Vocho said. "But why are you here in this room right now?"

"Because Licio has offered to be the prelate's new special envoy to Ikaras, supposedly to broker a deal about all the trouble on the border. Oh yes, and because he's bringing his magician with him, and Sabates is very pissed with you for fucking up his nice plan. He has, I'm told, an easy way to find you. The last thing he wants is for you to put another spanner in the works. This time he wants to make sure nothing goes wrong, and that means making sure you're not around."

"And what's it to you if he does find us?" Kacha couldn't help but remember a dark, dank prison cell and discovering that Dom, the person who she'd thought a friend — a bumbling fool perhaps, but a friend — hadn't been all that he'd appeared.

Dom laughed and smoothed away an imaginary crease in his silk sleeve. "Not much, I'll grant. But you and I, Kacha, we've a lot in common. Both beholden to Eneko in one way or another, both betrayed by him. I merely want to make sure it doesn't turn out for you as it did for me."

Dom stood up and bowed curtly to Kass, one equal to another, two ex-assassins with axes to grind. "I came to warn you because I thought I owed you that at least. What you do with the information is up to you. It might be a chance to clear your name at last, if you can find any proof, and keep it this time. Oh, and I brought this."

A flourish of his hand, and paper appeared. Not just a slip, several sheets folded together, and she could see the seal from here. Petri's seal.

"A gift," he said. "From a mutual friend."

Dom left as suddenly as he'd appeared, leaving Vocho confused and Kass looking at a bundle of papers as though they were snake about to bite. Vocho hoped she threw them into the fire. Petri bloody Egimont. Vocho had hoped he could live the rest of his life without ever coming across that name again, but no, here he was, even when he wasn't. Stirring Kass up just when Vocho had thought she was mellowing.

She had mellowed too, since their original ignoble exit from Reyes, leaving chaos and confusion in their wake. For months before that she'd been angry as a stirred-up bees' nest with everyone, and all because of Petri, because he'd left her with barely a word. Since their escape and Petri's small part in it, and also a whispered conversation Vocho had only heard part of, she'd calmed down. A bit. Kass was never going to be Mrs Serene, but at least she'd seemed quieter in herself, less likely to go off half cocked at some innocent comment. Vocho had often wondered what the two of them had said, but didn't dare to ask, at least partly because he was happy enough that Petri was far behind them. Where Vocho hoped he'd stay, for good, if only because now he and Kass could manage to get through a day without sniping at each other. Sometimes at least.

"Aren't you going to look?" he asked, not because he

especially wanted her to, but he did want to know if she was going to stay calm or explode.

She slid him a glare from behind a fall of blonde hair and stashed the papers inside her shirt. "Cospel, how much money do we have now?"

Cospel came out of the shadows, where he liked to lurk. He jingled faintly. "Five hundred bushels. A few coppers as well, and I, um, I found this." He held out a gold ring with a small blue stone in it. Vocho didn't like to ask where he "found" it. In someone's pocket or on their finger, probably. It wouldn't be worth more than a hundred anyway.

Kass considered briefly. "It's not really enough, but we don't have much choice."

"Enough for what? I mean, it's enough to eat for a couple of weeks. What else do we want to spend it on?"

"Didn't you listen to what Dom was saying? That bloody magician is coming, and the Ikaran king is looking for Reyen spies, probably us in particular. And here's you with a magical bull's eye on your back. I really don't want that to be around when Sabates gets here. We either get someone to take it off, which will cost, or I murder you and leave you in the gutter for them to find while I escape. Which would you prefer?"

She smiled as she said it, but he couldn't escape a little shiver. It was hard to tell if she was joking. She could kill him, especially if she caught him unawares or got lucky. He was almost sure she wouldn't.

"We need another magician to take it off, Voch."

Magicians, in Reyes at least, were as rare as lion's feathers. He'd only ever met two, and that was two too many. They'd framed him for murder and almost got him to murder the prelate, and his own sister. He really didn't want to be meeting any more. He wasn't sure his nerves could take it.

"And what is Ikaras but one big university?" Kass went on. "Magicians aren't banned here; they train them. We just need to find one that'll do it for the money we have. That's the tricky part. I had Cospel scope a few out. Far too expensive, at least the ones with any sort of good name."

"I don't like the sound of what you're suggesting."

"Neither do I, but there's bound to be a few who are, shall we say, a bit less respectable."

"That doesn't make me feel better, Kass."

"It wasn't intended to. Your choice though. Sabates can find you again, maybe do something to you, through you, with that tattoo on your back. Or we find a back-alley magician to take it off. Then we're well out of everything; we can go and find someone who wants to hire a couple of no-name ex-guild master swordsmen, wait for everything to calm down in Reyes, and when it's over see if we can find a way back in. Or just stay out."

Stay out – not something Vocho had ever contemplated, and he was pretty sure Kass didn't mean it either unless she'd had a soul transplant overnight. The guild had been everything to both of them. Kass might be disillusioned with it, and so was he, a bit, but the fame, the adulation, the glory. He wanted all that back, every scrap of it. Being a no-name sell-sword wasn't his idea of a good life. Still, Kass had a point. And life was all about risks, right? Had he ever worried about risks before? No point starting now then.

"All right. Let's see who we can find."

It didn't seem very promising when Cospel led them down a dark alleyway. Ikaras was famed as the city of light – vast structures of glass covered all the bigger buildings, cut and sculpted and placed to reflect and refract sunlight so that it shattered over the whole city. Smaller buildings, individual houses, had their own, smaller glass partitions and sculptures set into the roofs, making smaller globes of mirrored light that encased them. Once the sun rose, everywhere was light, in the summer so piercing that the locals had developed a hat whose brim could be angled so as to shade the eyes. At night, light stored somehow in the glass glowed red and blue and yellow to light rooms and houses and streets, making the city look like a flickering, living beast from the hills that surrounded it. Even now, on a day when wispy clouds scudded over the sun, the brightness was blinding to one not used to it, and Vocho had to squint away the pain of the wine he'd had last night. Ikaras, city of light, was not a place for the hungover.

The building at the end of the alley had a glass structure on its roof – a delicate rose shape, but one that was sullenly dark in the sun. Other buildings along the way might once have had glass atop them, but most of it seemed to be underfoot, long shards and tiny pieces that tried, and failed, to shine. No glass on the roofs, so no lights in the windows, making the alleyway a black stain on an otherwise bright street. Out from the old city, the bits with shining glass, they were in a swampy suburb. Houses stood on stilts, plain wooden houses over trickling streams and sucking mud. In between the houses mangroves shouldered for space, and more than one crumbling house was half hidden by vines.

Finally Cospel led them to what looked like a thicket, with a narrow path into it, where a dog sunned itself and looked them over idly as it scratched out a flea.

"Are you sure about this, Cospel?" Vocho asked as they

headed into the path, which looked more like an animal trail than anything else. Two paces in, the vines closed over their heads and Vocho had the oddest feeling they were watching him. "I mean, magicians can charge a king's ransom for a single spell, so what would any decent one be doing down here? No madman is going to touch me, I can tell you that."

Cospel shrugged in the green dimness and waggled his eyebrows in a complicated dance that probably meant something profound. "Not mad, sir, I promise you that. Well, perhaps. More sort of radical. I couldn't even get *in* the university, and even if I could, we ain't got the money for one of them fancy magicians. Not to mention that Sabates is a member of the university, like Kacha said, and we don't want to be found, right? So I had to be a bit creative."

Vocho narrowed his eyes as Cospel knocked on the door. "What do you mean, 'creative'?"

"I think he means," a voice said as the door opened, "that I am years ahead of my time."

Vocho turned to see almost exactly what he hadn't expected. The two magicians he'd seen close to before were serious, threatening even. The patterns that writhed on their hands were shapes of blood and death, and they had seemed matched by their faces. He'd seen one or two from afar, as far as bloody possible, around the university and all had held the same sort of menace.

This face was sunny and cheerful, and while there were patterns on her hands – Vocho took great care not to look too closely – there was no blood and death there. She was clearly a magician, the markings on her hands gave that away, but everything else was subtly wrong somehow, or at least different. She was short with a crop of dark hair framing a shrewd-looking face, and she, well, she'd never be called skinny, even by a liar of Vocho's skill, instead being solidly formidable. Unlike other magicians, her dress was bright and colourful with flowers around the edges, and she radiated a sort of calm no-nonsense goodwill.

She looked him up and down like a horse dealer inspecting a nag for soundness. "I suppose you're the one looking for the cheap fix. All right, come in. Make sure to wipe your feet." She spoke in Reyen, not well but well enough and certainly better than Vocho spoke Ikaran.

She pushed the door wider and let the three of them in. Vocho wondered why she'd bothered asking them to wipe their feet – the place looked like a whirlwind had gone through it. Plants covered every surface, waving in a non-existent breeze, and again Vocho couldn't escape the feeling they were watching him. Books lay scattered everywhere, loose sheets of paper hanging out of them or, in one case, stuck to the wall with what looked like blood. The markings that looped and spiralled on another wall were definitely blood, and the spot between Vocho's shoulders began to itch.

"I thought you said she wasn't mad," he whispered to Cospel.

"I said perhaps," Cospel whispered back. "And she's all we can afford."

Kacha shut the pair of them up with a glare and stepped forward to introduce herself. She didn't get the chance.

"Kacha and Vocho and . . . and Cospel, wasn't it?" the woman said. "What? I am a magician, you know. A proper one. As good as any up there in the university. Better, because I'm not stuffed so far up my own backside I can't see what's going on. Don't worry, I won't tell anyone who you are if you don't tell anyone I'm still practising magic.

One reason Cospel and I managed to come to terms, though he does drive a hard bargain. Now then." She rummaged among some papers on the desk, wiped one hand absent-mindedly on her dress leaving a dark red smear behind and looked up again from under her fringe. "I'm Esti, Esti du Bellan. You've heard of me? No? Well, perhaps that's for the best, all things considered. Right then, Vocho is the one with the problem, is he? Strip to the waist, please."

"What? But we've only just met, and my sister is . . . Oh. Right." Vocho withered in the face of Esti's grin. He got his tunic and shirt off and shivered in the draught while Esti paced around him, tutting to herself and tapping a pen on her teeth as she looked at the spot between his shoulder blades, poked and prodded and pinched. It itched something fierce, but at least it wasn't burning right now.

"Tricky," she said at last to Kacha, as though Vocho wasn't there. "It's a real piece of work, that. I can do it, maybe, but it may require more unusual methods, and it'll take some time. Good thing you came to me rather than the university. They wouldn't dream of interfering with another magician's work. Me, I have no scruples as long as the cash is right. Have you the money? Good. Half now, half when it's done. There are things I'll need to buy. There may also be things that money cannot buy, which you will have to acquire."

Vocho shuffled his shirt back on and tried not to see how Esti's mouth was twitching like she was trying not to laugh. He'd never felt less like Vocho the Great in his life.

The tattoo itched and nagged all the way back to their lodgings.

Chapter Four

Petri wasn't sorry to see Licio and Sabates go. Bakar sent them off under a scorching summer sun with a retinue of guards and a farewell waved from inside – Petri wasn't the only person not to have left the building in weeks.

He turned away from the window and back to the room of little cubicles, incongruous under the high, vaulted ceiling of what had been the old king's ballroom. If Petri shut his eyes, he could still hear faint stirrings of the music they used to play, see ghosts of the dancers, smell the waft of mingled scents from the gardens outside the window, which had now been replaced with an orrery that clanked and ticked as the background to his every thought. Listening to the ghosts was far better than opening his eyes and seeing the inside of the cubicle that was sucking his life out.

"Egimont, stop standing there like a stunned mackerel and get to work." His supervisor brought him back to the here and now. Odious, pumped-up prick of a man, lording it over his little domain worse than any noble had ever lorded it over anyone. "Just because you're the prelate's favourite doesn't make you mine. So get on with it."

Petri didn't say a word but went to his cubicle and sat at his desk and tried not to think about just getting up, walking out of the door and leaving. Nowhere special in mind, just going, leaving everything behind – name, reputation, chains. Kacha.

Just thinking about her made him sweat, but it didn't matter. He'd left her behind a long time ago, ruined his chance when he'd first lied to her. He wiped his forehead against the heat and tried to concentrate on the papers on his desk. Bakar had made his working life a living hell the last few weeks, more so than ever before.

These orders were madness. Yet no one else seemed to see it, or if they did were too afraid to say anything. He looked up, and one of his co-workers was staring his way. Back to the papers, whose words seemed to swim in front of his eyes. He'd been torn in two ever since Licio had first recruited him to his cause. Now the split seemed to reach down past his soul and into his balls. Nothing he did would be right. The prelate needed . . . something. Deposing, retiring. Yet was Licio, with Sabates at his back, really any better? God's cogs, no. What then?

He ran a hand through his hair and pinched the bridge of his nose. What indeed? He had no choice, and he thought perhaps this was where Licio and Sabates had wanted him all along – beholden to them for his life, just as he had always been beholden to Bakar. They'd promised him freedom then taken it away with the other hand. He glanced up again – the same woman hurriedly looked away.

What he needed was information, an ally. What he had was nothing. The only good thing he'd managed to do recently was get a note to Kacha. He'd had no idea who he'd get to take it, how he'd even get it out of the palace, but that ever-hated fate, or someone's planning, had dropped the perfect vehicle into his lap. Narcis Donat Chimo Ne Farina es Domenech had arrived in the palace like a perfectly turned out, and secret, whirlwind. Petri had returned to his rooms a few nights ago to find the whole floor in disarray, men and women shouting, in one case weeping hysterically, and Dom sitting in the lonely chair in Petri's room as though the world was something that turned about him.

"Ah, Petri," he'd said with a dangerous smile. "Glad you could join me. Do shut the door behind you."

It was, without a doubt, the same Dom that Petri had met as an ally of Kacha and Vocho. Yet this Dom looked sharper than swords rather than the bumbling fool of before. Still, that bumbling fool had managed to best Petri with a sword on more than one occasion. Petri shut the door quietly behind him and kept his hand ready, in case.

"You've done well for a man I last saw in the Shrive."

Dom inclined his head. "And you've done well to stay alive for a man playing both sides for what he can get. But I'm not here to pay compliments."

One step brought Petri across the mean width of his room. "No, I suppose not."

"I've made sure we won't be disturbed. Apparently some fool has put scorpions into some beds around here. Shame no one realises they're the harmless kind. But I think you have something for me."

"I do?" Petri couldn't think what he'd have that Dom wanted. He wasn't even sure who the man was, really.

Another smile from Dom, swift and sure as a knife in the dark. "You do. Maybe time for you to discover a thing or two. Who knows? You have a letter, I understand."

Petri sat down on the narrow unmade bed. Last night he'd written a letter, long and heartfelt, to Kacha. Despite what Sabates had said, he'd not intended to send it, in fact had no way to send it . . . and now here perhaps was a way. But could he trust it?

"I know what you're thinking," Dom said into the silence. "You're thinking, he works for who-knows-who but possibly a magician, and he probably can't be trusted. Why should I give him my letter?"

Petri started because that was exactly what he'd been thinking. Dom ignored the movement, seemingly bored as he inspected his immaculate nails.

"Because," he carried on, "Bakar is increasingly unhinged and sees enemies everywhere, even in his own household. I'm the only chance you have, and more than that, I'm a very well trained assassin. And you have upset a friend of mine very deeply. I do not like my friends upset. And yet, you still live. Why is that, do you think?"

Petri couldn't think; that was the trouble. An assassin – a job title until recently held by Kacha. And here, in his room, yet not to kill him. And Kass – Kass had seemed to trust Dom, at least a little. Petri's mind whirled, but his mouth settled on an answer before it was even fully formed in his head. "Because you don't work wholly for Sabates."

"Well worked out. Yes. I don't work for him, though at present it suits me to let him think I do. I know that before long, when he considers it the right time, Sabates, or perhaps Eneko or maybe even Bakar might ask me to kill you. If that happens, then I might. Depending on what you do now."

"If you can get in here, why don't they just hire you to kill the prelate?"

"You don't need me to tell you how he's keeping himself under wraps. Into the palace? Tricky but doable. Close enough to the prelate to kill him? Nigh on impossible at present. At least, not swiftly. That is what I've told those who asked, at least. Truth is, like Kacha, I've lost my taste for killing when there's a better, easier way."

"What do you want?"

Dom held up a packet of papers. "Your seal on this. I've read it. Very good. If anything will work on Kass, this is it. And it's fair warning for her. I was pretty sure you'd do that, at the least. She might even believe you."

"If you're going to take it, why not just tell her yourself?"

Dom shifted in his seat and smoothed an imaginary crease in his immaculate tunic. "There are things she needs to hear that I can't tell her, things only you can say to bring her back to where she belongs. I owe her, I think. No, I know I do. And Vocho, but mostly her. Please. Your seal, and then this uncomfortable interview can be at an end without bloodshed. Sad to say, I will kill you if I have to. I'd rather not, if only because I'd like Kacha still to be speaking to me."

Petri didn't think long. He took the seal out of his pocket, but wavered. "You're doing this for Sabates?"

The laugh was genuine, he was sure of it. "Gods, no. Wouldn't trust that bastard further than I could spit. Neither should you, if you have any sense, nor Bakar either. Sad to say, Petri, there is no one you can trust, not even a little. Not even me. We've all got our own plots and plans under the surface, our own wants that haunt our dreams. Haven't we? There, thank you."

Dom stood in a flurry of tinkling knick-knacks and scented silk.

"A last word of advice, Petri Egimont. Sabates never has just one plan on the go; he always has a backup. Maybe things won't go as planned with Ikaras. Maybe Sabates will change his mind. Keep your eyes open and your ears sharp. Licio had that priest killed because he was Bakar's favourite, because that would incense him the most and hit closest to home. Who is next in line for that favour? Whose death would cause Bakar perhaps to lose the little reason he has left and show all Reyes just how fractured his mind is? Leaving the whole province ready and willing to accept a new leader with almost no loss of life. Except yours. Your life is measured in days, maybe hours, if you're not careful."

"Why are you—"

"I told you, because we all have our own plans, our own wants. If I do this, if I go to Ikaras with another little job in mind, someone else may give me what I want, what I've wanted longer than I care to admit. Besides, Kass seems fond of you for some unfathomable reason, and I'd like to be able to tell her I did my best to keep you alive. I'll give her your love, shall I?"

Before Petri could even open his mouth to answer, Dom was gone, leaving confusion and consternation in his wake. Which had perhaps been his intention.

Petri considered that now as he sat in his overheated cubicle and watched his co-worker trying not to watch him. Dom had been right about one thing: Petri had no one he could trust. And about another: he needed to keep his wits about him. Matters were swirling to a conclusion, but what that conclusion might be he couldn't say, only that it didn't look good for him.

A shout from outside caught his attention, had everyone craning to see while pretending they weren't. Petri had no such inhibition and went to the window. Four guards were dragging a struggling man down the steps, and Petri was both surprised and not to note it was Bakar's personal valet, a man who'd served him loyally for almost two decades. Yet now blood flowed from under his hair and out of his nose, and a guard gave his head an extra clout so that the man passed out. Probably a mercy, Petri thought as the Shrive wagon pulled up, and shivered at that thought. Dom's words came to him again. *Bakar is increasingly unhinged and sees enemies everywhere, even in his own household.*

Petri's own position was becoming precarious. He was expendable, which was the problem. He looked behind him at his co-worker, who immediately buried her head in paperwork. Not the only one, Petri thought. Other odd moments came back to him, ones that had meant little at the time: feeling sure that someone had been in his room, one of the maids taking a sudden interest in his movements, his supervisor being more zealous even than usual in keeping Petri at his desk, the way Bakar sometimes looked at him sideways.

He was expendable and being watched.

Kacha was glad to see the back of Vocho the next day when he went to see Esti. Petri's letter was burning a hole in her shirt. She was itching to read it, but not while Voch was about.

They'd decided that she'd have a nose around, see what she could find out, see if what Dom had told them and all the rest they'd heard was true, while Vocho was off having whatever it was done to him. Cospel went with him, just in case, so it was only her.

She hadn't got used to Ikaras yet – she doubted she ever would. She missed Reyes, missed knowing exactly where she was at any set of the clock, knowing all the little back ways and underpinnings of the city, all the rooftop runs.

Here she was good as lost a few minutes after she left their lodgings, and it was only by working out where they were in relation to the spires of the university that she could find her way back. She hadn't got used to the glass either – shafts of reflected sunlight felt like needles in her eyes. She adjusted the brim of her hat and headed for the centre of the city. At least that was easy to find – just head for the university.

She'd dressed to blend in. Ikaran women didn't wear breeches, as she usually did. Indoors it was dresses, but on the street they wore loose tops and voluminous trousers in silk, more wrapped around than sewn into shape, to help with the heat. They didn't carry swords either, men or women, and she felt naked without one at her side. Still, she'd managed to scrounge up a sort of dagger with a thick curved blade and a horn handle. Not much good as a weapon – she missed her old stiletto – but at least it was something, and almost everyone wore one, though they were blunt and purely for show. She'd managed to get a half-decent edge on hers though, and the weight of it at her hip comforted her as she made her way through the crowds.

Unlike Reyes there was no main marketplace, but a maze of little alleys and walkways through the glass, hiding dim booths and shadowed kiosks, shielded from the reflected sun by mats woven from the reeds that choked the river.

On the outskirts of the trade area was a new thing, from what she could gather. Guns had never been widespread here, as they hadn't been in Reyes either until lately. Now cheap versions were coming in on ships – mostly not directly from Reyes but via middlemen from other provinces. Recently many businesses had lost workers to the army, taken to the plains outside the city to drill and train, but not the little broken-down forges here, one-room shacks. No one took their workers away, because the king had a use for them. The high-class artisans in the centre of the city made Ikaran-style guns, more ceremonial than useful, but out here they were producing guns that worked, by the hundred.

All day and night barges came along the river from the wooded interior of the province and from the disputed border with Reyes. Iron ore and charcoal were offloaded for the nearby bloomeries and fineries to churn out steel. Forges glowed cherry red all night, all day, and the constant pounding of hammers almost had Kacha feeling at home.

As she neared the city centre, the forges disappeared, replaced by copper workers, carpenters, then on to finer artisans – scroll makers and apothecaries and learned men who'd share their wisdom for a coin. Multicoloured strands of thread hung damply from the mats of reeds, showcasing dyers' skills. Jewellers and their wives sat adorned with their wares, carvers used toe lathes to craft incredible wooden structures, while other carvers used tiny chisels to pare out intricate scenes to be inlaid with gold and silver and ebony.

Maybe a third of the little kiosks that hid among the glass were shut – their owners drilling and sweating on the plain, learning how to use the new guns, how to hold blades without cutting their own hands off. Other traders had drafted in wives and children or were already run by women in any case. Other children ran after Kacha as she made her way through the maze. They grabbed at her sleeves, plucked at her trousers, offering cool water, fine silks, a cure for the clap.

Finally she escaped their clutches and emerged into a small open space. The Mouth of Ikaras was full of glass

and light. Sculptures, windows of all colours, even the
flagstones weren't stone but glass, so that she could see
through to an underground warren of offices – the king's
administration, supposedly open to scrutiny by all. They
were open about what went on in at least a couple of
dungeons too, in what was likely an effective deterrent
given the state of two poor bastards chained to a wall,
brand marks covering their skin.

The other thing the space was full of were religious
speakers – they'd kept the old gods here, after a fashion,
and there were men and women calling for people to revere
all of them. Priests of the goddess of war with red-painted
faces and tattooed eyelids, devotees of the god of the sun
covered in tinkling jewellery and jangling daggers.
Adherents of the twin god and goddess of purity and
sanctity staged a mummers' play, calling for people to abjure
sin. She was pretty sure that's what they were doing anyway
– she could understand more Ikaran than she could speak.
Mingled in with the sermonisers were crackpots and
madmen, ranting about just about anything you could think
of, and there at the end, what she'd come for. Every day,
at noon, a representative of the king announced the day's
news in a slow and sonorous voice. She liked slow. It gave
her some hope of working out what he was saying before
he got too far ahead.

She got there just in time to see the king's representative
take to his podium in front of the university gates,
resplendent in gold silk tunic and trousers, trimmed in
black to show his rank. If that was in doubt, his dagger
had an ivory hilt with half a dozen silver charms hanging
from it. He started his speech, his rich voice carrying over
the heads of the small crowd, while two scribes sat in the
shade of a sculpture, taking the words down, no doubt

for the sheets that made the rounds of the hostelries, inns and shops where men and women would sit in the cooler evening temperatures and gossip and drink scalding-hot chaat, just as they had for a thousand years.

He started off with the usual, which Kacha knew almost by heart by now – about the magnificence of King Orgull, his health, vast generosity, concern for his citizens. Once he'd got past that, the man moved on to what everyone was really here for – the news. The words rolled over her, a jumble of sounds that she could only pick some words out of. Enough to know that Bear had been right about the reward offered for Reyen spies. Something else about the border dispute – she thought an army had been gathered but wasn't certain – and then what she'd come for. Licio was coming to Ikaras to negotiate, and the king was hopeful that he could get favourable terms for Ikaras, if not outright submission. Something like that, anyway. She'd get Cospel to pick up one of the sheets so they could go over it in private.

The news confirmed what Dom had told them, and that was going to be a problem. Everyone wanted them dead, and there wasn't much of a way out. Except maybe to prove that Licio had been plotting against the prelate, wanted him dead in fact. A predicament, because all their proof had been destroyed. Except one piece. One paper that, on a whim, she'd offered to the Clockwork God in Reyes, and that he'd accepted and locked away in his brass heart. One paper that would also implicate Petri.

Kacha made her way from the plaza deep in thought, and found herself somewhere quiet to sit and look at the bundle of papers Dom had given her. Petri's seal, Petri's handwriting, but hadn't that been the case with the other note? The one she wasn't now sure had really come from him? The one telling her to have nothing more to do with Vocho, or Petri wanted nothing more to do with her. Yet Dom had given this one to her, and she trusted him, to an extent anyway. As much as she trusted anyone lately, which wasn't a lot. Whatever was in this letter, could she trust that? Could she trust Petri?

She turned the papers over and over in her hands before she put them away, unread. She wanted to believe all that business with Petri had been a misunderstanding, but there was no getting away from the fact that, to start with at least, he'd come to spy on the guild by getting close to her. He'd betrayed her trust before they'd ever spoken two words to each other, never mind the rest. And yet . . . and yet . . .

And yet she didn't want to start all that again. She'd finally stopped hating him for breaking her heart, and she wasn't going to get drawn back into that, into him. He might have helped her save Voch in the end, but he'd still been with Licio and Sabates, still been part of the plot to overthrow the prelate, to assassinate him using Voch as a puppet.

She kept that firmly in her head. Maybe she didn't hate him any more, but he meant nothing now. Really. No matter how much his letter burned a hole in her shirt, she wasn't going to read it, or risk her and Vocho's necks to save him.

They needed to get that one piece of paper back, however they could. How did you get an offering back from a god? She didn't know, but that one piece of paper was all that stood between her and the block. Which meant going back to Reyes. First though, they had to make sure that Vocho no longer had the magical bull's eye on his back.

Chapter Five

Vocho approached Esti's house with trepidation, though he wasn't about to show either her or Cospel that, and instead swaggered up to the front door and let himself in without a knock. Partly because the damned tattoo had started itching again and, just as importantly, it had hurt putting the thing on and he was hoping it would hurt somewhat less taking it off. He also didn't want to scream in front of a lady. Or Cospel. Or anyone, if he could help it.

He was taken aback by the state of the room and the smell of cooking blood, which had nothing but bad, if vague, memories attached. Where the room had been bright with sunlight before, whitewashed walls, a forest of plants, a few badly done watercolours and some more homely touches such as a home-made rag rug in every colour he could think of, now the windows were shuttered and the Ikaran-glass lamps were turned off. Despite the heat of the noonday sun outside, in here all was cool and dark, with a long table covered in a white cloth lit by a flickering oil lamp. Everything else was in shadow, including Esti, which was why Vocho jumped half out of his skin when her face appeared from the darkness.

"Oh, it looks proper eldritch, don't it?" Cospel said with a smirk and wiggle of his eyebrows that Vocho couldn't decipher except to conclude that Cospel was enjoying Vocho's trepidation a touch too much. "All ghosts and ghouls. Maybe of the people she's killed come to warn you."

"Dozens of them, I expect," Esti said dryly before Vocho could speak without squeaking. "Cospel, if you go into the next room, there's some food for you. We need to be alone for this."

Cospel's eyebrows leered at Vocho knowingly and he left with a sniggered "Good luck" through a small door at the far end, letting in a blast of light, smell and noise that suggested several children and some sort of stew.

"Right then." Vocho tried to be brisk but failed. How could you tell the difference between ghosts and ghouls, and what was that moving shadow in the corner? He pulled himself together and tried not to recall what had happened previously between him and magicians. "Where do we start?"

Esti smiled enigmatically and turned away. "Shirt off, on the table, face down."

He considered making some quip but for once common sense, or perhaps dread, got the better of him. He really hoped he wouldn't scream, but pulled off his shirt as though born to strip and hopped onto the table.

The smell of cooking blood got stronger until Vocho thought he might gag, but then it faded to almost nothing and Esti said something under her breath in Ikaran that Vocho couldn't catch. Strong fingers poking into his back made him jump, and the muttering was making him more nervous than ever.

"Who was it who gave you this?" she said at last.

"He called himself Sabates," Vocho replied. "He tried to—"

She said something that, by its tone, was some dire Ikaran curse. He was pretty sure he heard the word for "mother" mixed up with something that sounded much less complimentary. "I can guess what he tried. Bad blood, this. Very bad."

"But you can get rid of it?"

He felt the shrug in her fingertips. "Yes, no, maybe. Sabates, his magic, is very strong. Me, not so much, or not in the same way." She poked around some more, pressing her fingers so deeply into the tattoo Vocho wondered they didn't poke out the other side of his ribcage. "This may hurt."

She didn't even give him time to take a breath before a scorching pain in his back robbed him of it. It felt like a red-hot thread of lead was being pulled through his skin in some weird and intricate pattern. In his efforts not to scream he bit his thumb hard enough it bled. At least the blood might come in handy.

At last the pain subsided, Esti leaned back and told him he could sit.

"This will take some thought," she said as he tried to stop his hands from shaking too obviously. "And lots of blood. Special blood perhaps. It isn't Sabates controlling it now, I don't think, but someone just as strong. Close by too. You're being watched, Mr Vocho. Here, this will help."

She gave him a cup of something warm. He expected it to be foul and medicinal but all he could taste was honey and lemon so he drank the lot and the shakes soon went, along with much of his vision and any semblance of sobriety. His legs went rubbery; he couldn't feel his fingers, and he had a sudden stabbing worry that the person watching him through the tattoo was Esti.

A flip of a toggle on the wall, a yank of the shutters over the windows and the room was light again, though Esti's face wasn't. She frowned at Vocho like he'd done it on purpose, had this tattoo put on, then pushed him to the doorway at the end through into a kitchen, where Cospel was comfortably engrossed in shoving something fragrant down his neck. He grinned up at Vocho, winked in a devil-may-care way and turned back to the woman he'd been talking to.

The kitchen was full of people, mostly children. They scattered underfoot as Vocho stumbled in and sat heavily on the chair Esti pointed him at. The room was almost unbearably bright, with sunlight darting in from every angle through the windows. A range against one wall blasted out heat and baking smells, but the room was saved from overheating by the constant sea breeze that swirled through the windows, tinkling the chimes that hung before them.

It had surprised Vocho until someone had explained. In Ikaras there were no temples, and people didn't pray as such. The king didn't care if you worshipped one god or another or no god at all. No god, clockwork or otherwise, stared down from statues or tried to tell you what to do, though the sermonisers in the Mouth of Ikaras gave it a try. Instead, every home, almost every room, had a window-sill shrine. There seemed to be a god for everything, but Ikaras being a coastal city that suffered in the winter from gales and tempests, gods of sea and air seemed most favoured. Just about every window was festooned with a complicated array of wind chimes and charms which fluttered in the merest breeze, each jingle and jangle, each glittering, spinning charm a small prayer to save this house from harm. Often, underneath was a silver bowl full of saltwater, with odd rocks or bits of coral or even dried starfish and anemones dropped in each time someone asked a favour. The goddess of light, revered above all perhaps, had a sliver of the glass that covered all the buildings placed to catch the sun and reflect it onto chime and bowl, as though to appease the other gods. The people didn't pray, they got their things to do it for them.

A group of grubby children sat by the window, playing with the chimes, making them tinkle dischordantly. A woman, so like Esti they had to be sisters, plonked a bowl of something in front of Vocho with a cryptic look before turning back to the range. He hesitated – he'd been caught out once before, when they'd first arrived, and he'd been given something he thought was fantastic until told what it was. Blood sausage with added things that he hadn't noticed until they moved in his mouth. They'd said you knew it'd gone off when the maggots were dead. He hadn't been able to puke fast enough. He peered myopically at his bowl, poked it to see if there were any legs that looked like they were attached to anything alive, caught a disapproving look from the sister and picked up a spoon. Even through the fug of whatever Esti had given him, he knew that she was his best chance of getting rid of the tattoo, and Sabates' hold on him. Much as he wanted to, offending them by not eating would be a mistake.

The older children squawked when Esti began shooing them out, but calmed when she said they could come back for dinner. They scooted off, yelling something about last one to the docks was a ninny, which made Vocho smile. That still left four children, two babes in arms and two toddlers, one of which was happily on Cospel's lap playing with his buttons. The other sat on a rug by the range and stared up at Vocho in silence. He tried not to look at it — him, it was a boy — because children were an unknown quantity. He was aware they existed, he just wasn't sure what you actually did with them. Which meant that when the child crawled across the rug and tried to pull himself up Vocho's leg, he almost dropped the bowl.

"Sorry about that." Esti picked up the toddler and handed him to her sister. "Hazard of the job."

"Of being a magician? You get infested with children?"

She laughed and some of the tension left. "No, being the daughter of sailors. We end up looking after children whose parents are both at sea or who only have one parent, and that one is abroad. It's us or the orphanage, so it's usually us."

They both seemed determined not to talk about what was on his back, and Vocho was more than happy with that. Despite the effects of whatever she'd given him it was tingling like a bastard, and he'd rather not know what that meant.

Esti gave her sister a meaningful look, and the children were rounded up and taken for "a nice nap" in another room. Esti sat at the table, spread her hands over the tablecloth and cast a supplicating glance at the chimes over the window.

"How much do you know about magicians, either of you?"

Vocho and Cospel shared a look.

"Not much," Vocho said. "They're illegal in Reyes, and good riddance. Blood and bastards, that's all I know. Er . . . present company excepted, of course."

"Huh. Well, you don't know the half of it then. Just enough to get you into trouble. Which you have done. In style, I might add."

Vocho almost preened at that, until he realised it wasn't a compliment.

"Look," she said. "Magicians aren't all maniacs out to drain the blood of virgins, or even not-virgins. A load of old hokey, that is, at least in part, exaggerated to scare people. Magic does do funny things to people after a while, makes them all dark inside. It sucks you out and replaces you with someone else if you're not careful. But we hardly ever use human blood. Well, most of us don't. It's not forbidden, but it isn't usual. Except in certain cases or for certain things. But Sabates . . ." She broke off and shook her head.

"Is completely deluded," Kass said from the doorway, before she sauntered over and plonked herself down at the table, a familiar set of papers in front of her with Petri's now broken seal.

Kacha drummed her fingers on the papers and watched Vocho carefully. It had taken a long internal tussle before she'd decided that not reading what Petri had sent would be stupid.

She thought she was prepared for the excuses, the possible lies, had hardened herself, but he'd caught her off guard, again. How did he always do that? She put that one away for later, because there were more pressing things to worry about. The piece of paper inside the Clockwork God was the least of their worries now.

Vocho was pretending to look unconcerned but he must be losing his touch because his leg was jiggling and he kept squirming his shoulders.

"Did you get rid of it?" Kacha asked.

"Not exactly," Esti said before Vocho could speak. "Sabates is a crafty one, and strong too. Besides, something's happening with it."

"What?" A shaft of anxiety stabbed through Kacha's gut.

Esti's face scrunched up. "I don't know exactly, it's not really my thing, you know? I do a bit of healing and midwifery – all I can do now, without giving myself away. But even before I was more into the making side rather than the, well, the other side, like Sabates."

Vocho's spoon dropped into his bowl, and he turned a strange shade of grey. "And what does that mean, exactly?"

Esti eyed the pair of them as though weighing up what and what not to tell them before, with a surreptitious glance at the window, she said, "Magic is – do you know what it is? I doubt it. No one really does, although many have tried to pin it down. But like a butterfly, when you pin it, it dies. I can tell you this though – anyone can learn it if they can do one thing. And that one thing is to be aware on an – what's the word? Oh yes! On an emotional level of who and what is around you, always. You feel things, here." She thumped her chest. "Sounds stupid, I know, but that's the only way to describe it. Nothing solid, just a little twinge of feeling, and that's the basis of it all. Of course, just because you can feel things around you doesn't mean you like them or are a nice person. Sometimes it makes it easier for you to torture them, because you know exactly where to hurt them."

"And Sabates is—"

"No, that's the point. Or he never used to be. He was always a very powerful magician, but of course the more powerful tend to be also more, well, sensitive is perhaps the word. Your revolution, Bakar taking power, purging the magicians . . . Things changed in Ikaras, in the university, just as they did in Reyes. More subtly perhaps. Refugees turning up, not many but some. Sabates' son dying in Reyes, that changed him all right. Changed the whole magical arm of the university, a magician dying like that, murdered. No one had ever dared before. The magicians got scared, I think, pulled back, pulled themselves in. We closed ranks, didn't accept any new members except one. Sabates withdrew to his room as soon as we heard about his son, kept himself there in the dark for weeks. Then she came. Alicia that is. Came from Reyes, I reckon, though she never said. Never said much at all those first few weeks, and she was too old to start the training, but she offered Sabates something. I don't know what or how she got to him, but he took her in. And she was good, I'll give her that. Never said much back then, but by the gods she listened. She learned too, quicker than anyone I ever met. I was pretty young at the time, seven or eight, and I'd been training a year or more by then. She must have been eighteen or so. Others had been training for ten years by the time they were that age, but she caught them up in less than a year. Then she started pestering Sabates to show her more – different things, darker things. He was dark himself by then, dark inside, you know? So was she, always was, I think, and the magic eats away at that and makes it worse, twists it all up inside. We felt sorry for her to start with – thought she'd suffered under the revolt or lost someone, something like that – but there was always something sort of . . . dark and red at her centre. That's the best I can describe it."

"What's all that got to do with me?" Vocho said. "Sabates is deluded or deranged. Got it. Alicia is his apprentice. Check. We knew all that, if not the details. Now, how are you going to get this thing off me?"

"Well, if she's about, you could be in deep shit. She's not a pleasant person to cross."

Kacha took the opportunity of getting a word in. "She's

already here, I think." The look on their faces was at least partly satisfying, and now she had their attention, she carried on. "Petri, he, well he says lots of things here."

"I just bet he does," Vocho muttered under his breath, though he shut up when Kacha glared at him.

"One of which is that Sabates and Licio are on their way. I checked at the Mouth of Ikaras and it looks like Dom's right. And Alicia's already here, Petri thinks."

"So?"

"So, you plank, we already screwed them up once. Sabates isn't the forgiving kind and he wants to make sure we aren't around to screw him over again while he's 'negotiating'. They're looking for us, Voch. Sabates knew we were here, though I think he only just found out. And Alicia or someone has got the king to offer a reward for any 'Reyen spies'. We can't go back to Reyes openly because—" She shot Esti a glance. "Because. And we can't stay here. The way I see it, all we can do is try to convince the prelate that Licio's planning to kill him, and somehow manage to do that without getting arrested. Or anyone finding us through that thing on your back."

"Bugger."

"Exactly."

They sat in silence for a while, before Kacha said, "There is one thing we can use to help, one piece of evidence I left behind. Gave it to the Clockwork God – and don't look at me like that. One of the papers from the chest, but we daren't go anywhere right now because they'll know where we are. The tattoo, that's first. Get rid of that and we have a lot more options."

"That's easier said than done, apparently." Vocho slumped as if whatever Esti had done to him had sucked everything out of him.

Strangely it annoyed the crap out of Kacha when he was all ego, but life was only right somehow when Vocho was grandstanding and boasting and generally being a dick.

Esti looked thoughtfully between the two of them, took another look at the chimes at the window and then a deep breath. "I can stop them being able to track you at least. Do you think you could get into the university?"

Chapter Six

It had sounded so easy, but Vocho was coming to appreciate the subtleties of the defences around Ikaras University, in particular the mages' quarters. If appreciate meant lose blood over. He swore viciously under his breath, sucked the blood from his fingers and for the hundredth time reminded himself why he was here.

The lock was proving to be something of a trial, to put it mildly. When they'd decided on this frankly ridiculous plan he'd thought it would just be a matter of over the walls to avoid the university guards, who let no one in without a pass signed in duplicate by the deacon and the chief archivist, then a quick lock or two, get what they came for and away. Simple for a man of his distinction and talent, or should be. But it wasn't the main part of the university they needed to get into; it was the magical section, which made Vocho all sweaty just thinking about it. It also made getting in that much trickier.

"Voch," Kacha whispered behind him, "I think you might want to hurry up."

"Hey, you can't rush perfection."

"I would if I could see any. But there's people coming and I don't like the look of their gloves."

Not a phrase to instil dread in anyone's heart except in Ikaras.

He hurried up. The lock pick slid in his sweating hand, and something went click inside. It didn't sound like a very friendly click either. It sounded more like – "Duck!"

Vocho threw himself behind a nearby wall, and Kass all but fell on top of him. Something whizzed out of a suddenly open aperture above the lock, through the air right where his head had been and thunked against the stone the other side of the broad alley, bringing big fat sparks and a wailing screech that would wake the dead. The screech didn't stop when the axe blade did either – it carried on, the noise spiralling louder and louder until Vocho could see spots in front of his eyes. Kass said something, which was thankfully drowned out by the noise. He was pretty sure it wouldn't be complimentary.

She yanked him to his feet and with a quick look around they hared out of the alley, through a series of moving shadows conjured by the array of lights coming from the university and into the gardens at the centre of the main quadrangle, where Cospel and Esti were waiting for them.

"Went as well as could be expected then?" Cospel said.

"Pretty much," Vocho gasped from where he was bent over, hands on knees, trying to get his breath back.

Kass flopped down next to him, keeping a wary eye out through the bushes and trees. The quadrangle was suddenly full of people – students mostly by the look of them, young and rumpled from their beds. There were a few who looked a shade more noteworthy – older, wiser heads, professors maybe. Vocho recognised one from their endless reconnoitring. Coming from every corner, jangling in their bronze armour, a dozen guards headed towards the building they'd just left and servants galore ran to and fro, some shouting orders that everyone else seemed to ignore. Worse were a man and a woman who strolled through the mayhem like it was a picnic. Even the half-asleep students hurried to move out of their way when they noticed the way the shadows and light played across their faces, robes and most importantly their gloves.

Vocho had never been quite so breeches-soilingly scared of any piece of clothing before. "This was a bloody stupid idea," he whispered.

"Well, it was yours," Kass replied. "And we're here now. How else are we going to get that thing off your back? Ahh, shit."

Vocho whipped around to see where she was looking, peering through a set of thickly leafed branches. Shit indeed. The two mages had stopped and were peering very intently at the bushes.

"You don't suppose they can see the tattoo, do you?" Kass mouthed.

Vocho tried very hard not to suppose that. If it was true, they were sunk, but they had no real knowledge of what magic could do except be a pain in the behind and make you do things you didn't want to.

"Probably not," Esti whispered, and Vocho breathed a sigh of relief, "but I can't guarantee it," she continued, which made him suck it right back in again.

"Is there another way in? There must be, surely?" Cospel asked. "Place as big and old as this, I expect they've got a half-dozen ways in and secret tunnels too."

Esti shrugged. "I'm not sure. I never really needed to know because I always went in the front door. But perhaps through the kitchens? It's a long way around, but the back of the magicians' buildings butt up to the main kitchens, I think. I'm sure I remember a door there somewhere."

"There you are then, Cospel," Vocho said. "Off you go."

Cospel huffed and muttered under his breath but he knew his role well enough. He messed up his shirt and hair and stepped out of the bushes, fiddling with the ties on his breeches as though fumbling to do them up, and ended up right in front of the mages, whereupon he burped hugely.

"Beg pardon, I'm sure." Vocho winced at Cospel's accent, but to be fair it was better than his and Kass's put together.

"What in hells were you doing in . . ." the male mage began, until Cospel started rooting around in his breeches like he was trying to rearrange himself. "No, don't answer that. Gods' sakes, man, you don't piss in the deacon's bushes!"

Cospel moved around subtly so that the mages were facing the university not the bushes and who was hiding in them. "Oh, those are his? My apologies, I'm sure. Only just got here, see, and got caught short. An old war wound, it is, makes me have to go something terrible. I'm supposed to report to the kitchens."

The woman looked him up and down. "Well, that explains your ridiculous accent. It's that way, and make sure you wash your hands before you touch anything!"

"Yes, ma'am." Cospel bobbed up and down like a nervous housemaid. "Thank you, ma'am. And thank you for not frying me alive, ma'am. Much appreciated."

The male smiled condescendingly. "Lucky for you no one can stand the deacon or his stupid garden. Go on, sod off before I change my mind and have your blood."

Cospel hurried off in the direction of the main university building looming above them, subtly lit from within so that shadows became darker among the bushes, but it'd be easy enough to spot Vocho and Kacha if anyone was trying.

The mages didn't hang about, but went off towards the area that Vocho and Kacha had just vacated so hurriedly.

"Stupid bloody idea," Kass muttered again as she watched them go.

It was too, but while they'd argued for hours about the best way to get into the university and that tattoo off his back, none of them had managed to think of anything better. For some reason Esti was either unwilling to just walk in or, more likely to Vocho's mind, unable to, though at least she knew what they were looking for and where they were likely to find it.

Magicians kept records, she'd said. Reams and reams of records – of who invented what procedure, how they were performed, whether eyes of newts or tongues of dogs were required, that sort of thing, along with possibly how to reverse the spells. All the most powerful ones were written in an ancient red book that dated back hundreds of years, it seemed, locked up somewhere in the magicians' buildings. Surrounded by magicians. And magical locks. And gods knew what else. Three-headed dogs, probably. The only problem was, she wasn't sure exactly where the head mage kept the bloody thing because magicians were secretive bastards, or words to that effect.

Cospel, bless the scoundrel's devious heart, had managed to find and bribe an ancient magical archivist with a lot of booze and flattery, and had squeezed out of his sozzled brain where the safe was – in the head mage's office, set into the floor under the rug – and that the combination involved at least two number threes and a five.

The archivist hadn't been too clear on that last detail, probably because by then Cospel had picked his pockets and he was as drunk as ten lords in a gutter somewhere down by the docks. Luckily, locks and combinations had always been one of Vocho's accomplishments.

So there it was. Esti had been quite clear: the book was their one and only hope of getting this sodding tattoo off his back, or at least neutralised so that no one could track him through it.

After a time the furore that their hurried exit from the alleyway had caused died down. Students went bleary-eyed back to their beds, the guards jingled their bronze and leather armour in their usual patrols again, the lights that ranged across the glass exterior of the university dimmed, and Cospel sneaked back into the garden looking smug. Vocho wondered what he'd managed to thieve this time, and how it was he'd ever been caught when he was so good at it. Working for the guild, for them, had been part of his court-ordered rehabilitation after a stint in the Shrive, but Vocho could never stop him thieving. He sometimes wondered if Cospel's fingers were magnetic but had to admit his talents did come in very handy.

This time he'd come back with nothing worse than some roast beef and some information, as it turned out. Information, and the getting of it, was Cospel's speciality. Vocho thought this was because he looked like an exceedingly grubby and underfed spaniel with eloquent eyebrows and pleading eyes. He had the sort of rubbery face you just wanted to tell things to.

"Almost none of the servants are let out except on their days off, once a month or less, so I never had much of a chance to find one before now. Backstairs servants know everything. Probably why they don't like 'em going out much. Mind, at least they *get* a day off." He looked pointedly at Vocho.

"Yes, yes, but what did you find out?" Vocho had to work hard to keep his voice down. Maybe it was being this close to so many magicians, maybe it was his imagination, but the tattoo was burning his back like someone was drawing on him with a red-hot poker. He was sure he could feel Sabates' eyes through the damned thing.

Cospel slurped down the last of the purloined beef and licked his fingers. "Well, now, looks like Esti may have the right of it. Even magicians got to eat, right? And seems even some magicians get midnight hunger pangs too. So I found out how they get their food. In particular, how they sneak it in and out of the kitchens where they think Cook won't notice. Even magicians are afraid of Cook, and I don't blame 'em. I've served a few in my time, and they're terrifying, every last one. You don't mess with Cook unless you want to live on gruel and piss for the rest of your life. Come on, I'll show you."

"Er . . ." Esti said.

"Er what?"

"If I go into the kitchens someone will recognise me. That's, um, not really a good idea."

Vocho gave her what he liked to think was a penetrating look. "I'd have thought it was great – you can order them to show us in. Right?"

"Wrong. Look, I thought we weren't going to see anyone, or I'd have stayed at home. If anyone sees me, well, let's just say I left under a bit of a cloud."

"What sort of cloud?" Kass asked.

"The sort where you've kind of accidentally killed a few people, plus all the goats, and the cloud is their ashes blown in the wind?"

A short silence followed. Half of Vocho had just decided that the sooner they got away from this loony the better, and that he was never asking Cospel to find someone to help them ever again because they always seemed to be mad. Also, never trust a magician. The other half was looking at her in a new way and thinking that he could understand the killing-people-accidentally thing, having done it himself. And that someone who could do that might be a worthwhile ally.

"I can see how that might be a problem," Kass said slowly, "but I don't fancy going into a nest of magicians armed only with a couple of swords. You were going to be our fallback, in case it all went wrong." Her tone intimated, even if she didn't say it, that she fully expected it to all go wrong. Vocho couldn't help but feel stung that she looked at him while she said this.

"Oh, I can help with that," Esti said and pulled out a scalpel, a brush and some scraps of paper. Vocho winced as the scalpel sliced her forearm, bringing just enough blood to wet the brush and let her draw some strange twining symbol on the paper. She handed it to Kass, who took it like it was a gun about to go off.

"If you get into trouble, just throw that onto the floor and try to make sure you're not standing too close."

Kass held the damp paper up. "Why? Wait. Stupid question. Don't answer that."

They'd seen the effect a piece of paper like this could have. Vocho really didn't want to be near another one, but it was the best they were going to get.

"It'll be fine," Esti said. "Magicians aren't noted for their late nights, so the place should be good and quiet. Hardly any guards even, because most of them get jittery around magicians. I'll draw a map of where the office is."

Vocho and Kacha shared a look, but it wasn't like they had a better sort of plan or even much of a plan at all because they'd not been able to find out much about the inside of the university. Even Esti knew little about the parts that weren't ruled by the magicians. Kacha shrugged and Vocho thought, what the hells, and they made their careful way through the gardens until they were close to a door.

"Are you sure about this, Cospel?" Vocho whispered, but Kacha dug an elbow into his ribs, and he remembered who he was. Vocho the Great, Vocho the duellist, the guildsman, the undefeated. OK, almost undefeated, but Kacha had cheated so that didn't count. Main point, he was bloody good at what he did, and what he did was beat people with panache. His confidence might have taken a bit of a battering lately, but he could count on that. "Lead on then."

Kacha led – of the three she was by far the best at fading into the shadows. They waited till the patrol at the far end of the quadrangle had been and gone, and made their move. After earlier the guards were more alert so they had to be careful.

It was only as they reached the door, behind a pane of glass that shimmered red, that Vocho realised he was enjoying himself. Weeks they'd spent cooped up in a room over a cobbler's in Ikaras. Kass had never been one for sitting still at the best of times, and Vocho, despite his recent experiences, wasn't happy unless someone was watching him be fantastic and sisters didn't count. Leaving their rooms had been a problem, what with everyone looking for them. They'd only started that business with Bear because they were desperate, and look how that turned out. Now, outside and with the chance of being fantastic even if it was only in front of Kass and Cospel, with the added prospect of this damned tattoo coming off, Vocho had cheered up immensely. He had to stop himself humming.

The narrow door – Vocho had to go through sideways – led into a corridor that was just as cramped, not to mention musty and slightly damp. It led off in two directions before splitting into more corridors, but Cospel never faltered. Subtle coloured lights played over every glass surface, and inside them too. One wall glowed in intricate geometric patterns, now blue, red, yellow, green, that last making Kass look like she needed to throw up.

It wasn't long before the corridor led away from the glass and into the depths of the university. Instead of glowing glass, little lamps lit their way until Cospel motioned he should go first. "And put the swords under your cloaks. We're supposed to be servants, right?"

"Servants? But I—" Vocho protested.

"You keep telling me what a noble and honourable profession it is being your servant," Cospel said with a triumphant smirk. "Now, are you all mouth and no trousers, or are you willing to show me how true it is?"

They did their best, but swords weren't the easiest things to hide, even with a cloak.

Cospel was greeted in the kitchen like a long-lost friend. Two serving maids, either up early to start the day's baking or up late to finish clearing from yesterday, giggled and whispered behind their hands, making eyes at Cospel and making Vocho wonder what he could possibly have done to earn them. Especially as the same two girls didn't even give him a second glance. A man elbow-deep in suds gave Cospel a bubbly clap on the shoulder, and even Cook – Vocho could see what Cospel had meant about her being fearsome – smiled and nodded.

No one seemed to mind as they sidled through the chaos, though Cospel muttered something which brought them some sympathetic glances, and then they were through into an even narrower corridor that led off at a right angle. The lamps were few and far between, and the smell of must got worse until Vocho was stifling a sneeze every other step. Finally they arrived at what looked like a dead end with a small door halfway up the wall with odd-coloured staining around the edges.

"Cospel," Vocho said with a frown, remembering those sympathetic glances. "What exactly did you tell Cook that we were doing here?"

Cospel grinned sheepishly and shuffled his feet. "You wanted to get in, right? And you couldn't the other way. So this is our only choice. Probably best if we leave it at that for now."

"Cospel." Kass looked like she was on the edge of snapping, but Cospel didn't answer, only opened the door.

The smell that came out was indescribable, except in relation to goat shit. Vocho looked more closely. Some sort of compartment, like a dumb waiter with a plain shelf on top and what was undoubtedly a cage underneath. Next to the door was a lever, presumably to work the thing.

"Correct me if I'm wrong," Kass said, "but that's goat shit in there."

"Might be, might be." Cospel fingered his grubby collar. "I didn't say it'd be a nice way in."

"You said even mages get midnight hunger. You did not say, 'and this involves live goats'."

Cospel withered under her fierce look. "Well, not always. See that shelf on top? They seal up some food and put it on there. Head mage is partial to ham and eggs at three in the morning, I'm told."

"And the cage?"

"Is for the, um, other sort of hunger."

Vocho and Kacha stared at him until he said, "I don't

know, all right? She said they just need goats sometimes, and it seemed as good a place as any to get in, and sometimes they send people down there in the cage . . . and . . . and . . ."

"And they don't come back because mages use blood," Kacha said in a flat voice. "Are you sure we won't get minced on the way down?"

"Well, one of the girls says she goes to clear up sometimes, and there's no blood at the bottom of the shaft. Mostly."

Kacha raised an eyebrow Vocho's way. He shrugged. "It's this or nothing, and I want this bastard thing off my back. I say we make Cospel go first. If we hear screams, we can think of something else."

For a second Cospel looked like he was going to argue but then his shoulders slumped. "All right. Tell my mum I tried my best to be good, all right?"

"I'll tell her you died the king of Five Islands rolling in gold, if you like," Vocho said. "Let's go before someone realises their mistake. Is there a handle on the inside of that thing?"

Cospel got himself wedged inside, wrinkling his nose at the smell, and looked around. "Aye."

"Good. Off you go."

It didn't take long before Vocho and Kacha found themselves in a dank and unlit room.

"Are you sure this is the right place?" Vocho asked. It seemed to him there should be something a bit, well, magical about the place, and all he was getting was a strange smell and something crunchy under his boots.

"Have I ever steered you wrong?" Cospel asked, hurt clear in his voice.

"How about the time you forgot to mention the magician

in the coach? Look how that turned out. Or when you told me that young lady was unmarried? You almost steered me to an early grave."

"Look, you can't expect miracles on what you pay me. How about when you left me up that bloody tree with all them dogs hungering for my blood while you went off drinking? Or the time—"

Kacha hadn't said anything while they argued, but now she let out a whispered curse that shut the pair of them up. Finally, after some fumbling she lit one of the lamps, an oil one, and its muted glow showed the room in all its glory.

Vocho was tempted to curse as well. The whole room was full of bones, was made of bones. A table was made of long straight-ish bones, with smaller ones polished and inlaid on the top. The floor was more polished bones, set in a precise and mind-bending geometric pattern that made his eyes go strange. Just to top it all off, an oil lamp in the corner was made from a human skull with the top taken off. Underfoot lay bones not set into anything, not polished, hence the crunch under his boots. Some of them still had bloody meat on them, which explained the smell.

"God's cogs," he whispered. "Hey, how about we get the fuck out of here?"

For once Kass didn't argue and neither did Cospel. The door had a lock, but it was a mundane one this time, no booby traps, and Vocho had it open in moments. Then they were in a dim corridor taking deep breaths.

"Let's leave a different way," Kass said.

"If we can. Come on, get the map out."

She slid the scrap of paper out from under her tunic. Esti's map was detailed and precise. All they needed to do was work out where they were in relation to everything else.

After a short time and a whispered three-way argument which Vocho won, they headed right down the passage. The place was quiet as dead mice around them. Not even a snore. They risked moving faster, if not as quietly — it was getting late, or early, and they didn't want to be caught here once the magicians started waking up. Or at all.

Kass ghosted ahead, always quieter than Vocho could ever hope to be. Around corners, down steps, up steps, past open doorways with strange shadows and odd smells emanating from them. Their earlier escapade had obviously stirred something up because as they came to an unexpected cloister — unexpected because Vocho was looking at the map wrong — movement swirled in the centre.

A paved courtyard lit by a large lamp at the top of a stumpy pole was surrounded by arched walkways. Fountains tinkled somewhere in the shadows, but that wasn't the problem. The problem was the six guards looking alert in the centre of the courtyard, where they could see in all directions, along with what looked like a magician if the gloves were anything to go by.

The three intruders faded back into the corridor they'd just come from, and a hasty whispered conversation ensued.

"How far have we got to go?" Kass asked.

Vocho consulted the map, squinting in the dim light. "Other side of the courtyard. They'll be protecting the head mage's rooms, probably. We've got no chance of getting past them unnoticed, and there's no way around."

They both turned to look at Cospel.

"Don't go looking at me. You don't pay me enough."

"Think of it as recompense for the goat shit," Vocho growled. He was never going to get the smell out of his tunic.

Cospel's eyebrows wiggled all over his face, but finally he said, "Fine. But I get a day off. Deal?"

"If you live, you get a day off, after you've got the goat shit off my clothes," Vocho said. "Now look at the map. Draw them off and then see if you can make it to where we were supposed to come in. Here." He jabbed at what he hoped was the right point on Esti's map. "We'll meet you there. I'm betting we can open that door from the inside without an alarm going off. From there it's just a hop over the walls, and we're out of here. Easy for a man of your talents."

"Easy, he says," Cospel muttered. "Just draw off a load of guards and a magician and try not to die while you're about it. Easy-peasy. Do I have a choice?"

"Well I would do it, obviously, but Kass will need my help. I mean, there could be anything in that office, and two swords are better than one. You, Cospel, do not have a sword."

"Them guards do."

"But you can run faster than them. Good man. Off you go."

With a sour look Cospel straightened his shoulders, loosened his knife in its sheath and walked out into the courtyard as though he had every right to be there.

"Hey, you," the magician called, but Cospel didn't even wait for the "you" to leave the man's mouth before he was haring off down another corridor, away from where Vocho and Kacha needed to be. Cospel had a swift turn of speed, and the guards were caught by surprise so he had a good lead as he turned a corner and was out of sight.

Sadly, he didn't draw them all off — two guards stayed right where they were. Still, Vocho wasn't a bloody good swordsman for nothing, and when it came to it, there were only two of them, and they weren't up to much. A thrust, a clumsy parry from the first that almost tipped him over as he followed Vocho's line. A crunching elbow as he lost his balance, a twist of a wrist and a smack on the back of the head. Disarming them and rendering them unconscious, if slightly bloody, was an easy night's work.

They stashed the two guards out of sight and hurried away from the fading noise of the rest chasing Cospel. Around one corner and, "There. That one."

Surprisingly, and a little worryingly, the door wasn't locked. It should have been – it always was, according to Esti, especially when Sabates was away. Something didn't smell right, and it wasn't blood.

Kacha got out the little broad-bladed knife she'd found to replace her stiletto – she complained about it, but it was better than nothing and she'd always preferred the two-blade approach. Vocho hefted his own sword. One was more than enough for him, a point of pride that he only needed the one, as he reminded Kass at regular intervals.

"Stop posing and open the sodding door," Kass hissed.

Really, she had no sense of style at all. He opened the door. Quietly.

The first hint of daylight filtered in through a high window but didn't illuminate much. The lamp on the desk did, and it showed Vocho someone sitting behind it, scrabbling in its drawers like a mad rat, short dark hair falling over her face.

She looked up as Vocho opened the door wider and lifted his sword, though he had no real intention of using it. Until he saw her hands, anyway. Dark marks wriggled across her fingers, over her knuckles, up onto her wrists. The marks resolved into pictures. Long vines, intricate flowers, a sapling bending in the wind. He dragged his eyes away – he'd been caught that way before, and never again – and lifted the sword with more purpose.

Kass came in behind him, and she and the woman behind the desk both swore at roughly the same time as Vocho realised it was Esti.

She recovered quickly enough: leaped out of the chair and put her back to the wall, her hands out in front of her. The vines and flowers became thorns.

"You just stay there," she said. "Stay there and I won't do anything rash."

He stepped forward till he was up against the desk, gave the sword a flashy twirl that had the tip whip across an inch from her nose, and put on his best show-off smile. He didn't even get the chance to say something witty.

"I can explain," she said in a rush. "I never thought you'd get this far."

"You thought we'd die, you mean? Handily tying up all the guards so you could get whatever it is you're looking for."

Kass came up on his flank, blades at the ready. She had almost as much cause to be wary of magicians as he did. If Esti *blinked* wrong, he was going to make sure she couldn't cast any spells. Now or for ever.

"Yes! Well, maybe." Esti lowered her hands. "But you said you were good, so I thought you'd be fine and perhaps, you know, just to make sure . . . Did you get rid of all the guards?"

Kacha turned her head at a noise from the corridor. "No, and here they are."

Just when it had all been going so well too. Vocho couldn't decide which way to go, who to poke with his sword – the magician in front of him or the guards that had just reached the doorway behind him.

He'd just decided on Esti – he was never going to stop hating magicians, especially ones that were devious, and besides Kacha had turned to deal with the guards – when Esti burst into action. A scalpel appeared from nowhere, and even before Vocho could flinch she'd slashed a line down her own arm and blood ran freely. A great cracking sound from the doorway made Vocho turn despite himself. For some reason, a tree was growing there, with long twining branches full of thorns, tangling up the guards and drawing more blood from them. More trees sprang up in its shade, coiling through the first, inextricably trapping the two lead guards, whose muffled curses echoed around the room.

A neat trick. When he turned back, Esti was halfway out of the window.

"Hey!" he shouted after her.

"Never mind her," Kacha said. "Let's find the bloody book and get out of here. Even if we can't get her to use it, maybe we can find another magician."

"Now that's a plan I can get behind."

She rifled through the already messed-up drawers to see what Esti had been after while Vocho dragged up the rug from the floor and found the safe. Three-number combo, and hadn't the archivist said two threes and a five?

"Voch, you want to get a move on? Only I'm pretty sure there's a magician the other side of that tree now."

"I'm hurrying, I'm hurrying!" There were only a few ways this could go, and he'd tried them all. The safe refused to open.

He glanced up at Kass. She had her sword in one hand and a drawer in the other, which she flipped over, spilling pens everywhere. God's cogs, yes. A previous employer had once the 'brilliant' idea of writing his combo on the bottom of the drawer, which, while not the first place any decent safe-cracker would look, was certainly not the last.

"Four six four," she said.

"Cheeky bugger lied to us," Vocho muttered and spun the lock. *Click*.

Too late he recalled that this was a magician's safe. He recalled at about the time he scraped himself off the wall, head ringing and eyes blurred. Kass, with perhaps more sense, had ducked behind the desk and missed the worst of it. Vocho staggered to his feet, pulled himself together at the sound of guards getting altogether too close to getting in, and counted himself thankful no bones appeared to be broken.

The contents of the safe, after all that, were a disappointment. While there were some interesting-looking books with risqué woodcuts that presumably Sabates didn't share with anyone, he found nothing like what they were looking for. Nothing bound in red, nothing that looked very old.

All the while the guards were hacking away at the instant forest, and there was a distinct smell of cooking blood.

"Shit," Kacha said when she looked in the safe. "Come on. We need to get going before they get through."

"There must be something." Had to be or why would Esti have risked all this?

"If there is, we haven't got time to find it. Come on!"

Only there was. Under the woodcuts lay a small brown book full of tiny writing that Vocho couldn't read and a sheaf of papers with some complicated-looking plans on them. He shoved it all into his tunic and followed Kass.

Esti had left the chair under the window, and within moments the two of them had climbed out and dropped onto a small lawn surrounded on all sides by a path and then blank-faced buildings. Only one door broke the glass surfaces, and they headed for it as fast as they could. By the sounds of it, not a moment too soon. A crossbow bolt skipped past Kacha's head and through a pane of glass ahead, which shattered in a shower of blue and green shards.

They made it through the door with no idea what they'd find on the other side and slammed it shut behind them. What they found in the corridor beyond was Esti, leaning against the wall with a twisted look on her face, and some guards advancing warily.

Vocho didn't stop to think – he rarely did – but rushed the guards, who pulled up short, just for a moment. Long enough for Kacha to join him and hiss something at Esti.

The lead guard hefted a short spear that looked more ceremonial than anything else, a heavy *palla* blade in the other hand. At least only one of his companions had a clockwork gun, which was a relief. Vocho leaped in, took out the gunman first and whirled on the leader. Out of the corner of his eye he could see Kacha holding her own against two more.

It wasn't fair really. He and Kass had spent a couple of decades training at the duellists' guild, and by the look of it these men had received a few weeks training in the park and a spear. Ikaras was known as a peaceful city, so no doubt no one ever expected them to have to do much.

Sad for them, but Vocho went a bit easy because of it. Only one gave him much trouble, the leader, who was a crafty bastard. The *palla* was a weapon Vocho was learning to loathe. It had no art to it, just sheer chopping power. Half his fancy moves were so much dust before it.

The man feinted left then aimed for Vocho's groin with the short spear. Vocho knocked it away with inches to spare, dodged an overhanded blow from the *palla*, and had just enough space and time for a slash to the man's face that missed but pulled him up short. They circled briefly, both unsure of the other's weapons. The man came, double-handed again. The spear was ineffective held in only one hand, but it'd be enough if it caught him. In the end the weakness of the *palla* – no defence, just all-out brute attack – told as Vocho swerved away and used the greater reach of his sword to its best effect, got in under the man's guard and took out the spear arm. After that, he didn't last long before he was a pile of groaning on the floor. Vocho had to wonder at the laxness of the security. If they'd known how bad it was, they would have just walked in.

When he turned, Kacha was bending over Esti.

"Don't get too close," he said. He didn't like the look of the markings on her hands, thorns like daggers. "You never know what they'll do, and she's already lied to us."

Kacha got Esti up. It was clear she'd hurt her leg somehow, possibly in the drop from the window. "She's the only bloody hope we've got, Voch."

"If she doesn't do anything to us," Vocho muttered. The tattoo on his back was itching like crazy, and looking at the magician just made it worse, made all the shadowy memories come back. "Or make us do anything."

"I won't, I promise!" Esti said. "You help me out of here, and I'll help you with whatever you want. I really will."

The woman looked pleadingly at Vocho as the echoes of more running feet came to them.

"I'll take the tattoo off, for free."

Vocho would do almost anything for that.

"All right. But if you try anything, you'll regret it. Now let's get out of here."

Chapter Seven

Kacha helped Esti up the steps to her house. Vocho was being a right arse, but she supposed she couldn't blame him. Esti clearly had plans of her own, ones she hadn't bothered to share with Vocho and Kacha. She'd used them and lied to them. But she'd done nothing that either of them wouldn't have done themselves. Hells, they'd sent Cospel off with guards on his tail armed with nothing but a knife, though they'd found him safe and well — the man could get out of a bear trap if he had a mind, Kacha often thought. Esti hadn't done any worse than they had, if you thought about it. Besides, Kacha thought she had been telling the truth about some things. Thrown out of the magicians' little cabal, just as she and Vocho had been thrown out of their guild. Kacha was at least prepared to hear what she had to say.

Esti's house was small and dank under its coating of vines. Esti got herself to a stool by the mean little fireplace in the front room and shuffled onto it. Her leg was swollen but not purple. She'd probably be able to walk on it in a day or two. Vocho came in like a bad cloud behind them and rounded on her.

"So, what was that all about? No, you keep your hands in those gloves and where I can see them. You tell us about some big red book you want, that can help me, but basically you were using us to get what you wanted. Did you get it? Because there was no red book. I did, however, find this." He slapped the little brown book on a table, along with the plans for what looked like a clockwork heart. "And I can't read Ikaran, but I can read your name clear enough on the front of that book. So you start telling me what's really going on here and maybe this room won't end up with a whole lot of blood in it."

Esti glowered up at him from under her fringe, but soon sighed and relaxed her shoulders. "I suppose that's fair enough. I was desperate, all right? Sabates had me thrown out of the university, and he was blackmailing me too. Using that book, among other things. Did you see what else was in the safe?"

"Well there were these plans and some, um, interesting woodcuts. Oh, I see. I think. My word. And sideways too. Gosh, how acrobatic." Some of the anger leached out of Vocho, though it still bubbled underneath. He was never going to like a magician. "But what does that have to do with me and Kass? And can you actually help me or not?"

Esti blushed and wouldn't look at either of them. "I needed money to get away from him, as far as I can because he can reach a long way. He always wants me to do things for him! He won't let me say no. And there's quite a big reward for Reyen spies, in case you hadn't noticed. I don't earn any money, or not much. I'm not in the university any more. If I use more than the smallest bit of magic other than what he gets me to do, Alicia'll find out where I am and then, well, and then it's the dungeons. The ones under the Mouth. If I'm lucky. And I've got my sister to think about, my brother, the children. I had to get these things back so he'd stop blackmailing me."

"And you used us to do it?" Vocho, usually so blasé, was looking anything but as he kicked at a table.

"You're using me too, aren't you? Who else do you think would take off that tattoo without reporting you to the king's men? Or worse, the magicians. Or do it so cheaply? You wanted my help, and this is my price."

She picked up the book and opened it. "This is everything. All my notes, my charms, my spells. Everything – it's my whole life. This book can get that tattoo off your back."

Vocho strode forward as though he was about to wrench the book from her hands. Kacha had never seen him like this before. Vocho wasn't an angry sort of person, usually being too busy showing off, but that tattoo had done strange things to her brother. Esti held her ground with an icy stare and he stopped at the last second. She looked to Kacha, but she wouldn't find much help there – she was almost as wary of magicians as Vocho.

"What do you need?" Esti said at last. "If I help you, take that tattoo off for starters, will you promise I can keep the book, and you won't take me back to Sabates?"

Vocho looked like he was on the verge of grabbing the book anyway, maybe grabbing Esti and giving her a good shake, but this might be their best chance.

"Well, promise might be a bit of a strong word," Kacha said, ignoring the glare from Vocho. "But we'll certainly give it a try."

Petri tried to walk normally, but the temptation to look over his shoulder was almost overwhelming. No doubt about it now, he was being watched. A co-worker, a maid, one of the guards. They were careful about it, mostly, but not careful enough. Maybe there were others who were more careful. But he was sure; wherever he went, someone was watching.

A guard tracked his movements as he took the grand staircase three steps at a time, past the orrery, up into the wide corridor, dim at midnight, that led to Bakar's rooms. He'd been sent for, again, and the tone of the note didn't bode well. Metallic disharmony greeted him as he opened the door. Clocks chimed and clicked and ticked and tolled the top of the hour. He gritted his teeth, pasted a smile on his face and went in.

Bakar's room was black as pitch. Shutters closed, curtains drawn. Old sweat and new fear saturated the room.

"Bakar?"

A light flared in the corner, then bloomed as it was touched to a wick and the glass set in place on a lamp. The glass rattled against its brass base as Bakar put the lamp on a table.

"Petri, you came."

"Of course."

"Of course? I suppose. Sit, sit."

Petri took a chair by the cold fireplace and watched Bakar as he came across the room. The public man projected to the world was gone. In its place was a husk. Dry skin cracked over sunken cheeks; hair that had once been thick and full and dark now wisped around a knobbed forehead. But the eyes – the eyes were as bright as Petri had ever seen them, as bright as the day when Bakar had brought down a king and changed the face of Reyes for ever. Petri had thought then that the man burned. With injustice, with passion. Now that fire had used him up, leaving just the eyes, just the passion, which had now twisted into madness.

Bakar took a seat opposite, his shaking legs almost collapsing him into it.

"Tea." He waved a bony hand at a tray set on the low table between them. Apple tea, Petri's favourite. Even as he was, Bakar never forgot little details like that.

Petri poured for them both, though Bakar took none until Petri had sipped and remained alive, unpoisoned.

"I know who it is, you know." Bakar's voice was as dry as his skin, but as burning as his eyes. "I know who's trying to kill me, take Reyes for their own."

Petri's cup stopped halfway to his lips before he forced himself to take another swallow. "You do?"

"Oh yes, I think so. I have suspected for a while, in fact, but every man has frailties, flaws. Only the clockwork is perfect. My reading of it was, well, imperfect. My reading of you."

Petri's cup rattled in its saucer. Bakar couldn't know. *Couldn't*, not with any certainty. "Me?"

Bakar's eyes grew ever brighter, seemed the brightest thing in the room until Petri could see the cogs behind them, in Bakar's head, endlessly whirring. "Trust is my flaw, Petri. Always I trust in my fellow man. But a leader of men cannot trust, not even one he looks on as his own son. The Clockwork God provides."

He drew out a much folded and battered piece of paper.

"I trust, but men in my employ do not. There is, in the cellars of this palace, a room where three men work day after day. Sifting through the truths that men and women give to the Clockwork God. Trying to find truths for me. Here is one."

He opened the paper and smoothed it flat on the table next to the teapot.

"Tell me what it says, Petri Egimont."

Three words in, and Petri knew what it was. Knew how it ended.

Lord Petri Egimont, Duke of Elona and Master of the Duelling Guild of Reyes.

Written in a fit of idiocy, on a day when he thought both those titles might soon be his. A day he'd betrayed this man.

"Why, Petri?"

What could he say? Nothing that wouldn't seem self-serving, ungrateful, stupid. He'd betrayed a man he'd looked to as a father for what? For lies. And yet, looking at him now, the insanity glowing behind those burning eyes, knowing what Reyes had recently become under his guidance, he thought he'd do it again.

And perhaps, yes, perhaps he was even lying to himself.

Quiet feet behind him. A faint jingle. There would be a gun, no doubt, tightly wound and pointed at the back of his head.

"Just tell me why, and with who." Bakar's sorrowful voice was at odds with the heat of his eyes. "That's all. Was it Kacha and Vocho? Kacha, no doubt, though I suspect you've little liking for her brother. Her, though? You think I didn't see? Think I didn't know about you and her? Was that all it was, that you thought you loved the scheming witch?"

Petri forgot whoever was at his back, the gun that was certainly ready to kill him, and shot out of his seat. Another gun, held by a silent man in black who stepped forward from the darkness behind Bakar, pulled him up short.

"Not to worry," Bakar said. "I know where you sent your little letter. She'll be dead soon enough. Then perhaps you'll see sense, hmm?"

That was when Petri realised that Bakar had slid so far

past sanity that he could no longer see it. Even Sabates might be preferable to this. He couldn't seem to find words to speak except, "Why not have them just shoot me?"

Bakar rose to face him, and the heat of his gaze was a lunatic furnace. "Because you're my son, Petri. You always were, and a responsible father chastises his son. He doesn't kill him." He looked over Petri's shoulder to the man behind. "Take him to the Shrive, but be no rougher than you need."

A gun jabbed into the back of Petri's neck, and he didn't resist when other hands dragged his arms up behind his back, when they cuffed him, even when they thrust him into the corridor and then out of the building on the way to the terror of the Shrive.

Chapter Eight

Alicia made her careful way through the maze of the magicians' part of the university. It had taken her painstaking years to learn where everything was; she could have walked the halls blindfold and still got to where she needed to go.

She had her instructions from Sabates and she intended to carry them out, though maybe tweak them a little for her own ends. Sabates had been focused on this one thing for so long, he was blind to almost everything else. Maybe that was his one weakness, and she'd spent a long time looking for weakness in him, somewhere she could force in a blade and crack him open.

She turned a corner straight into a commotion. A group of the rather ineffective university guards milled about, unsure what to do. Only one seemed to have any clue – an older man who seemed as out of place here as a shark. He still stood tall and proud, the three interlocking scars on his cheek vivid in the light. A life-warrior, one sworn from birth to serve his lord, his only god, who thought dying for him the greatest honour he could earn. Under a sleeve she could make out another scar from the cuffs that had bound him to his life-mate, another warrior, for many years until they proved their worth. As this one had, if the cheek scars were any testament. Proud and honourable to a fault, all of them, barely even looking at any not in their caste. Only their king had their devotion. Yet this one had betrayed that. His most prominent feature was his nose, or lack of it. Now it was just a scarred and gaping hole, the worst fate for any life-warrior, leaving him open to ridicule and scorn, to debasement and a life of drudgery. Had left this one with the task of overseeing men the army wouldn't have or the courts had decided needed some discipline in their lives. Poor subordinates for one who'd once been one of the best warriors that Ikaras had to offer.

She wondered what he'd done to earn it and how she could use it – him – for her own ends. Honour, she'd found, was an easy thing to twist.

"Wind and sodding water!" a sergeant shouted at a group by Sabates' door. "Stop, just stop. You. Yes, you with the face like a bag of spuds. Start at the beginning."

"I – I – I –" The potato-faced boy couldn't get any words out to start with, until he looked at the floor and took a deep breath. "The alarm went off on the south door about one in the morning. We searched everywhere, but we couldn't find anyone."

"And no one thought to come and find me?" The life-warrior's voice came softly from behind the sergeant, spooking even that bluff man to silence. Alicia tried not to smile at how the boy tried to shrink back but was subtly pushed forward by the ones behind him. A life-warrior, even a disgraced one with no nose, was not a man to be trifled with.

"Um, no, sir. Two of the magicians came to look, but

they couldn't see anyone either and they said the alarm was probably just faulty, so, um, well they *are* magicians, sir."

"And you didn't want to get fried to a crisp." A world-weary sigh from the warrior as though the magicians he was supposed to help protect were the bane of his existence. "Then what?"

"And then," Alicia said, moving smoothly between Spud-Face and the warrior, "even though they stepped up patrols, someone got into Sabates' office. More than one someone. Your name, warrior?"

His eyes snapped to her, took in the gloves and he nodded, eyes alight – with that one title she'd offered him a hint of his former glory, as though she hadn't noticed the ruin of his face.

"Gerlar is my name," he said. He didn't back down, not even from a magician. "You knew and did nothing?"

She allowed herself a slow smile, which made Gerlar look as though he wished honour would allow him a pace backwards, but he checked himself as she knew he would. Gerlar had lost enough dignity, and he'd do nothing that might make him lose more in front of these green boys, that might make his hold over them weaker. "Oh, not nothing. But I wasn't here, so what could I do? I only learned of it when I got back here this morning. But I can help you. If you'll help me."

Gerlar narrowed his eyes, but he grunted what might have been a yes and growled at the guards to "Leave us alone, and get and do your jobs."

It didn't take long before they were alone next to a ruined door and the vestiges of what looked like a tree.

"Well?" Gerlar growled.

Again she smiled. She might need this gruff bastard

before she was through. "Let me see in there and then perhaps I can tell you more."

He studied her for some moments before he answered. "Sabates is away until next week. Escorting the delegation from Reyes. Orgull had to send someone important. Annoyed him no end."

She chuckled – everything pissed off Orgull, as Gerlar no doubt well knew. "Well then. Looks like someone or several someones knew that he was away and took their chance. Wait, just a moment."

The scalpel was, as always, within easy reach, stashed in a little sheath in the cuff of her glove. Only a small nick – she didn't need much. She was pretty sure who'd been in here anyway; she'd already spoken to some of the servants and had a good description of Vocho and his sister and servant. A life-warrior would never think of talking to lowly servants to find out what they knew. Subterfuge and subtlety were dishonourable and anyone not a life-warrior beneath notice except their king.

Alicia, on the other hand, found it helpful always to know the person who knew the most in any place. Here, it was Cook, whose staff told her every little thing they knew, everything they saw and heard when they served dinner in the private rooms. Cook was like a spider, feeling a tingle on a thread and reeling it in, baiting webs with kitchen maids or butlers, manipulating students who owed her money or favours. Armies were ruled by their stomachs, and so were servants and universities. And who did Cook owe? Exactly. So Alicia had a good idea about at least part of what had happened, and the tree gave her another clue. Esti had been a thorn in her side for years, in more ways than one. Who else could make a tree grow from a seed in moments? Who else had a grudge against Sabates?

Really, it didn't take a genius to figure it out, but Gerlar likely wasn't a genius in anything except bashing heads together no matter how elegantly or honourably. The magic would make a good show, might get him on her side, and might even help her track down the little bastard that was Vocho. A few drops of blood on the floor by the remains of the tree. Alicia muttered under her breath, and there, plain as plain. Esti had been in here. How had she got in? Didn't matter. Another few drops over by the desk, and Vocho's face wavered in front of her eyes.

"What's missing?" she asked Gerlar, but she was fairly certain she knew the answer.

"Don't know yet, ma'am. Won't know until Sabates gets back."

"Oh, I think we can guess, Gerlar." Alicia straightened up and wiped away a stray smudge of blood from the sleeve of her dress. She had a good idea. Esti's book, her life's work, which she was desperate to get back. What Sabates was blackmailing her with perhaps – he thought Alicia didn't know, but he always had underestimated her. She wondered if there had been anything else in that safe, what secrets the old bastard was keeping from her. Worth finding out.

"Yes, ma'am."

"Good. Get your men, and I use that term loosely, to see who they can find. They'll be looking for a man and a woman, Reyens. She'll be easier to spot, as she's fair haired. Whatever you do, don't let your men attack them. They'll die in heartbeats. I think perhaps they may have a magician with them, a renegade. Find them, and when you do report back to me, and me alone. No taking them to the king's dungeons, no charging them as spies, no alerting them to the fact they've been found. Understand?"

He nodded and left her on her own in the office. She closed the door with care, stepped around the remains of Esti's tree and sat herself at the desk.

She drummed her fingers. This wasn't quite how she'd intended it, but she could make it work. Of course she could. She'd spent years planning this, and one little glitch wasn't going to stop her now. All she needed to do was find Vocho and Esti before Sabates did. The tattoo was being irritatingly hard to find — shoddy work by Sabates, she thought. Perhaps she just needed to concentrate harder. She pulled the scalpel from its hiding place and set to work.

Kacha rubbed at the bridge of her nose and took a deep breath. No matter how much she tried to persuade Vocho they needed Esti's help, as far as he was concerned, the sooner every magician died, the better. Against his protests, sulks and outbursts, they'd left for their rooms with the promise that Esti would see what she could do. Cospel was to wait with her, keep an eye on her. It'd take some time, she said, and Kacha and Vocho had plenty else to do.

After trying to pick a fight with Kacha, Vocho had finally left their rooms just about sunset, when the dazzle of the light lessened, turned into mellow reds and yellows across the city, and the lamps lit up, festooning the buildings in blue and green and gold. Kacha was pretty sure he was going to get himself rip-snortingly drunk but didn't blame him. The only reason she didn't join him was because, without Cospel about, one of them needed to keep a clear head.

Besides which, there were things to think about, and she did that better without Vocho around. She opened a window and sat on the wide sill, enjoying the breeze that wafted up from the docks, which were far enough away not to smell too rank. From here she had a good view of the bar over the road where Vocho was trying his best to show off in a language he couldn't really speak. He was doing pretty well with sign language and posing.

Oh yes, lots to think on. Tattoos, magicians, trust. She was still thinking hard when the sun finally set in a shower of sparks in the glass, and a figure came along the alley. Kacha didn't pay too much attention at first. The woman came slowly along the way, as though looking for something. Or someone. Kacha sat up and paid more attention. Gloves, the woman was wearing gloves. Anywhere else that would mean nothing, but right here and now it meant trouble. Especially when she paused outside the bar and peered in to where Vocho was using the thrust of a full jug to make some drink-addled point.

Kacha didn't hesitate — out of the window, up onto the roof, quiet as a cat. The tiles were glass but dark enough. The lights in them had failed years before, and apparently no one knew how to fix them, which was one reason Kass had decided this was where they were going to lodge. Just in case of an event like this. The glass was slippery under her boots, but she'd trod on worse, and a handy chimney for her hand helped her balance.

No doubt about it now. Kacha moved until she was above the woman and could see the writhing marks on her hands when the gloves came off. A quick glance showed her that Vocho had noticed the magician too, though he was making a good effort at not showing it. He flicked a look at the window Kass had been sitting in, noticed her absence, let his gaze travel upwards. She nodded and, without a moment's hesitation, leaped from the roof.

The fall jarred her, but she rolled, let the momentum

carry her along and pop her up right behind the magician, sword already half out of its scabbard. Perfect positioning. Just in time to see Vocho barge out of the inn, sword in one hand, jug swinging for the magician in the other. Light spilled out with him, and he got a good look at the woman, which stopped him in his tracks.

"Vocho, dearest," the magician said. "If you're there, then Kacha is right behind me, correct?"

"Bloody right I am." Kass aimed a blow for the back of the woman's head with the hilt of her sword, but it never connected because the magician wasn't there, leaving Kass off balance for all of half a second as she recovered.

Half a second Alicia used. She ducked forward and to one side to avoid Kass's next blow, neatly avoiding Vocho's jug, which was trying to connect with her forehead, and she already had her scalpel out. The stench of cooking blood made Kass gag but it was the light that stopped her. Uncountable pinpricks of light stabbed out of the glass surrounding them into her eyes, leaving her blind and groping.

She swung her sword anyway, and it connected with something but she couldn't be sure what. Vocho swore viciously and something shattered – the jug because now sour beer mingled with the smell of blood.

The lights dimmed and Kass could see again, but it wasn't encouraging. Alicia stood with blood dripping down one arm, her lip curled. Black marks wriggled over her hands, and Kass tried not to look but it was impossible. Noose, sword, guillotine. None of the pictures had anything to do with living, and the feeling came over her that death was inevitable, not just in some far future but right now.

Vocho's voice cut in, shouting but faint as though he

was far away, edged with panic. "You just stay away from me. You stay the fuck away and I won't slice you to bits."

The markings changed, turned into Vocho and Kacha, no doubt about it, before they exploded into little shards of nothing. Her eyes were full of the markings, couldn't seem to see anything else, so she went for them, for the hands. Take a magician's hands and what was she good for? Kass lunged forward, not thinking about anything except stopping those hands, slicing away the markings that seemed to be mocking her. Again, the magician wasn't there; she was ten feet away, laughing.

"Stupid duellists, always thinking with your swords, not your heads."

Vocho edged sideways and, seeing what he was about, Kacha moved the other way. Trap her in the middle and quickly.

Kacha managed to drag her eyes away from the markings to see what was actually in Alicia's hands. A scrap of paper, with something smeared in dark blood on it.

"Voch."

"I see it." His voice had lost all its bluster, came flat and heavy across the alley.

"You misunderstand me," Alicia said. "I haven't come to kill you, or you'd be dead already, dead as soon as I saw Vocho."

A fair point, Kacha had to admit, if it were true, but that didn't stop her. If only they could shut her up, they might have a chance.

"What do you want then?" Vocho asked. "An invitation to tea?"

Alicia laughed at that, but it sounded forced. "Hardly. Maybe you'll find out, maybe you won't."

A sudden flash, and what felt like a hot hand drove

Kacha against the wall behind her, smashing all the breath from her lungs and even making her drop her sword. She bent to grope for it even before her eyes recovered from the purple and blue splotches that wavered in front of them.

A hand on her arm made her swing, but she stopped just in time to avoid punching Vocho.

"Cogs, Voch, you almost scared me silly. You OK?"

"Yeah. Booze kind of numbs things a bit. Probably hurt like blazes tomorrow though. You?"

Kacha gave herself a quick once-over. Nothing seemed to be broken, though she was going to have a bruise like a dinner plate on her hip tomorrow from where her knife had got caught between her and the wall. "Good enough." She blinked hard to rid herself of the last of the splotches and peered down the alley. Nothing. No one. Not for long though. Alicia knew where they were living. The Reyes delegation was due in the city tomorrow at dawn, and with it would be Sabates, she could almost guarantee it. Perhaps Alicia didn't want them dead; with that tattoo still on Vocho's back maybe he would be used again.

"Come on. Time to pack up and move," she said.

Alicia watched from the darkness as Vocho and Kacha packed their meagre belongings. It was all starting to fit together rather neatly. They would go to Esti's, she was sure of it, and then she'd find out where the damned woman had hidden, what had been in that safe and what Sabates was planning. Something he was keeping from Alicia, she was sure of it. Some plan that left her by the wayside and Esti in her place, which she'd worked very hard to avoid.

She'd get rid of Esti permanently, then Domenech, who she was sure would find this pair of scoundrels. Domenech and Eneko were the two men she most wanted dead. When she had what she wanted from them at least. Eneko was easy to find if not easy to persuade to give her what she wanted. Domenech . . . he'd come to these two, she was sure, he seemed to have grown fond of them for some unfathomable reason. Just a matter of waiting. Alicia beckoned to Gerlar, who'd kept out of the way during the fight.

"Watch, follow, see where they go. They'll be looking for me but not for you. Do try to be discreet, won't you?" She took a hard look at the missing nose, the man's way of standing, the scars that would mark him as a life-warrior to any Ikaran. "All right, that may be difficult."

He stared straight ahead. "My job is now at the university, not working for you."

She paced around him, noting the lack of even a wooden ceremonial knife. Lower than the night-soil men in the scheme of things. There were dogs that had better social standing than a life-warrior with no honour, or at least he'd think that way, as would every other Ikaran. Ikaran life involved a thousand little jugglings of rank a day, judging whether you were higher, lower or equal to the person next to you and adjusting your manner accordingly. Alicia found it fascinating to watch in others, interesting to manipulate but utterly boring to have to follow herself.

"Gerlar, how would you like to get your honour back? Things will be changing at the university. Soon enough you'll have a new master. Besides, these two broke into the university, stole from Sabates right under your nose and escaped with barely a hitch. Surely it's your duty?"

He turned a cold eye on her. "My duty would be to arrest them now."

"Ah, but then the third one would escape your grasp.

What honour in that? If you had a knife you'd lose many rings from it for that, yes?"

"I have no knife, no rings or honour to lose. I have only duty."

God's bloody cogs, he was hard work. She'd not had much to do with life-warriors before now, but she was coming to appreciate how single-minded they were. And how annoyingly, stupidly stubborn. But every man has his price. It was just a matter of offering the right thing. Riches and glory wouldn't do any good with this one. More earthly pleasures weren't likely to work either, given the life-warriors' famously ascetic nature. Denying themselves was an art form to them. There was only one thing he'd want – his old partner back, the left hand to his right. One was nothing without the other. It was merely a matter of making him think she could provide that.

For now she didn't have time, but having someone whose loyalty was utterly unquestionable was always useful. She'd work on him later, use a little blood, some persuasion. For now a little misinformation would do.

"Gerlar, what is your current sworn duty?"

"To protect the magicians from any threat, at all costs," he said promptly.

"Well, now, what if I were to tell you that I suspect these people to be involved in a plot to assassinate Sabates. More than suspect, in fact. They're two of the duellists' guild, sent by Reyes to destabilise Ikaras ahead of the negotiations. I can't follow them because they know me. But you can, and find out who else is working with them – one of the magicians, I know that. I just don't know where she is. Of course, if you were to foil a plot to assassinate Sabates, maybe even Orgull, and expose a traitorous magician, then perhaps your honour would be somewhat

restored? Or maybe I would be grateful enough to give
you what you most want – your partner back, alive and
well. Oh yes, I can do that, a simple matter even. If I want
to."

Yes, that dart hit home. He hid it well, but his shoulders
straightened and his eyes warmed, although a curt nod
was all she got before he took up his position hidden in a
doorway opposite Kacha and Vocho's lodgings.

Minutes later they clattered down the steps and hurried
up the narrow street, with Gerlar trailing at a safe distance.

Chapter Nine

Petri savoured his brief taste of free air after weeks cooped up in the palace and let his mind roam. One of his escorts shoved him down the steps and out across the clanking clockwork garden. Illuminated stars and midnight planets slid past on rails, always going the same way, to the same end. Like his life, only he hadn't expected his personal rail to end in the Shrive. There had to be a way out of this. There always was a way out, he had to believe that. He couldn't escape the Shrive the way Kacha had – Bakar had plugged that particular hole. His only chance lay in escaping before he was taken through the vast doors into the twisting maze of corridors and cells.

Escape now didn't look likely either – Bakar's men met with four masked escorts, all with sword and gun, and handed him over. When they reached the end of the clock-work garden, they didn't turn him towards the Shrive. Instead he was yanked through a dark gate where a watchman lay unconscious – sleeping or knocked out, Petri couldn't tell – and out into the city. He opened his mouth to say something, but a gruff voice growled, "Shut up and keep moving." A gun pressed into his kidneys, so he did as he was told. Wherever he was going, it had to be better than the Shrive, surely.

The looming bulk of the guild ahead changed his mind on that. He was pushed, struggling, over the bridge that separated the duellists from the city, thrust through the open gates into the courtyard, where the clockwork duellist watched him with passionless bronze eyes. He knew where he was being taken as soon as they entered the cloister, and clamped his mouth shut on the words that wanted to come out, clamped his fingers over the sweat on his palms. Reyes seemed to be nothing but prisons and the threat of execution.

Down stairs, round corners, up stairs in a pattern Petri knew by heart, and then he was shoved through an open door to stagger in front of Eneko. The guild master sat behind his desk and regarded Petri solemnly. He'd aged in the weeks since Petri had last seen him, his once firm stomach now straining at his tunic, the skin around his eyes looser. Yet he still had all the arrogance that Petri recalled.

"Good of you to join me," he said and nodded at a chair. Petri took it, wondering whether this was any better than a cell in the Shrive.

"I thought you'd be in Ikaras," Petri said.

"So did I. A small matter of a price on the head of all guildsmen found in Ikaras. King Orgull doesn't like our involvement on the border. For me to take part in the negotiations would be . . . indelicate."

Whatever Petri did, wherever he went, he was a dead man. The inescapable finality of it gave him a curious sense of freedom and loosened his usual laconic tongue. "So instead you save me from execution? I'd have thought you'd be more likely to help them pull the lever."

A shrug from Eneko. He picked up a trifle on his desk and passed it from hand to hand as he spoke. "Not my first choice, obviously. But I see which way things are going. Licio will be king again before the end of the year; Bakar will be dead and good riddance. Licio is much more easily manipulated. I find it politic to side with him, at least secretly. And he and Sabates want you alive. For now. Besides it'll piss Bakar off no end, and I live for that."

"Playing both sides?"

"Just like you. And I'll play my part. I'll keep you alive, for now. Just as long as you tell me all I need to know about inside the palace. Of course, I only said I'd keep you alive, not intact. I'm sure you can imagine how a lifetime's work with a blade has given me much experience in non-fatal wounds. Have a little time to mull it over."

He rang a small bell on his desk, and Petri's escorts yanked him from the chair before he had the chance to stand by himself. Petri had moved from one prison to another, via the threat of a third, and counted himself lucky.

Vocho hurried along behind Kacha, her back illuminated blue and green by the dimly glowing glass. That they needed to leave their lodgings was beyond question. Where they were going was open to argument as far as Vocho was concerned, so that's what he did.

"I am not sharing a bloody house with a magician. It's bad enough you offered to help the woman, worse that we need her help. Now you want to play all cosy with her! I'd rather keep as far away as possible for as long as possible. Let her get the tattoo off, soon as she can, then get going. Somewhere, anywhere, I don't care as long as no magicians." He'd even stopped caring about rejoining the guild and getting his good name back. It'd be nice, but for now he wanted any life back, his old one or otherwise, just as long as he was alive to enjoy it, which was looking increasingly unlikely.

"That's exactly what we're going to do, Voch." Kass stopped under the light of a late-night café that still had a few dozy-looking patrons. "But where else are we going to go? We've tied up just about all our money with her, or had you forgotten?"

"Fine, so we get the tattoo off. And then what? Because I get the feeling you've got something in mind, and I'm pretty sure I'm not going to like it. Does it involve us relaxing somewhere warm with a raft of money and no pressing need to run away?"

She laughed at that. "Probably not." But for once Vocho wasn't trying to be funny.

"No, I didn't think so. You forget, I know you. I know how you think – you get all these bloody ideas about being noble and honourable and whatnot into your head, and then look out everyone else."

"That is how the guild trained us, Voch. 'What seems good to you' – right? I seem to recall a few thousand classes on that and how to decide what's good and what isn't."

"I slept through those."

"No, you didn't; you're just choosing to ignore them. And you may be able to live with that – with the thought we could have done something about Licio and Sabates and all the lives that are going to be snuffed out when they try to take Reyes – but I can't."

"Don't give me that shit. It's Petri, isn't it? What was in that letter? Just when I thought we'd got rid of him, oh no, he pops up like a fucking jack-in-the-box."

The light was dim, but he could have sworn she blushed.

Which was unnerving all by itself because Kass wasn't the blushing sort.

"It's nothing to do with Petri, not really."

"Bollocks it isn't. You're going to help me get the tattoo off, and then you're going to run back to Reyes and play the heroine for Petri and get your old job at the guild back, get all the fun and glory, because *you* can of course; *you* haven't been found guilty of murder. I however have, and I'll be stuck fighting illegal duels or robbing people until I die penniless in a gutter somewhere. Or maybe I'll be stuck with this bloody thing on my back, and I'll end up a gibbering wreck, and then at least you won't have to feel guilty about anything."

"The more you talk like that, Voch, the more tempting it sounds, because then I won't have to listen to you talking like that. Maybe I could have some peace and quiet for a change."

"Kass——"

"This isn't the place to talk about it, not in Reyen anyway, because in case you'd forgotten all Reyens are to be handed over as spies, and if you look behind you, we're getting some very interested looks from people who appear to be in dire need of the reward money."

Vocho snatched a glance behind them and, sure enough, some passers-by were looking at them with interest. He gave them a cheery and entirely fake smile, waved an airy hand and then turned back, grabbed Kass's arm and hustled her along the street until no one was behind them.

"Look, Voch, I know it's not ideal. The thought of dealing with magicians doesn't fill me with joy either. But where else have we got to go? Anyone hears our accents, we're handed over. Anyone recognises us – and with the delegation turning up any time, who knows who might — we'd be dead before we were handed over. It's Esti's or nowhere."

He really hated it when she was right.

"Fine. But when the tattoo's off, what then?"

Kass didn't say anything for a while as they hurried on down the quiet streets. Vocho kept a lookout behind, but all he saw was some old duffer shuffling along with a scarf over his face. Finally, when they reached the street where Esti's house sat, and the old duffer had dropped out of sight, Kass said, "I don't know, Voch."

The swamp houses and Esti's vine-covered home were dark compared to the glowing city behind them. They stared at the thicket of vines for a while, and Vocho wondered what was going through Kass's head. He couldn't even be sure what was going through his. What did he want to do next? Apart from stay alive, obviously.

What seems good to you.

The motto of the guild that had ruled him almost his whole life, until they'd thrown him out. He'd lived and almost died by that damn motto, though what seemed good to him and what seemed good to others weren't always the same. What seemed good now? The Clockwork God only knew, because Vocho didn't. He shook his head and started into the vines to Esti's. He'd probably do what he'd always done — wait and see, react to events more on instinct that anything else. It had only rarely steered him wrong. Of course when it had, it had been pretty spectacularly wrong.

But the tattoo, that was first. Esti said it was going to hurt, but he'd live with that if it meant the thing off his back. Then maybe he could do something to get his life back on track.

*   *   *

Kacha stopped at edge of the thicket and looked around. No one in sight to see them go in. Good. She followed Vocho in. He was acting very strangely, even given the circumstances. Thing was, she knew what she needed to do after the tattoo. What seemed good to her. There was revolution coming, war whether she wanted it or not. It was time to pick a side, and she didn't think Vocho was going to like which way she went.

Esti limped out from the back when they knocked and went straight in. "I didn't think you were—"

"Slight change of plan," Vocho said, looking out of the door before he shut it firmly behind him. "Alicia found us, so we thought it prudent to move."

Esti sat down hard. "What do you mean, she found you?"

"I mean she found us – what else would I mean?"

Esti's fingers twined around each other, and the markings there grew darker, more violent.

"How might she have done that?" Kacha asked, because just stumbling across them seemed unlikely in a city the size of Ikaras.

"Blood – if she had any of yours or Vocho's. Doesn't even need to be fresh. More likely she's taken over the tattoo and found you that way. If she found you once, she can do it again as long as you have that thing on. She could find you here." Esti got up and limped jerkily around the room before she glanced at a chest in the corner and seemed to come to a decision. "If I take the tattoo off now, will you leave?"

"Well, yes," Vocho said. "But I thought you said —".

"Never mind what I said," she snapped. "Now I'm saying let's get the damned thing off and you out of here before Alicia walks through the door and kills us all. Now don't just stand there like dummies. Help me with this chest."

Esti began dragging things out of the chest, throwing some behind her, putting some on the table, all with a haste that bordered on desperation. "Alicia! That name's a byword for torture around here. Looks like you've heard of it too. Well, respect what you've heard. Here, Vocho, take this." She handed him a mangled leather strap.

"What's that for?"

"For you to bite on so your screams don't wake up the entire neighbourhood. Kacha, hold him down."

Chapter Ten

Vocho greeted the dawn sweating and quivering, with a throat red raw, a back that felt like someone had whipped it with razors and no guarantee that anything had actually worked.

Just as the sun hit the first of the glass atop the tallest spire of the university on the other side of the city, spearing his eyes with light, he heard someone bustling about in the next room, which he vaguely recalled was the kitchen. He got himself up from his position, lying prone on his stomach, on the third try and had to hold on to the bed until his head stopped swimming. A lot had happened to him over the last weeks, and night, enough to strip away almost every dignity, but he was buggered if he was going to let Esti, Kacha or Cospel see that. He was Vocho the bloody Great and he was going to go on being him.

A sentiment which faded a little as he tried putting his shirt on. Just raising his arms made spots swim in front of his eyes, but in the end he was dressed and looking as dandy as ever. He took a deep breath, remembered not to square his shoulders at the last moment and headed out.

Kacha looked up from a steaming cup of tea, relief as plain as the nose on her face. Cospel waggled his eyebrows in what Vocho thought might be an approving manner, and Esti stopped stirring a pot on the stove. The scent of melting sugar and vanilla filled the room, and Vocho thought he might actually kill for something sweet.

"I told you he'd wake up eventually," Esti said, but she smiled at him as she said it and poured the liquid in the pot into a big bowl. "Here, try this. It should help."

Vocho breathed in the aroma and felt something settle inside. "What do you mean by 'eventually'?"

Kacha's hand twitched, which made Vocho want to twitch too. He took a sip of Esti's concoction, burned his mouth and tried again after blowing on it.

"She means you've been out for three days."

"Three days? But . . . but Alicia . . . everything . . ."

"The delegation has arrived in high style, Sabates among them. Alicia has been conspicuous by her absence, but there's some old fart hanging around with a scarf covering his face so I think it's safe to say we're being watched, which is making Esti very twitchy. Three days. I was starting to get worried, Voch."

He was quite touched by this. His prickly sister usually told anyone within hearing what an annoying arse he was. "Only starting?"

"You're tough enough, normally. Remember that sword thrust from Ballan? Through the ribs and out the other side, never seen so much blood. And you were in an inn starting, and finishing, a brawl twelve hours later."

"It's a hell of a scar."

"And you'll have another to match it on your back. Esti had to take the skin off, and we still don't know if it's entirely gone – she says it might never be all gone, some sort of built-in failsafe or something, though no one should be able to track you any more. But I'm glad you didn't die."

From Kacha this was an admission akin to professing undying love, which made Vocho wonder just how bad it had been.

"Me too, funnily enough. Now come on, spill it all. Three days. If I know you, you know a lot more now than you did then."

"Oh, I do indeed. Come on. You need to get up and about, work the kinks out, and I'll tell you all about it."

There was something sly about her manner, but he didn't push it. He got up without wincing and managed a small swagger out of the back door after her. Taken the skin off? God's cogs!

Outside Voch couldn't see a damned thing that wasn't some shade of green, and there must have been a hundred shades. Nothing not green except the flowers draped over every available surface, delicate ones, big thick fleshy ones, one the size of his leg that smelt worse than Cospel after a week without a bath. A clearing in the centre was the only open space. It was quiet this early in the day, though the far-off sounds of the city waking up drifted over them.

"Our little watcher isn't here right now," Kacha said, "but I know who he is, or at least where he usually lurks."

"The watcher, watched?"

She laughed under her breath. "Oh yes. All that training came in handy. What do you know about Ikaran life-warriors, Voch?"

"Not much."

"Neither did I, but I do now. Professional soldiers, a bit like the guild, I suppose. Only they don't hire themselves out. They serve one man or woman only, the king or queen, and give not a shit about anyone else. They come in pairs – linked together when they first join, or rather are made to join, at about age eight. They're cuffed together, and they stay cuffed for years until they earn the right to call themselves warriors."

"You mean they, well, you know. All the time?"

"Yeah, all the time. God's cogs, Voch, I'd have killed you years ago if they'd done that to us."

"I'd have died of embarrassment first. There are some things a man should never see his sister do. Or anyone, come to that. I wouldn't have pissed for *years*."

"Me neither. But they say it means they bond closer than brothers and sisters. They know everything about each other. Everything. And when the cuffs are off, they stay together. They serve their king and queen, like I say, and it's drilled into them that honour is the only way they have. The thing the Ikarans have about shades of rank, of gaining and losing respect, it's in them tenfold. A hundredfold. By the time the cuffs are off, I reckon they can't think of anything other than how to gain honour and glory for their master. It's, I don't know, who they are. No honour, no life."

"Which is a nice story, but what's it got to do with our little watcher?"

"Everything, because he is one. Or was."

"Was? It doesn't sound like the sort of thing you can just quit."

"Oh, he didn't quit, Voch. He wears a scarf because he's got no nose – they cut it off to mark him as a man who betrayed his pair."

"That's . . . pretty fucking gross."

Kacha shrugged. They'd reached the edge of the clearing and a vicious-looking bush with purple flowers that Vocho would have sworn moved to follow their progress. They turned about and Vocho was glad because even the short walk had tired him, and his back was throbbing so hard he thought he might have to sit down. He wasn't about to show weakness to Kacha though, not unless he passed out. Which was seeming increasingly likely.

"Gross to us, not to them. They think we're a bunch of feckless idiots without a shred of honour between us. Anyway, he had no master, not after what he did."

"What exactly did he do?"

"No idea. Doesn't matter, probably. But the important part is, once he was dishonoured, the king didn't want him; no lord or lady would take him, and he got shunted off to a lowly job, just to grind into him how he had no honour left. A guard. At the university."

"Ah. Back to Alicia again? So, she's watching. What for? Why not just come and kill us? What's she waiting for?"

Kacha nodded towards a clump of bushes at the far end of the garden, still shrouded in the night's shadows. "Best guess, him."

Him? Vocho took another look at the bushes. Just bushes. Except that one shivered in a breeze that wasn't there, and the next moment Dom was strolling across the clearing past beds of herbs and odd-looking vegetables.

He swept his hat off in Kacha's direction and nodded at Vocho. "Good morning," he said, like finding an assassin in your garden was to be expected. "How's the invalid?"

"Grouchy, as I'm sure you can guess. How's the assassin business?"

He spared Kacha a brief smile. "Busy, as I'm sure you can guess."

"Come to kill us?" she asked.

"Not today. I'll wait for you both to be on form. Unsporting otherwise."

"Good of you. Then maybe some tea?"

He laughed at that. "Certainly. Tea. Though I'll be sure to drink only what you drink in this house."

Vocho followed them inside and wondered what exactly that meant. The kitchen was empty except for Cospel, who was dozing by the range and started when he heard them come in. He caught sight of their guest and cocked his head in a way which Vocho took to mean, "Oh crap, shall I start packing?" Vocho shook his head and Cospel relaxed a touch.

"Cospel, could we have some of that tea, please?" Kacha said and dropped into a chair. Vocho followed with rather more care, glad to be off his feet.

Cospel bustled about, handing Vocho a cup of the sweet whatever-it-was that Esti had apparently left for him, and tea to Dom and Kacha. Vocho took a long draught and breathed out as the pain began to subside.

Dom waited for Kacha to take a swallow of hers before he even touched his cup.

"A brave thing to do here," he said.

"Seems you know something we don't. Then again," Kacha said, "maybe we know a thing or two you don't."

Dom nodded agreeably. "That could be true. You read your letter?"

Kacha flicked a glance Vocho's way and back again. "Yes. But that's not it. You first."

"Well, shall we start with the fact that apparently you are not aware that you are staying in the house of Ikaras's foremost poisoner? Whoops. I'm sure tea stains come out. Not to worry."

It must have been the first time Vocho had seen Dom anything other than pristine, with Kacha's tea all over his fine jacket. He tried not to gloat, but only managed it by choking on his own concoction.

"Poisoner?" he croaked when he got his voice back. He stared at his cup and put it down hurriedly. "I thought she was a magician. She is a magician."

"Well, yes. Specialising in, among other things, the magical cultivation of plants, most particularly poisonous ones. She's very good. I've heard she can grow anything, anywhere, and make it grow better than it does in the wild. A while ago she devised a way to make sugar grow better. She's working for Sabates now, in a roundabout way, I'm fairly sure."

"But she—"

"I didn't say she *wanted* to work for him. I'm pretty sure she hates his guts, actually. But Sabates does have a way of getting people to work for him, as Petri knows to his cost. As do you. And like you she was cast out of her 'guild' for it, and is paying for it still, even as she continued to work for him in secret."

"So what did she do?" Kacha asked. "Kill someone? Do magicians care about that?"

"Not really. Killing someone is irrelevant as long as it's not another magician. Which sadly it was. Nasty business, and officially the king wants her dead and so do all the other magicians. Sabates has other plans for her, though. If she's caught, she'll hang. She has to work for Sabates or suffer the consequences. She's trapped, just like you, so might well make a present of two fugitives to the king who wants her head, in order to save it. So, there you are – my piece. And yours?"

Dom sat back, though Vocho had an inkling he had other things to tell them. It seemed Dom always came with secrets.

Kacha took a sip of her tea and set the cup down carefully. "I suppose you know we broke into the magicians' quarters in the university?"

"Oh yes, I'm sure Esti was very relieved to get her life's

work back. But what I came to tell you is that Esti's been poisoning Bakar. Well, she's not been giving it to him, obviously, but she makes it, I'm sure of it. Sending him quietly, or not so quietly insane. Don't know how they've been getting it into him, but someone has."

That made Vocho sit up. "So all that with Bakar being a bit, well, loony is him being poisoned? All those stupid taxes and the bit about the purple flags?"

"Almost positive. Almost. Esti's involved in this somehow anyway. Maybe willingly, maybe not. Partly why I'm here – to every poison there's an antidote. And that's not all. You know Eneko threw in his lot with Licio in secret? Aye, well, I had my suspicions. I've got a spy or two of my own in the guild. Looks like Eneko's preparing for a small coup of his own."

"Has someone been poisoning Eneko as well?" Kacha asked. "Because he must be mad. Half of Reyes is getting ready for the war they think is coming, Licio negotiating or not. The guild is big and full of good men and women but a coup? A reach too far, at least now, surely?"

"You'd think so, wouldn't you? But guildsmen have been protecting the border for a long time now, augmenting the council's regular troops. Eneko's had plenty of time to work on those troops. The councillors won't work together if their lives depend on it, which they might. So Eneko's presenting himself as Bakar's saviour – the only man who can protect Reyes. Bakar is far enough gone that he'll believe Eneko's false promises. And Bakar's already uncovered one 'plotter' and had the guild deal with him as a gesture of good faith. Petri."

Vocho risked a look at Kacha, but she gave no sign of having heard; she was looking up at the wind chimes playing at the window.

"What did they do with him?" she asked at last.

"I don't know, yet. But I thought you'd want to know."

"Yes. Thank you."

Dom frowned but said no more and got up to leave, motioning to Vocho as he did so. Vocho pushed himself out of the chair and just about managed to keep the grimace off his face as he followed Dom to the door.

"Is she all right?" Dom asked in a whisper before he left.

Vocho thought about it for a while. "I don't know. I don't know what's right with her these days."

"And you? You're walking like a bloody duck, man. Esti get the tattoo off?"

"Supposedly. Apparently there are bits left, but at least no one can make me murder anyone against my will now."

"Well, she's good at what she does, I'll give her that. But don't trust her or anything she gives you to eat or drink. She's killed more men than I have. What are you two going to do next?"

"Well, now you've given us that little speech about Eneko, I suspect Kacha will want to go back to Reyes and save Bakar and Petri in a blaze of glory. So thanks for that."

"Vocho the Great is complaining about a blaze of glory?"

"No, I'm complaining about the fact I'll probably die before I get the chance to see it."

Chapter Eleven

It was something of a relief when they came to take Petri to Eneko. He wasn't sure how long he'd been left in pitch-black silence, gagged and tied. Days, he suspected, with nothing but himself for company, leaving thoughts scattered around his brain like confetti. The lamps outside his cell were muted but still blinded him as they left so that tears soaked his face and dripped from his chin. The two men escorting him prodded him along, and he stumbled down the corridor like a drunk. By the time they reached what he assumed was Eneko's room and he was shoved into a chair, Petri could see blurred shapes but not much more.

Someone removed the ties from his hands, the gag — Petri couldn't make him out, but he knew the voice well enough.

"Petri, so glad to see you. I thought we might have a little chat." Eneko, trying his best smooth voice though it seemed harsh as clanging bells to Petri after the silence of his cell. He sounded so ridiculous that Petri laughed and, once started, couldn't stop for some time.

"Yes, that cell does do strange things to people," Eneko

said when Petri had subsided, weak from his outburst. "But I've found it very useful over the years."

Petri blinked hard and tried to focus, but it was difficult. Half his mind was back in the cell, where there was no light, no sound, yet he had still been able to see things, hear things. Clocks, god's cogs, there had been clocks everywhere, the sound of them driving him mad. He could still hear the ticking, recall how it had sounded so loud he thought it might crush his head. He'd seen the bone clock hanging in front of him, and after a time he'd come to realise the bones were his, that he was dead and that was his only monument . . .

The only thing that had kept him sane was his hands, even though they were tied behind him. His fingers knew every inch of his tiny cell, barely bigger than he was. Even his belief in that solidity had started to waver at the end, until he wasn't sure whose face this really was, who he really was, where he was.

"Petri?"

Something cracked across his face, and the shape in front of him was talking. He tried to concentrate, tried to focus on the real sounds, but the whirr of the clocks drowned them out. Another whack rocked his head back, something cold and wet swept across his face, and when he opened his eyes again he could see more clearly. He wished he couldn't.

Another blow from the back of Eneko's hand made him bite his tongue so that he could taste blood. Even that was something – he was glad of anything real. His vision had begun to clear, though past Eneko's blandly smiling face things were still a blur of red and yellow and blue.

"What?" Petri muttered, his voice sounding slurred and somehow old. "What do you want?" Because Petri was coming to realise he'd say quite a lot, anything in fact, to avoid going back into that black box. Something Eneko seemed to have anticipated.

"The only problem with that particular cell," he said, "is that when they first come out, our guests tend to babble any old thing, and it's imaginary as often as not. So we've found that a little something extra is needed to help them concentrate on what is really true."

Eneko stepped back, and Petri saw what had been turning the world behind him red and yellow — a brazier, good and hot. Atop it sat a blade, and one Petri recognised — Kacha's stiletto, its edges glowing as red as the brazier.

He tried to shake away the sound of the clocks in his head, the phantom voice of Bakar saying he'd read Petri's future in the gears.

Eneko pulled on a thick glove, picked up the stiletto and came towards Petri, who tried to be stalwart and stoical, to be the brave and noble man he'd always thought himself in his head, but that heat, that blade . . . It was only when he tried to get up, tried to pull back, that he realised he'd been tied to the chair and that at least one of his escorts was behind it because they held his head still.

"Now, just a few things, and then all this unpleasantness can be over." Eneko's voice was hardly more than a whisper. "Firstly, what was it Sabates asked you to do?"

Petri's scrambled brain groped for an answer but all he could think about was clocks, about bones and skulls — his — and clocks. Only wasn't that the answer? He didn't care about Sabates or Bakar or anyone else; he only cared about getting that blade away from his face, getting these thoughts out of his head. Not going back to the black cell. Anything but that, and the clocks that haunted him there.

"The clock. I had to do something to the clock."

"Well now, that's very vague. Bakar has a lot of clocks." The point of the hot blade touched Petri's temple and he had to clamp down a scream. "I don't have much time, so I'm afraid I'm going to have to go a bit faster than usual. You choose, Petri. Eye or hand?"

The blade pressed down the side of Petri's face, outlining his cheek in fire, trailing the smell of burned skin behind it. He couldn't stop the scream this time, even when the look on Eneko's face made him want to be sick.

"The clock! The bone one. I was supposed to make it run down, I don't know why." All pretence at bravery burned away with his skin and he babbled, only stopping when the blade reached the edge of his mouth.

Blessedly, the stiletto had cooled, but that merely meant Eneko placed it on the brazier to heat again.

While he waited, Eneko said, "And how do I know that's the truth, Petri? You were born a noble and a liar. You were adopted by and work for the prelate, also a liar, and you also work for the man trying to kill him, making you a liar. You trained in this very guild, and yet you fold at the first hint of pain. You'd never have made a guildsman, a master. Never. And you wonder why I let you go, *made* you go? You're weak, Petri Egimont, weaker than bad steel, softer than lead." He picked up the stiletto again and inspected its cherry-red tip.

"Tell me the best way into the palace, into Bakar's rooms."

"You already had men in there. They brought me here, remember?"

"Not the directions to his rooms, Petri, the method to get past his defences. Besides, the men who escorted you from inside the palace were Bakar's, not mine. I have bought Bakar's trust by dealing with you for him. Can't trust a man who can be bought, isn't that so? You should know.

First Bakar bought your loyalty, then Sabates. What was your price?"

"I was never—"

He got no further as the hot blade sank into his skin and drew down next to the first burn. Pain shot up his face and centred in his eye, in his brain. The sizzling, the smell of his own burning skin made him want to throw up.

"Oh, you were paid, or were due to be. Leadership of the guild, wasn't it? That's what Sabates offered you. That and my head, I don't doubt."

A twist, more pressure, and the knife burned through Petri's cheek to the bone. The hands holding Petri were hard as iron as he twisted, silent, beyond screaming.

"The best way in, Petri, for someone quick and quiet, where no one can see. In, a swift blade, and out, and no one the wiser as to who did it. I have a man, an assassin, who'll do anything for me, because only I have what he wants. Or maybe one last job for myself. Not as good as our dear Kacha though, neither of us."

The thought of her seemed to spur Eneko on, made the blade push further, burning under the skin now, slicing his cheek away or that's how it felt. Blood lay on his tongue, and the taste of burned pork hitched his throat so that he couldn't breathe.

"Years I spent training her, making her trust me so she'd do as I asked without a thought. *Years*. She was my perfect assassin, the pinnacle of my achievement, like my own daughter only better, and what happened? You. That's what happened, Petri. You took my perfect, obedient assassin and ruined her with your questions, with your doubts and lies. I should have your eye just for that. Or maybe your hand. Both, if you don't give me what I want. Tell me how to get to Bakar. Tell me how I can end all this with one swift, quiet thrust, and no one the wiser. Then maybe I'll take pity on you, have mercy and kill you quickly."

"There is no way."

Eneko might be getting on in years but he was still quick as a snake. The stiletto flew across the room to bounce off a wall as Eneko smashed his fist right into Petri's mess of a cheek. Pain exploded in his head like a clockwork gun so that Petri barely noticed falling back, his head hitting the floor, hardly tasted more blood in his mouth.

Petri had once thought himself a brave and noble man. Not any more. Now all he wanted was for this to stop. He'd say anything, betray anyone, if only Eneko would stop. But he wouldn't, Petri knew that. Eneko would not stop even if Petri told him everything he knew.

Hands yanked him up by his hair and set him back in the chair. Eneko was breathing hard, face flushed and hair awry, and the stiletto was back in his hand. The blade was cool again now, but that didn't stop Petri flinching away as Eneko touched it to his other, as yet unblemished, cheek.

"Tell me, Petri. Tell me and all this will end."

Petri had nothing to tell him. Bakar was too paranoid, too clever. Yet there were some, Petri was sure, that Bakar knew, or thought, or hoped, he could trust. That would be the only way – to buy those men.

Petri stared at Eneko. He was lost, along with his thoughts. No one knew where he was except perhaps Bakar. No one would be coming to rescue him. It was just him and Eneko and the blade for as long as it amused the guild master, and then Petri would die. Unless he gave Eneko . . . something. When it came to it, Petri was no better than any other man, wanting to hang on to life to the last possible second even if it was as a man with half a face living in a silent black cell. Just hoping that something would change, maybe. Willing to beg if he had to.

"Bakar's second valet." The words dripped out, unwilling. "No one's been allowed out of the palace in weeks without permission. But the second valet has a wife outside. She comes to the kitchen door sometimes, to see him."

Eneko patted his still whole cheek. "That's a nice story. Is it true?"

The knife again – it hung before his eyes like a sharpened sun, ready to burn his will away, burn his soul away and leave nothing in its wake but a broken man.

It wasn't, but Eneko wouldn't believe the truth – that there was no way, not that Petri knew of. "It's true, I swear."

"Swear on what?"

What did he have to swear on that Eneko would believe? Nothing, nothing left to hold dear except one thing.

"Kacha," he whispered. "I swear on Kacha's life."

The sting of his tears was the worst pain of all.

Until Eneko brought the hot blade down into his hand.

Chapter Twelve

Dom had left, quiet and secretive as always, and Kacha was drumming her fingers and glaring at the wind chimes when Esti came back. As soon as she opened the door and took in the way Kass was wound like a spring, a hand came up, fluttered by her face and dropped again as though in defeat.

Kacha lifted up her cup of tea. She had spent the time waiting, thinking about whether Esti could have poisoned them – almost certainly – and taking some hope from the fact she hadn't already. "I take it there's nothing in this I need to worry about? Nothing that might kill me, for instance?"

Esti closed the door quietly behind her and put down the toddler struggling in her arms. He immediately launched himself at Vocho, who greeted his arrival with a pained "Oof."

"Nothing in here, where the children might reach it. And nothing in the tea. Who told you? I knew it wouldn't be long."

Kacha shrugged. Esti seemed resigned. To what, exactly? Them finding out? Something else? "A friend."

"Nothing in that jollop you've given me?" Vocho asked from under flailing toddler limbs.

"No! Or nothing harmful anyway, I promise. It's just . . . Look, you helped me; I helped you. Fair's fair."

Kacha wanted to believe her, she really did. She liked Esti, and besides she'd looked after Vocho with more care than he probably deserved. But recent experience had taught her one thing – no one was to be believed all the way through. No one. She'd taken a risk with Esti because they'd needed her help, but it had been a calculated one. She hoped she could add up.

"Are you still a poisoner?" she asked because someone had to, and Vocho had his hands full.

Esti sat down at the table wearily and poured herself a cup of tea. "I don't have much choice. A bit like Vocho and his tattoo, I suppose. Sabates took my brother last year, so I do what he says."

Kacha sat opposite and tried to reconcile the part of her that was screaming not to trust a damned soul, and the part that believed Esti and wanted to hear her out. Maybe even help her.

"And what is it, exactly, that Sabates wants you to do?" *And why are you telling me so easily now?*

Esti fiddled with the edge of the tablecloth, shredding it with her fingers. She didn't seem able to look at Kacha. "He said I was going to be helping the king. I mean, that's what magicians *do*. Reyes has its duelling guild, and they say they'll work for anyone, but who they mostly work for is Reyes. And they all swear to protect Reyes, if it comes to it. Well, magicians are the Ikaras version. Or magicians and life-warriors anyway. So he told me I'd be serving the king, and that my brother and sister and their children would be all right. If I did what he said.

Said I could practise my magic again, properly, get me a pardon."

Kacha had a brief flash of what that might mean – to her it would be like being back in the guild, back doing what she was always supposed to. She got the feeling that was the real nub of it for Esti. She didn't want her family to die, but she also dreamed of doing what she was born to do.

"So you did what he wanted?"

Esti's mouth worked, a corner of the tablecloth turned into tatters. "I did. But then he killed one of my brothers anyway. Slaughtered like a traitor in the plaza. Took all his ranks away, took his knife and broke it. Made him die like nothing. So I ran. I took the children and my family and I ran. Couldn't go far – no money. So we hid. Easy to hide if you've got a magical knack for it. He'll find me eventually, him or Alicia, and maybe she's worse. He always gets what he wants. So I do what I can to earn money so we can leave for good. Somewhere far enough away even he can't find me."

"Yes, but—" Kacha said.

"Poison, that's what he wanted. I didn't think I had any choice, so I made it. Lots of it before I managed to get away. Tincture of mansbane. It gets absorbed through the skin if you touch it."

"And does what?"

Esti shrugged and applied herself to the tablecloth. "Depends how much over how long a period. Doesn't do much to start with, but a sustained dose over a number of weeks? Insomnia, paranoia, delusions. That sort of thing. It'd be hard to get enough in someone to kill them – he knew I'd never agree to that!"

"You're the king's poisoner."

"Who told you that? I am — or rather was — the king's *botanist*. Plants, that's where my magical skills lie, and the king's always had a keen interest. Up at the palace he's got as fine a collection of flora as you can find anywhere. Plants from all over the world. Left over from the empire — the Castans' gardens here were famous, and even after the Great Fall a few kept them up. King's gardener is a rank almost as high as prince, though more popular with some kings than others. They must have lost some plants, but there's still a thousand or more species up there. It was like heaven. Anyway, the current king is especially keen, always pushing for better crops, quicker-growing sugar, strains that are resistant to mildew, that sort of thing. But when a magician died, they said it was me, only it wasn't, I swear, and the king wanted me dead and Sabates helped me to start with, kept me hidden even from Alicia, if only I'd work for him and . . ."

She broke off, but Kacha didn't need to hear any more. The king wanted Esti dead — she knew how that felt — but she wasn't sure how much to believe.

"A poison that sends men mad," Vocho said, having finally disentangled himself from the toddler and distracted him with a biscuit. "Sounds familiar."

Kacha didn't like how pale he was, or how quiet. It was unnerving her. "Doesn't it? Esti, how long before Voch is well enough to travel? Say, quite a long ride."

"Today, if he takes the drinks I made him."

Vocho groaned but Kacha ignored him.

"Can you promise me there's nothing untoward in them?"

"I promise you. As soon as I knew that tattoo was of Sabates' doing, I only wanted to help. He's got me in the same net as you. And what can I do? Oh, I could poison him perhaps, use my magic, but don't you think I've tried?

The man's impossible to kill, or impossible for *me* to kill. But you two can do more than me. You can expose him to people who might believe you. Maybe even kill the bastard. You get him for me, make it so I don't have to hide or run away, maybe so I can even openly practise my magic again. And I promise you there is nothing in those drinks except something for the pain."

Kacha gave Vocho a once-over. Pale, quiet, slightly clammy but noticeably better after the drink. "Well, I suppose you haven't turned green yet."

"Thanks. I think." Vocho turned to Esti. "So you're probably not trying to poison me. I appreciate it, really I do. But look, trust isn't something we come by easily. Especially lately. We've only got your word for all this, against the word of someone who, while I don't trust him much, it's more than I do you. He at least has not made my back a flaming pit of hell."

Esti sat up straight at that. "He hasn't removed Sabates' means of finding you either, has he?"

"I've only got your word for that. Haven't I?"

Esti's mouth flapped open and shut as though she was desperate to say something, but no words would do justice to her rage. She stood up, shoved the chair out of her way and stormed out of the room.

"Nice one, Voch. Pissing off the one person who's helped us in this godforsaken place."

"Are you saying you trust her?"

"No. No, not exactly. But I don't not trust her either. She did what she said she would, and we're both still alive. Which, given that she's fed us for a couple of days, means I don't think she wants us dead or we'd be foaming at the mouth."

Vocho tried to sit up straight, winced and gave the toddler

another biscuit to forestall the next sticky-fingered assault on his person.

"True enough."

Kacha sat down opposite him. "Look, Voch, there isn't much choice. This place is being watched. And why didn't Alicia finish us off when she got the chance? Well, maybe so she could follow and watch. I get the feeling there's not much love lost between her and Esti, and if Sabates really is looking for her, we just led him right to her door. Why in hells should she trust us? But I tell you one thing: she might not be being honest about why, but I can tell you she hates Sabates' guts as much as you do. So why not trust that? Anyway, we've got to leave; you know it and so do I."

"To Reyes, and Petri, no doubt."

"Not just Petri. Eneko trying a coup is our business."

"No, it isn't."

"It's guild business. As is the fate of Reyes itself. You're a fickle bugger, Voch, and I know it, but I can't believe you'd just let the place go to hell without even trying."

"Can and will, given half a chance."

"Fine. You stay here, and Alicia can catch you and flay you alive."

"Or we can get flayed alive in Reyes."

Kacha sat back with a sigh. He had a point. Wherever they went, whatever they did, flaying was a distinct possibility.

Esti slammed back into the room and banged a small clay bottle on the table.

"What's that?" Vocho asked suspiciously.

"That," Esti said, "is the antidote to what I gave Sabates to use. It's mostly sugar — a good dollop of that will help if you can't get anything else or lose this — plus a dose of goatsfoot trefoil."

Bakar, whose fevered dreams had led to this, all of it if indirectly. Kacha looked at Vocho and could tell he'd had exactly the same thought. "The antidote?" she asked.

"You'll need to find out how the poison is being administered and stop it, and you'll need to keep using this for a while after that. But it'll reverse the effects sure enough. And Kacha?"

"Yes?"

"Sabates. You get him and you get him good, for me."

Kacha looked at her long and hard. To trust her or not? Even if she was only telling them the half of it, the antidote might be enough to get Bakar back into his right mind and them a pardon. If they could get the antidote to him, of course.

"All right."

"Kass!" Vocho's mouth had dropped open, and he looked comical in his dismay.

"You don't have to come," she said. "You can stay here and deal with Alicia if and when she finds you. Or any number of other people who'd love to turn you over to the king for the reward. Or you can hide away with Esti here, and I'm sure she won't put a damned thing into your food, will you, Esti?"

The botanist grinned at Vocho. "Well, I can't promise anything. Old habits die hard."

Vocho raised his hands in defeat. "All right, all right. I suppose being flayed at home beats being flayed in a foreign country. Reyes it is."

Chapter Thirteen

Alicia stared out of the window and watched the play of light on the glass of the university as the sun rose. Behind her Gerlar stood still as stone, waiting for her to speak, to say something about what he'd just told her. She took her time.

"So, Vocho and Kacha have left. No one visited them?"

"No, ma'am, not that I saw."

Damn. She was sure he would have done. Then again Domenech was too good to let just anyone see him. Still, he'd turn up wherever the damnable duellists went, she was sure of it. And at least she knew where that little traitor Esti was hiding.

"Where did they go?"

"Livery stables on the edge of the city, ma'am. Looks like they'd had their horses there a while. Cheap place, and they didn't look too happy with the state of the horses, but they paid up and left. Heading south."

Back to Reyes. Well, that was a stupid move. What did they think they could achieve?

"You saw no one else? Are you sure?"

"No one went in or out except that Esti woman and some children."

Alicia snapped out her fan and tried to move the too-hot air around with little success. "I thought life-warriors were supposed to be the best."

"At fighting, ma'am. Not as spies."

Alicia watched the play of light as she contemplated. She couldn't track Vocho any more. She'd tried over the last few days, but while he was a tickle in her mind, even that was gradually fading. Esti, no doubt; the woman had an irritating way of thwarting her whether she meant to or not. The end result was the same.

Well then. Kacha and Vocho were gone, but it seemed clear enough where they were heading. Good luck to them. The plains to the south were alive with soldiers – new recruits, all moving as quietly as possible to the border – not to mention farmers and an army of slaves. The king had bought every one he could find, and now they were taking in the sugar harvest, replacing the Ikarans he'd drafted into his army. And Vocho and Kacha with prices on their heads as possible Reyen spies. Kacha in particular would stand out, even dressed in Ikaran clothes, and neither could speak Ikaran well enough to pass.

Where they were heading wasn't the important question. The real question was, why? Why back to Reyes, where they were even more likely to be recognised and lose their heads than they were here? What did they hope to achieve? What had changed?

She snapped the fan again. Ikaras was very pretty in the dawn, before the heat fell like a hammer.

Gerlar hadn't seen who she'd hoped, but he was so very good at not being seen, at disappearing into shadows. Maybe Esti knew something useful, and she knew where the little witch was now. Alicia smiled behind her fan. And she needed some blood as well. Now there was a plan.

She pulled a jar of leeches from a shelf and got to work.

Alicia had to admit it — the place was well disguised. No wonder she'd never been able to find Esti. If Gerlar hadn't told her, she'd never have even known it was there. He showed her the way now, silent and watchful.

The thickets of vines and mangroves weren't unusual in this quarter of the city, where sparkling glass gave way to houses built wherever some wretch could hack out a space at the edge of the swamp north of the shallow harbour before the land rose sharply. The stink of stagnant water coiled through what she supposed must be called streets, if only because they connected houses, but they were ankle-deep in water that grew darker and deeper the further out you went. Dark shapes moved in the water under the stilts of some of the far houses.

Alicia picked her way with care yet was still stained with swamp mud when she reached it. The only hint that this tangle of putrid vegetation was anything other than what it appeared was the mud-streaked dog sitting in the shade of a mangrove as though at attention and a dark tunnel that led off into the deep green of it.

She and Gerlar watched from the shadow of a tangle of driftwood on stilts that seemed to serve several families as a house. Alicia prepared herself mentally, not that Esti was especially powerful. Not as strong as Alicia anyway, but it wouldn't do to underestimate her. Not as strong, but she was unusual. Manipulating people, persuading and nudging them in the direction you wished them to go, that was every magician's skill. A few could use animals in much the same manner. Alicia had never seen another who could manipulate plants.

A pathetic skill, she'd once thought it, as pathetic as its owner. They'd all thought that right up until they'd found Harnet hanging in a vine forest that had sprung up overnight in his rooms with a branch grown through where his heart had been. Esti, found in the corner with a strange smile on her face, had claimed self-defence. It had been only her good luck that Sabates had seen something in her odd powers, and while he couldn't go against the king, he had hidden her away from non-magical eyes. Lied about her to the other magicians, kept her and his plans secret even from Alicia. Esti had escaped that confinement too, and it was only then, as Sabates had raged about her, that Alicia had become aware her biggest rival was still alive and in Ikaras.

No, strange as she was, and weak, it wouldn't do to underestimate Esti at all. She'd used Kacha and Vocho to steal what she needed from the safe, kept herself hidden from even Sabates' prying gaze for a long time now. Kept herself alive for long years before that, and that was no easy task among magicians.

"Gerlar, wait here and listen for my call. In the meantime, let no one in or out."

"Yes, ma'am."

Alicia approached carefully, her fan her only defence from the heat that had bludgeoned everyone to stillness. Even the dust that coated the mangroves and hung in the air seemed to droop. The dog panted in its shade and watched her warily, as though expecting a kick at any moment. She stared it down, and it whimpered and slunk off into the darker recesses of the thicket.

The tunnel was low so she had to bend, and deeply

shadowed. The air was so close that she found her breath caught in her lungs and sweat dripped from her. The vines seemed to close in on her, and she couldn't be sure whether it was the heat making her see things, making her think they were trying to clutch at her, or whether Esti's hand was behind it.

She'd come prepared – half a dozen scraps of paper, folded or rolled, daubed in still-damp blood and kept where the markings wouldn't smudge and change their meaning. She wouldn't use them yet. No need to announce herself so early, on the off chance Esti wasn't aware of her. Along with the more usual tools of her trade was one that was peculiar to her. The leech sat in a little bottle.

A vine fell on her shoulder, and she brushed it away. Another and she drew her knife. The last green-tinted shafts of light shone from the charms that hung from the haft. It cut through the questing vine, causing the plant to drip sap and shiver away. She slashed around her, thinking it at the same time ridiculous but also practical. The twisting vines drew back, and she moved on.

When she looked behind her, she was startled to see she'd barely come a few feet from the open ground – it seemed further – but here was a door under what she could now see was just a thin cloak of vines. She didn't bother to knock but pulled out a scrap of paper in readiness. The first room, a cramped sort of sitting room full of plants that somehow gave the impression of looking at her, was empty, so she crept through it to the far door and pushed it open.

A kitchen, with a cold range and chimes at the windows. Also empty, but now she could hear sounds coming from further on. It didn't take long to find the source. She peered through a last door into what looked like a laboratory up at the university. Odd contraptions, a few glass beakers.

But a laboratory with a difference. The beakers held soil and plants, not volatile liquids, and other plants grew over and around the contraptions or, in one case, actually was the contraption. Among all this was, at last, Esti. She was shoving random-seeming items into a bag. A toddler sat on the desk, babbling to itself and "helping" by taking things out of the bag when Esti had her back turned.

Esti hesitated, clearly torn between two plants.

"I'd take the purple one, if I were you," Alicia said from the doorway. "Such a pretty flower."

Esti whirled to face her, plant in either hand, her face paper-white with eyes like two holes cut into her skin. Her glance slid to the toddler, who'd found a shawl and was busy trying it on as a hat. Then she took a deep breath so the plants in her hands stopped shivering. Not for long, if Alicia had anything to do with it.

"I knew you'd come. You or him," Esti said.

"And you thought helping those two, getting rid of that tattoo, would stop me?"

A shrug, a sneer. "You always did have an inflated idea of the usefulness of such things. Much like your ideas about yourself."

Alicia gritted her teeth – she wasn't going to let Esti get to her. She was above that now, above her. In a blink she was by the toddler, picking the snotty brat up, her scrap of paper at the ready. Not quicker than Esti though, and they tussled over the screaming child for a moment.

A moment that broke when Alicia said the word that unleashed what she'd written on the scrap of paper. A blinding flash – more for show than anything – a push of air, and Esti was in a heap by the far wall and clothes and plants were scattered everywhere. The toddler giggled in Alicia's arms and shouted, "Again!"

Alicia put him down and ignored him, even when he tried to climb up her leg. Instead she strode over to Esti just as she was struggling to her feet, wrenched the plants she had grabbed from her and ripped their leaves so that sap dripped over her hands. It occurred to her that perhaps Esti used the sap much as she herself used blood.

"Now then," she said. "You can tell me all about Vocho and Kacha later; for now I want to know about your other visitor."

Esti looked genuinely puzzled, but Alicia knew from years of being lied to just how false that look was.

"Yes, your other visitor. I know he came. He must have done. Tell me all about Dom and his visit." She picked up the toddler and bounced him at her hip, making him giggle. "Or I shall have absolutely no compunctions whatsoever."

An hour and one leech later Alicia was sure that Esti had told her all she knew about Dom, which was nothing. She kicked a pot, sending earth and leaves scattering everywhere. The toddler sat where Alicia had left him tied to a table, happily eating spilled soil. Esti had told her what little she knew about Kacha and Vocho too: that they were on their way back to Reyes – for their stupid guild honour, a motto or something. And for Petri. Alicia was surprised. She hadn't thought Petri Egimont anything like attractive enough to warrant anyone putting themselves in danger.

"Just let me and the baby go," Esti said.

Alicia considered. "No. I'll have someone come and take the child to a house more suitable to him. You are going to do a little something for me."

"For you? I . . ."

Alicia wagged a finger. "Remember what I told you about

the leech?" Esti sagged back into her corner. "Good, much better. Now then, tell me all about what was in the safe."

Esti blanched, but with the leech on her she didn't have any choice. Not unless she was a lot stronger-willed than she looked.

"My book," Esti began. "My book was there and some . . . Look, please. I won't cause you any trouble. I'll leave Ikaras; you can be next in line after Sabates. That's what you want, isn't it? To be the next head mage?"

"It's one of the things I wouldn't mind," Alicia replied. "But you're offering me nothing I haven't already got or could have with just a few words. What else was in there? Do you still have them?"

A grimace as the stupid woman tried to resist, a gust of breath as she failed. "I packed them already."

Alicia rifled through the bag with a grimace of her own, scattering clothes and plants over the table until she found some woodcuts and a sheaf of what looked like plans. The woodcuts were very revealing. She'd probably never look at Sabates the same way ever again. The plans were what held her attention though.

"Tell me about these," she said. "The truth, and quickly. I'm running out of patience."

Esti twisted her hands in her lap. "Sabates sent a copy of those to Eneko. He found the basis for the plans in the archive. Orgull had a new lot opened up last year. A clockwork heart, at least mostly clockwork."

Did he now? This was something to take a little time over, time that Gerlar might spend on other things. She could think of a use or two for Esti as well.

"Gerlar!"

The life warrior appeared, silent and impassive.

"Gerlar," she said without taking her gaze from Esti,

"catch them up. They won't be travelling fast." Vocho would be tender for quite some time – the after-effects of removing the tattoo could even be fatal, she understood.

"When I find them?"

She shrugged. She hoped Dom would find them too, but perhaps he cared as little for them as he seemed to for everyone else. Maybe it would take a more direct threat to flush him out. He was a careful man. She flapped the plans to move the still air and wondered how far she could push Esti under the influence of the leech.·

"Follow them. And if you find a nice quiet place . . ."

"Kill them?" The gleam in his eyes made even Alicia shudder.

She gathered herself and told him what she wanted.

Petri lay back in silent darkness. There was nothing else to be done. Nothing to see, nothing to hear. Nothing to feel except the pain of course, which while merely excruciating wasn't as searing as the regret or the shame.

He'd thought himself brave once, and honourable, someone who could hold a secret to the grave. A man who wasn't afraid to do what needed to be done, even if it was distasteful or painful. Shameful how quickly Eneko had disabused him of those particular notions. How quickly he'd caved in, told him everything he wanted to know. All he knew about Sabates and Licio, about their plans. About Vocho, and more shameful than all the rest, about Kacha.

He grimaced in the darkness and had to fight back the blinding pain in his face where an eye had once been and the urge to be sick that came with it.

Not quite all about Kacha. He'd managed to keep one small kernel to himself. Everything else had been laid bare like the bone in his cheek.

Silence slowly drugged him, as did darkness, taking his thoughts and twisting them into mad patterns. He never knew if it was day or night, never saw light, never heard the thrum of the city around him, except three times he'd felt or thought he'd felt a rattle through the floor. But he couldn't be sure because he was seeing and hearing things that could not be there. A faint rumble again, and he was sure, as sure as he could be of anything. The change o' the clock, the slick movement of the city through its turns. He groped around him with his left hand – his working hand – tied now in front of him, and relished the touch of stone under his fingers, the scent of the rank straw that lined the cell floor. His only points of reference, the two things he knew were real, and he wasn't sure about the straw.

His questing hand found the bottle. They'd left him a bottle of foul-tasting water which left a greasy film inside his mouth and a scrap of bread so stale he couldn't eat it without his face screaming for mercy, even when he tried softening it with the water. Not even if he broke it up, and that wasn't so easy to do with one hand, so he went hungry, and that made the images ever more vivid as they danced in front of his eyes, crept up his arm, sat on his shoulder, whispered in his ear.

Strange thoughts had begun to torment him down there in the dark, odd visions that couldn't be real. Could they? Sometimes he thought he heard things – the ticking of Bakar's bone clock, slicing seconds off his life. The hiss of hot blood, the rattle of the clockwork duellist at the guild, the soft warm sounds of Kacha as she slept in his bed. He couldn't be hearing any of them, but his mind insisted that he did. Then it wasn't just sounds, but voices, and he *knew* they couldn't be real because they were the voices of dead people.

He became aware of a hectoring voice that he knew and shrank from – his father's. "Show some backbone, boy. You're above that guild, above that classless oik Eneko. You're a duke, not some wretched dock rat, like that whore-spawned fishwife you insist on hankering after. Eneko should have been proud to have you in that guild of his. Now show me what you're worth, that you're my son, because this is where you will be forged."

Should have been, should have been . . . The thought echoed around Petri's head long after his father's voice had faded back into blackness. Should have been a duke, should have been a master duellist. Should have been making a good marriage to some woman he was probably related to, should have been what his father wanted. Should have been loyal to Bakar, should have been smarter than to get mixed up with a magician. Should have been honest with Kacha when he had the chance. Should have beens were the bane of his life. Never quite measuring up to what people expected of him – his father, Eneko . . . Kacha. Never given the chance to show what he knew was inside him.

"A good man. A brave man," a voice said. It took a moment to recognise it because Petri had barely known him despite the fact his presence, or absence, had ruled much of his life.

"Kemen?"

"You were a good man, a brave one despite your circumstances, and you can be again."

"Why am I talking to dead men?" His brother had been dead for years, like his father, yet now he heard them as plain as the sun that he hadn't seen in days.

"Who else is there?" Kemen said. "Who else is in your head, wanting to talk?"

He fell silent then, no matter how Petri called for him, no matter how the panic grew and coiled in his gut, how he grabbed frantically at the stone – the real, all that he could be sure of.

A good man. He hadn't been that for a long time, if he ever had. Now he didn't even have the illusion of being a brave one, or a noble one. Eneko had taken even that, sliced it away with his hot knife, taken it so easily that Petri couldn't believe it was ever there in the first place.

"A pumped-up mountebank," Vocho said. "Too quiet you are, Petri bloody Egimont. Too sneaky, too underhanded. A backstabbing double-dealing little prick, not near enough to a man for my sister. So why don't you fuck off, my dearest duke, and leave her be?"

Under usual circumstances Petri would have rather put out one of his own eyes than agree with Vocho, but going quietly mad in the dark was not usual circumstances and besides he only had one eye left, a thought that left Petri suddenly weak with laughter that had a metal edge to it.

"I concur: a craven coward and no more," Eneko said in Petri's other ear. "I knew it as soon as you joined the guild. Oh I took your father's money and agreed to train you, but there was always a flaw inside you waiting for a knife to slide in, twist and fracture you. You were too much like the worst parts of your father, and none of the good parts, none of the incisiveness, none of the determination. Only the vanity, the cruelty, the ability to sacrifice anyone for what you wanted."

The laughter stopped in Petri's throat. "No, I—"

"Why do you think I let you go to Bakar so easily, why I *gave* you away? The least worthy of being a duellist of all I had. I want no weakness in the guild, Petri, not among my masters. And you are weakness."

Strange shapes reared in front of Petri's eyes. He tried to ignore them, told himself they were just phantoms in his head born of too much silence and darkness, which had lived with him almost from the start of his time here. Little spiders of fire, crawling up his arms, across his face to burn the marks there, burrowing into his now useless hand.

Now they crawled over his eye, blinding him with light. He tried to slap them away, but a hand stopped him. A real hand, warm and strong on his. He grabbed it with his own, hung on to it as the one real thing in this place of delusions and opened his eye.

He was in light, in warmth. A lamp dazzled his eye, then the wavering shape in front of him resolved into Eneko . . . but was he real or just another part of Petri's fevered mind?

"Weakness," Eneko said again and showed Petri a knife that glowed red at the edges. "If I find that flaw in you, slide this in and twist, you'll shatter like glass and tell me everything. Shall we see?"

And yet Petri's new screams were better than the darkness of his own mind.

Chapter Fourteen

It was three days' hard ride from Ikaras to the edge of Reyes, another two to the city itself. Vocho wasn't sure he was going to last that long. They'd reached the foothills of the mountains that split Ikaras from Reyes and were the source of much of their bickering, lately turning to the prospect of war. Iron, coal, gold – all and more could be found in some measure at one point or another along their length. The iron in particular was a sticking point because neither country had any deposits anywhere else.

It was getting harder to move. In the lowlands, among the sugar plantations that gave Ikaras much of its wealth, the road had been oddly lonely. The only people they'd seen were slaves working the crops and an occasional overseer, and slaves wouldn't say a word they weren't bidden to. They'd now left that behind and entered a poorer part of the country where they stood out like nuns in a brothel. They rode horses, and no one had more than a donkey, and that for pulling a cart. Yet they weren't dressed right for nobility, and besides the swords were hard to hide in a country where no one carried them. The few people they passed looked at them askance and whispered among themselves.

If Vocho had any doubt that they needed to do something other than hide away somewhere until this whole mess blew over, it vanished at a dusty crossroads between two narrow valleys. The sugar had given way to tea as the land crumpled into steep hills punctuated by knife-sharp ridges and hidden valleys. And here between two of them was the first real indication of what Ikaras – with the help of Licio and that bastard Sabates no doubt – was up to.

Around the crossroads a swathe of tea plants had recently been cleared and sat in fragrant burning piles. The sweet smell of the smoke permeated the air. In the clearing little clots of men and women clustered together, armed as no one was armed in Ikaras, with guns at hips, or holstered on their back with slip-rings to bring them in hand in a blink. Not just guns either – along with the gaudy ceremonial knives that every free Ikaran wore, there were long daggers and swords that looked ill-balanced and hastily forged. Some had armour, though if any armour was proof against a gun or even a good sword at close range, it wasn't these cobbled-together affairs made out of bits of leather. Who knew what these people had been last week or last month, but Vocho was prepared to bet it wasn't soldiers. They were soldiers now though, or playing at it, picketed in wonky rows, and so many of them. The emptiness of the plantations they'd passed through made more sense now.

To one side, two men sat on scrawny horses with faces to match.

"Officers, if I'm any judge, and I've met a few. Not many good ones neither," Cospel muttered and Vocho agreed. These two didn't look confident though, more scared with a veneer of swaggering bravado.

Kacha pulled her recalcitrant horse to a stop, where it jigged and snorted, knowing full well how these sorts of meetings generally went. Even Vocho and Kacha would have difficulty dealing with this many men, but the horse looked like it was itching to try anyway. Vocho's horse stamped a foot as one of the officers kicked his scrawny beast towards them, while the other cantered down a line of grubby tents shouting something in Ikaran that Vocho couldn't catch but was pretty sure meant bad news.

The officer brought his horse to a stop insolently close, which almost cost him a chunk of flesh as Kacha's horse whipped its teeth towards him, but he reined back just in time.

"Your business?" the man snapped at Vocho, ignoring Kacha and Cospel.

Vocho painted on a bright smile and nodded towards the mountains, where he could now see plumes of smoke rising over the ridges and valleys, no doubt signalling other encampments such as this.

"Reporting for duty."

The man snorted in disbelief, ran his gaze over them both and didn't much like what he saw, if the curl of his lip was anything to go by.

"Reyens?" He turned and shouted something incomprehensible except for its tone, which had "Come and arrest these spies immediately" written all over it.

Vocho slid a glance Kass's way, got a nod of agreement and, while the man playing at being an officer was still turned away, they both rammed their heels to their horses' flanks. Kass's beast shied, looked like it was going to argue and then plunged towards a still standing field of tea. Vocho's horse, permanently exhausted as it usually was, ambled after it and only broke into a canter with another jab of his heels. Cospel's dogged little pony followed.

The lush green plants hid them from view, at least partially – they couldn't avoid the noise or the bushes shaking as the horses barged through. Behind them someone was screaming orders at someone else, and the crash of another horse entering the field had Vocho urging his horse on, as did the sound of a bullet whizzing through a bush to his left.

His horse was no match for Kass's great beast, and Vocho wasn't much better – his back was still on fire, and the removal of the tattoo had left him weak. He fell further behind, leaning forward in the saddle to urge the horse on, desperate now. His horse pitched forward unexpectedly on the uneven ground, sending Vocho up its neck and almost unhorsing him entirely. He scrambled back into the saddle and risked a look behind. He could just make out a plumed hat above the plants, scything through them like a boat through water, scattering leaves in its wake. To his left, another; more to his right. They'd had more than the two horses then. And of course, if he could see them . . .

He took his horse in hand, muttered dire imprecations under his breath and kicked so hard it shot forward like a cork out of a bottle. A few yards later the tea bushes came to an abrupt end and Vocho found himself in clear ground, which was exactly where he didn't want to be with a load of guns behind him. The horse, all pretence at exhaustion disappearing as it picked up on Vocho's desperation, jigged under him as he reined hard about with a grimace at the pain in his back, searching for Kass. He found her on a steep stretch, waiting for him on a snorting impatient horse, Cospel beside her. His own horse struggled to make it up the slope. It was slathered in white sweat by the time he made it, and his shirt was wet with his own. Kass gave him a look shot through with exasperation, turned and dropped down the other side of the ridge out of sight of their pursuers. For now.

The other side was tea, tea and more tea – still not quite tall enough to hide them on horseback. In the distance, up another, steeper, incline, the waving bushes gave way to woods that might at least hide them for a time.

Kass pulled up her horse just below the ridge so that she couldn't be seen by anyone until they had breasted it. Meanwhile Vocho's horse panted and blew, gasping for breath as he turned to see what she was about, drawing his sword as he did. He regretted that almost instantly and struggled to keep the blade up. The only way he managed was by imagining how great it would be to drink some of Esti's jollop and neither feel pain nor care about it.

The first of their pursuers fairly flew over the ridge, driving his almost spent horse for all it was worth. Too quick, because he was on Kass before he knew it, and on the ground an eyeblink later. The scrawny horse galloped on, eyes white, sweat streaming from its neck.

"There's more," Vocho gasped. "Too many." His back was on fire, and where his shirt was stuck to the wound with sweat he was pretty sure he could smell burning.

Kass leaped down, checked the unconscious form at her horse's feet and grabbed the gun from his waist.

"It's not that desperate yet," Vocho said. Kass had a bad history with guns. "Just put it away, please?"

She shot him a look but grudgingly tucked the gun away where it probably couldn't do any damage, to anyone else or more importantly them.

The Ikaran's horse was below them, plunging through the plants as though it had wolves on its tail, all but obscured by their tops so that all they could make out was movement. So when Kass led her horse off to one side, quietly and carefully, mindful of the steep slope that kept her feet slipping to the left, Vocho slid down and did likewise, Cospel close behind. Dismounted, the tea plants towered over them, and it wasn't long before they were hidden completely, and they stopped so the plants' movement didn't give away where they were.

Horses crashed through plants, men grunted as they were jolted against saddles, the whisper of protesting leaves, and then they were gone down the hill, following the now riderless horse.

Vocho's horse struggled to catch its breath and Vocho didn't feel much better. He fumbled blindly in his pack for the jollop and got a good glug down before Kass's hand stopped him.

"No telling if those men can actually track," she whispered. "We need our wits about us, because it's not just them." She nodded to where he had earlier, to the other plumes of smoke towards the mountains. "We need to get away from here before they realise their mistake."

Right now Vocho hardly cared. He laid his head on his horse's sweating neck and waited for the jollop to do its work. First came the light-headedness, which he welcomed – while it didn't dull the pain in his back, it did make him care about it less. Then came the heaviness and with it numbness, so he could stand straight without breaking into a pain-racked sweat.

Kass watched him with a frown, but she said nothing, only took the reins of his horse with hers and led them away, not downslope but not up either, for which Vocho was thankful. She took them around the lip of the valley, stopping every once in a while to scramble their tracks behind them or to clamber onto her horse and look carefully about.

By the time Vocho began to get his senses back enough to ride rather than stumble blearily after her, it was long past noon and they'd come in a big loop to almost opposite where she'd downed their pursuer. Apart from a few far-off calls and once the crash of a horse close by to their left, they'd had no sign of the pursuit. The horses had cooled by now, and Cospel saw to rubbing them down and checking their feet. Vocho's horse had a knee that was swollen and warm after its pitch on the uneven ground, but seemed sound enough provided he didn't ask too much of it. That didn't seem likely, given Vocho felt like he'd asked far too much of himself today. Every bone dragged with weariness, and even through Esti's jollop there was a faint remembrance of pain as though it was just biding its time.

Kass gave him an appraising look and said, "You wait there. I'll see if I can find some water for the horses and take a look around. Cospel, try to look after the silly bugger."

Vocho didn't argue, which only made her frown the more. Instead he fell to his knees, trying to stay alert while Cospel fussed over the horses. She wasn't long, and he groped his way back to his feet.

"No sign of them now," she said. "And they're pretty bad at covering a trail, so I doubt they're much good at following one either. Still, better safe than sorry. Come on. There's a wood not far and a stream."

"Kass . . ."

"Out here's no good. Come on, Voch. It's not far."

They started off in a silence that only grew between them, broken by the snorts of the horses, the jangle of harness and Cospel muttering under his breath about days off, getting shot at and how going back to the Shrive might be preferable and more peaceful. Fire grew again in Vocho's back, and he kept casting furtive glances at his pack, though he made sure Kass didn't see. No more of the jollop until sundown, he'd promised himself, and that was hours away.

He didn't like it when Kass was this quiet − it meant she was thinking. No pointed remarks, no needling him, none of the usual things that drove him mad and, when they weren't there, he missed. He supposed he wasn't being much like himself either, but damn, he just wanted a moment to sneak some more jollop. Just a swig, just a small glug. Just something to take the edge off.

They came to the end of the plantation, where it merged almost seamlessly into a wooded slope. He groaned at the thought of climbing, but better that than stay where there was no water and little cover. Not with all those fires he'd seen and the number of soldiers that must be around them.

She stopped just before they left the tea bushes behind for good, and he joined her in scanning for any sign of . . . well, anything. People, ambush, wolves, surprise magicians. Once they were satisfied the way was clear, Kacha led on to the stream she'd found, and a small clearing bounded on two sides by near-vertical slopes and on the third by brush so impenetrable Vocho thought rabbits might have trouble getting through it. They debated a fire, and decided not. It wasn't cold; they had enough food that didn't need cooking and, though neither of them said it he knew they were both thinking it, there was an army massing around them. An army that probably wouldn't be too friendly. They were Reyen by accent, by looks in Kass's case, by the harness on their horses and by their swords − spies.

Kass looked at him carefully before she spoke. "Can you ride without taking any more of that stuff?"

He shrugged but not too hard because even the slightest movement made him wince now. His hand twitched to his pack, but he snatched it away. "Maybe."

"Voch, you're going to need your wits about you if we hope to get through all that. And that stuff . . . it leaves you worse than when you're drunk. If we get into trouble, I can't get us both out, not even with Cospel's help. I need you with me."

He'd rarely seen her so serious, and he had a sneaking suspicion he knew why. "You're planning something, aren't you?"

She looked up guiltily. "Maybe."

"Well maybe you could tell me what? I'm not so far gone I can't see straight."

A snort of laughter that was better at least than her silence. "Well, OK. Let's start with, what does all that mean?" She waved a hand towards the shadowy mountains, the plumes of smoke between them.

"Oh come on, Kass. I'm in pain and dosed up with the-Clockwork-God-knows-what, but that's easy. Given the, er, gentlemen we met earlier, it looks very much like a lot of people who don't normally live here spread over a large area. Probably for reasons of warfare."

"I saw a few things while I was looking for water earlier. The road up to the pass is all churned up, like a lot of horses and wagons went past not too long ago. Old fire pits, that sort of thing."

"Forward does not seem like a good option right now, then. Even less so than before."

She fidgeted with the gun she'd stolen, and Vocho leaned back out of the way and noticed Cospel subtly doing the same.

"Not really, no," she said.

What is wrong with you, Kass? What aren't you telling me? It struck him that he'd never before had cause not to trust her, but the feeling in the pit of his stomach was like someone had dropped a stone in it.

"But you want to go anyway." Not a question – he knew his sister far too well. "Why are we going, or rather why do you still want to go?"

"Same reason as you, Voch. Undying devotion to Reyes, not wanting to watch her burn or her people's blood run in the streets. You know, the good thing."

"Sod the good thing. I mean, I'm all for saving Reyes – I quite like the place even if it currently doesn't like me – but what are we talking here? An army sat right in our path. Eneko planning his own little coup if Dom's right. Sabates and Alicia behind and probably catching up. Us with an antidote but probably no way to get it to the person who matters. I'm not liking this plan of yours much."

"It's all I've got. Give me a better suggestion."

"We could go around, go back, lie low somewhere. There's a fucking big army out there if you hadn't noticed, Kass, not a half-arsed bunch of nobles playing by the rules, not Orgull doing a bit of posturing to put pressure on the negotiations, even if you and I know those negotiations aren't what they appear. Not just a few soldiers got together in case negotiations fail. There's too many fires out there for that, too many tracks in the dust, too many empty fields in a country that relies on exporting what it can grow, because you aren't the only one with eyes in your head."

"I realise that, but—"

But Vocho was too far gone to stop now. Too much pain in his back, and tiredness making his eyes spin. "Kass, out there, right where we need to go, is a big, proper army, just waiting for the go-ahead. I mean, yes, I love Reyes as much as you do, which is why I agreed to come in the first place, but not so much I'm willing to die in some stupid wood because I don't talk with the right accent. Why are you so all fired up to do this?"

A sharp glance, so quick he might have missed it. "We swore, Voch, didn't we? Swore to protect Reyes if it came to it."

"I never swore," Cospel muttered, and they both raised an eyebrow, which he answered with a mysterious semaphore of his own. "I never! Never swore to the guild. I may have cursed the bloody thing for giving me you two as employers, and may be inventing new words for it as we speak. If it weren't for the fact I'm up to my neck in as much shit as you two, then I'd have hightailed it a long time since. Because I never swore. I didn't have much choice, did I? This or swing for thieving, and some days I ain't so sure swinging would be worse."

"Fine, you never swore," Vocho said. "Kass, *we* swore all right, and look where that got us. Reyes broke faith with us when no one even questioned my guilt, when we had to leave like sneak thieves in the night. When the prelate put a price on our heads – and that hasn't been revoked, has it? No, Reyes left us before we left it. I was willing to go along because, well, because Reyes is home and maybe we'll get a pardon, but I don't owe it a damn thing. Not against an *army*, Kass. There's reckless and then there's downright stupid."

She still had that stubborn look to her face, the one that meant she was going to do it anyway, whether he liked it or not.

"Come on, Kass. Why do this? Why not sit this one out?"

It took a long time coming, her answer. "Because we're better than that, aren't we? I always thought we were. We're duellists, Voch, whether we're in the guild or not. Think of the glory if we help prevent a war."

But her gaze went everywhere but him, and he knew. Kass wasn't like him, couldn't lie as easily as breathing, in fact as far as he knew had only lied once to him, and that was only by not telling him something. She was not telling him again, and it'd take a team of horses to drag it out of her most like, but he could guess.

Only one thing could make her lie to him now, and that was Petri bloody Egimont. Had to be. Damned man always made her go all noble, like Petri liked to think he was. Vocho didn't give a crap for noble.

He blew out an exasperated sigh and, despite Kacha's glower, got Esti's jollop out of his pack and took a swig, felt the pain in his back along with a lot else melt away to nothing much.

The trouble was, he did give a crap about Reyes. And glory – glory was always good. But what in hells was going through his sister's head? He knew her better than anyone alive but suddenly felt like he didn't know her at all. She was lying to him, he was sure of it, and that made his whole life sway in front of his eyes. He'd fucked up before and sworn he wasn't going to do it again. Besides, she was his sister, and he was going to make sure she didn't do anything stupid. Like believe anything Petri told her. The glory, if there was any, would be a bonus, his muddled mind told him. A whole boatload of glory if they managed to stop a war – oh and brought the prelate back to his senses. Maybe they'd even get back into the guild. Not under Eneko or Petri though. He'd eat his sword before he did that. Maybe . . . Now there was a thought. With Eneko and Petri both having betrayed the prelate, who would be guild master? Not Eneko's apprentice and once closest confidante, surely. Maybe a certain glory-filled young man with a bit of dash to him? A thought to warm the coldest recesses of his heart. He might even share with Kass if she got her head out of her arse about Petri. If she stopped lying to him about it.

There was only one way he could think of in his addled state to make her see sense. He had to know what she was thinking. What Petri had told her. He had to see that letter.

He fumbled at his horse's saddle and went through all the rest of the routine – brushing the sweat from the gelding's back, checking his feet, which had his back screaming through the numbing jollop. Cospel offered to help, but Vocho shook his head. Water from the stream, grain from the bags, hobble the gelding so he could at least graze. All through this he said nothing and neither did Kass, and that made him only more sure she was lying. Finally he slumped down next to where a fire should have been and cocked a weary eyebrow her way. She looked up from where she fiddled with a bit of harness and looked him over, not seeming to like what she found.

"You and Cospel go first," she said. "I'm not sleepy yet."

Another lie, because he could see the weariness in her eyes, but he said nothing. She lied because he'd had the jollop, saw he couldn't hide the clumsiness of his movements. They weren't safe here, and at least she was alert enough to see trouble coming.

The lies coming so thick and fast worried him, but he wasn't going to argue so he found his blanket and lay down – not on his back. As he shut his eyes he had time for one clear thought – *Thank god for Esti's jollop* – before he was asleep.

*   *   *

Alicia flipped the pages and flung a look at Esti, who trembled in the corner. "A clockwork heart?"

"N-not just clockwork," Esti stammered. "I had to add a little to it. I only know they had me make the living part – it's an organism I created. Eneko said he could use it for whatever they were doing. Sabates did something with it too."

And Alicia hadn't known a damned thing about it. Wasn't she supposed to be Sabates' confidante, wasn't he supposed to be sharing all his plans with her? He'd certainly led her to believe he was. He'd led her to believe that Esti was dead for quite some time as well. And Sabates plotting with Eneko of all people, that was just too much. This was going to take some pondering. In the meantime she had her original aim: use Vocho and Kacha to lure Dom to where she could kill him. Such a shock to discover he'd been their ally in Reyes, that she could use that alliance for her own purposes. If not, if Vocho's current state and the army in their way did for him and his sister, she'd find another way. And if they did make it to Reyes that would be a splendid distraction for Sabates.

She looked over at Esti and at the leech on her neck, keeping her under Alicia's control.

"What does Sabates want this for?"

Esti shrugged and then flinched. "I don't know; he just made me do it. This is only a copy. The originals went to Eneko weeks ago."

Eneko? What were those two bastards up to now? And why hadn't Sabates told her about this? How many more secrets did he have? And just what was he planning?

She strode over to Esti, who tried to press herself into the wall, but there was no escape from Alicia, not now. Maybe not ever. The leech pulsed under Esti's dress at the base of her throat. Just a word, a thought, and she could end Esti right now. The little witch had stood in her path every second of her stay in Ikaras. Always better, always more favoured, thwarting Alicia's ambitions at every turn and without even seeming to try, which made it rankle all the more because magic didn't come naturally to Alicia. She had thought she'd got rid of Esti, made herself prime in Sabates's confidences, when she'd set Esti up for murder, made sure the king knew about it, and had him sentence her to hang. Even then Sabates hadn't been able to let go, hadn't been able to confide his best secrets to Alicia. He'd kept this witch in secret, in blackmail too knowing the bastard for what he was. Now here was part of a plan Alicia knew nothing about.

"What was he doing giving it to Eneko? He hates the little shit as much as anyone."

"I . . . I don't know! I swear. He just made me do it. He did say . . ."

"Say what?" Alicia whispered, and the leech twisted under the cloth, bringing a gasp from Esti.

"Eneko hates the prelate as much as Sabates does," she said in a halting voice, not wanting to speak the words but having to. "That Eneko could be a tool to bring down Bakar for good, and discarded afterwards. But I don't know how, or what the heart has to do with that. I swear it!"

Alicia grunted and brought out her scalpel. She gripped Esti's hair and yanked her head forward. One quick slash where it would bleed profusely but not show, on the back of her head, and suddenly the room was full of the smell of blood. It was the work of moments to fashion a circle of it on the floor. A few more seconds, and she could see Reyes. Some fine tuning . . . There was another circle in the guild. In a private room. She peered out of the circle and saw a room made for nasty work, implements on a table, some heating in a brazier, a blood-soaked chair in the centre. The circle was Sabates' work, she was sure.

Someone moved across her vision, a familiar figure. An idea came, and she acted on it at once.

"Eneko."

The figure stopped what it was doing and turned to the circle. Eneko's face loomed large, close enough for her to see every wrinkle and wish she couldn't. She wondered that he didn't recognise her from before, as opposed to knowing her as Sabates' associate. But it had been a long time ago and only the once. Maybe it had been a minor thing to him, not the world-shattering event it had been to her. She'd been not much more than a girl then, and maybe he'd never even known her name. She supposed they'd all changed in the years in between.

"Alicia." His tone was formal, wary but curious. "What can I do for you?"

"Progress report. Sabates has his hands full at present, but he wants to know how things go at your end."

A raised eyebrow. He hadn't expected her, she thought, wasn't aware she'd known about the circle. Finally he inclined his head.

"They go well enough. Those plans . . . genius! Sheer genius."

"Naturally," she said dryly. "But more details, please. You know how Sabates likes his details. I can't just report back that you're pleased."

A smirk at that, at the thought she had to do as she was told. "Certainly. Tell Sabates that the automatons will be ready by the time he reaches Reyes. They should be more than enough for me to prove my worth as the new leader of Reyes, and enough to make a show of this 'war'.

Sabates will get what he wants. Bakar will be the first to die. A few skirmishes; my automatons will kill Orgull, and then Ikaras and Reyes – or rather Sabates and I – will come to terms as agreed. Impress on him that I'll be true to that agreement."

Crafty bastard, although Alicia had no doubt as to Eneko's life expectancy once Sabates had what he wanted out of the man. "Certainly. Thank you."

The face in the circle winked out, and Alicia sat back in thought. Clockwork hearts for automatons. Secret agreements with Eneko. Bakar dead – well, she'd known about that plan. Orgull's death was a different matter, but how could she use this to her advantage? She had her own ambitions. She didn't care if Bakar lived or died, if Reyes won the "war". She cared about Eneko, getting what she wanted from him. And then killing him for all he'd put her through whether he'd known it or not. Sabates killing him before she could get what she wanted – no. That would not do at all. Maybe she'd have to bring parts of her plans forward, change others.

She looked down at Esti, who cradled her bleeding head in her hands. Maybe she could use Esti to do that too. Wouldn't that be fun?

Kacha listened to the snuffles of the horses – hers in particular would let her know if anything disturbed him, possibly by the screams as he did his best to bite any available flesh. Too many people around for her liking in a country that had been as rural as they came, with the occasional house and silent groups of slaves working fields here and there. Now it was positively crowded, if the fires were anything to go by. They winked down on her from the foothills that led to the main pass, too many to count. And how many men had King Orgull at each fire? All poised on the border, and more joining them, from what she gathered from the tracks she'd seen. Horses, wagons, men on foot. That group earlier, who'd given up the chase and passed by half a mile to their side late in the day. No woodcraft, or they'd have spotted them, but that was hardly unexpected from what looked like a bunch of plantation workers.

They wouldn't be the only ones, so she kept sharp and listened. She glanced at Vocho and wondered just why it was he'd changed. Maybe it was the pain – Esti had said he'd take some time to heal, and Voch had often been a bit of a baby about physical pain – or maybe it was something in the jollop Esti had given him. Kass wasn't inclined to trust her, for all she'd helped them, and she looked at the bulge in Vocho's pack, nestled under his head, where the bottle lay. She could pour it away. She probably *should* pour it away, but she'd have to prise it out of Vocho's hands first. And maybe there was nothing wrong with it.

But he'd been unnaturally quiet for most of the day and peevish when he wasn't quiet. For the voluble Vocho, this counted as well past strange and into suspicious. It worried her – he worried her. And what worried her more was that she'd begun to doubt him. Oh, not about the usual things, like whether he was lying, because he often was. OK, always. More about whether he'd have her back if she needed it. She'd never not been sure of that – even during the fallout from the whole priest debacle she'd never really doubted it. Now she did.

He was here under protest, she knew that, because she'd asked him and tempted him with the thought of glory, but she didn't know how far she could push it. Not very far if he knew her real reason for wanting to go back to Reyes.

Oh, all the others, the ones she told him, were true enough. But they weren't the real reason.

She got up to stretch her legs and left him sleeping like the dead even if he snored rather more noisily.

The clearing they'd camped in was almost perfect for keeping hidden. Only one side was relatively open, and that's where she watched because she was sure they'd been marked leaving Ikaras, but she hadn't seen a damned thing since to confirm it. Either she was paranoid or they were very, very good.

She saw nothing now either, just shadows and trees shifting in the breeze. A silvery owl ghosting through the woods in search of dinner. The horses snapping at snatches of grass, her horse bullying Vocho's out of its fair share. She looked down at the sleeping Vocho when the moon came up and fitful beams filtered through the canopy to light his face. He lay curled on one side, leaning on an arm and his pack for a pillow, and looked so gaunt she felt a pang of guilt for all she hadn't told him.

Not enough to not wake him when she felt herself start to nod, though she gave him as long as she could, as much to make sure he wasn't clouded by the jollop as anything else. He sat up groggily but readily enough, and she slid into the warm space he'd just vacated, though she waited until he was fully awake before she shut her eyes.

It wasn't much that woke her – a rustle that seemed too loud for any woodland creature that would risk getting so close, followed by a muffled jingle which was certainly no animal.

Close on the heels of that came a prod in the shoulder and a hiss. She came upright in a rush, hand already on her sword, the other at her knife, and looked about. Without a fire, without the moon, which was obscured by clouds, it was dark, but after a few moments she could see well enough. Her horse stamped and snorted behind her, snapping its teeth at something. Vocho was to one side of her, still haggard, but at least he looked alert under the sheen of sweat. He had his sword out of its scabbard and was peering into the darkness.

Suddenly the moon shed its cloak of clouds. In that light she saw her pack at his feet with paper poking out of it.

The slightest of sounds away to her left, the whisper of a breath and then a glint of metal. For the first few seconds all she saw was the sword, all she was aware of was getting her own up in time to save her head and a quick, random thought — maybe this army weren't all amateurs. She managed a hasty parry that juddered her arm as she caught her attacker's sword awkwardly. Then she was rolling away, getting her feet under her as Vocho leaped to her undefended side. Whoever had attacked had melted back into the shadows just as Cospel sat up, blinking sleepily.

"What the fuck was that?" Voch whispered as they came back to back.

"The bloody tooth fairy? What do you think?" she snapped back. "Looks like Orgull has a few professionals with him."

"Oh good. I need a bit of practice." Despite his words Voch sounded bone tired. "And that trip across the mountains through an army had sounded so boring. I bet hiding—"

"Voch?"

"Yeah?"

"Any chance you might shut up so we can hear whoever it was just almost took my head off?"

A short silence and then, "Good point."

Kass strained to hear over the rasp of her own breath.

Vocho fidgeted with his feet, and she looked down to see him trying to poke the papers back into her pack, but that was going to have to wait for later, when no one was trying to kill them.

Whoever he was – she was pretty sure it was a he, she'd caught a half-glimpse of a face – he was good. She strained her ears but heard nothing. A glance towards the horses showed them alert, ears pricked and listening but not alarmed. She didn't like this at all.

A flicker of movement to her left. She whirled to face it, only to find nothing. Behind her there was a grunt as Voch did something – parried most like as the sound of steel on steel echoed around the clearing.

She turned again, and Vocho was defending against a savage overhanded blow from a *palla*. It thundered into Vocho's slimmer sword, staggering him and bringing a screaming sound from his blade. Then the attacker was gone, leaving Voch looking pale and shocked, just before the heavy blade came for her, from the other side.

This guy was good.

She managed a dodge and a parry – so late it was almost useless, but it turned the blade just enough, and then she was on the back foot, defending against a heavier blade and a much stronger opponent. She caught glimpses of him in the fitful moonlight – an impression of a tall man, heavyset, ideally suited to his weapon. A face with odd markings or possibly scars marring one cheek. A hole where his nose should be. The heavy blade whistled through the air towards her and missed her by the breadth of a hair, so close she could feel the slide of it across her skin.

But the attack had left an opening for her, one she was trained to use. She ducked under the still swinging blade and came up with the knife in her left hand arrowing for his armpit, a thrust that should have skewered him if he'd been there to receive it. Something – the hilt of his weapon, she thought – slammed into the side of her head. Her vision blurred for a second, and then the man was gone into the dark just as Vocho came up on his flank.

She knew who he was now, the same man who'd been watching Esti's. Marked too that there had been a hint of awkwardness to him. Nothing much, favouring one side like she did when she knew Vocho had her flank and she could ignore that side and concentrate on the other. A life warrior.

"Aim for his—"

"Left, yeah. I'm not blind," Voch said. "That's if I see it in time."

They stood, as they often had before, back to back and watching every shadow. Cospel huddled by the horses with a heavy pan in one hand, as much for his own protection as to protect them, and kept out of reach of Kass's horse. Vocho seemed more like his old self, and having him there, knowing he had her back, made knots in her neck she hadn't realise were there loosen. They waited but no further attack came. Only the first stirrings of dawn and with them the chorus of waking birds that told Kass that no one was close. Or probably anyway, remembering that her normally hostile-to-everything-that-moved horse had barely stirred until their attacker was on them. Whoever this man was, he had more woodcraft than either her or Vocho, who'd lived and worked in the city almost their entire lives.

He was almost certainly something to do with Alicia, she thought as she scanned the area in front of her again. Only Alicia had good reason to kill the pair of them. It didn't make any sense that the man was playing with him, and she was clear on that. If he'd wanted it, she'd be dead.

This was not a prospect she'd often had to face, and one she didn't want to now.

"I say," Voch said after a time. "I say we pack up and ride the fuck away. It's altogether too lively around here."

It was hard to disagree, except perhaps on which direction they should go.

"Let's go," she said.

They packed up their belongings hurriedly, one hand hovering over blades, one eye on the fading darkness, and Kass didn't fail to notice that her letter from Petri was out of order. Her horse complained bitterly, but that was nothing new, so she dodged his lunging teeth with ease, strapped everything to his back and mounted.

Alicia was playing with them. Why? What the hells had she achieved?

They moved off into the gloom of the trees, trusting the horses to find a path though they had to beware low branches. Kacha itched all over, expecting attack at any moment. Vocho seemed just as twitchy as dawn melded into day. She watched his back as they rode and thought a great deal about trust, at the same time turning over all she knew about their attacker.

They came carefully out of the shelter of the trees into a rocky defile that was still filled with grey light and led towards the nearing mountains. A road ran nearby – over to their left plumes of dust rose over the ridge, and the sound of men and horses filtered through the air – but without saying anything they knew the road was a risk too far. Two against ten? No problem; they'd done it before and won. Two against twenty; trickier but doable. Two against what might be ten thousand . . .

The defile led them towards a gap in the fires, to what must be an area too inhospitable to camp. The way became steep and rocky, finally too steep for the horses with them aback, so they dismounted and led them. Kacha looked back often, kept sharp watch on the lines of the ridges to either side, but saw nothing and wondered whether that was a good thing or bad. In front of her Vocho struggled along over the rocky terrain, his hand going often to his pack, to the pocket where he kept Esti's jollop. Then he'd turn, see her watching and take his shaking hand away. His face was haggard, but there was a set look to him and accusation in his glance.

The way got harder, so that even she was winded and sweating, while Vocho only held himself up by a hand on his horse's stirrup. She called a halt, but he gritted his teeth and carried on, so she followed, and Cospel came behind too tired to grumble.

They reached a long steep slope of fallen rocks and brush. Vocho cast her a look, one she knew of old, though with none of the humour that was normally there. "Dare you," it said. "Dare you to beat me." Then he tied his horse to a stunted oak and went on, pulling himself up the slope by the straggling shrubs and warped trees. She followed, leaving Cospel to watch the horses, not trying to beat Vocho, only to stay with him.

At the head of the defile stood a small stand of pines, and Vocho sprawled in their shade, panting. Kacha flopped down beside him, and they stared over a small plateau, one of the high pastures that dotted these mountains, this one dark with men and tents and the smoke of campfires.

"And you want to go through that, for him," Vocho said at last, when he'd got his breath back. The jollop appeared in his hand. He took a long swallow, grimaced and then relaxed a touch. Only a touch because he was wound tight as a bowstring. It took her a while to recognise his mood for what it was, because she didn't think she'd ever seen Vocho truly angry before. Angry was her, not him.

"You read the letter then." She scanned the camp below her and began to think Voch had a point, only giving up wasn't in her nature and she was damned if she was going to start now. Not to mention going back was about as safe as going forwards.

His back stiffened but he said nothing.

"Well?"

He faced her, briefly, his face darker than the storm clouds moving in across the peaks. Then he set his face forward again. "What do you want me to say? Petri's a self-aggrandising pompous dick, but that's nothing new."

"So are you, Voch, and I haven't killed you either."

He ignored her. "Nor is the fact he makes you stupid in the head. What is fairly new is he almost got the pair of us killed. He was spying on us for both the prelate and —" he paused to shudder "— Sabates. He's swapped sides more often than I lie, and that's a lot. You can't trust him, Kass, not at all, less than any magician, and you can't see it because he's blinded you. If you want to throw yourself away, be my guest. Just don't expect me to go down with you."

Anger came off him in waves she could almost feel on her face.

"If that's what's behind all this stubbornness — not Reyes or because it's the good thing or anything else — if the thought uppermost in your mind is him, well, you can go on your own."

She stared at him, at his serious face when nothing was ever serious to him. All the new hollows under his cheeks, the shadows gathered around his eyes. She'd known he'd take it like this, which is why she'd said nothing about the letter or what was in it. He'd not been the same since Reyes. More serious, like now. Less reckless. Twitchy at times, and yet steadier than she'd ever known him at others. All of these things had only grown more pronounced since the tattoo had gone, since he'd started to rely on Esti's medicine, even more now he was trying to keep secret how much he was taking. This wasn't the brother she knew.

"Not just for Petri," she said now. "For us too. We're dead if we stay, you know that. We've got that life-warrior after us, though why he didn't kill us I don't know. Life-warriors and a nest of magicians behind us, a price on our head. In front we've got a chance, Voch. For us."

"For us, bollocks. Swan in, save Petri, thwart a revolution, fame and bloody glory. That's not you, Kass. It's me − except the save Petri part − or at a push even Petri on his better days, but it's not you. And I'll do it just for the glory, like you knew I would when you suggested it. And for the possibility of a pardon, because I'm a Reyes man, born and bred, and I want to walk down one of its ridiculous shifting streets without worrying for my head and because I love that place in my bones. I belong there where I don't belong anywhere else. But don't try to tell me this isn't about Petri, that you'd be riding this hard, not planning on charging through a bloody army. God's cogs, an *army*, Kass, and you just think we'll ride through. Don't tell me it's not for him. Not after that letter. I know, you see. Better than he does, because I know you better than he does. All that fancy talk in there, all the long words and protestations, it's got you thinking. I know because you aren't fidgeting, and it's always one or the other with you, always something in motion, and if it's not your hands, it's your head. So you do it for Petri, if you have to, and I'll do it for the glory, but don't expect me to cheer when you find him. And don't lie about why you're here. I do the lying in this partnership. If there still is one."

With that he levered himself to his feet and staggered on, not even trying to hide how Esti's bottle came out or how his hands stopped shaking after he'd taken some. She got up to follow him and called out softly, "I can't give up on him. Like I couldn't give up on you, even when I tried."

He didn't even turn to answer. "Looks like you're going to have to give up on one of us, Kass. Because he hates me even worse than I hate him. But you've got plenty of time to think about it while we're trying not to die."

No, this wasn't her brother at all. She followed him, looking up at the clouds and reckoning they'd be soaked before the hour was out, but up this high clouds became fog, and that could only help them.

It was probably a mercy Vocho hadn't had time to read the entire letter.

Chapter Fifteen

Petri no longer had any notion where he was or how long he'd been there. No one came; no lights disturbed his eyes; no sound came to his ears. He was truly alone.

All he had was what he could touch, and pain, and what was left inside his head. Apart from the pain, then, of which there was much to spare, not much. He'd given it all to Eneko in the faint and muddled hope that would make the pain go away. No, not quite all, and he held on to one tiny thing in the mad darkness. Kass would come – she would. He thought of all he'd poured into his letter to her, a part of himself that was now hers utterly.

She'd come. She had to.

One thought strayed into another. Smell – all he could smell was himself. Nothing to taste. He only got water, and a little bread when they came, which they hadn't for . . . it must be days. Sometimes he shouted just to know he wasn't deaf, but he couldn't be sure even his own voice was real. He raised a shaking left hand to his face, towards what had been his eye, but couldn't bring himself to touch it. The pain faded at times, but any touch would flare it to

life, have him screaming all over again. Yet sometimes he
did just that, because at least the pain was real. He felt for
his eye with his left hand because the right was useless.
Tendons cut, muscles severed, bones cracked, fingers now
only limp slugs. A marrow-deep throb where once he'd
known only deftness. He'd known, as soon as Eneko had
started there with his hot blade, cauterising even as it
sliced, that he'd never duel again, that the hand would be
nothing but dead flesh.

Like him now, without that hand, his one true skill in
life cut away with the muscles. His hand was like he always
had been, perhaps, but had just never been able to see:
useless, cowardly, insignificant, worthless. As his father
had always said, as Eneko had said later.

A scraping sound in the dark. And again. Someone at
the door. He sat very still and listened, needles of fear
prickling everywhere; at the same time he wanted nothing
more than to see something, anything. Another human face
even if it was coming to take him to Eneko. He heard words
and only belatedly realised he was babbling, pleading with
them to come in. Take him, don't take him, whatever they
liked, just come. Just let him know he wasn't alone, wasn't
mad. Even the prospect of Eneko's knife couldn't dull the
desperate need for someone, anyone, to come. The noise
stopped, and panic gripped him worse than the pain – the
thought that they'd go away, leave him.

The door cracked open, let in a sliver of light that blurred
his eye with pain, but he didn't care. He hated the men who
came and threw bread at him, whispered threats of what
they would do to him, naked in the dark where no one
would ever know. He feared them, would do anything they
asked for a scrap of hard bread, a word, something that was
neither silence or Eneko's voice scraping across his nerves.

They came, and he cried, begged as he'd known he would, held out his one working, shuddering hand, everything stripped from him, every pretence that he was noble, brave, good. All he had to look forward to was begging.

Unless . . .

She'd come. She would. He held the thought, determined that Eneko wouldn't take that one last grain of hope from him.

Alicia moved smoothly down the rows of tents, picking her way through the mud, fan at the ready in the humidity of hot mountains after rain. The rain had passed swiftly, as it always did here, and now the last of the heat was mercifully dying with the sun as it dipped behind a peak. The camp sat on a shallow sloping plateau. She was impressed despite herself. She'd hitched her star to Sabates because he'd been her best hope of getting what she wanted, but until now she hadn't truly believed he could persuade Ikaras to go to war purely to fuel his own revenge fantasies.

At the centre of the camp, in a wide clear circle, sat two tents, as different as sun and moon. One tall and white, simple yet impressive due to its size, with a purple and gold dragon banner hanging limp in the heat. Next to it a complicated affair in blood red, squat next to its tall neighbour, mushrooming with small side tents and extra doors, dripping with gold braid and all kinds of ornamentation. Licio and Orgull. The tents that crowded around showed similar differences. More Ikaran tents than Reyen, that was clear at a glance, the plainer white tents an island in the middle of colourful chaos.

She stepped into the cool dimness of Licio's tent, where the guards glanced at her before moving aside to let her through into a series of flimsy-walled rooms lit with hundreds of tiny brass lamps. Voices ahead – Licio's brash, youthful tones, Sabates's smooth words, the staccato imperiousness of Orgull. She took a few moments to prepare. Brush and papers ready, several vials of various types of blood hidden where she could easily reach them in bodice and cloak and secret pockets. She took a few more moments to concentrate on the marks that oiled slowly over her fingers, the darker permanent ones, the redder new ones she'd laid on earlier. Her only true defence against Sabates and his power.

The silken door gave way under her hand and Sabates came to his feet with what looked like genuine pleasure in his smile. An incline of Licio's head acknowledged her, no more. A seated shallow bow from Orgull and a secret look that faded almost as soon as it was there.

She listened with half an ear as Sabates greeted her, fussed about getting her some wine, found her a seat. Orgull, bar that one bow, barely bothered with her, but she was watching his two guards, two life-warriors with matching, mirroring scars on their faces. They returned her look with an implacability that made a tiny shiver run through her, of delight mixed with some other emotion she couldn't name as she thought of Gerlar.

"A small change of plan," Sabates was saying. Such an oily sort of voice, she'd often thought, though she kept that behind shuttered eyes and her swishing fan. Sabates had been carefully cultivated, much like Esti grew her little plants. He went on, "I knew Eneko would prove to be a problem."

Alicia cocked her head. "I thought as much myself."

"Then you won't be surprised to learn he's preparing his own little coup. To take the city before we return, get all the population behind his guildsmen."

Is he now? No, not surprised, but it makes my life a little harder.

"No match for an army," Orgull said.

Sabates smoothed his robes and glanced at Licio before he replied. "Perhaps. Perhaps not. You've life-warriors, yes, but not many. The rest of your army is made up of farmers, artisans and the like. No match for guildsmen. And if the guild wins the city, they'll get an army much like yours. Besides . . ." He hesitated, caught Alicia's eye before he carried on. "They have something else. A new contraption, new clockwork. It will be quite devastating if he manages to finish them before we get there."

You know that I know about the hearts, about your little deal with Eneko, that I can see now that you are betrayed.

"So then?" Outwardly she stayed calm. Inwardly every cog in her head was whirring. Sabates knew, and that was dangerous. In all likelihood he knew that she'd spoken to Eneko. Maybe even knew about Esti. Did he know why?

"If it was just that," Sabates said "there'd be little problem for magicians of our calibre. But it's not just that. Eneko has Petri, has done for some days. We have to assume he knows as much about our plans as Petri did. Eneko's not a kind man when he wants something. Petri will break, as others have done before him in Eneko's hands. Probably he has broken already, because Eneko has some skill in that area."

No, Eneko had never been a kind man. "Then what do you suggest?" she asked.

"Exactly what we were discussing." He handed her a glass of wine and managed a brief secret touch as he did so. She fussed with her fan to cover the grimace that she couldn't entirely keep from her face. "Any thoughts?"

Yes, you fool. I don't care except for how this affects my plans.

"Eneko may suffer some disruption to those plans of his," she said. "Vocho and Kacha are on their way back to Reyes even now, and they bear him no goodwill. I don't doubt they intend to pay the guild a visit. And Kacha always was a fool over Petri. If I were Eneko, I'd be sleeping with a blade under my pillow and one eye open."

Sabates raised an eyebrow. "You let them live?"

"For now. They may prove useful. At the least they'll be one more thing Eneko has to watch out for."

"I see," he said in a tone that she knew meant that she'd be asked for a thorough explanation later. He drummed his fingers on the arm of his chair. "Perhaps fortunate. Perhaps not. Our plans need to adapt, nonetheless. Especially as there's more than one guildsman in this camp."

Her turn to raise an eyebrow.

"They were guarding the mines until they were persuaded, by fair means or foul, that it was the 'good thing' to join us and stop Bakar in his madness. But when this news about Eneko becomes known – and it will – then it becomes trickier."

"No match for my life-warriors," Orgull said with a smugness that just begged for a slap she couldn't give.

Aloud she said, "It's only a problem if you want to keep them alive."

"Ah, but I do, at least some of them. Reyes is well defended, and there's all that damnable clockwork to consider. Eneko knows we're coming, so we'll not have the advantage of surprise. I need them to help us find a route in that won't kill half our men." Sabates shifted irritably and took a sip of wine. "At any rate, we need to move sooner than we'd hoped. And without Petri in the palace, no matter how coerced, at least part of our plan will have to be redesigned."

Ah yes, his plans for the truly hideous bone clock the prelate loved so much. Alicia had thought all his manoeuvring stupid, though she had to admit that the poison they'd been administering through Bakar's precious clocks had done wonders to help them destabilise both the prelate and, by extension, Reyes. The best way to get any population behind a change in rule was to make the current one abhorrent, and how better to achieve that than to make the ruler insane?

"I could get in, perhaps," she said. "Bakar might remember me." Though not for the reasons Sabates thought.

A smooth, knowing smile from him with a hint of jealousy. She'd danced him around her so long, promised much and given little, but he'd grown weary of waiting for her final yes. As if that would ever happen. Many men had thought so, and none had got what they wanted, though she had allowed them to believe they might for her own purposes. And Sabates jealous of Bakar, a man so addled from all the poison he'd been given that all she'd needed was a bit of flattery and a friendly ear rather than the seduction Sabates assumed.

"Oh, who could forget you?" Sabates oiled. "Good. Still, we'll need to make a few other adjustments, bring things forward." He turned to one of the guards by the door. "Inform the commanders we leave tomorrow, as soon as is practicable."

Licio, Orgull and Sabates stayed talking and planning until it was late, but finally Sabates rose and took his leave. He slid a glance her way, a look she'd seen for coming on twenty years. She'd ignored all of them with more or less grace. But she wasn't sure she could ignore this one, when he thought he had her, had caught her going against him . . .

"Let me show you to your tent," he said, and she nodded, fluttered behind her fan to hide the racing of the pulse in her throat and the way her mouth clamped down on her sudden fear. He'd caught her out, knew what she'd discovered, what he hadn't meant her to know about his deal with Eneko. He was powerful, more powerful than her, and he'd never taken lightly to his pupils getting too smart for their own good – the university gardens flourished on what was left of those pupils. She'd danced him about, and now she'd made a possibly fatal misstep.

The camp thrummed with life around them as he led her. Even now, as her mind was whirring on how to get out of this one, she took in details. Details helped you live. There were only a few Reyens: Licio's men with their coloured flashes, guildsmen here and there in gold and green tabards with the sort of stunned smiling faces that occurred after a magician had spent a lot of effort persuading them, the sort of persuasion that may or may not take long. They were far outnumbered by the Ikarans, and she wondered if Licio realised how much danger he was in, or whether Sabates had perfected his control of him. She rather thought he had, but maybe he didn't know just how much she had worked on Orgull on her own behalf. Maybe there was a way out of this after all.

Smoke from the fires curled around them as they turned off the main path and out into darker areas where men looked up fearfully as Sabates passed. Sabates' stock in trade. Not outright terror, no direct threat, just a shifting unease that made a person think that he should follow the magician because it was better to be on the winning side, surely? That being on the losing side, even if it was right, wasn't for a man who wanted to stay alive and feed his family. Someone who could offer them that, when the alternative was a deluded prelate, was surely the right side. They muttered among themselves, but when didn't they? Was any ruler really better than another? If not, then did it matter whose side they were on?

"Here we are." Sabates strode past two guards, who straightened up when he came into view, and pushed back the flap of a tent only slightly less impressive than Licio's.

She tried to think as he fussed around, lighting a few small lamps, before he turned to her, unnervingly close so that she could feel the heat of his skin.

"You've dangled me on your thread for long enough with your promises of tomorrow," he said, all soft and smooth with implied threat. "It's time to come good on them. After all it is, very nearly, tomorrow."

She raised her fan, but he batted her hand away and gripped her other wrist, pinching the skin and squeezing the bones. She wasn't going to be able to fob him off as she had the others, not this time.

"As you wish." She let her body go loose, smiled up at him full of promises and let him pull her inside the circle of his arms. She caught sight of the pallet behind him covered in furs and silks and most certainly made for two.

Sabates was breathing hard, making her neck shiver with it. His hand crept around and deftly filched the vials of blood from her cloak and the little pocket on her bodice, the scraps of paper from her sleeve. He slid them out of every hiding place one by one, and threw them onto a small brazier in the corner. The glass smashed, the blood evaporated. The papers with their stored spells burned with a green flame. He took the Ikaran knife from her waist and threw it into a far corner.

"Just in case. I know you," he murmured. "And I'd like to live long enough to enjoy the experience."

He leaned in to kiss her, and she strove not to recoil or turn aside, but instead slid her arms around him so that both hands grasped the fan.

"Sabates, you think yourself so clever. More fool you. I wonder, how much blood do you have?"

He jerked back, and the thin blade she'd slipped from the fan slid between his ribs.

Quite a lot of blood, as it turned out. Quite a lot.

Chapter Sixteen

From the tumbled rocks of a high ridge Vocho looked down over a deep hollow full of fires in the dark. He was screwed and he knew it. No matter what he said to Kass, there was no going back because the dark behind them was as full of fires as the front. And what was there for him back in Ikaras anyway? Nothing except the prospect of being hanged for a spy, and he'd worked hard to keep his neck rope free.

That and Esti and more of her jollop, but he knew that for a bad idea even as he found his hand reaching for it. Kass kept looking at him strangely, and not just because of their row earlier, he was pretty sure. More at the way he couldn't keep his hands still, or how sometimes his mouth trembled.

Concentrate. Easier said than done when all he could think about was the fire in his back, the ache in every joint and how another slug of jollop would make it all fade away, for a time.

"How many, do you think?" Kass said now.

"Too bloody many," he snapped. "So what's your grand plan, Kass? You have got one, I suppose?"

"Not as such."

She kept glancing over her shoulder. Vocho didn't blame her. Whoever he'd been last night, he was still around, Vocho was sure of it. Oh the horses were calm enough, even Kass's nightmare, no stamping or snorting or clacking of teeth, but he couldn't shake the feeling he was being watched, and by someone who had given every indication he could beat the pair of them without breaking a sweat.

"Not as such," Vocho repeated. "Well, that's helpful."

He kept looking though. There had to be a way.

Right in the centre of the hollow was a fire ten times the size of the others, and by its flickering light he could make out two great tents, one white and ghostly, the other darker and more substantial. No one seemed to be moving, which wasn't surprising given it was the middle of the night, though he was sure they'd have patrols or watchmen at the least. Still, night seemed to be the best bet, when they'd not stand out too much. Although . . .

"Kass, you see those tents over there? To the left of the big fire?"

She peered down. "What about them?"

"Well, looks to me that the tents on this side aren't familiar but those ones are. Very familiar."

She looked more closely then swore under her breath. "Guildsmen? What the hells are they doing here?"

"Don't know, but I do know that if they're here, we won't stand out so much. How many Ikarans are going to worry about two guildsmen if they've already got some in camp?"

"It doesn't make sense. The last Ikarans were ready to hang us for spies, and now here they are all cosy with a bunch of Reyens."

"A bunch of Reyens surrounded on all sides, Kass. And, let's face it, probably under the influence of magic."

"And guarded very well, even if they are being subtle about it," a new voice said. Kass leaped to her feet, sword already out, and Vocho struggled to follow. Dom was the last person Vocho expected to saunter out from behind their horses, looking dapper as ever.

"Of course this is the kings' camp, both of them, rather than the rabble, who haven't a clue what's going on. Licio isn't so flush with allies he'll turn friends away, and Orgull, well, he's got enough trained men here to take Licio's out if he needs to, I don't doubt. I don't rate the Reyens' chances myself, but I don't think they had a lot of choice. Not with Sabates around."

Kass's sword sagged, and Vocho managed a weak laugh at the mention of the magician's name in the hope it might ward off the shaft of dread that had just turned his stomach over. "God's cogs, Dom, you almost gave me a conniption. What are you doing here?"

"Same as you, I rather suspect. Trying to get home. Maybe thwart a war. Not making it easy, are they?"

Vocho was about to make some smart-arsed reply when a noise from the camp stopped him – a man's drawn-out scream of rage and pain which tapered off into the night. As Vocho watched, people scrambled out of tents, running in front of fires so that he could track their shadows as they struggled into clothes and armour. More torches were lit and gathered off to one side of the camp, by a tent almost as impressive as the main two. In moments the whole camp was alive with people, most of whom were only paying attention to one thing – what had caused that scream.

"But that might help," Dom said. "Nothing like a good distraction. Come on."

The way down was steep but not impossible, if they led

the horses. Dom went ahead while Vocho took the reins of his horse as well as his own. He was glad of his horse because his legs felt rubbery, and he had to hold on to its patient neck more than once to make it to the bottom.

They found Dom spying out the way. The camp was pandemonium. Men clotted around campfires, whispering; others ran to and fro; still more buckled on armour and tested the edges of their weapons. They spoke in Ikaran, and Vocho couldn't follow what they said.

"What's happened?" he asked.

"Can't say for sure, but it sounds like someone important just got a knife in the back." Dom nodded in the direction of the most impressive tents and handed over a small telescope, something Vocho had rarely seen before as they were both expensive and easily broken. "Someone is just waking Licio up, by the look of it. Ah, there he is. He doesn't look happy, does he?"

Cospel snickered evilly. "He's walking like someone just shoved a stick up his arse."

Vocho fiddled with the telescope and got it focused. Licio looked like a man who'd just heard the worst news imaginable – pale and staring as his guards went ahead and pushed people out of his way. The man behind him, an Ikaran in the most sumptuous silks Vocho had ever seen, seemed likely to be Orgull. He followed Licio with a grave face, but there was a hint of smugness about him. He was followed closely by a pair of life-warriors – those scars, the way they mirrored each others' actions. Just like their attacker in the woods. They moved with the same sort of fluid threat too, as though they took it for granted that anyone who stood against them would die.

"Something is most definitely amiss," Dom said, taking the telescope back, folding it up impossibly small and sliding it into a pocket. "Which is all to our advantage. Let's go."

They moved off, not drawing as much as a glance from soldiers bent on looking to see what was causing such an uproar. Vocho thought he could probably have killed half of them before they even knew he was there. One or two had kept their wits, but they were easy to spot and dodge in the chaos. Even so, it took them some time to work their way around the edge of the camp. They made a brief stop by the guildsmen's tents at Dom's insistence. Most seemed abandoned.

"I'm hoping they've taken the same advantage we have, and got away," he said. "But if they have, they've left a lot behind."

They took a look, Kass and Cospel ducking in and out of tents and finding armour and weapons, food and clothes strewn about in a haphazard manner.

"Not one," Cospel said, and Kass nodded her agreement.

Vocho stared at the tents, at all the men and women had left. No guildsman would do that, not unless . . . Vocho felt sick. Not unless they had no choice. Not unless they weren't coming back for them.

A figure stirred at the end of the row of tents, and Vocho moved back into the shadows with Dom by his side. No guildsman this, nor soldier unless they'd started wearing dresses, and he relaxed. Until the ice-fair hair came into view, and the ice-fair face. Alicia.

The hairs on the back of his neck prickled, and he turned to Dom to say something – let's get the fuck out of here was favourite – and stopped dead. Dom was staring at her like she was an apparition, his own face as pale as hers.

"Dom?" Vocho whispered.

No response. Alicia came closer, and now Vocho could

see what Dom apparently had: the blood down her dress, coating her arms, the odd faraway look to her eyes. With anyone else he would have thought they'd witnessed some terrible thing and were now shocked to the core. Not Alicia though. He'd bet a large amount of money she was the cause of all that blood.

Kass swore softly behind him, but Dom seemed utterly stricken by the sight of her.

"Dom, we really need to—"

Dom took not a shred of notice and stepped forward into the faint light from a fire. "Cee?"

Alicia jerked as though stuck with a pin and whirled to face him.

"Cee?" he said again.

"Dom," Kass whispered from back in the shadows, "what the fuck are you doing? She's got enough blood to kill half an army there. She's a magician, Dom."

Dom stood as though struck dumb, ignoring Kass, ignoring Vocho, the only movement his hands opening and closing helplessly. Vocho's consolation was Alicia seemed almost as shocked as Dom, though she recovered quicker.

"Finally," she purred. "I've spent a lot of effort trying to get you to show yourself."

Vocho had seen Dom in several different guises – the bumbling idiot, smooth and sophisticated, graceful killing machine. He'd never seen him like this, like a teenage boy struggling to ask a girl to dance, and failing. All that came out of his mouth was a stutter that went nowhere.

Alicia stepped up to him and raised a bloodied hand, though she stopped short of touching him. "It's been a very long time. Too long."

"I thought . . ." Dom seemed to be speaking in a dream. "I thought . . ."

Alicia stood on tiptoe to kiss him, and what Dom thought was lost. Kass looked away, Cospel coughed, but Vocho, while he wanted to do both of those, wanted more to make sure this witch wasn't going to stab Dom in the back. Even so he felt helpless as the moment dragged on until he thought one or the other must surely pass out for lack of air.

Not so helpless he didn't spot the knife in her hand. He dived forward, barging into the pair of them and knocking the knife from her surprised grasp. Dom took a second to look bewildered, but Alicia never even paused – she was reaching for a scrap of paper even as the knife fell.

"What . . ." Dom said, but Vocho didn't stop to answer. Kass was beside him on the instant, sword drawn, and Alicia backed away with a hiss and a wicked grin. Her thumb smeared blood on the paper.

Vocho led with a thrust that almost made him pass out with pain. Dom gasped and tried to grab his arm, but didn't do more than send the move awry as Kass moved around to Alicia's back.

"Voch, what are you—" Dom said.

"She's a magician," he replied, shaking Dom off and advancing on Alicia. "And I'm trying to save your life."

"No. No, she's not."

Alicia herself proved that wrong when she threw her scrap of paper. The flash blinded Vocho for a second and left strange purple marks in his eyes; the bang almost knocked him on his arse. All he could make out were vague shadows. Three shadows, and Kass he could tell with his eyes shut just by the way she moved. He shifted so they could protect each other's flank, and peered into the darkness as Kass muttered under her breath next to him.

Things gained clarity, slowly, as his night vision came

back. Too slowly. Two shadows, and the taller one had to be Dom, only he was . . . What was he doing? Never mind, because the shorter one was doing something complicated which he suspected involved blood and he tried a stab in that direction.

His sword met another, Dom's. What the hells? It didn't matter, because Alicia said something, the smell of cooking blood filled the air and he, Dom and Kass were thrown backwards into the wall of a tent.

The horses went berserk behind them, and he recognised the sound of Kass's bastard kicking everything within reach, sending Cospel diving for cover. Which was helpful because the noise had brought a couple of Ikaran soldiers running, and the horse caught one right in the gut and the other in a knee so that they added their screams to the rest of the hubbub. Cospel took the opportunity of relieving them of a few oddments while they were distracted and then made sure they weren't getting back up for a while.

Sadly there were more soldiers behind them. Alicia shouted something to them in Ikaran. Vocho didn't catch all of it, but enough to know they were in serious shit. *They killed Sabates.*

The air around him was suddenly full of Ikarans and swords. Kass was already heading for the horses and the clanging sound of Cospel thumping someone with the heavy and by now rather dented tankard he'd taken to hanging from his belt. Someone swung at Vocho's head, but he managed to duck the blow and wind them with a shoulder to the gut that almost blinded him with pain. He dived for the horses but hesitated when he realised Dom wasn't behind him. A man came for Vocho, but the hilt of his sword to the man's mouth put a stop to that as teeth and blood flew around the scream.

Dom hadn't moved. Despite the noise, the soldiers, the everything, he was standing as still as the Clockwork God when he'd been dead, staring at Alicia. She stared back with a gloating kind of look like a cat that had swallowed the whole dairy. The knife was still in one hand, dripping with blood and looking thirsty for more.

If they didn't go now, there would be no going at all. Kass manhandled her prancing horse past, leading Vocho's more placid beast. She threw him the reins and let her mount do what he lived for – terrorising as many people as possible. In mere seconds every soldier in the vicinity had gained a healthy respect for the beast and had backed off, leaving them a small but significant path.

Unfortunately these were proper soldiers not farmhands, and they were drawing clockwork guns. The weapons looked like the cheap knock-offs that had flooded the streets of Reyes a few months back, but some of them might work, and the soldiers hadn't drawn off far enough that distance was going to be a problem.

Kass kicked forward into the gap, ducking low over the saddle, leaning so far to one side she almost slid off the horse, but she was a smaller target that way. Vocho's started to follow, and he got a foot in a stirrup just in time, swung himself up and landed in the saddle with a jolt that shot a rod of pain up his back and made his eyes cross.

Still Dom just stood there, hands opening and closing, opening and closing. A shot whizzed past him with an inch to spare, and he didn't even flinch, nor when Alicia smeared a bloody thumb across another piece of paper.

Vocho dug his heels in, and his usually indolent horse, unused to such measures, sprang forward with a startled snort. Kass had cleared a space, but there was no telling how long it would last or whether the guns would do for them anyway. No telling, so time to just do. Vocho made a grab for Dom on the way past, missed the back of his tunic but got the powdered pigtail that lay curled over one shoulder. That woke him up. Dom yelped like a kicked dog but took in the situation in the instant it took Vocho to let go and grab something less painful – his arm. Vocho slipped his foot from the stirrup and Dom grabbed the saddle and got his boot in. The horse staggered with the extra, unbalanced weight, but plunged on, knowing his place – behind Kass's horse. Cospel followed on his pony, leading Dom's own horse and dinging anyone who got too close with his tankard.

The path Kass had cleared didn't last long – soldiers flowed towards them like water. One made a grab for Vocho's reins, and it was all Vocho could do to keep the beast going. To stop now would be to die, that was clear. Vocho risked one hand free to punch the man in the face, but he was stubborn and leaned back, trying to overbalance the horse, which stumbled, maybe from the weight or maybe from a guy rope as they passed a tent. Didn't matter which, because the stumble lost Vocho a stirrup and almost bounced him from the saddle. A hand grabbed for him and flailed for his knife – a sword was no good at such close quarters – and then the saddle was slipping under him, his back was fire, his blood was ice, and all he could think of was the rushing ground below the horse's hooves and Esti's jollop in his pack – that if he lost the horse he'd lose that too . . .

A thud sounded; the Ikaran fell away with a cry and the horse staggered on, doing its best to reach Kass, who'd reined in and turned to see if he was there. Dom, fresh from thumping the Ikaran off the horse, grabbed hold of Vocho's arm and dragged him back into the saddle before lunging for his own mount as Cospel galloped it into range. He vaulted across into the saddle; the poor beast staggered, and then they were off, trailing Ikarans and badly aimed bullets behind them.

The whole camp was in uproar, and once the four of them were free of any immediate threat the place was in too much turmoil to notice three horses and a pony galloping to keep up with a muttering Cospel on its back. Kass took no quarter and barged her beast over and through anyone in their way. Vocho's horse recovered and managed to keep up, even if it had less bile when it came to any obstacles. Before long they were into areas where everyone had gone to see what the fuss was about or soldiers were preparing for who knew what, with guards at each tent row and stoical men putting on good working armour by fires while they talked among themselves.

Kass reined her horse into a walk and the rest followed suit. No temporary army this; Vocho saw among them men such as he was, or liked to think he was anyway, when he was working – professionals to a man. It showed the calculation behind their eyes as they weighed up a threat, a ready hand on a sword as the four of them rode past. At the centre of these soldiers, sending more shivers up Vocho's spine to mingle with the pain there, stood two men so alike as to be twins. Matching marks on their cheeks and eyes that glittered cold and deadly, mouths that brooked no mercy and heavy *palla* swords. Maybe only Vocho noticed how Kass tightened, and that was only because Vocho felt pretty tight around the bravery bone himself right then. Professional men and women, Vocho thought again. Not starting a fight unless necessary, unless ordered to, but ready, always. Doing as they were told.

Like him. Hadn't he always done that? Done the jobs

he was told to, not noticed other things, other causes that he might have helped? He followed Kass away from the uproar, away from less professional soldiers who also did as they were told but were bad at it. Cold eyes watched them go, and Vocho wondered just how much he was like them or how much he would give not to look like that, like clockwork mannequins come to life for the one and only purpose of killing.

He couldn't see that it had got him very far as yet, except into more trouble than he ever wanted, so perhaps it was time, as Kass said, to do things because they were the right thing to do.

Chapter Seventeen

Alicia glowered at the quivering man who'd drawn the short straw and had to report to her, but like much else the glower was false.

"They disappeared, milady. An army is a fine place for a few soldiers to hide. We'll keep looking but I don't hold out much hope."

She waved a blood-streaked arm at him and he left, looking grateful that he was still alive.

Vocho and Kacha turning up just then had been a fortuitous happenstance, and she wasn't going to waste it. And Dom . . . A faint thrill at that. All right, more than faint. Years she'd been searching for him. *Years*. All that messing about with Kacha and Vocho, hoping he'd turn up to help them had paid off. Now she'd found him, and for a moment there she'd almost had him, had what all this was about. Would have done if not for that annoying Vocho. Still, he was close and wouldn't get far, not if she had anything to do with it. She had unfinished business with the Domenech, but Esti was going to help her there, with the three of them if she could. And if not, well, one more thing for Eneko to deal with.

Ah yes. Eneko. With Sabates dead, Alicia felt free of every constraint from the last twenty years. He'd always held her back from what she wanted, counselled patience, patience. And she'd been patient, but Dom turning up and Eneko plotting with Sabates . . . too much to resist. The time for patience was gone. Now was the time to get what she wanted. Besides, she had all this blood going spare.

It was the work of moments to lay out a circle of blood on the table, to fine-tune it to where she wanted – Eneko's rooms. And there he was, busy over some poor bastard in that chair. Not so busy he didn't respond to the circle. It was still working well enough, so she suspected he'd been topping up the blood, probably by way of whoever was the focus of his attentions with the knife in his hand.

"Alicia," he said warily and put down the knife. "Where's Sabates? He said he'd contact—"

"He's not going to be contacting anyone now or ever. Now you have me to deal with." She let that sink in, amused as he tried his utmost to hide his feelings at the news. Tried and failed. She'd spent a lifetime studying people in order to manipulate them all the better, and he couldn't fool her. "Come closer and take a good look, Eneko. See if you don't know me."

A frown at that. "Of course I know you; you're Sabates' assistant."

She let herself smile at that dismissive thought. "Was, Eneko. Was. And not just his assistant. Oh, I am so much more than an assistant. I was his student; I am now his better, his successor, his killer. Look closely. Think back. Remember letters you received and ignored or were dismissive of, laughed at. A desperate woman you turned away from your gates rather than admit any wrongdoing, and not just once. Think back to when you were younger and ruined a young girl's life with a word. Ever since you've refused to even see her, to respond to her pleas, to make amends, to say just one word that might help her. One word is all I asked, and you wouldn't give me even that. Think back and who do you see?"

His lip curled up into a sneer, but there was a tremor there, a sudden twitch of the eyes. She had the bastard rattled. Good. Everything, everything, had been for this.

"Could be anyone," he said with an attempt at nonchalance that didn't fool her for a second. "You think I recall every man or woman I cross?"

"A tall order perhaps, there have been so many. Well then, do you recall a certain young man, a favourite of yours once, by the ridiculous name of Narcis Jokin Donat Chimo Ne Farina es Domenech?"

The flinch wasn't slight this time; his whole body jerked with it. That he remembered Dom and not her . . .

"Cee?" Eneko said after a pause.

"Indeed, good of you to recall. Cee, or Alicia, or any number of variations on the theme that I've used over the years. I suspect you can now guess the reason for me contacting you?"

She was expecting any number of things – denial, contrition, argument. Not laughter.

"You expect me to tell you? Now? Sabates is dead, and my only, and very tenuous, loyalty was to him, not some sugar-brained girl who, if I recall, did nothing but cry. Jokin broke the rules and he knew it – knew the consequences. I owe you nothing. And that's what you'll get. Take it out on Jokin if you must."

"Oh I intend to. But on you as well. Tell me, and I won't bring down Reyes and your beloved guild. Maybe I'll even let you live."

This laugh was more genuine. "Oh, my *dear*." Maybe she'd let him live long enough to regret that choice of words. Maybe not. "Oh, you killed Sabates, and you have no idea what that means for me. He gave me what I needed, because it suited him. The downfall of the guild or Reyes wasn't his aim, only the death of Bakar in this phoney war, in which I supported him for my own purposes. In return he gave me a little trifle. A clockwork heart with a little magical something extra. I don't suppose he cared what I intended to do with it as long as Bakar died. But have no doubt, my dear, with it and with the combined talents of the clockers of Reyes, I can beat off even a host of magicians such as yourself. And when I rule Reyes and Ikaras is beaten, you can still sing for what you want because even if I wanted to, I can't tell you what I no longer know, if I ever did. But I can take the opportunity you just gave me, for which I thank you most profusely."

The last thing she saw was his hand sweeping across the circle, disturbing the blood and severing the connection. Her own hand dashed blood from the table, splattering it across the walls of the tent. She calmed herself. No point getting angry. Had she ever really thought he'd just tell her? No, it would take the direst threat he could imagine before he gave in, she'd always suspected that. The destruction of his precious guild, his beloved city. She drummed her fingers in what was left of the blood. Now she was glad that she'd let Vocho and Kacha live. They would certainly want their own reckoning with Eneko, and that would give him another threat to be wary of. A distraction perhaps, if she could finagle it. And there were ways . . .

She gathered what was left of the blood of Sabates, using it to bolster her will, and wiped her hands as people began to file into the tent. Gerlar entered, blank-faced and seemingly implacable, though she knew what it was he craved, knew he stayed only because she'd promised to give it to him when all this was done. But a shiver ran down her back at the thought – if she didn't, or couldn't, fulfil her promise of a new life-warrior partner for him, made from the scrap of dried blood his old one had left behind on the armour Gerlar had carefully kept . . . if she couldn't, he would kill her, she was sure of it. Life-warriors swore to protect their ruler from anyone, and that had included magicians in the not-so-distant past.

Orgull on the other hand was as easy as the pliable Licio, who was panicked and lost at the thought of being without Sabates – all that influence the departed magician had put on him gone, leaving him floundering in a current not of his own making. Leaving him susceptible to any new influence she might contrive, which was all she needed. Licio was pale and trembling, partly the after-effects of Sabates's disappearing magic and partly because, bar a few guildsmen and some of the king's own guards who even now were being dealt with, he was on his own. Alicia shared a look with Orgull.

"Who did it?" Licio whispered. It was all he'd said since he'd heard.

"Guildsmen, your highness," Alicia said in her most gracious voice. "I saw three of them in the camp, but they've escaped. No matter, we know who. And possibly who for."

"Guildsmen," Licio repeated in a faint voice. "Eneko?"

"Possibly, though the guildsmen we saw are, ahem, not in Eneko's favour at present. Perhaps they're trying to regain it."

The young king looked up at her with red-rimmed eyes that seemed to stare through her as though she were a ghost. "Who?"

"Vocho and Kacha. And that other fellow, Dom."

"Vocho and . . ." Licio's head wobbled as though his neck was suddenly too frail to support it. "No, not for Eneko. For themselves. Revenge? Or so that tattoo will no longer have power over him? How did Sabates not know he was close?"

Alicia hid behind her fan, fluttering it against the warmth of the rising sun. "I think he was distracted, your highness." That was the truth at least, or part of it.

"But how could he . . ." Licio blinked hard, rubbed a hand at one eye and sat up straight, looking like a small child resolving to be good if that's what it takes to get sweets. "No matter. He's gone. The question remains, now what?"

Orgull smiled and spread his hands. "Everything is still in place. We still have an army and the redoubtable Alicia to provide what magical assistance we might need. We still require all speed, in order to get to Reyes before Eneko can rise against the prelate. What now is, we carry on."

A short silence followed as his words sank into Licio's shocked brain before he nodded slowly. "Yes. Yes, you're right. Is everything ready?"

"As Sabates ordered it," Alicia said.

Licio gripped the arm of his chair and found some resolve. "Well then, perhaps a fitting send-off for our friend and then we leave with all haste. Alicia, are there riders still looking for these guildsmen?"

"Naturally." Not very hard, mind you, but the Ikaran guards who served the magicians were looking. Her plans for Kacha and Vocho had changed since Gerlar had performed so well against them on the road, since Esti had told her all about the antidote she'd sent with them and Dom had turned up. Now she rather thought she wanted them to get to Reyes, though that would take some explaining. Orgull's life-warriors, on the other hand, might well be looking for them very hard indeed – he wasn't stupid for all he looked like the butt end of a donkey. They might well be a handy failsafe in negotiations with Bakar should this assault fail, and Orgull was a safety-minded man.

"Good," Licio said. "Send for a fast rider, one of my men to take a message to Reyes."

Another glance passed between Alicia and Orgull. Licio had no men here, not now. The uproar last night had been good for covering up more than one misdeed. Alicia hesitated and then wondered if Licio would recognise any of his men anyway. Possibly not, not all of them anyway.

"Certainly."

"Good, see to it. Now what's the best way to send off a magician?"

Alicia gritted her teeth at his tone, like she was some maid to order about. But he had a point. No matter how she'd loathed Sabates, used him for her own ends until it suited her to get rid of him, he would be expected to have a fine send-off. She had her owns reasons for her suggestion as well.

"Fire, my lord."

"Really? That doesn't seem very . . . fitting."

"Oh, most fitting," Orgull said. "Only the very noblest Ikarans get that honour; burial is for peasants." Alicia noticed Licio wince – his family had their own cemetery – but he said nothing as Orgull carried on. "As head of the magicians in the university, he had that right. Besides, much quicker than burial, especially here. Not much soil, and with all these woods so near we can make the finest pyre a magician has ever known. It's also Ikaran tradition. Before a battle we make a sacrifice, which we then burn."

Besides which, they could make sure the bastard was good and dead.

"A sacrifice to who?" Licio asked, seemingly quite recovered from his shock. Such a fickle youth. She sometimes looked at him and thought of another who'd be about the same age, wondered whether they were fickle, or shallow, or any of the things so disappointing about Licio. But then she'd see Licio's naïveté, his trusting nature, and wonder whether she was the problem for thinking these weaknesses. Whether that other would hate her for what she'd done when it was all she could have done.

"I thought you didn't worship any gods," Licio said.

"We don't. Worship them, that is, or think of them as gods as such. Merely people of different powers, like magicians yet more remote. Sometimes we ask, as one equal to another. We offer a favour for a favour. So, a sacrifice. Cows, sugar, maize. But a magician will do well enough. Even if he is already dead. I find they don't care one way or the other very much."

A nod from Orgull, and servants scurried off to do his bidding.

Alicia turned to go while Licio was occupied, but stopped dead at his next question to Orgull. "If Sabates was head of the university magicians, who is now?"

She held her breath and caught Orgull's eye as she turned to see what he'd answer.

He turned away with an arrogant shrug. "Traditionally, there's a contest to help the dean of the university make his choice. He's not a magician, but he holds the power to grant or rescind university titles. However, for practical purposes there are only two worthy of consideration. One is the resourceful Alicia here, who is, or will be in time, as powerful as Sabates ever was, albeit in slightly different ways. The other is named Esti. A very unusual woman, and a very unusual mage. I think I can safely say that Alicia will win that battle."

Alicia smiled behind her fan. Truly Esti was very unusual but would be no threat to her at all. In her head Alicia sneered at how easy it was to manipulate her – anyone who cared about other people. She'd been like that once, had let herself be influenced by her care for others. But not any more. Now there was only one who she would die to protect. She just needed to find her first, and Eneko was going to tell Alicia where she was if he wanted his precious guild and city safe.

Chapter Eighteen

Kass kicked her horse on and tried to put as much distance between them and the roused army as she could. Sounds echoed around the little plateau behind them as they rode headlong into a steep gorge, risking the horses' legs and their own necks in the dark. They'd be followed and quickly, and not by one man as before. Their only hope lay in the dark and that the pass before them wasn't a single track but many winding among the shattered peaks.

Her horse stumbled, and she let it slacken its pace till they were trotting – still too dangerous, but not half as much as what came behind. But they couldn't keep up even this for long. The horses had been tired from the day's travel already, and those that followed had fresh horses.

A glance behind told her that Vocho's horse was struggling – sweat frothed on its neck in the faint moonlight, saliva at the bit. Vocho didn't look much better himself, holding on to the pommel of his saddle like that was all that was keeping him upright. Cospel's pony coped better with the terrain than the horses, but it wasn't built for speed. Dom's horse kept up effortlessly, as graceful and surprising as he was, but Dom himself was swaying in the saddle, and for a moment she thought he'd taken a wound she hadn't seen.

They had to stop — and couldn't stop. They'd killed Sabates, Alicia had said. Licio would send everything he had against them for that, even if it wasn't true. Small consolation that the magician was dead when another looked to have taken his place and his death had unleashed half of Ikaras against them. They had to stop but couldn't. Not here.

They reached the top of the defile and, once over the lip where they stood out against the sky, she pulled her horse up. The plateau behind them was like a pack of dogs fighting over a bone, lights moving this way and that. A spur of lights headed their way, and she didn't doubt there'd be others in front, scouts and warriors used to working in the dark. Once she'd not have worried, would have thought herself the most dangerous person on the mountain. Now she knew better. Eneko, damn his soul, had spoken a lot of truth in among his lies, and one truth had been *No matter how good you are, there is* always *someone better*. Those life-warriors gave her the shivers.

She'd heard of them before, but to see them properly, not just a dishonoured one who she'd only glimpsed, was something else. She and Voch fought together well enough, knew each other's moves for the most part, could guess what the other would do before they did it, but these were inhuman. Mindless almost, though they looked like men. And the one who'd followed them had caught them unawares in the woods and almost beaten the pair of them even on his own. They needed to be careful. More than careful.

The horses caught their breath and they moved on at a slower pace, no one talking, content to follow her lead. She looked ahead, saw fires dotted along the various tracks of the pass and wondered if the army had any way to communicate in the dark. Most likely it did, and even if it didn't any guards worth their cogs would have seen the commotion and would be alert.

There were smaller paths up here, narrow cracks through the crags that had never been mapped, but most of them were no good to anyone on a horse. Walking and leading the horses, perhaps. And maybe they led only to blank walls or sheer drops. She knew none of them well enough, only knew that they were there. Another glance ahead saw movement by the fires, caught glimpses of men on horses moving down towards them and decided her. Lost was better than caught between the hammer and the anvil.

She pulled her horse to a stop and waited for the others. Cospel and his pony seemed bright enough, but the other two . . . Dom sat in his saddle like a sack of wet fish and Vocho was slumped and whey-faced. His hand groped for his pack as soon as they stopped and brought out the bottle that Esti had given him. He took a pull on it and a deep breath afterwards, then his whole body seemed to relax. Just one more thing to worry about, but she had no time now, and wouldn't know what to think if she did.

She sidled her horse up to Dom's. He kept taking little sideways glances back down into the valley behind them before his eyes shied away as though they'd seen something dead and rotting, something he'd killed himself perhaps and was now haunting him.

"Dom? Dom!"

He looked at her finally, and she flinched back in the saddle at that look. He'd always seemed so carefree, even in the midst of armed men trying to kill him. Always there with a faux-bumble to make her laugh, or a grin as sharp as daggers drawn, hinting at who he was underneath all the pretence. Now he looked every one of the ten years he had on her, and more. It was in the slump of his shoulders, the twitching of his mouth in the faint light, the hands that kept opening and closing, opening and closing. She was glad she couldn't see him properly, but she could see enough to give her pause.

"Dom," she said again, and finally he seemed to see her. "Do you know any of these paths?"

"What? I . . . I . . . Maybe." He shook himself like a dog and seemed to get a grip then, became his usual sharp-eyed self yet with an undercurrent, as though he'd let slip the real him. He wouldn't look her in the eye when he spoke, but kept his gaze behind them, maybe hoping to catch a glimpse of someone, something. "I know a few paths, the less used ones. But for all these cracks are a maze for us to lose people in, there's the long narrow part at the other end, in Reyes, the Throttled Neck, they call it. No other way but that, and all they need do is set enough men there and there's no way through for us."

Kass's horse flicked its ears forward then twitched one to the side, stamped and sidled, gearing up for a fight, and she trusted his hearing better than any of theirs. Cospel whipped his head round, and she was kicking her horse on even before he said anything – he didn't need to. She could now hear the jangle of harness, the snick of a bit between teeth, the breath of horses hard pushed.

"Pick a path," she said to Dom. "We'll deal with the Neck when we come to it. Just pick one!"

He hesitated. For a second she was reminded of Dom the bumbler as she'd first known him, pretending to be the idiot. He looked utterly lost until a man shouting up the defile galvanised him to action.

"This way." He didn't stop to see if they followed but reined his horse about and spurred it into a crack between the rocks so small and dark she thought he'd lost his cogs. Then his horse's quarters disappeared into the gloom so thoroughly she wouldn't have believed it if she hadn't seen it. She kicked her own on, with Vocho and Cospel hard on her heels. Her beast tried for Vocho's with a hind leg and caught it a glancing blow that made it more careful as any faint light ceased in the narrowness of the crack.

The way widened after a short time and she almost barrelled into Dom as he waited in silence. The sounds behind grew louder, louder still until it seemed the men that hunted them must almost be on top of them, before they gradually faded to murmurs and the spang of steel shoe on rock. It wouldn't be long before there were more. Finally there was silence except for their own breathing – Vocho's was a staggered hitching breath that sounded odd – the soft movements of the horses, the hiss of wind across stones.

When all sounds of their followers had gone, Dom led them on at a fair pace – not fast enough to make too much noise, but not too slow either. The way opened up further, letting in a little moonlight, just enough to see the way once their eyes were accustomed to it. All of them stayed silent, for reasons of their own. Kass nudged her horse up next to Dom's and watched him a while from under her eyelashes.

It seemed to her that Dom was not one thing or another, that she was constantly peeling back layers to see another underneath. First a bumbling fool, then an assassin, now . . . now what? Now a man with a furrow in his brow, a silence that lay on his shoulders like the weight of years, and a hand that opened and closed, opened and closed as though grasping for something that wasn't there, that had never been there.

The crack twisted and turned, widened and narrowed, branched so often Kass was hard put to name which way north lay. Finally she broke the silence but in a hushed tone that made her wonder what she was afraid of – hunters behind or the quiet of the trail.

"Dom, do you know the way?"

He laughed at that, a sad and hopeless sound swallowed up by the rocks that towered over them. "I've never known my way. Has anyone? I'm only groping as blindly as the rest." He grimaced at that and spared her a glance that told her nothing at all. "Not the answer you wanted. No, not really. Not even the goats that live here know all the paths, I'm sure."

"I'm sure I can hear a but in there somewhere."

The laugh was brighter this time, and his shoulders lost some of their tense droop. "Indeed. *But* I think I can get us where we need to be. I just can't be sure what we'll find once we get there, or that no one will find us in the meantime. Come dawn they'll find our trail. A scuff of steel-shod hoof on stone, a disturbed bird, a stray wisp of smoke if we dare a fire, or the smell of horses if we don't, an echo out of place. The men they'll send aren't woodsmen, but some *are* mountain men. They can see a goat's bleat across the valley. And . . . the life-warriors." He hesitated, cast her a look that debated whether he should say more and plunged on. "They aren't just people, not just men. They don't stop. Ever, unless they're dead. It's easy to think they don't have a heart, that maybe they have cogs instead like the Clockwork God. Like they're battle machines. They certainly fight like it, and it's a mercy they're so few. Only one weakness, so far as I know."

"They have a weakness?"

He looked at her quizzically but only said, "Yes. Of a kind. It does rather depend on you killing one of them, which is a drawback seeing as it's so damned difficult. They have this, what's the word? Geas? Basically it means if one dies, the other is honour bound to follow him to the afterlife as soon as he can. A lone life-warrior is a man with no honour and no soul. That's what they believe anyway. All to do with the two warriors being two halves of one soul or somesuch. So –" he smiled brightly as though suggesting a nice picnic "– all we have to do is kill one of each pair. Which is, er, about two dozen life-warriors in total, and I'd say Orgull will have all of them with him. Nothing to it."

Kass stared blindly ahead, remembering a sudden sword in the dark. "So if there was one life-warrior on his own . . ."

"Impossible. They'd rather die than live without the other. They've been known to take the matter into their own hands – they carry a blade for just that purpose."

"Just say there was. What would that mean?"

Dom raised an eyebrow. "Well, I'd say you've got a man who knows how to gut an opponent silently twenty different ways, who thinks he has no honour and no soul, a man who thinks those two things are everything that matters. A man with nothing to lose and everything to gain, a man unafraid of death even more than he was before. Not a man I'd chose to fight, to be honest." He pondered a moment. "It'd probably be quicker and more painless just to gut yourself and have done with it. Now, tell me why you ask."

Was it her or had it gone suddenly cold? Her hair prickled with the itch of a thousand biting ants; the rock walls seemed to close in and at the same time seethe with shadows that could hide a man determined to do whatever he needed to.

"Before we reached the army," she said at last. "He'd followed us from Ikaras, I'm sure, watched us at the house there."

She told him the rest too, how she thought he was something to do with Alicia, how he'd played with them, how helpless she'd felt – and that last was a wrench to admit but somehow with Dom it was OK.

When she'd finished, he was silent a long time. She looked back at Vocho and Cospel, saw one only barely holding on to his saddle, white with pain, the other nodding and waking himself up on the apex of his snores. Dom followed her look and, with an unspoken agreement, they began to look for somewhere safe to stop, as safe as anywhere could be in mountains swarming with people who wanted to kill them.

Dom kicked his horse on ahead while she dropped back next to Vocho, who said no word when she appeared at his side, only stared at his horse's ears, Esti's fast-emptying bottle and reins clutched in one hand, the other white on his saddle. It was the silence that perturbed her. Vocho could always be relied on to say something annoying, but now he was silent as the rocks above, as the waiting night. Beads of sweat popped out on his forehead like berries before they broke and rolled down his already drenched face. Yet he'd not complained. If he had, she'd not have let Dom take them so far before they tried to find a place to hole up.

She talked to him as they went on – of nothing much,

her mind distracted by how old he looked. He was bent as an eighty-year-old docker, shoulders stooped, hands clawed. She was glad when Dom dropped back and told her he'd found a good spot just ahead, though again they shared a look – this was not the time to stop and probably no place counted as good, only the best he could find.

It was the best she could have hoped for in the circumstances – a widening of the trail, open at each end so they could see down the path and there was little chance of ambush. To one side was a hollow in the rocks, not a cave exactly but a deep overhang which would shelter them from what felt like another storm coming in and hid them from above. It wasn't going to be comfortable, but it was as safe as they could hope to be.

They had to help Vocho off his horse, and that was when Kass really started to worry. They tried talking to him but all they got was a wan "I just need to rest. And the jollop, so I can." So they made him as comfortable as they could, bedded down on a patch of grassy soil among the rocks. Cospel saw to the horses, fed them from the dwindling supply of grain in their bags, checked their legs, rubbed them down and slipped their bits so they might find what they could to eat – a few hardy bushes and tough grasses scrambled for a life in cracks and nooks. Kass's horse was even worse than normal, and in the end she had to tether him as far from the others as they could before he took a chunk out of one of them. At least she could be sure anyone trying to attack from that direction was going to get more than they bargained for.

When she came back under the overhang, Vocho was in a twitching, clenched sort of sleep, Esti's bottle in one hand, and Cospel had fallen asleep sitting up with his back to the rock wall. Dom was waiting for her. He leaned back against a rock, and she thought that she'd never seen him nervous before – when he was acting the idiot didn't count. Now he was fiddling with a bit of harness and trying not to look at her while looking at her. He made a mess of the harness, swore, apologised for swearing and started on the harness again.

"So, you're too polite to ask, but you want to know," he said in the end. "Correct?"

She sank down next to him and watched him carefully. She was dying to know, but it hadn't been politeness that had stopped her – more wanting to get out alive coupled with not knowing how to bring it up. "Correct."

He blew out a breath, threw the bit of harness and ran a distracted hand through his hair before he chanced a grin. "I have this friend, you see. He's not very smart and gets into trouble. I could tell you about him."

She couldn't help but laugh at that. "All right."

"So, this friend. Bit of an idiot when he was young, all those romantic notions, you know? How the world is supposed to be, what's good and right. What justice is. Poor fool. Well, there he was, bound not to hold anything above his oath to the guild. You know the words – no spouse, no children, nothing to distract you from what you've sworn to. Dalliances, OK. Flings, no problem. Full-blown affairs, absolutely fine and dandy, just as long as you recall who your master is, and it is the guild. But this friend . . . well. This poor fool of a friend had to go and fall in love. And because he had all these romantic notions of, basically, stupidness, he went and married the object of his desire. It took a lot of lies – to her, to the guild, to Eneko – but he did it and thought himself ever so clever, and that a few lies for something so . . . so *grand*, so bloody world-shattering was a small price to pay. And he was happy for a while, deliriously so, and so was she, and all was right in the world. True love conquers all, star-crossed lovers make good, cosmic justice — all that sort of crap."

He shook his head at that, laughed ruefully and ran the hand through his hair again.

"So, what happened?" she asked when it looked like he wasn't going to carry on.

"What happened? Well, what happened was he got careless. Even more stupid than he'd been originally. Two sorts of stupid even. The worst, the *stupidest*, was thinking he was above the guild and its oath. That Eneko would make an exception for him because, well, because he was Eneko's apprentice and personal assassin, and we know how very loyal he is, don't we? I thought I knew how loyal, much like you thought you did. I learned fast and hard. The worst part was so did she. Cee. Alicia. Whatever you want to call her. My wife."

"You married a magician?" She stared at him, aghast.

"God's cogs, no. Do you take me for that much of a fool? She was no magician then. There's a lot of things she wasn't then. We were both very young, and she was . . . well, not innocent exactly, but we shared the same sort of romantic, idiotic notions. And it hit her harder when that all turned to shit. I'd lied to her, you see. For noble reasons — to protect her because I loved her. She'd never known I was a guildsman, never knew that, legally, our marriage was invalid. That she was now mother to a bastard. Eneko went to see her, and I don't know what he said or did. I know I came home and there was no baby, only her ready and waiting with a knife. Something turned in her then, and she found the hard place inside her. It was always there, perhaps, underneath, waiting for the right circumstances to bring it out. We were very alike in many ways.

But that it should come out like that . . . She tried to kill me. Almost managed it, gave me a scar on my belly that reminds me of her every day. I deserved it too. I still deserve it. She left – who can blame her? And I went to Eneko, to try to work something out, find out what he'd said, where the child was. My little Maitea. All I got for my trouble was thrown out of the guild, and Eneko gave everyone some bullshit reason. He'd sent our daughter away, he said, and I believed that. I still do, live in hope that it's true and I might find her again. But then I'd no one, nothing left. No wife, no child, no guild, no way to get any of them back. My father disowned me for the disgrace; he still hasn't forgiven me, as you might recall from our little escapade in the Shrive. He had to move out to the country, become someone new to escape the shame I'd brought on him. But the worst was no Cee, no little Maitea with her dimpled smile, and that crushed me. I thought I could make it right. I could find what Eneko had done with our daughter, bring her back, make Cee love me again. Only I couldn't – can't. I thought maybe Eneko had sent her with the slaves he was selling to Ikaras, so eventually I followed, went to Ikaras and the university, met Bakar there even, that much is true. And Cee was there already. I saw her once, and she was, well, she wasn't the girl I married. That girl died the day she tried to kill me. But then I'm not the boy she married either, not any more. So no, I didn't marry a magician. I made her one, perhaps. Made her bitter enough to take that route. I tried to find her again but it was like she'd vanished. So when I saw her again, after all this time . . ."

He sat up straight and took a deep breath, ran a hand over his face and ended by pinching the bridge of his nose. "Well, that went on a bit longer than I expected. So there you have it." He looked at her oddly, shyly almost, as though worried what her reaction was going to be.

And what was her reaction? She couldn't be sure, felt all kinds of things but said, "Funny how love makes idiots of all of us." She thought of Petri with a shiver that wasn't all regret, of how blind he'd made her just by being there. Blind and deaf to everything else. She couldn't be sure she'd not do it again either if − no, when − she saw him. Because Vocho was right, damn his eyes. She was going back to Reyes for Petri. Because she'd once loved him, and he'd once loved her and, god's cogs, she wanted to feel like that again. And love was making her blind.

She looked over at Voch, where he lay all twisted up and muttering in his sleep. She'd pushed him too far, too hard, she knew that. Knew that he'd been right, that this was madness, and yet she couldn't stop.

"All kinds of idiots, yes," Dom said. "What's in that bottle of his?"

"Something Esti gave him for the pain − his back still looks like a butcher's shop." And yet here he was, following her anyway. Yes, love made idiots of them all, even weird and twisted kinds like the love she and Voch shared.

"Did she now? I think we might want to take a look at that."

Only even asleep Voch wasn't letting go.

"You *do* recall me telling you she was a poisoner?" Dom asked. "And yet here he is, drinking something she made."

"By the time you told us that he'd already been drinking it, and seeing as he hadn't turned green and frothy at the mouth, something for the pain was better than nothing. He'd never have managed to get this far without it."

Dom gave her a penetrating look. "Yes, but how much further is he going to get? What about when the bottle runs out? Or when he can't do without it? Though I think he's already there."

"Tell him, not me. Bloody stuff makes him act strangely, I know that. But I wasn't leaving him behind. And Esti gave us this too."

She went through Vocho's pack, found the bottle of antidote and told Dom that he'd been right about Esti making poison, and for who.

"I hoped there might be an antidote," he said when she was done. "What I came to Ikaras for, as it happens. I'm glad I didn't entirely fail. But I wouldn't trust it, or her. Not for a second. She's a magician and not a single one is to be trusted."

She packed it away again, in her pack this time. "That includes Alicia, don't forget. Dom, why are you here? Why are you helping us? I mean, not that we're not grateful, but I don't see why. Everyone has their own reasons, wants, needs – like Esti, like Alicia. Like you." Like me, she thought. "So what is it?"

Dom shrugged and frowned in Voch's direction. "Lots of reasons. Pick any one you like." He flashed her a grin, the old Dom, the sharp one, back again as though he'd never been away. "Maybe I see someone about to make the same mistakes I did, and want to help them."

It seemed all she was likely to get from him, but Dom, for all his mysteriousness, was one person she found she trusted.

He took a look around, listened keenly for a moment or two and said, "We can rest here for a while, but we need to move, and sooner rather than later. Life-warriors aren't to be trifled with, and I don't like the sound of a single one after us as well. This needs thinking on. Go on. You sleep, I'll watch."

Chapter Nineteen

Alicia sat in her tent and frowned down at the table. Blood, and lots of it, bottled and smeared and everything in between. So much blood, and all hers for the using. This bit though, this little bit here, that was what she wanted. No more than a smudge on a corner of her dress, obtained when he wasn't paying attention, but enough. Orgull and Licio and all the rest, they were a distraction now. This was what had been at the back of her mind all this time, all these years, driving her on, and yet now it was here, it seemed empty of promise.

Another bottle sat on the table, but the contents of this one moved. Sabates and his tattoos, so very crass she'd always thought. No subtlety, no sense of natural justice. She cut away the corner of her dress and laid it on the table, smoothed it down carefully with a gentle hand. It hadn't been what she'd expected, seeing him again. She'd known he'd be older – as she was – but there was something else about him. Different, she thought, something very different. Narcis Donat Chimo Ne Farina es Domenech. Such a silly name, she'd always thought, and not even his full one. Something she'd teased him about a long time ago, and it made her smile even now, though she'd allow that the smile was different after finding that the extra part of his name meant he was a guildsman, the most famous they had, that their marriage had been a lie.

But she'd thought she'd feel something, seeing him. Her younger self would have expected fireworks in her head perhaps, the vestiges of what she'd felt for him before Eneko had stolen away Maitea and her heart with the child, told her who and what Dom really was, exposed all the lies that he'd had fed her. And she'd been so happy she'd believed every one, thought her life was charmed. Her older self knew that the world doesn't work like that, that *people* don't work like that, and everyone lies, that hate sits inside and festers, solidifies after time until it's a stone ball in your heart. She'd expected to feel that hate but instead . . . she didn't know. Perhaps she'd gone so far past hate she'd come out the other side, but still she needed to do this. Needed to lay that particular ghost to rest, even if she should be oddly grateful to him for altering the course of her life. She could have been a wife and mother all these years and never reached for anything else, never realised what potential she had. And now here she was, head of the magicians of Ikaras, adviser to kings, more than that even in time.

So, a peculiar sort of thanks to Dom for making her this way, for showing her she didn't need to rely on anyone, that she should never trust the words out of anyone's mouth. She took the stopper out of the bottle and reached for some tweezers. The leech wriggled in their grip, maybe scenting the feast of blood around it. A particular spell for a peculiar thanks. She dropped the leech onto the little square of cloth with its smudge of Dom's blood and watched it feed. Not much there, just enough for it to know, to taste. It wriggled and sucked, and then it was done.

She lifted it carefully with the tweezers and found a new bottle to put it in, a small one that would fit in a pocket.

"Gerlar," she called, and there he was. Silent, watching, waiting. Waiting for what she'd promised him, for his life back, for his reason to live.

"Take this," she said. "Carefully! I've set it to him, but it can be turned if too much temptation comes its way."

He took the little glass vial carefully, as she'd said. Such an obedient man.

Something shimmered over his face as he looked at the leech. "How do I use it?"

"You know where they are?"

He shrugged, a curious gesture that was part not caring and part caring desperately. "My kin know, at least know where to look, but they don't share information with me. Not any more."

"They will now. Here is my personal order. Show it to them and find out. And when you find the man I'm after, the new addition to their happy little band, use this on him."

His lip twitched ever so slightly – the only indication that she'd just asked him to do something that dishonoured him. A life-warrior fought with edged weapons not subterfuge, but this one . . . this one wanted something from her so badly it coloured every thought. Even dishonour was worth what she offered. Find a lever, Sabates used to say, find the lever that will shift a man, and you have him. She'd learned well, maybe all too well for Sabates himself. His old partner back, that was what Gerlar wanted. His life-partner in blood and more. And she could give that to him with a little help from Sabates' blood. Maybe she even would.

"Just make sure the glass smashes and the leech lands on his skin. I will do the rest. And here." She indicated the other glass bottles red and pregnant with power. "Here is what you want. A new warrior, one to be your twin, exactly as the old one. Just do this one little thing for me, and what you want will be yours. Honour returned, a new chance to do things right."

He hesitated, but it wasn't long before he stashed the little vial in his tunic, bowed stiffly and turned away without a word.

A pang twitched at her. "And if you don't . . ."

He stopped, his head dipped, and he took a deep breath. "I will, ma'am. I will. For my soul."

When Vocho woke up the grey chill of dawn was in his bones, his legs were made of glass, his head stuffed with cotton, his back on fire. Getting up seemed like the work of a thousand years. The bottle was in his hands, and he went to take a crafty pull before Kass, over at the edge of the overhang, could notice. A strong hand stopped his. Dom.

"I think that's enough of that, don't you?"

Vocho struggled upright and glared at him. "No, I really don't. Maybe you'd like me to scream the whole way down the fucking mountain, bring everyone chasing us down on our tails. Maybe you just want to torture me. Or maybe you're paranoid. But I'm using this for as long as it lasts. Hopefully by the time it's done, so will the pain."

Dom shook his head. "I told you to be wary of her. Not everyone wants the same as you and some people are prepared to go to great lengths to get it. Why is it, do you think, that a bottle of syrup given to you by a known poisoner makes you feel this way? Like you can't go another hour without it? Let me look." His hand snaked out. Vocho was too slow to react, and . . . and wasn't that telling? He was quick, quick as anyone, so quick they told stories about it. Yet Dom just reached out and took the bottle, and it was then that he noticed how his hand wouldn't stay still, how panicky he felt without it in his hand.

Dom sniffed at the bottle, grimaced and rolled his eyes. "You two are entirely too trusting, you realise that? How you ever survived as guildsmen I can't imagine."

Vocho eased himself into a position where his back was merely agony and wished he was back asleep where things didn't hurt. "We didn't have much choice, really."

Dom snorted. "Always a choice." He took another sniff. "God's cogs, man, you know what's in this?" Before Vocho could react, Dom had thrown down the bottle, which smashed with the whiff of dark-smelling herbs.

Vocho stared at it, at the one thing keeping him on this damned trail. The only thing that had made it even bearable.

"Now get up," Dom said, dragging him to standing. "And let's get the hells out of here, preferably while you aren't herbed up to the eyeballs. Turn round and take off your shirt."

"What?"

"You heard."

Vocho wasn't feeling his best just then, so he felt, all in all, he'd be better off doing what Dom said, especially when he had the sort of look on his face Da used to have just before he reached for his belt. Besides, his brain didn't seem to want to cooperate in listing all the reasons why he didn't want to.

He turned and, eventually, with a few gasps as he twisted his back, took off his shirt. Dom and Kass stared at it like he'd just grown a new head there or something. Dom touched the skin to one side of where the tattoo had been, and it was all Vocho could do not to scream. He held on to a handy rock to keep himself on his feet.

"All right," Dom said at last. "Now I can see what we're dealing with. We're going to need to risk a fire. Cospel, make it small and as smoke-free as you can. Over there, that channel of rock might dissipate the smoke somewhat. Boil some water. Kass, have you got a spare shirt or anything like that? Good. Fetch it."

A finger probed Vocho's back gently, and white spots whizzed across his eyes.

"What do I do?"

"You?" Dom said. "You concentrate on how embarrassing it'd be to cry and faint in front of your sister when I start. And how stupid you were not to show me this before. She didn't just take the tattoo off. If only it were that simple. You really know how to land yourself in trouble, don't you?"

"It's a talent, I guess," he managed. "Do you know what you're doing? I mean, you aren't a magician. How do you know how tattoos work? And what are you going to do?"

"Make it so you don't need that stuff Esti gave you any more. Make it so you can get to Reyes alive. Because like this you'd have been dead inside a day, you know that?"

"I do now!"

"If I were you, I'd get down on your knees with something to hang onto. This may hurt quite a lot."

"When doesn't it?" But it had to be better than the flames that seemed to burn across his back, to reach out for other parts of him, vines of agony working their way across his body. He got gingerly to his knees.

Dom did his best with hot water and compresses made from some foul-smelling leaves he found in his pack, scattered on hot linen and pressed onto the wound. He did his best to be gentle, but it didn't do much good. Vocho dreamed of getting that bottle back, no matter what was in it, and he soon learned how embarrassing it was to cry in front of his sister.

When Dom was done, they didn't give him much time to rest. Kass came scrambling down from a low ridge where she'd been keeping watch with the news that she'd seen movement behind them.

"How many?" Dom asked.

"Twenty at least."

Dom swore quietly and helped Vocho up. "I've done the best I can. Just keep on your saddle for the next day or so, try not to make it any worse, and maybe you'll live. You've got as much chance as the rest of us."

"Are you going to tell me what it was?"

Dom turned away, but not before Vocho caught a quick and knowing glance between him and Kass as Dom started getting the horses ready – they'd kept them saddled, though with loosened girths, and now Dom set about tightening them for the race ahead. "There's many types of poison, Voch. Fast, slow, fatal, not so fatal. Esti knows them all."

Vocho made his way to his own horse, who greeted him with a headbutt and a warm and grassy snort, and didn't mind when Vocho leaned on him for support.

"Luckily for you," Dom went on, "I know a few as well. That one, *if* it's the one I think, enters an open wound and creeps gradually towards the heart. Something was certainly heading that way. The bottle she gave you would have numbed the pain enough you wouldn't have noticed until maybe a day or so from now, when boom! No more Vocho. It still might, but there's no time for me to do any more now. If you die, then she thwarts Alicia. Do you see?"

Vocho didn't see. He couldn't manage his horse's girth by himself but was past all shame. Cospel had to do it for him and help him into the saddle. He sat, shivering and feeling helpless, and concentrated just on staying atop the horse. Once Kass had kicked her own foul beast on, and his horse, knowing what was expected of him, followed, that was more than enough to occupy every waking second. He held on to the saddle horn and didn't worry about reins or steering the horse up the rocky trail, trusting it to know best. Everything felt numb, and not in a good way. Pain was still there, buried beneath, waiting to break free and take him with it.

What had Esti done to him, and why? He found he didn't give much of a shit past the fact that she had, especially once the trail got steeper and the jolting got worse. Kass led them on, pushing the pace, with Cospel following Vocho, and Dom bringing up the rear.

An arrow spanged off a rock to one side, followed closely by a bullet pinging off another. The way here was steeper, almost too steep for the horses to climb with riders, but they dared not dismount.

The track branched three ways. Kass didn't hesitate to take the right-hand path, which seemed to lead towards the top of the pass, so close now Vocho was certain he could see the notch they were aiming for. His horse's ribs were going like a bellows, but he held on tight and kicked on. When he turned round, Dom was nowhere, and all that greeted him was Cospel's well worn and long-suffering face and a plume of dust back along the trail, too close for comfort. Another bullet, closer this time, enough to make his horse shy and almost have him off. Sweat made his shirt cling uncomfortably and slicked his hands as he gripped the saddle horn. That bullet had come from above.

He twisted as far as he could to look up, and the sweat turned cold and clammy on the instant. The rock walls on either side of the trail ended far above their heads, but not so far they were out of range. A series of movements told him everything he needed to know, which was how much shit they were in.

Vocho's horse baulked as he tried to urge it faster up the slope, slipped on some loose scree and almost fell to its knees, sending him sprawling over its shoulder. All the world went dark, reduced to his back and the vines of molten lead that crept from the wound there. He couldn't breathe, couldn't see, and would have killed anyone, anyone at all for another pull of Esti's jollop, until a hand fell on his arm.

Kass yanked him back into the saddle none too gently. "Hold on, just hold the hells on," she murmured.

He nodded, about as much as he could manage apart from fumbling for the saddle horn again. His horse was spent, lathers of sweat on its neck, head bowed with effort. He heard Kass swearing as she urged her beast on, and if that bastard was in trouble they'd all had it.

A quick glance behind – they were gaining, no doubt about it. Cospel dug inside his tunic and brought out a tiny crossbow. Vocho wished with a kind of dizzy fervour that he'd got the hang of guns because one would be handy about now, though he drew the line at Kass using the one she'd filched even when they turned another bend and the way ended in a wall of crumbling rock. The upper pass, or at least one of them, was just above it, so close Vocho could almost touch it. It was just they couldn't reach it, or not from here, and here was as nicely boxed in as you could hope for.

Kass reined her horse about and luckily for everyone seemed to have forgotten the gun at her belt. Instead she pulled her sword, and Vocho fumbled to follow suit. He could do that, if nothing else. The sword felt heavy in his hand and pulled at already screaming muscles, but he could fight, always.

Twenty, at least, behind them on horses as spent as their own. The only good news was that the trail was narrow and they'd have to come in threes or fours at most. But they had men above, men with guns.

A man fell screaming from the top of the rock wall and landed with the thud of broken bones and a splash of entrails at the feet of the first rider. Who forced his reluctant horse straight over the body as though it was of no consequence.

"Plan?" Vocho asked Kass, who sidled her horse next to his. Like old times almost. Except he couldn't feel his arm apart from where it hurt like buggery, and he seemed to have quite lost his effortless not-giving-a-shit ways. He wiped sweat out of his eyes and glanced sidelong at his sister.

She took in the scene with a series of glances, tongue between her teeth as she thought rapidly.

"We hope that Dom kills a few more up there, try and bull our way through here and find another path, one that'll take us out of this maze. Take out what we can on the way."

Not a great plan, but it looked like all they had.

Kacha's horse flung its head up as she shifted in the saddle, its eye rolled and it blew froth from its mouth, and then she let it have its head. With a wild yell she shot forward, the horse with its head out and teeth at the ready. The lead rider never stood a chance. He tried to rein aside, but the crunching impact of Kacha's mount threw his horse off balance just as Kass brought her sword round to slice across his neck, and he fell in a splash of bright blood. Vocho wasn't sure what the rest of them had been expecting, but he didn't think it was that from the way they milled about.

Another body fell from above, dead before he hit the ground behind their pursuers, whose horses threw up their heads and danced about some more. Not only the men weren't trained in warfare, Vocho had the time to think, and that gave Kass the opening she needed. She didn't so much fight as bludgeon her way through, using elbows and sword hilt and blade and her horse, and then there was a gap. Vocho took a look behind, saw Cospel right at his back doing his best to protect it, and headed for the space she'd made. He kicked his horse forward and everything else was forgotten – there was only the slice of blades, the pant of his breath, fire on his back and sweat in his eyes, all melding with the dull throb at the end of his arm, the pull of the sword's weight on his shoulder, and another man replacing the one he'd just slashed.

It was too close for arrow work, but more than one of them had a gun, though the men above seemed to have no clear shot, or perhaps Dom was having his wicked way with them, because, to his surprise, Vocho didn't get shot. Passing Kass, he didn't stop once he found himself out in the open either – with a glance to make sure she was still there, he sheathed his sword, held on to the saddle with one hand and used the other on the reins, slapping them on his horse's shoulders to urge the poor beast to greater lengths. It staggered down the slope with a series of jolts that made Vocho feel his insides had come loose but then they were on smoother ground.

He risked another look behind, found Kass right on his heels with Cospel not far behind, his pony taking all this far better than the finer-bred horses. Most of their attackers were trying to get themselves untangled, though a tall man on a roan horse had turned on the head of a pin and was even now after them. Vocho cocked an eye skywards because the three of them were fine targets now. Nothing, except two figures against the sun. One was certainly Dom – he could tell by the way he held himself – and then the second figure dived at him, and they fell out of sight. Vocho wasn't unduly worried, given that Dom was a trained assassin and all-round sneaky bugger. He could look after himself and would catch up when he could.

They reached the place where the path split and Vocho hesitated. Kass didn't, but bulled past him, reined her horse around a corner and down a new path so quickly the horse almost fell, before recovering and stumbling on, stubborn to the core like its mistress. After what seemed like an age of jolting and swearing, of pain and sweat and fleeting visions of darkness across his eyes, the path split again, and Kass took one that turned into a wider way before the walls of the maze gave out entirely. A small plateau ringed with wizened trees opened up before them. On one side the ground fell steeply away down a scree-filled slope that would test a mountain goat, on the others paths led away through more rocks, while the main trail led towards the notch they were heading for – the pass. Reyes. Home.

Kass pulled up by a small spring among some stunted trees, jumped off and did her best to make sure her horse didn't drink too much of the ice-cold water in one go.

Adding colic to their predicament would help no one but their enemies. Vocho slid gingerly from his saddle and tried to do the same, only every hurt came back with a vengeance, and he stumbled and fell to one knee. He grabbed a stirrup to pull himself back up before Kass noticed, but not quick enough.

Her hand went under his elbow, and he was grateful and ashamed all at once.

"We can't stop long," she said with an apology in her tone.

"No. It'll be fine. I feel better, honestly." And he did, but "better" was a relative term. He no longer thought he would die at every breath, only every time he moved. He gripped the stirrup leather till his knuckles cracked but couldn't stop shaking. His mind went to his pack, to what was in it, before he remembered what Dom had done with his only comfort. A chill took his stomach, making him shiver violently so that Kass lost her grip.

"Voch, are you going to make it to the top?"

What would she do if he said no? Leave him for the Ikarans? Once he would have known without hesitation; once she would have stayed with him no matter what because whatever happened they were two, always together. But now . . . now he didn't know. Now she had other things on her mind, like Petri fucking Egimont. And Dom, let's not forget him, and the two of them being all cosy about something last time they stopped.

Speaking of which: "Did you see what happened to Dom?"

Kass wiped sweat-damp hair back from her face and shook her head. Her eyes kept darting to the side, out across the plateau, to see if anyone had followed. "He can take care of himself better than you or me."

Under normal circumstances Vocho would have agreed, but that last man who had gone for Dom – there had been something about his silhouette or maybe the way he moved, like he was favouring one side . . .

"Kass—"

A noise like thunder echoed through the peaks that surrounded them, a wild yell amidst it. At the far end of the plateau, where the trail they'd taken bled out onto the dusty grass, a dozen galloping horses appeared. Only three or four had anyone riding them, and "riding" wasn't strictly accurate; more like hanging on. All except the man at the front. A wild-eyed Dom, who urged a horse not his own to greater speed.

Kass whirled to her own horse. Voch tried to mount his and barely even noticed the shame when Kass had to help him up. Her horse had something to say about being mounted, and said it with feeling, but she avoided the teeth and launched herself onto his back unscathed. "What's he doing?"

The riderless horses spread out over the plateau, slowing down, some of them stopping, flanks heaving and mouths flecked with foam. Dom, low in the saddle to avoid arrows and bullets, Vocho had to assume, opened up a lead before the few riders got their mounts under control and began to follow. He led them unerringly towards the little grove where Kass, Vocho and Cospel waited, out of sight.

"Only four of them left," Kass noted.

Cospel grunted. "Had enough of this," he said and swung out of his saddle and up into one of the trees near the edge of the grove while Kass held his pony.

Dom was almost on them, and his hunters almost on him when the first flew backwards over his horse's rump with a bolt in his throat. The horse shied and turned circles around the already dead man, whose foot was trapped in a stirrup. A couple of riderless horses milled uncertainly, muddling with the three riders left. Another of them got a bolt, in the top of his shoulder this time.

"And he always pokes fun at me for not being able to aim a gun," Kass muttered and readied her sword.

But that was enough for their would-be killers. Only two were left unhurt, and no doubt they knew who they were chasing, at least that they were three guildsmen and one more who was a dab hand with a tankard and a little crossbow. They whirled about as best they could among the milling horses and left as fast as their mounts would take them.

Dom came to an abrupt stop, his horse gasping for breath, and slid down.

"Closer than I generally like," he said.

Cospel clambered down from his tree looking smug. "See, at least one of us can aim."

"A crossbow, Cospel?" Kass said with an arch of her brow. "Conduct unbecoming a guildsman, surely?"

"If I'd ever been a guildsman that might matter, miss. But I ain't, and you ain't neither now. I pinched it off that lady what Dom seemed so taken with. My tankard's all very well, but if we're on the run, Cospel, I thought, maybe we could do with something a bit better. Something with a bit of range."

Dom sagged against a tree and put a hand to his face. "You stole that off Cee?"

"Well, you was doing such a good job of distracting her, I thought I might as well. It's a right good un, and all. Bet you're glad I did too. Besides," he added with a sly grin, "it's made of ivory and proper old Castan steel, inlaid with gold and everything – look, you can see the maker's mark. I could retire on this."

"And how many bolts do you have left, Cospel?" Dom asked.

Cospel's face froze and he slid a glare at Dom. "None now."

"Then it's very pretty but useless. Except, perhaps, to her. And magicians do get very attached to their possessions, and they find ways to protect them. See any funny marks on it?"

"There was some," Cospel admitted. "But they rubbed off on my hands."

"And what colour are your hands now?"

Cospel looked down at his fingers. A rusty-looking red was smeared all over them.

Roughly half a second later Cospel's retirement fund was tipping end over end down the scree slope and Cospel was scrubbing his hands in the stream and muttering dire imprecations.

Chapter Twenty

Petri was never sure if he slept or not. He thought not. They hadn't come for him for . . . days? He couldn't be sure, only that it seemed a long time, weeks perhaps. She hadn't come, and now neither did they.

Only, only what was that? A new noise in the silken darkness, a sliding sound, the scuff of leather on stone, a soft breath, a laugh he knew, which echoed dimly off unseen walls. His heart seemed to shudder to a stop before, reluctantly, it started again. Another step and a blaze of light that blinded him. Another, and a human voice that sounded strange after so much silence, so he couldn't understand what it said. And then, blessedly, a cup of water at his lips, a hand behind his head to steady him. It hurt to drink, the water so cold it stabbed into his brain, sending icicles to where his eye used to be, but he drank greedily and only afterwards wondered who'd given it to him and why.

He began to make out shapes in the brightness and then a few blurred details. The face of the man with the cup. Petri gripped it so tightly that it broke, cutting his hand, but that was no matter. If Petri was a man shattered by events, Eneko was little different. Grown grey and gaunt, his mouth hooked up into a wry smile with no strength behind it.

"Hello, Petri." The voice sounded monstrous after the silence, the sound of a giant breaking rocks in Petri's ears, but he now understood. "I'm afraid I need your assistance. I assure you I wouldn't bother you, but I need what's in your head."

Petri couldn't look at Eneko, nor towards the light, which hurt his remaining eye so that tears bathed his face. He said nothing. He had nothing left to say, no words left inside him. Eneko had cut with hot metal and let them pour out like a lanced boil.

"Come on, up," Eneko said, and there was gentleness in his voice so Petri hoped. For what, he couldn't be sure, though possibly for no more pain. A hand under his arm steadied him as he got to numb feet. His legs wouldn't hold him to start with, but Eneko held him up until feeling, and with it pain, began to come back. No sound came from Petri though; his screams had all gone with his voice, sucked into the knife that hung at Eneko's belt. Petri shuddered at the sight of it, but he could stand at last, though not without cost.

Eneko led him out of the cell and up three steps, which almost confounded him, past two guildsmen. Eneko barked an order at them, and they helped Petri, leaving Eneko free to lead the way. A way Petri knew all too well. Up a winding stair, through two doors, along a cloister, where the fresh air revived him and sent waves of pain through the wound at his eye so that he staggered, blind and gagging with it, until they pulled him back up, pushed him on, gentle but insistent, with the hint that they could stop being gentle any time they liked.

The cool night air on his wound blurred much of the rest of the journey. He recalled the Clockwork God, resplendent on his pedestal, mainly as a blaze of light he had to look away from. A broad avenue he only belatedly recognised as the way to the palace. Even at night it should have been full of people – hawkers, beggars and thieves, clockers strutting about in their finery. Tonight it was empty except for them, a flick of wind turning dust into whirling dervishes along the cobbles the only movement.

The palace ahead was dark except for a few lanterns at the windows, and that too was strange. Bakar hated the dark. Not afraid, he just loved light and so put lanterns in every window, had kept some of the grand chandeliers, added more modest ones of his own so the whole place shone out over the city – a beacon of light against darkness, thought against ignorance, enlightenment against the barbarism of the old king, Bakar had once called it. A symbol, like his Clockwork God and his orreries spinning along their axes. Now the facade was largely dark, the vast orrery in what had once been the gardens stuttering in its rhythm. One of the planets spun past, squeaking slightly as it wobbled on its rail.

Eneko eyed Petri in the dark and seemed to come to a decision. "Sabates is dead," he said. "Killed by Vocho and your precious Kass, if reports are to be believed, which they shouldn't be because it wasn't them. Licio is a little boy, nothing without the magician behind him. Ikaras can be . . . dealt with. Bakar is, by now, almost completely insane. It won't take much for the guild to take control with me at its head. With us holding the city, Licio will collapse, and Orgull will sell him out for not much at all, I should think. But Alicia is now a problem. I need to hold the city, and for that I need you, young Petri. For the good of Reyes."

The news of Sabates' death was like a physical blow. He sagged and but for the guildsmen would have fallen. All he had sold his soul for, gone. Eneko was right: without Sabates behind him, Licio would like as not crumble. Everything Petri had sacrificed would be for nothing. And yet he couldn't feel anything other than relief the man was dead. The rest of Eneko's words washed over him except that last sentence, said in a tone of menace he'd come to know very well. He raised a hand to his ruined face, but stopped short of touching it. He knew that Eneko would not fail to follow through with the intent behind his words. His life was measured only by his usefulness now, if it hadn't been before.

Words came back to him, not ones he would ever have spoken before, when he'd been a different man to the cripple who stumbled along. When he'd had dreams of being noble and brave. She hadn't come. She wasn't coming. He was alone. He wanted to live but above all he wanted never to see Eneko's knife coming for his flesh again.

"What do you want me to do?" he said in a voice that sounded like someone else's. Like his father's.

Kass stared down from their vantage point, a goat trail that led from one sharp outcrop to the next on an angel's hair of track.

The Throttled Neck, they called it. All the trails led to this one point everyone had to cross if they wanted to make it to Reyes without trekking a hundred miles out of their way. Some weeks ago when they'd first come to Ikaras, it had been a simple matter to cross. A few guards on either side looking not for one or two travellers but for bands of armed men as they glared at each other over the border. All they'd had to do was tell the guards some tale of petty trade, and through they went. A cursory search had been made, but three people on horses were hardly likely to be smuggling quantities of coal or iron, and so it had taken only moments.

Now an army was camped in the Neck, crammed between two sheer cliffs impassable even for goats. There was no sign of the Reyes post; instead Ikaran soldiers sprawled everywhere, filling the air with the spicy scents of mountain food, Ikaran style. A corral to one side meant at least they knew what they were eating – sheep mostly, some goats and one or two scrawny cows. At either end of the pass a solid mass of men stood alert and ready.

Dom stood next to Kass, shading his eyes against the setting sun.

"How in hells are we going to get through that?" she asked.

"With great difficulty," he said. "How's Vocho holding up?"

She glanced back at her brother, who was sitting in a little nook trying to sleep and, by the look of it, failing. "Not well. We need to get him some proper medical attention. But first we need to get off this bloody mountain."

"Proper medical attention . . . " Dom frowned and scanned the ravine below. After a minute he put a hand on her arm. "Look down there. Just this side of that reddish outcrop. See it?"

She looked at where he was pointing. More soldiers were coming in from behind them on the main trail: an army on the move, with all the attendant shouting, swearing, mud, carts getting stuck and messengers whipping horses through the crowds. A not very organised army either. These were not professional soldiers, and for them marching consisted of being sworn at until they all moved in the right direction at roughly the same rate. Different units met, intermingled and separated again but not necessarily with the same soldiers they'd started with.

At the beginning of the Neck the army was met by a phalanx of tents. As each unit arrived, a man went to the largest one, presumably to report. Other tents spiralled away from this one, and these had more comings and goings. A mess tent, for sure, that one. Smoke and steam drifted out of a hole in the top, and at the back was a vast vat of hot water, or possibly soup, with half a dozen men toiling over it. Another was little more than a shelter next to a picket of horses, where every now and again a messenger would storm in, swap horses and race on. Gradually Kacha identified them. This was a weapons store, that some sort of quartermaster's depot. The largest was clearly the headquarters. Everyone had to show a chit to enter.

When the man returned from the headquarters tent, he'd hand a chit to his commander and men would be dispatched — some to go to the mess tent with a handful of pots each, some to the other tents for whatever reason, while the bulk of the unit would move on into the Neck. One tent was set further back, nestled right up against the rock wall near a stream that straggled down its sheer sides. Kacha couldn't immediately see what it was for — not many went that way. But, after a lot of shouting when a particularly shoddy and ill-disciplined unit pitched up, a junior officer handed a chit to his commander, who immediately gave orders to a little knot of men huddled at the feet of his horse. Four of them lifted the fifth and jogged off to the far tent carrying him between them.

"A medical tent," she said. "Which would be great, if we could reach it without getting killed."

"The main army isn't here yet," Dom said. "They've had

messages, to be sure, but Licio and the rest are still on the march. No one here knows what we look like, except a couple of really bad likenesses of you two on a pamphlet."

She looked at him sideways. "No, and that's fine for you to say, but I'm really going to stand out, aren't I? How many blonde women do you see down there? Besides, our clothes are a dead giveaway."

"Training for assassination also gives you the skills of a sneak thief, don't you find?"

"I try not to."

"No, well, needs must, Kass. Look at the messengers. They gallop in, change horses and gallop out. No one looks at them, not closely anyway. They just try to make sure they don't get run down."

"So we pretend to be messengers? When Voch can hardly stay on a horse let alone gallop it through a bloody army? Even Cospel, on his pony?"

"It may present a challenge, true. It's not much of an idea, but it's the only one I can come up with." He pulled out his telescope, took a look and then passed it to her.

Campfires dotted the ground, and smaller tents and more makeshift arrangements sprawled everywhere along with more men and women than Kass had ever seen in one place before. Not just soldiers, she now saw, but all kinds of camp-followers as well. Traders were selling weapons, clothes, food. Dogs lurked in the shadows, looking for scraps. A blacksmith had set up a temporary forge over by one rock wall and was doing a roaring trade in sharpening blades, as was a clockworker making repairs to guns. There were more than a few women soldiers, and many more women taking care of other things, cooking and mending clothes and bits of leather armour, tending to the sick and those with minor injuries from the trail. There were even some children scampering about, getting under everyone's feet.

Over by the big tent at the entrance to the Neck huge lanterns were strung across the ravine, leaving no shadows to hide in. Hard-eyed men stood under the lanterns and glared at anyone crossing an invisible line until they showed a chit.

"It's a safe bet they're just as vigilant at the other end," Dom said. "More so, perhaps, it being the Reyen end."

They watched closely as a messenger galloped across the invisible line in a cloud of dust and headed straight for the horse picket. Two men leaped to untie a fresh horse, while another ran to get him a canteen of water before he swapped horses and was on his way again less than a minute after he'd arrived.

"They don't ask for any orders or anything," Kass said.

"They don't need to. Did you see the flash on his hat? I noticed it earlier. All the messengers seem to have one."

Kass twisted the eyeglass to take a closer look at a poster outside the main tent.

"You know what, I think I have an idea. Cospel likes distractions, doesn't he?"

Only it seemed that suddenly Cospel had gone right off distractions.

"But, miss, they'll know me."

"No, they won't. That leaflet had our pictures not yours. This is Ikaras. As far as they're concerned you're not much better than a slave, and who cares what they look like?"

Cospel bridled at that. "Slave! As if. I'm a respectable working man, with respectable employers who pay me and everything. Or I was," he muttered as an afterthought.

"And you will be again, just as soon as we manage to

save the day and restore our reputations. But if we don't, then you'll stay being not very respectable at all. Or turn into being dead, if we don't get out of here. They'll find us soon enough, and if they do . . ."

Cospel eyed the horse they'd stolen. Well, hijacked was probably a better term, along with the messenger they'd found on a lonely and less populated part of the tracks that led over the mountain. He glared at them from where he sat tied up and semi-naked, Dom having stripped him of his clothes to give to Cospel.

"Huh," Cospel said. "Dress up like the enemy. I mean it's not like they won't be expecting that, is it? Four people turn up looking just like them leaflets only with different clothes on, that'll fool them for about half a second, that will. Wouldn't fool my blind old granny for any longer than that."

"Ah, but it won't *be* four of us. Just you. And your face isn't on the leaflets."

He narrowed his eyes in the gathering darkness. "What do you mean, just me? What are you going to be doing, miss, if you don't mind me asking?"

"Waiting for you to make everyone run in the wrong direction, Cospel," Dom said. "The professional soldiers are all up by the entrance to the Neck; the rest are draftees, farmers and such, who by the look of things have brought plenty of rum with them. They don't care who rides through the camp, or not much. Once we're in past the professionals, who will be chasing in entirely the wrong direction thanks to you, we should be able to avoid trouble till we get to the other end, especially as only their officers have horses. But we need to get in first. Hence you, this fine horse and a set of clothes with a messenger's flash on the hat. A very fine horse, Cospel, all for you."

Cospel folded his arms and adopted a haughty look. "Don't hold with horses. A pony was good enough for my da, a pony is good enough for me. Can't say I put on airs and graces, like. My pony is a good, honest animal, and that horse looks like it's got mischief in it, you mark my words."

Kass looked at the horse, a docile chestnut wiffling its lips over the ground as though hoping to find a stray bit of hay. It looked about as far from mischief as possible.

"Will your pony keep you alive when the Ikarans find us? That life-warrior? No. Fancy waiting here until he finds us?" Dom asked. "Exactly. I thought you'd see sense."

Cospel disappeared behind a rock with the clothes, muttering all the way. While he was busy Kass hunkered down by Vocho.

"Hey, Voch. Time to go, eh? Time to ride to glory and infamy. Can you get on your horse?"

He turned a sour eye in a face dank with sweat on her. "Glory and infamy, my arse. But I'm not staying here for that bastard to find me. Get me up and I'll stay there."

Cospel looked the part at least, and Dom had him repeat what to say, had him change it a little to try to get the accent right before he declared he was satisfied.

"One last time then, what are you going to say?"

Cospel glared at him. "Tempting though it would be to say, 'Hey, you stupid buggers, this is a distraction,' I'll wave at the poster on the tent and say" – here he switched to Ikaran and Kass was grateful he was better at it than she was – "'Back there, on the trail, riding hard this way. Orgull is giving a year's pay to the man who kills them!'"

"Excellent."

"I don't suppose that messenger had a gun on him, did he? Because I'm going to feel a bit naked down there on my own, and I miss that crossbow already. No?" Cospel's shoulders slumped. "Of course not. If we get out of this alive, miss, I think I'll be asking for some time off for the good of my nerves."

"Here," Kass said, handing over the gun she'd stashed, forgotten, at her waist. "I picked this up but Voch always looks like he'll pee himself if I look like using it. And if we get out of this alive, I'll be wanting some time off myself. We'll meet you in the camp by that black outcrop, all right?"

Cospel went, muttering, "This is never going to bloody work," under his breath.

Kass didn't dare admit even to herself that she agreed with him, but it was this or nothing, and they were trapped. She went to help Vocho up onto his horse.

Chapter Twenty-one

Vocho sat hunched in his saddle and stared down through the night at the tents, at the brightly lit picket of horses and the knots of officers. It seemed like for ever before Cospel came down the road like a sack of potatoes bouncing around on the back of his unfamiliar horse. He reached the main tent and began to ham it up good and proper, pointing at the poster and gesticulating wildly back up the path.

The only hope they had was that, while there were a few professional soldiers down there, most of the officers had qualified for their posts only according to how much money or influence they had.

Cospel generated quite a fuss – it was a talent of his, one which had stood Vocho in good stead on more than one previous occasion. Officers went to fetch more officers, and they seemed very animated. Some sort of argument erupted, which Cospel seemed to fan quite nicely with the odd comment. Vocho could almost see his twisted grin from here. If they got out of this, Cospel was getting a day off. Maybe even a pay rise.

The argument descended into blows, with one man, taller than all the rest, picking another up, giving him a good shake and throwing him to the ground. With that he called for a horse and jumped into the saddle, yelling something over his shoulder. A mad scramble for horses followed among the other officers, and the shouts of orders drifted up even to where they waited among the crags. Young boys – runners – scampered to and fro with messages, and the real soldiers camped out in precise lines near the entrance to the Neck were roused. Soon they were up and out, loping up the slope after their officers, leaving only one grizzled officer shaking his head by the main tent and a few to guard the Neck, plus a load of men and women who could just about tell one end of a sword from the other. Most of the horses were gone too.

Cospel looked up their way, then mounted his horse in the suddenly quiet area before the tents. The grizzled officer said something to him, to which Cospel shrugged. He trotted off, just another messenger off to look for a bed for the night.

"Ready?" Dom murmured.

A curt nod from Kass. Vocho sighed inwardly and held on to his saddle horn. He could do this although one arm was numb already and his hands were shaking. He had to stay on, had to ride, because if he didn't he was dead. "As I'll ever be."

Dom led, and Kass brought up the rear without a word, ready to help Vocho. He felt every jolt as his horse scrambled down the dark hill after Dom. Every step was a shock to his back, a stab in his lungs, so that before long breathing was all he could think about, the fire of it. He couldn't be sure how long they'd been going, or even where they were, when Kass brought her horse up next to his. "Fine," he assured her, though that was gasped out of a raw throat. "I'm fine."

A loud bang close by startled his horse into a shy, jerked his hands from the saddle horn and almost saw him off onto the rocks. Another bang, and it was only then that he realised what they were – guns going off. His horse recovered and sped up, trying to catch Dom's horse with no urging from him. More bangs. His horse shied again at something in front – a man, he saw at the last moment, wielding a sword. The horse half-reared and spun in the dark, disorienting him. The man was still there, only on his right side now, the sword already coming for him. He could barely feel his hand as it reflexively grabbed for his own blade, pulled it out smooth as silk and parried on instinct. Then he was past, but other men stood ahead and to the side. Speed was the only way. There was no other path through this camp but hell for leather and hope for the best, trust to luck and put enough distance between them and any horses left at the picket.

Something slashed at his leg, cut through his breeches but not deeply, no more than a scratch compared to every-thing else. He gave the horse a kick and they shot forward, knocking men aside, the horse screaming as something caught at it, but not enough to stop its wild gallop. He kicked again, bent as low as he could over its neck, as another volley of shots came, further back now.

Then they were free, clear of men, the shots rapidly fading into the distance. Past the strangling pass of the Neck, the vista of Reyes before him, laid out below like a blanket. The lights of little villages, a faint glow on the far horizon that would be Reyes itself. He kept going, down one of the several paths that would take him back to where he wanted to be and didn't want to be. Back home.

It was only then that it came to him. In the rush, the confusion, the white haze of his pain-filled vision, he'd not seen, not noticed; he'd been too busy just living. Kass wasn't beside him, Dom was nowhere to be seen, even Cospel was conspicuous by his absence.

He was on his own.

A whirlwind surrounded Kass – of people, of swords, men shouting, women yelling, children screaming in the chaos.

The plan had worked well enough, up to a point. They were careering through the haphazard tents of the camp, not caring whose dinner they trampled or whose laundry got stamped into the dust. Dom and Voch were right behind her, following the path her horse made with teeth and feet, speed and sheer terrifying weight. Once they'd passed the line of lanterns, where soldiers had fired shots at them and scrambled for the few horses left, it had been easier. They entered a darker area, one with few campfires, and she took a moment to pull up her horse and take stock. Dom brought his own horse to a hard-breathing halt beside her.

"Where in hells is Voch?" she asked after a moment, breathing hard herself. "And Cospel? He should be here too."

Dom shook his head, and then they had to move on as a gaggle of soldiers came around a tent. A bullet winged its way past. Where was Voch? She wrenched her horse round but couldn't see him anywhere, Cospel neither. They had to keep moving, and she could only hope they'd find them both. It was darker here, which helped and hindered. The Ikarans couldn't see them except perhaps in flashes, but they couldn't see their way, couldn't avoid holes to break a horse's leg, or guylines to trip them.

Kass bent low over her horse and urged it on anyway

– there was nothing else for it, because death surely lay behind. The beast took the dare of the touch of her heels and flew, seeming always to know where not to tread, Dom's own horse half a pace behind so that she could feel its ragged breath on her leg. And always, always she was thinking, where's Voch?

Her horse jinked left, almost spilling her from the saddle with it, a half-second before another bang signalled a bullet. Ahead a body of men arranged themselves into a crude line. Not professionals, but they didn't need to be.

With them stood the life-warrior who'd found them in the woods, his disfigured face flickering in the light of torches lit from the campfires. Something so implacable about his face, it gave her the shivers. The worst had happened already, his eyes said. A heavy *palla* blade hung in his hand, loose and ready. Her horse baulked at the sight of the line, but being the stubborn bastard it was – and her sort of horse – for only a moment, and then snorted and went on. The bloody-minded thing was smarter than she was because it headed for two young men who look scared out of their wits.

She had her sword out, ready to cut down anyone who got in her way; Dom beside her let out a cry and waved his own sword over his head. The line held for a second before the man on the right broke and ran, the rest scattering in the face of a snapping set of teeth and a ton or so of horses bearing down on them at high speed. All except the life-warrior, who came for her as silently as before, heading her off. He dodged a vengeful hoof and brought the heavy blade around for the horse's leg, hoping to dismount her and take away her best advantage. Kacha's desperate kick made her horse leap forward and avoid the worst of the blow, but blade struck flesh along its flank.

Her horse screamed and turned to bare its teeth at this new threat. One it had no hope of beating.

Neither did she.

They were past the wall of men now, which had fallen away in confusion, and into a clearer area. She turned the horse as well as she could, peering into the darkness to see where the life-warrior was, where he was coming from. A sudden bright light blinded her, some sort of shuttered lantern shining right in her eyes. The horse came to a juddering halt, favouring one leg and shaking its head at the invisible threat. Blades clashed, Dom shouted something, a dying horse screamed and the lantern went out, leaving her in darkness. The sounds of blades again, the lantern coming back on – it hadn't gone out, only the shutter had come down – to sear her eyes with brightness. She slid down from the horse, wary and keeping its comforting bulk at her back, just as the lantern turned away and let her see.

Not much though – a glint here and there, a movement in its beam too quick to pin down before it was gone, the shadow of a sword that flickered out and back. Dom's face, there and gone into the darkness. The light shuttered off and on again four paces to her left, catching Dom unaware and showing the life-warrior right in front of her. She slashed on instinct, but he whirled to block her, numbing her arm with the force of it and knocking her back into the horse. She caught a glimpse of a face dead except for a grim glint, and then the shutter came down and they were in darkness again.

The soft scuff of boots on stone, but whose? Other sounds, the not-soldiers gathering their courage and moving back in, another set of hooves behind her and a whispered "Miss?" that could only be Cospel. The sigh of a slim blade in front of her aiming for something vital, and a strange sucking sound, a gasp, the clang of that blade hitting the ground. Dom — what the hells had he done to Dom?

The light came on further away as the life-warrior retreated, but he'd left Dom on his knees. She ran forward, pulling him up as she looked at the hesitant mob in the unsteady light, which was gathering the courage to come on under the exhortations of a man who sounded a natural-born sergeant.

Dom came to his feet, oddly ungainly for a man who seemed made of grace. She cast around, looking for the life-warrior, the hint of a heavy blade coming for her back, but there was nothing except Dom's horse, dead at his feet. Nothing ahead either, except Cospel looking worried and the end of the Neck, the lights of Reyes far away down on the plain. And somewhere in all that, Voch, only barely able to sit his horse. She had to hope he'd managed to get through, that they'd find him before anyone else did.

She manhandled Dom into her saddle, where he sat like a man hit with a sledgehammer. A glance behind told her there was no time to spare. She clambered into the saddle in front of Dom, the horse trembling but answering her nudges, grabbed the reins and with a word to Cospel they shot off down the path, out of the Neck and towards home. The not-soldiers didn't follow them, and as far as Kacha could tell the life-warrior had vanished after he'd done whatever he had to Dom. He was waxen faced and barely even nodded when she asked if he was all right.

She stopped them far down the trail, where the path widened out, much as it did on the other side of the pass, into numerous little trails among craggy rocks and towering cliffs so that following them would be difficult. She'd asked Cospel about Voch, but he didn't have much of an answer.

"Saw him, miss, but he barrelled past me like a man afeared for his life. Never saw me, I reckon, never saw nothing perhaps. Shot off down the path, his horse all lathered up, him hanging on like it was all he could do, and that was it. He's out here somewhere though, I seen him make it through."

Alicia raised an eyebrow at the fresh bandage over Gerlar's face and the fresh hatred in his remaining eye.

"You failed with the leech." Not a question. She'd felt it latch on, but then . . . gone. She supposed she could expect nothing less from a man so slippery.

Gerlar shifted uneasily, teeth gritted against what she'd say, do. "Yes, ma'am. But he's injured, I made sure of that, and they're one horse short."

"Injured," she said and blew out a breath rather than take it out on Gerlar — he was useful even if he didn't always succeed. "And losing a horse should slow them. Well then, they should be easy enough to find. I suppose it will have to do. And I want them found, before we reach Reyes city, before they can reach Reyes. Understood?"

A flicker of his eyelid, the merest hint of a nod.

"Good. Don't fail me this time, if you want what I promised. Now, come here and tell me. If you were to assault the city of Reyes, how would you do it?"

He approached the table, and the detailed map of Reyes laid out there. She let him ponder while she sent for Licio and Orgull.

Licio blustered in, but the wind was out of his sails, the bluff gone from his voice. When he thought she wasn't looking, there was panic behind his eyes, which she did absolutely nothing to dispel. A foolish boy, she'd always thought him, too likely to do whatever Sabates told him.

Easy to blind with the promise of his kingdom back, a promise she'd reiterated, and expanded on, and had as little intention of fulfilling as Sabates had.

Orgull sat back with his usual carefully blank face. She'd changed the rules, that care said, but he was content to see what she'd make of this, what she'd offer him. A pragmatist to the core, and one who knew how valuable the magician's guild in his city was, working at least nominally for him.

The map, of necessity, was an intricate piece of work. Reyes wasn't always the same city, it was three cities, each with its own vagaries and things to beware of. Gerlar studied it with the same detached calm he studied everything but she had no doubt that behind that his mind was working furiously.

"Men inside," he said now. Much as Sabates had planned.

"In the guild, for preference," she agreed, and signalled a guard. Two men came in, not by their own choice, who'd lately been guarding the border on the Reyes side. Leeches pulsed on their necks, latched on without hope of cutting them free. Not if they wanted to live, at least.

"What do you want them to do?" she asked Gerlar, but Licio interrupted the reply, and she noted the twitch of Gerlar's eye as he did.

"They do what you tell them?" Licio asked with a shudder.

"Oh yes. This works so much better than tattoos. I doubt even Esti could remove one without killing the host. And they work for more than just that, too."

"And you can suggest, as Sabates did with Vocho? Better?"

"Oh much better, my lord. Sabates had a crude way about him. These work so much more subtly. As do I."

Orgull hid a smile behind a sip of tea at that. *Oh you may smile, my lord. You may think you know. You have no idea. You think magicians work for you, but I could smear you across the ground with little more than a word. Why should magicians obey your orders? If I have my way, I'll be giving the orders and you'll be saying "yes, ma'am". If I let you live.*

"Very well, slave. You may continue." Licio gave a lofty wave of his hand, and she wondered how much Gerlar would enjoy killing him, how much that disdain burned at the man inside. It was impossible to tell.

"Thank you, my lord." Alicia said before Gerlar could say anything rash, and gathered herself. "Two men, inside the guild. Others will be inside the city. Reyes will be on First Threeday, meaning this is the layout. Our men will disable the clockwork at this gate here, giving us safe passage through to both the palace and the guild."

"You're quite sure of this news of the guild?"

She smiled and snapped her fan out. "Quite sure. Eneko means to take over the city as we march, and confront us with a rallied populace to defend the city. I have taken steps to ensure he doesn't. But he will need dealing with, and carefully."

Chapter Twenty-two

Vocho didn't know exactly where he was or why he was going on anyway. If he had a sensible bone in his body, he'd probably get the hells out of Reyes and stay out. He considered it as he let the horse go on at its own pace down a road that was more a dusty track along the bottom of a valley. The Spice Islands were nice this time of year, he'd heard, and had the added advantage that no one would be trying to kill him. He was getting very bored with that now.

But there was Kass – there was always Kass. She was annoying as hells, but he couldn't go anywhere without her. Even now there felt like a gap at his side where she should be, defending his flank as he defended hers. Scowling at him for not taking things seriously most likely, but he thought he'd probably even miss that.

Do what seems good to you.

It seemed a very long time ago he'd sworn that, and with it to defend Reyes, the guild the city's last defence. He'd never taken it especially seriously, instead been more concerned with outstripping Kass in the glory stakes and making a name for himself. But things were different now, and so was he.

Sweat dried on his skin, crusted his shirt to his stinging back. What was it Dom had done, and before him Esti? At least the pain had gone, mostly anyway, though he'd been left with the shakes and a damnable thirst for Esti's syrupy jollop.

He reached the end of the valley, where it opened out onto the hills that would, he hoped, lead him down onto the plain and Reyes. Home. To start with he'd wanted nothing more than to get his name back. And Kass's life for her. He didn't think he was ever likely to get either of those, not now. Now he'd be content with not getting involved in a war, maybe stopping that war if he could. And he could, couldn't he? He had Esti's antidote, if that's what it was. If he could get close enough, he could do it – cure Bakar of the poison that Sabates had sent leaking through him, turning his mind. He might not be the best ruler ever, but Bakar sane had to be better than Bakar mad, and averting a war . . .

He perked up as a thought struck him. Vocho the Great, fighting magicians at every turn, saves the day and the city. That seemed very good indeed to him. All he had to do was do it. He nudged the horse into a faster pace and tried to ignore the remnants of pain in his back.

Kass had to be out here somewhere, didn't she? If she'd made it through the Neck, she had to be here somewhere. She *was* here; he wasn't going to start thinking about the alternative. And she wouldn't wait – she never waited – and besides waiting with an army about to march through here would be stupid at best. She'd expect him to get to Reyes, if he could. She'd got past, and she'd be heading for Reyes as fast as possible, just like him. He'd find her and, no matter the whys of her motivations, the end result would be the same. They would both get what they wanted, and, what the hells, he'd even be grown-up about it and not complain about Petri being back in his life again.

OK, not much.

Kass called a halt at dawn, when it was clear both her horse and Dom couldn't go much further. He'd held on to her with a grim determination and a grip that was both close and oddly disturbing, but his hands had slackened this last half-hour, and the horse was stumbling with weariness. She couldn't honestly say she was much better.

She found a hollow at the end of a valley and slid from the horse, helping Dom down after her. He looked worse than ever, but he managed to keep his feet and give her a wan smile. Cospel all but fell off his horse and set about taking care of the two animals with a dreamlike slowness, paying special attention to Kass's where it had taken a blow. The beast was too tired to put up a fight. It didn't take Cospel long to pronounce the wound "Not so bad, miss, but the horse needs rest, not you two on its back."

There wasn't much she could do about that because time to rest was something they had precious little of. The Ikaran army would be heading down these valleys any time now, ready to swallow them up if they stayed there too long, and that chaffed. By rights she should wait for Voch . . .

Cospel's eyebrows waggled in a comforting manner as he went on, as though she'd said that aloud, "He ain't stupid, miss. Vocho, I mean. He got through and so did we. But we can't stay here and wait for him, same as he can't stay and wait for us. Ikarans will be through that pass any minute, and none of us can afford to be here when they come. If he's got the sense he was born with he'll be hightailing it to Reyes and look to find us there. Which is what we should be doing."

"Yes, but—"

"No buts, miss. You know I'm right. And he can take care of hisself good as you or I can, mostly. Now you go and sort that Dom out. I got work to do with these horses, miss, and you fretting about don't make it no easier. Vocho's got as good a chance as we have, but we won't have none if the horses give out."

"Thank you. I think a month off with double pay if we make it out alive?"

"Won't say no, miss. Now bugger off; you're right in my light there."

While Cospel got on with rubbing the horses down, humming and clucking comfortingly under his breath, Kass dealt with Dom. He'd sunk down onto a grassy bank and was poking gingerly under his collar with one finger and wincing.

"Are you hurt?" she asked and made to look, but he flinched away.

"Not as such, no. That life-warrior works for Alicia, that's for sure. With Sabates dead, I suspect she's running things now, directing Licio. She was always good at that, and learning magic won't have made her any worse."

He poked some more, and a stream of blood soaked his collar.

"Let me look."

He did, reluctantly. A wound like she'd never seen before – not from a sword or a bullet. "What is it?"

"Bastard had a leech."

"A leech?"

"Blood magic, Kass. And how better to get to me? He

tried to put the bastard thing on me, but I managed to kill it before it latched on properly."

"To do what, exactly?"

"Anything. For all I know, she's taken a leaf out of Esti's book and wanted to poison me slowly. Maybe she wanted to get me to do something like Sabates did with Voch, or it'd kill me at some point, nice and quick. Or maybe it'd just tell her where I am. You try taking it off or cutting it out . . . Well I've heard of people trying, but the person with the leech never survives. So I'm pretty glad he didn't get it on properly."

They stared at each other.

"Not our most pressing concern, however," Dom said. "Which is getting out of here, finding Voch if we can. Maybe stealing another horse. Avoiding the army that's about to land on our heads. You let me worry about this and Alicia. You worry about the rest of it."

What was there to do? Nothing except snatch a bit of rest and go on. She found a spot where she could look back over their trail while Dom and Cospel tried to rest. The mountains loomed behind them, still shadowed in places from the rising sun. Little plumes of smoke and dust told her all she needed to know – the army was moving. Their only hope was in staying one step ahead, somehow reaching Reyes in time. Avoiding any scouts that they sent out. And they needed to find Voch. How in hells were they going to do that?

She turned to look the way they were heading. Rolling hills fading into a plain dry with dust. Patchy woodland. Farmhouses. Villages here and there. They needed a horse. Cospel was right: Voch was bound to head for Reyes, if he could. It was all she had.

She woke the pair of them after an hour or so, gave

Cospel her complaining horse and took Dom up with her on Cospel's horse. Turn and turn about was the only answer for now.

Once his head cleared properly, Vocho realised he felt better than he had in a while. Whatever Dom had done had worked, mostly. He was still bone-achingly tired but now he had a fresh sense of purpose. The track led to a more well-travelled road, which he followed. With a fresh horse it was a day or so's ride to Reyes. With his tired beast it'd be longer, but armies couldn't travel that fast.

Some time later he came to a patchy wood. On one side was a cottage all tumbled down, its garden a mess of weeds and small trees, with vines snaking out over the road. Someone was in the garden, someone familiar . . .

The vines snapped around his horse's leg as it went to step over them. Another shot up and yanked Vocho from the saddle, dumping him in a heap on the road, winded. When his head cleared, a familiar face was leaning over him, looking concerned.

"Esti?"

She held out a hand and he took it before his brain got into gear. By then he was on his wobbly feet.

"What the hells did you do to me?"

She backed off, hands out as though to ward him off. "What I needed to. I'm on your side, really I am. I had to make sure you'd go through with it."

"Through with what?" He patted himself down and found he had no new injuries past a bruise or two. Still, given his old injuries had not been helped in the least by Esti, he wasn't feeling very charitable. He laid a hand on his sword hilt and repeated his question.

Esti sagged at the shoulders. "Damn. I thought you were

just some scout. If I'd known it was you I'd have let you ride on." She took a furtive look up and down the road. "Look, there's not much time. Come with me, off the road. And where's your sister?"

She backed into a tangle of plants that moved out of the way to let them past, and back again to hide them. In the middle of what had once been a garden was a camp, where she'd been for a day or so by the look of it. She waited for him to tie up his horse, then gestured for him to sit, but he stayed where he was, ready to run if he had to.

"You're the magician; you tell me where she is," he said when she asked again. "And what are you up to? Try the truth this time."

She twisted her hands until she realised her supposed nervousness wasn't having the desired effect. "The truth? I was waiting for you. More truth – I was waiting for you in Ikaras too. I wanted you to find me because I knew I could get you to help if I just gave you a nudge, the right incentive. I want what you want, indirectly. You need to stop a war. I wanted Sabates dead; I still want Alicia dead. We can do both if you just listen to me. Because your sister is in serious trouble."

"Who isn't? I mean I've only got a whole army trying to find me, and kill me. Along with some freakish one-eyed warrior who looks like death itself couldn't beat him. And the Clockwork God only knows what you did to my back or put in that jollop. What makes you think she's in any worse trouble?"

Esti's hands started twisting again, and Vocho now had the feeling she wasn't acting. The way her eyes went wide and sad, the way she pinched her lips as though to stop the words coming out wrong – if she was acting, she was a hell of an actress. "You know that man you were travelling with? Dom. You know he's Alicia's husband?"

Oh so *that* was it! It explained quite a lot but posed more questions than it answered. "Why are you telling me?"

"Because you and Kass trust him. Do you think he doesn't care for Alicia any more? That he might even be working for her?"

Well, he'd certainly looked like a love-struck sheep. "He didn't know it was her; I'd swear it was as much a surprise to him as anyone."

"Huh. I wouldn't put too much faith in that. You still have the antidote?"

"Of course, safe in my pack."

"Give it to me."

"Now hold on. You poisoned me! Why should I trust you?"

"Because . . . Look, Vocho, we all have to do things we don't want to sometimes. But I didn't poison you; I was saving you. What happened with your back – the tattoo – it's like a failsafe in case someone tries to take it off. It'll do what it can to kill you. The jollop, yes, it's not that good for you, but it's the only way. Like Bakar's antidote. The jollop was the only way to stop what's left of the tattoo. I took away as much as I could, but there were remnants, and those are the danger. They'll worm their way in until they reach your heart, and then . . . You stop taking that syrup before the tattoo's totally gone, I can't answer for what'll happen."

"No choice. I haven't any left. Dom threw it away, said it was poisoning me – *you* were poisoning me. That the jollop was what would reach my heart."

"And what does he know about magic? About tattoos

and wards and what happens when you take them off? And he hasn't exactly been entirely truthful with you either, has he? I don't know much about him except what you've told me and that he's married to Alicia. I bet he never told you that, did he?"

No. No, he hadn't. And he'd not told them who he really was for as long as possible and . . . and, come to think of it, there was more he didn't know about Dom than there was he did know. Like, what was it he wanted? Why was he so very damned helpful for no reason that Vocho could see?

But the pain in his back was better today, after Dom had done whatever it was, and he said so.

"Because the jollop worked, I suspect," she said. "Fortuitous timing. It saved you; *I* saved you. Without that jollop the remnants of that tattoo would be eating your heart right now and I'd be trying to decide where to bury you. Yes, it has side effects, but at least you're alive to feel them."

Vocho sat back and tried to think, and Esti let him. It wasn't easy when most of his brain was thinking so, can we have more jollop now? Just a bit, just a nip. He tried to shake the thought away and partially managed it.

No bugger was telling the truth all the way, that was all he could be sure of. Maybe Esti had tried to poison him, maybe not. He couldn't think why it would help her at all. After all, if she wanted him dead she could have poisoned him good and proper before they even left Ikaras. And Dom hadn't been entirely truthful about Alicia, had he? Or quite a lot else, in fact. Besides, if he helped Esti, he might get more jollop. *Stop it. Think, man, think.* Why would Esti poison him? What would that achieve? Nothing leaped to mind. But helping him so that he'd help her . . .

"The question is," she said into the silence, "are you going to go on and leave me here? Or let me help you? I swear on anything you want to name we are on the same side. It's Alicia I'm after, and so are you now Sabates is dead. She'll carry on, head for Reyes, do her damnedest to get what she wants. It was always two things with her – she wanted to rule the magicians and get revenge on Eneko. This is her way of getting both at once. Now that Sabates is dead and she'll probably become leader of the magicians, all that's left is Eneko, and what does Eneko value the most?"

"The guild, the city, himself. Not necessarily in that order."

"So she'll destroy Reyes, or at least threaten to, to get what she wants. Eneko won't give her what she's after, give in to her for anything less. Don't you think she's tried every other way? If you want to beat Alicia you're going to need another magician. Got any others willing to help, for free?"

"No, I can't say we have."

"You said you still have the antidote. Get it out and let me see."

Vocho hesitated but not for long. Looked like it didn't pay to trust anybody, so he wouldn't. But he might play along for a bit until he could figure out who was lying the least. He grabbed his pack off his horse, but no matter how hard he looked, there was no little bottle.

"Gone?" Esti said with a look of panic. "In the wrong hands . . . gods damn it in the wrong *place* . . . I made that especially for him. Not pleasant but better than being poisoned. For anyone else . . . If they take it too close to me . . ."

"I thought you said it was just an antidote."

Esti scrunched her eyes up. "It is, if you give it to someone poisoned that way. To anyone else it could be fatal, and not just to them. To *me*, if I'm too close. I put a bit of myself in everything I make, and that . . . Oh gods. Please, Vocho, you have to find it, make sure Bakar takes it. And I'm not too close. Its effects . . . leach out to me." Esti was shaking, hands moving up to her lips in horror and back down to twist in her lap.

"Who could have stolen it?" Vocho asked. "There was only me, Kass, Cospel."

"And Dom. Her husband. Who has stolen the one thing that might have stopped this war before it properly starts. *Now* do you believe me?"

The palace loomed ahead, dark and forbidding as it had never been before to Petri. But things had changed and so had he.

Eneko half dragged him through the south gate, past the slumped forms of two palace guards and the more upright forms of a couple of guildsmen who nodded at Eneko but said nothing.

Petri could only guess why Eneko had brought him back here, but none of his guesses gave him cause for hope. The palace was almost the last place he wanted to be, Bakar almost the last person he wanted to see. He'd spent years wanting to be free of them, but he'd ended up in a far worse place than the cage he'd thought himself in.

He stumbled as Eneko pushed him on, head spinning, the eye that was gone nevertheless flashing weird purple blotches in his head. The clock room, he realised at last, they were heading for the clock room.

The sound of them ticking and tocking the seconds off his life pulled him up short, made him want to scream at the insidious scratching noise they made inside him. Eneko opened the door and shoved Petri so hard he fell to his knees. He tried to save himself with his bad hand, and yelped when it hit the floor. He crouched there, shivering and wondering where all his courage had gone, whether he'd ever had any to start with. If he had, Eneko had burned it all away.

The clocks ticked on.

"Which was it? This one?"

Eneko stood in front of the hideous bone clock with a sneer.

"Do whatever it was he wanted you to do."

Petri stared up at the clock, at the skull that topped it. If he did what Sabates had wanted . . . No, he'd decided he wouldn't. Because of Kass, because she would hate him if he did. Because all he had left was her not to hate him, to come for him. She'd come for him, she would, but she'd be too late. Sudden tears robbed him of breath, washed his face in bitterness and made his eye fire until Eneko kicked him back to the room, to now. A deep hitching breath did little good, another did better.

Eneko was as mad as Sabates was, as mad as Licio, he was sure of it. He'd written so in the letter to Kass, that he'd decided not to do what the magician wanted, what all of them wanted. Instead he'd told her he'd do the good thing, the *right* thing.

Eneko's boot ground into his bad hand, and all thought of good or right fled, replaced with doing whatever it took to stop this, whatever he needed to do to survive.

"Weak as dishwater – you always were," Eneko growled. "Get up and do whatever it was."

Petri was on his feet. He stared at the clock, at the bones hands moving round, ticking his life away. Unwind it,

Sabates had said. Make it stop. Why? What would that achieve?

"No one is coming to save you," Eneko whispered. "Bakar knows you betrayed him; Sabates is dead, and Alicia, Licio, they don't care. And Kass . . . she won't save you. Why should she? Why would my Kass give a toss about a little shit like you? The answer is, she doesn't. She's worth ten of you, and you're on your own. If you want to stay alive, you do this, now, for me. That's your only value. Do this or die right now."

A knife against the back of his neck.

Petri shut his one eye against what Eneko said, how it only confirmed his own fears. She wasn't coming; why should she? She'd left him to this and in that instant love twisted inside. The good thing, the right thing, had changed. Now it was do what was good for him. No one else was going to. Everyone else had abandoned him. He couldn't understand why the clock had blurred. He gritted his teeth, blinked to clear his vision and did as Sabates had said and unwound the clock. The bone hands stopped.

"Now what?" Eneko hissed.

"I . . . I don't know."

Now what, was the creak of the door, Bakar walking in looking lost and shaking. Dawn, it must be dawn, when Bakar came to wind the clocks and, lately, talk to them. Eneko dragged Petri back into a far corner still dark with night and hissed at him to be quiet. Petri did as he was told, one hand tracing where an eye had been, and wished, wished . . . *Kass, please . . .*

Bakar began at the end of the room near the door. He greeted the first clock, stroked it lovingly, took a key from the bunch at his waist and wound it before cocking his head as though listening. Finally, after talking to every clock between and winding those that needed it, he came to the bone clock.

"Well, hello, why have you stopped?" He found the key and put it in to wind the clock back up. Instead, a stream of liquid squirted out from the innards of the clock, turning into a fine greenish mist that Bakar couldn't avoid inhaling as he gasped in surprise.

Petri found he was holding his own breath as he waited to see what would happen. It didn't take long. First Bakar frowned as though puzzled, then wiped sweat from his brow. Further sweat followed as he began babbling to the clock, asking it why it had done such a thing. Finally, muttering about petticoats and periwinkles, Bakar ripped his clothes off as though he was too hot to stand them and stood naked in front of the clock.

Not for long – he stared wild-eyed around the room, taking in the ticking and tocking. "I see now," he whispered. "I see what's in the gears, what's behind the clockwork universe." He ran for the door, threw it open and launched himself into the corridor beyond, shouting all the while that he knew the truth now, that the only comfort was the truth he'd seen in the clocks.

Eneko let out a breath behind him, turned it into a chuckle. "Oh, that Sabates knew what he was about, eh? Let's go see how this pans out. Favourably for me, I'm thinking."

Outside the clock room there was chaos in the swirling of clerks and aides roused from their beds by the shouting, fear in the eyes of the guards, who couldn't seem to decide whether to restrain the prelate or let the man who gave them their orders do as he would. Bakar left a confused and rudderless trail of people behind him; no one noticed Eneko or the ruined man with him. Then the doors of the palace banged open and Bakar ran naked and screaming out into the dawn.

Eneko waved over two guildsmen lurking nearby. He pointed at Petri. "Take him to the Shrive. You know the cell. He'll have some company soon enough."

Petri didn't complain, didn't say a word as Eneko strode off, looking purposeful, after Bakar. Men and women breathed sighs of relief as the guild master passed, leaving behind a word or two of comfort, that the guild would see that things were put right, not to worry.

Petri was manhandled towards the grey bulk of the Shrive. To struggle was useless; everything was useless. He was lost, dead. He saw Bakar take a hammer to the Clockwork God, saw Eneko gently prise him from it, have Bakar taken away by kindly-looking guildsmen and address the crowd.

A temporary measure to restore order, he called it, in this time of coming war. The stress of command had obviously proved too much for Bakar, who he would have looked after by the best doctors available. In the meantime, the guild stood for the city, had sworn to protect it, and now Eneko would honour that promise.

As a purely temporary measure.

Kacha and Dom hired a barn from a farmer who was packing his things onto a cart ready for morning, when he and his family were making for safer pastures, at least for now. The horses were safe enough, with enough hay and water to last several days. Cospel didn't like leaving them – neither did Kass – but there wasn't a lot of choice.

By the time they approached the city, day was twined with dusk, and shadows, the assassin's friends, grew in all the nooks and corners. Even for that time of day, it seemed unnaturally quiet; usually there'd be a queue of people, carts, wagons, horses, all waiting their turn to move through the clanking gate and brave the vagaries of the clockwork traps inside. Tonight there was no one, no sounds echoing from the other side of the walls. No catcalling, no one hawking their wares, no one fighting, or singing, or anything. Only the quiet of a city waiting for an army. It made Kacha's shoulders shudder.

They made their wary way to the gate, as watchful as a pair of assassins knew how to be from long and careful habit. By rights she should have heard the grumbling of the guards by now, the whirr of the tower traps that protected the inner city, or used to at any rate. Now there was nothing – no muttering about having drawn the late shift, no jingle of sword harness or crank of gun, no sound at all from the towers through the gates.

Kacha slid round a corner like a shadow and found a dark nook to wait in while she watched, Dom following and finding a similar place the other side of the narrow way, Cospel close behind.

"OK," Dom whispered after a short while. "This is very strange and a bit creepy. Where is everyone? Why aren't the towers moving? Trap, do you think?"

"Maybe, but not for us." She shook her head – they were wasting time. "Come on, up." She jerked her head towards a ledge above them, and Dom's grin came swift and sure before he followed her. Cospel muttered a few choice words as he scrambled up behind them and in the end had Dom pull him up.

The walls and roofs of the city were, Kass had often thought, arranged as if to help anyone trying to sneak across them, if only you found the start. To begin with they were just roofs, with the city walls looming on one side. Then, nip around a chimney here, sidestep behind an innocent-looking panel there, and there you were, on a thoroughfare across the city that changed as the rest did with the clock.

Paths ran out before her, shielded from the view of the street. If you followed the paths right, the gaps over streets and alleys were an easy jump. A narrow squeeze between two houses, skirt a flat-roofed building bristling with the shacks of the poorest, who could be relied upon to see nothing in case it got them killed. Even this little village within the city was silent, with not even a candle to light any shack.

The city had never been this quiet, not even at the dead of night during a storm. There was always someone moving around. Only tonight it was just them, and it was starting to get disturbing.

They halted on a ledge where they could see the guild – lit up like the starry night – and the palace, which lay in darkness but for one lamp at a high window. Shapes passed in front of the light, jittery and agitated. And not without cause. Come dawn, the Ikaran army would be in sight, but Kacha had the feeling that all would be decided before then if they were even half right about Eneko.

She slid a glance towards the guild, to where Eneko plotted and planned, and had for years in secret. Not so secret now. The farmer who'd rented them his barn hadn't known much, but he'd known enough to make her sick that she'd once looked up to Eneko as she had her da. No one knew what, but something had happened in the palace, something that had turned the prelate from a paranoid fool into a ravening madman. No longer concerned with bizarre edicts and swingeing taxes on the oddest things, he'd burst naked like an avenging angel from the rooms he'd imprisoned himself in, shouting about spies and subversives everywhere. He'd had his guards execute a half-dozen of his own staff before he'd turned to the thing that had made him, that had held him in power and regard all these years.

As citizens watched aghast and guards hesitated to obey his order to attack the god that sat between palace and guild, Bakar had taken a hammer to his own Clockwork God. The farmer had been distressingly vague after that and had started shoving all his cured ham into a sack for his cart. Kacha thought she could guess. Eneko would have been on hand, being overtly dependable, trading on the history and good name of the guild, and on people's fear. Bakar would have gone to the Shrive, or perhaps been dealt with right there, in blood and blade.

The city was quiet because Eneko wanted it quiet. That was all she could think. They were too late.

"Where to?" Dom whispered beside her, but he knew the answer as well as she did. Too late, she thought again. If they took down Eneko now, what would become of the city come the morning when an army came across the plain? The city needed someone, and he was as devious a fighter as they came. What seemed good to her, for the good of Reyes? And yet that wasn't her only thought. Petri was here somewhere, and Eneko had never had any love for him. Had he sent Petri with Bakar to the Shrive, or to the blade? She shook that away or tried to.

"We can't do anything against an army that Eneko's not already doing. We need to know exactly what's going on. The guild," she said in the end. One way or another, this would end in the guild.

Dom twitched at that, but his nod was firm enough. "My thought entirely. And nothing to do with revenge at all."

They shared a shaky grin. "Not at all," she said.

It was eerily quiet all the way to the little plinth between the palace and guild where the mangled remnants of the Clockwork God stood, surrounded tonight by a dozen lamps that made what was left of him shine like gold. Surrounded too by silent men and women, heads bowed as a priest spoke in low tones. Some sort of blessing for the day ahead, from what Kacha could gather.

Mingling with the crowd were guildsmen in their green tabards with crossed swords, their fine shirts and foppish hair. Comforting the crowd or controlling it? She couldn't be sure, but there were tight mouths, tense hands, nervous feet.

They slid through the crowd, heading for the guild gates.

Kacha peered up at the guild walls and the two men hanging from them. Or rather, what was left of two men. But she could still recognise the faces, just. Blood ran down their mangled legs to drip into Reyes' river. A few children were throwing stones at the corpses from the bridge.

"Spies?" Dom asked.

"I know those men. If they were spies, it wasn't willingly."

Dom fingered the blood-splattered collar of his coat. "Possibly not."

The crowd struck Kacha as very different from the mob they'd left behind when they'd fled Reyes that last time. Then the city had seethed with anger, just waiting for something to spark it off. Bakar had been the spark. Bakar going mad because he was being poisoned. OK, maybe Bakar hadn't been the best ruler a city had ever seen, but sure as shit stank, he was better than Eneko, a man for whom morals were a handy tool to manipulate people with and for whom slavery and assassination were simply means to an end.

This crowd wasn't angry – nervous maybe, but that was no surprise when you considered the approaching army. And that was better than seething resentment or panic as the city's ruler went mad. Especially given that army.

"We need to find Bakar," Dom said.

"Not now," she said. "For now maybe Eneko is best left where he is. A temporary measure. At least until Ikaras and its army has been dealt with. We just need to make sure it is temporary."

"How?"

"Eneko will be busy with the Ikarans. While he is, we can find out what he's got up his sleeve, how many guildsmen are with him, or not, ready for when we give the antidote to Bakar."

"Isn't it a touch too late for Bakar?" Dom asked with a sarcastic slide to his voice. "I mean, he's already gone round the twist. People aren't going to forget that."

"No, but they may understand when they find out why."

"Of course, they'll listen to us – a bunch of exiled guildsmen who couldn't possibly be holding a grudge. That is if they don't chop our heads off before we can open our mouths. Maybe my father—"

"Dom, the last time you had anything to do with your father, he sent you to the Shrive."

Kacha stared up at the walls of what she had once called home. To the tower where she used to meet a man she considered a second father, more real, more *there* than her own da. A lot had changed since then. Or rather, it hadn't changed; she'd just discovered that the world and people weren't what they appeared, that everyone had secrets that drove them to do things that looked like madness to others.

What seems good to you.

To protect Reyes if it comes to it.

Maybe everyone else was a conniving bastard out for themselves, but she'd sworn that once, and she was going to keep on living by it if it killed her.

"No more lies," she said. "Reyes has had enough lies for ten lifetimes. We let Eneko fight this battle – he's got the city behind him now; they're as ready as they'll ever be. He's a crafty fighter, always has been. He'll have a plan to keep Ikaras from the door. So we let him. And while he's doing that, we find out all we can, because I don't trust him not to have something up his sleeve. Then we get Bakar, we give him the antidote. And then we tell the truth. All of it. We tell the councillors, we tell the story-tellers down in Bescan Square, we tell everyone. And let people decide for themselves."

"All of it? Even about Petri?" Dom said quietly. "Treason, Kass. Think about it."

She fixed him with a look, but he didn't flinch. "Yes, even about Petri. I think he's as much a victim of lies as everyone else. As manipulated. He just didn't have a tattoo on his back, that's all. Look at it this way," she said. "If we help Bakar regain power – and his right mind – we might get a pardon out of it and keep our heads. So might Petri. If we don't, we might as well start thinking about another country to live in, because Eneko will surely see us killed. And he'll find us. It may take him time, but he'll find us. You too, Dom."

"Well that's settled then." Dom stood up and dusted an imaginary speck of dirt off his coat. "So, where do we need to go? Is Bakar safe for now, do you think?"

"Oh, he'll want Bakar as safe and sane as can be for his trial and execution. And I know exactly where to look.

The only problem is going to be getting to it. Ah, Cospel, there you are."

"Yes, miss." Cospel limped up, out of breath and looking like he wanted to murder someone.

As the least recognisable of them, he didn't need to lurk in the shadows, and as always he'd gathered all the pertinent gossip.

"Bellows are going like the clappers down in Soot Town," he said. "Only in the one smithy though. No one goes in or out, except that a guildsman lets them. There's been some funny orders filled there lately – for the guild. Reckon Eneko's been planning this for weeks."

"Years," Kass said. "Sabates and the rest just sped things up for him. What else?"

Cospel shrugged. "Gates are still open. Towers aren't going; easy for anyone to walk in or out. Some people are watching though, up in the secret bits. Got a lot of guns."

"And Eneko?"

"Strutting around like cock of the bloody walk down near the main gate."

"Good. Then he won't be anywhere near the guild."

"And how exactly do you plan to get inside?" Dom asked. "I'm good with locks, but I'm not that good."

"No, but you and I are very recognisable, very wanted people. So, we're going to walk right up to the guild and cause a big fuss."

"That doesn't sound like the best plan ever."

"And here was me thinking you were the renowned Jokin, best duellist the guild has ever seen, unless you listen to Voch."

"Have you always been this stubborn? OK, yes. I am quite handy with a blade. But the guild's full of men and women like us, and I never fought all of them at once, Kass."

"And you won't now. Most of them are out in the crowd or down by the gate. The guild is the fallback position. Eneko is not expecting it to be attacked before the Ikarans get into the city."

Dom sighed. "Fine. After you."

Vocho stared up at the guild from the safety of the crowd in the square by what was left of the Clockwork God. That was where Kass would head, he was sure of it. The guild. Home.

"I could use magic to help us get in," Esti said.

"No magic. Except in emergencies." It was bad enough she'd talked him into letting her come with him, worse that he now wished he had eyes in the back of his head to keep watch on her. And the suspicions about Dom . . . he didn't like those one bit, but they had a ring of truth to them. He didn't trust Esti, but then again he was pretty much through trusting anyone. He wasn't even sure about Kass now, and having Esti with him took the edge off the empty space at his side. Besides, she could do dire things with her magic, and dire things might be required before the day was out.

The problem with trying to break into the guild was that it was a sodding fortress, Vocho thought but didn't say. *Think of the glory, Voch, think of that.* Well, yes, but he was finding that the thought of glory didn't have quite the same allure as it once had. Possibly because getting it seemed to involve him experiencing a lot of pain. Not getting executed, however, he could get right behind.

It was just starting to get light, turning the city into a grey ghost of fading shadows. The crowd had calmed. Guildsmen had walked among them, quietly reassuring, issuing orders from Eneko. All able-bodied men and women to congregate by the Clockwork God. Some of the clock-workers were separated out, taken off to do something mysterious that Vocho felt sure didn't bode well for the Ikaran army that the whispers said could now be seen from the city walls.

The streets around the Clockwork God were thronged but it wasn't hard to make their way through to the bridge spanning the river that separated the guild from the city. The guild was for the city, not of it, that had been drummed into him from the day he'd arrived. It stood sentinel, but it wasn't part of the city, its men and women a breed apart.

Walking over the bridge to the guild after so long away, after such an ignominious send-off, was a curious let-down. Still, he wouldn't be the person he was if he didn't add an extra bit of swagger to his walk. Even before they were halfway across a knot of men and women had assembled at the open gates. It didn't look like a welcome committee though, judging by the way they had their hands on their swords. That at least half had guns too was a shock – guns had been banned as unsporting and not becoming the guild. More of a shock was the fact that blood soaked the ground between the gates, and no one was even looking their way. There was a shout, and some of the guildsmen ran for the cloisters with swords drawn.

"What's going on?" Esti asked in a whisper.

"I suspect my sister has already been here. Ah, yes. See the wound on that man? She loves that move."

"Then we need to hurry."

"Style can never be rushed."

If they were going to do this insanity, they might as well do it properly. They strolled up to the gate like they owned the place, and Vocho swept off his hat with a mocking bow so that its – by now rather lacklustre – feather brushed the ground. It made his back sing with pain, but hells, that was the cost of panache.

Eneko's second in command, a stocky woman in her fifties who could eat most guildsmen for breakfast, looked them up and down as if they were joints of meat she was thinking of buying. Only with less enthusiasm.

"Hello, Mother," Vocho said with an inane grin he knew could be guaranteed to aggravate her. "Is this party for us? I'm touched."

"Touched in the head, more like," she replied and nodded to the four duellists behind her. Which was better odds than Vocho had been expecting. "Knew you'd be along after *she* turned up."

Mother came for him, flanked on each side by two men who Vocho knew to be solid, if a little unimaginative, duellists. It might take more than panache to get out of this. The two to her left didn't take much bar a few flourishes, a feint, a thrust they weren't expecting because it came from the wrong side. Solid they might be but they were no match for him. The two on her right were soon engulfed by twisting vines, leaving only Mother. Who would be a test all by herself – lightning quick and with years of experience in putting even the best students on their arses. She attacked with the sort of controlled vigour that explained her extended nickname of Holy Clockwork Mother of God, Help Me. Vocho was hard put to defend himself but managed it with his usual style – by the skin of his teeth.

He tried desperately to remember all the lessons she'd given him, the techniques she'd taught him – and the ones he'd learned later that she wouldn't know perhaps. All the ones he could think of were technically illegal in sparring, but then he figured he was no longer a duellist and they weren't sparring. A slash to the face that she danced away from, a kick to the groin that ended with him being flipped over and scrambling to get up before she skewered him. He had a longer reach, better weight, but she was so twisty it bent his brain. For a time it was all he could do to stop her dispatching him like he was a first-year student.

He was tiring. Though so was Mother, and Esti had dealt with her two and came to back him up. Mother's sword tip hovered between the two of them as she weighed her options. He feinted, lunged and turned that into another feint. Mother parried but picked the wrong feint. Vocho's sword slashed across her shoulder deep enough to hit bone. Hopefully not deep enough to kill her – she was a tyrant who'd ruled his childhood with a firm and often applied hand, but he was fairly sure she was a well-intentioned one.

Mother fell back against the door to the guardroom and the way was clear, at least for now. They'd kicked up a bit of a fuss, and more duellists were running across the courtyard towards the gate. Vocho had no intention of being there when they arrived.

He and Esti dived for the open doorway that led towards Eneko's rooms. Down stairs, up stairs, around twists and turns. Finally a stout doorway they could bar behind them, which they did and stopped to catch their breath.

"So far, so good," Vocho said. "Now what?"

"We head for Eneko's rooms." Kass said. "Where he kept all his little secrets. His little secrets are exactly what we need."

Dom nodded as though dimly remembering. "Lead on then."

Down more stairs, around more bends, through other

doors that they barred behind them until they came to a corridor Kass knew as well as any in the guild. Eneko's rooms lay on the left, and around the corner lay another stout door with a bar, the guild master's rooms being one of the most defensible places in a building that was a fortress to start with. Kass sent Cospel to drop the bar and keep an ear out for anyone trying to come that way.

Between Eneko's door and the bend was a blank expanse of stone wall.

"I bet you're going to tell me there's a secret room behind there, aren't you?" Dom said.

"A whole suite of rooms, in fact. When they built this place, it was for defence, and this was the last line. If the place got overrun, the king or emperor or whoever could hide in there."

She found the toggle, and there was a smooth whirr from the wall before part of it swung in, revealing a well-lit chamber beyond. Kass crossed the room to another door. She opened it and pulled up short.

"What?" Dom asked and went to look.

Kass had expected a bedroom or some sort of study. Not this.

The room had been stripped down to its walls, which held a dozen oil lamps that lit the place up like day. Kass wished they didn't. Against one wall a table groaned under the weight of various contraptions, some clockwork, some not, most of which she couldn't name. Or work out what they were for. She didn't want to know, either; they were crusted with blood and what looked very much like bits of skin.

Across from the table was a chair like the one in the barber's Vocho used — it tilted back so its occupant was half lying down. Only this one had straps on it, and more blood, more bits of skin. Next to it was a cold brazier with a knife balanced on top. Which explained the smell — burned flesh. Kass shuddered at the cold feeling that wormed its way up her spine, more so when she saw that knife was hers, her old stiletto.

She didn't recognise the thing on the chair for what it was at first. Just a clump of black hair tied with a dark ribbon, like many Reyes men sported. Only the colour of a ribbon and how it was tied were as distinctive as a man's nose, and this one, beneath its coating of dried blood, looked familiar. More than familiar. She remembered buying that ribbon down in the night market on a starlit evening that seemed very long ago as though it had happened to someone else.

Petri. God's cogs, what has he done to you?

Dom swore softly behind her. "What the hells is this? Kass? Kass?"

She was sitting on the floor with no memory of how she got there because her head was full of other memories, of days of laughing and nights full of whispered words, of sweat and want and wishing dawn would never come. Of a smoke-filled room when she'd made her choice, and so had he. Her skin prickled with cold, but her head felt hot and stuffy.

"Kass?" Dom had a hand under her arm and was pulling her up.

"Petri," she said through numb lips. "It was Petri in that chair."

It's too late now. It's been too late for me for a while. Almost the last words he'd said to her. *But I meant this.*

His ring seemed to burn on her finger, accusing her, and she couldn't breathe for the aching heat in her chest.

If it hadn't been for you, showing me, I'd never have joined Licio.

Would never have ended up here with his blood splashed over half the room. Dead. With that much blood – it was everywhere – he had to be. Petri was dead. That thought clanged inside her, cleared everything else out of her head but the need to find Eneko and kill him, right now. Right fucking now. Sod him being the best man to defend Reyes. Sod Reyes itself and what seemed good to her. Suddenly, being in the middle of a war about to happen seemed very good to her, because she was in the mood to kill every bastard who got in her way.

I wasn't lying when I said I loved you.

She took a deep breath which seemed to crack open something inside her and gripped her sword, reassuring in its solidity when everything else seemed vague and dreamlike. All this politics shit, all these devious manoeuvrings could go to hell. Swords she knew. Swords she could use.

A last look at the chair, at the crushed and bloody ribbon that had shattered her head – *Oh, Petri* – and she got herself in hand.

For the good of Reyes or not, Eneko was going to die tonight.

Chapter Twenty-three

It wasn't too hard in the end to find out where Kass was, and where she was, that was where Vocho needed to be. All they had to do was follow the trail of bleeding guildsmen. There were one or two tricky moments when some eager young pup recognised him and had a go at bringing him to justice, but nothing that Vocho the Great couldn't handle.

The barred door was more of a problem until Esti came up trumps.

"It's only wood, and wood is only dead tree. And I'm good with plants. Stand back a second."

She leaned into the wood as though listening to the complaint of its grain, the whirl of its knots. One hand ran across the wood lovingly and she shut her eyes. A faint rattling creak from the door. Vocho backed off a pace. Magic wasn't something to hang around in his experience. A twig wormed out from beside the lock, swelled and grew and twisted towards the faint light from a window. Another came, and another, until the door was a swaying mass of branches and leaves.

"I'm not sure—" he began, but an almighty crack stopped him. The door, or rather tree, twisted, revealing a very surprised Cospel on the other side, hanging on to what had probably once been a cudgel but was now a leafy branch.

"Ah, Cospel. There you are. I hope you weren't planning on braining me with that?"

Cospel stared at the branch, then dropped it. "Course not. Glad you're here." A twitch of a glance at Esti. "And not on your own, neither."

"Esti has some very important news. Where's Kass?"

"In there." He jerked his head back along the corridor. "Trying to find out what the old man is up to."

"Kass left you here to guard the door?"

A truculent nod.

"Well, perhaps you'd better, er, guard the tree then?"

Vocho hurried on, wondering what he'd find. Kass had complicated feelings about Eneko, he knew that, though his own were less so: he just hated the bastard. Esti followed, muttering under her breath. They reached a spot where the wall was hinged open, turned into the chamber beyond and hurried across to an open doorway.

The smell coming through the doorway was disturbing, but no more disturbing than many another smell even if it was familiar. The sight of Kass stopped Vocho dead. Oh, he'd seen her angry before – sometimes it seemed like her natural state – but this was something else. Her glare felt like it could melt flesh at twenty paces.

He shifted awkwardly, more to deflect that look from him than anything else, because he was afraid of it. She was stubborn, and he could live with that or coax her out of it. But the look in her eyes now – of utter grief and burning hatred – there'd be no coaxing her out of that.

She'd told him once she was sick of killing, but the look in her eyes told him she might make an exception, just this once.

A sound behind Vocho made him whirl, sword out and at the ready. He was completely unprepared to see Eneko, who took in the room in a glance and then focused on Kass. As he always had. Vocho had the wildest urge to do something, show him what he'd missed by overlooking him, but stayed his hand. Now was possibly not the time. Mainly because suddenly Eneko looked old. He'd always been older, of course, his hair sprinkled with grey even when Vocho first met him, and that had been almost two decades ago. But until recently Eneko had still seemed strong, vital, dangerous. Now he had old man's hands, lined and studded with prominent blue veins, shaking slightly. His hair was shot through with great bands of white. His eyes were pouched, his skin sallow. He looked like a man who'd suffered much in a short space of time.

"Kass," he said now, his voice the tremulous tones of an old man. "Kass, I did it for you. He took you from me, filled your head with lies, betrayed you. He betrayed us all. I needed what he knew, I admit. But I did it for you."

Did what?

Kass flinched back at these words, seemed bewildered, then her whole body clenched as though it was only by a great effort she didn't kill Eneko where he stood. "Not for me," she ground out through gritted teeth. "For yourself. Always for yourself, everything you've ever done. Oh, you like to pretend it's for the greater good, but we know, don't we, that it's always all about you."

Eneko laughed at that, a vicious rasping sound that made Vocho's shoulders twitch. "If only that were so. But it's true, no matter what you tell yourself: I did it for you.

And yes maybe for me as well. But Petri's not the only reason you're in Reyes, is he? I hear tell of an antidote of some kind."

Vocho shot a look at Esti but she shook her head. Instead, it was Dom who spoke.

"And here it is." He pulled a familiar-looking bottle from an inside pocket. "For you."

"Dom, what are you . . ." Kass said, but he silenced her with a look that Vocho couldn't interpret. Esti moaned behind them.

Eneko reached out for it, but Dom kept hold of the bottle. "You keep your end of the bargain. Tell her, *us*. That's all it would take, maybe. Licio and Orgull have other magicians, but it's Alicia with the power, and you have the means to stop her if you tell me, her, what we want to know. If you'd told Alicia or me, things might never have come to this."

Eneko snorted derisively. "Are you still harping on about that? Almost twenty years ago, and you won't let it go. Give that bottle to me, and I'll tell you."

Esti gave Vocho a "Told you" look.

Dom looked long and hard at Eneko and finally handed over the bottle.

Eneko gloated over it. "Yes, I heard about this, Kass. I heard about a lot of things. Takes a long time to brew, I'm told. It won't be getting to Bakar, at any rate. Shall we see what it does? You told me such marvellous things about it, Dom. Even I've heard of Esti and her renowned concoctions."

Before Vocho or any of them could do a thing, he'd ripped the stopper from the bottle and downed the contents, smacking his lips as it slid down.

Vocho heard Esti whisper behind him, "No, oh no! I'm too close!

"I really did do it for you, Kass," Eneko said. "Petri betrayed you, didn't he? Lied to you, used you, and you're still too blind to see it. Well, I removed the blinkers from your eyes. And now Dom has betrayed you too. Everyone betrays. Everyone. That's my last and best lesson for you."

Kass lunged for him with a snarl, but Dom caught her, pulled her off balance. She whirled on him with an elbow, smacked him in the side of the head and spun back towards Eneko with a savage look that twisted her face out of all recognition. Sword up and ready, tongue between her teeth.

"Don't try it, girl. Even now you'd struggle to beat me."

Dom whispered something to her, and she subsided.

"Tell me, and maybe we can end this and concentrate on saving the city," Dom said.

Eneko laughed. "Stupid boy. I don't know where your daughter is. I did once, but that was a long time ago. She could be anywhere by now."

Then it was Kass holding back Dom, her gaze pinned to Eneko as the antidote got to work.

A sheen of sweat popped out on his forehead, and his mouth worked but nothing came out. He staggered back a pace, recovered and fell to his arse with a thump. The bottle smashed on the floor. Vocho and Dom shared a glance, confusion on Vocho's part, some unnameable emotion on Dom's.

Behind them Esti moaned in pain.

"She . . ." Eneko said, all he seemed able to say, though his eyes were on Esti.

"She's a world-class poisoner," Dom said. "Not always in the way you expect. And Eneko trusted what I told him about it, before I went to Ikaras. Why wouldn't he? He thought he held all the cards I wanted."

Eneko was going a funny colour. He raised a shaking

hand in front of his face and screamed at what he saw —
his fingers writhed like vines, their tips a vivid green. His
boots burst open and more vines wriggled out into the
open. Eneko's breath became strangled, great heaving gasps
past whatever was happening in his throat. Vocho took a
step forward and hesitated. What could he do? And did
he want to?

Similar things were happening to Esti, until the whole
room seemed green and the scent of earth and leaf mould
stung Vocho's nostrils. Kass swore viciously and went for
Eneko, but again Dom caught at her and had her this time.
She elbowed and kicked and bit and used every crafty
trick she knew, but he held on, just, whispering in her
ear until all the fight went from her.

The masses of vines reached out to each other, grabbed
hold and drew the two writhing bodies together, enveloping
them in greenery, then began to retract. One body reap-
peared but only one. The vivid green faded from Eneko's
skin and he blinked as though the past few minutes had
been some kind of vile nightmare. Then he looked up at
them and smiled, only it wasn't his smile. It was the cheerful
and good-natured grin of Esti.

At which point a great clamour arose in the distance,
coupled with a faint boom which might have been something slamming into the walls. The Ikaran army was here.

Chapter Twenty-four

Alicia sat in a tent pitched on the top of a small hill where she could see Reyes laid out before her. On a table sat vials and pots of Sabates' blood, a mound of paper, bundles of brushes. Orgull waved another unit in front of her – a sorry lot, farmers, weavers, men who ran stills making rum. Poorly armed, barely disciplined enough to stand in a straight line. Not a soldier among them except for the officer. But they were going to have to do, and she had the means to make them a force to be reckoned with.

She poured a measure of blood into a clay pot in front of her. No longer fresh, it had the reek of festering scabs about it, but it hadn't dried so still kept all its potency. A clean sheet of paper, a new brush, and she set to work. It didn't take long – she'd worked out the method a long time ago, against such a day. When she was done she beckoned the officer forward.

"Ma'am?"

He was very young, she thought. Still keen, but with a terror about him as he stood in front of her and Gerlar.

She wasn't sure who scared the poor boy more, and found that thought pleasing.

"Take this," she said and gave the paper for Gerlar to pass over. "Be careful with it. You've been instructed as to the proper method of implementing it?"

He took the paper as though it was, and very poisonous, snake. "Yes, ma'am. I'm to say——"

Gerlar's hand hard on his arm and a warning growl shut him up.

"Get your men close to the walls and then use it. You'll find things much easier then."

"What does it, er, I mean, ma'am, what can I expect?"

She cocked her head at him, and his voicebox bobbed up and down in utter panic, but he didn't back away.

"You can expect your men to become fearless. You can expect to find great joy in battle and a fierce lust to kill all who stand in your way. You can expect to *win*. This is not my only magic for the day."

His shoulders slumped and he sagged like a balloon with a leak as the terror abated somewhat. "Thank you, ma'am."

He marched smartly back to his men, ordering them away to the front of the line.

"How much of that is true?" Gerlar asked in his growling voice.

She looked up sideways at him. He had his uses, but she could push him only so far, she knew that. Especially when Ikaran men were involved. Duty, obedience, servitude, those were his watchwords, and while he'd lost all honour when he'd not died with his partner, he sought ever to get it back, not tarnish himself still further with lies or manipulations.

"All of it is true," she said. "When he says the word,

those men will become like you. In a way. Not experts, not good with weapons, but they will be unstoppable."

She smiled inwardly at his confused grunt. "Here, let me show you."

They walked a short distance to the top of the hill from where Licio and Orgull were directing the army. It spread out like some weird growth on the plain, darkening it with people.

"I think we're ready," Licio said hesitantly. "Are you sure—"

"Positive, your highness. Gerlar, fetch a signaller."

A signaller duly arrived, a young lad with a pair of flags and a bugle.

"Signal the first unit to use its paper," Alicia told him.

A quick burst of flag-waving, a return wave of a flag, a short delay and then an intense flash of light.

"Is that it?" Licio said. "I expected something a bit more dramatic."

"Just wait, your highness."

They didn't have to wait long. After a minute or two a man broke from the line and rushed towards the city walls, then another. Then a half-dozen all shouting so loudly Alicia could hear them even at this distance, a blaring wordless wailing. And then the whole regiment went, waving their weapons, screaming mindlessly. They fell on the main gate like a storm-driven wave.

Dim figures moved across the tops of the walls, flitting between crenellations.

"Archers. Or gunmen." Gerlar's scowl threatened to engulf his whole face. "Our men will be—"

The faint crackle of gunfire sounded, but the Ikarans didn't stop. Alicia saw one atop the gate arch clearly take a shot to the stomach before he leaped at the man who'd fired at him, thrust him from the walls before he dived into the knot of men behind him with a wild yell.

Licio watched through an eyeglass with a growing smile, as did Orgull, although his smile was rather smugger. "And you've given this to all the regiments? Signaller, send in the next!" Orgull said.

"All except the life-warriors, your highness. They need no bravery from magic. And we also have this."

She drew a paper from her copious sleeve and carefully unfolded it. Dark, decaying blood glistened on its surface, and Licio's face grew pained.

"Is that Sabates' blood?"

"Oh yes. I'm sure he would approve, your highness."

"Well, perhaps. What does it do?" He leaned towards it, but one upraised hand from her stopped him.

"Oh, now this, this may well be what wins you your city back."

Persuasion, that was what blood magic was all about, when you got right down to it. Most magicians could persuade people; some could persuade animals; Esti could work miracles with plants. But Sabates had discovered, and hinted to Alicia, that sometimes even the elements themselves could be persuaded with enough of the right sort of blood. And this was exactly the right sort of blood. *I don't suppose you ever expected it to be yours, did you, you old bastard?*

The traceries of the design were hair thin, delicate as angels, deadly as demons. Alicia half thought she could see them squirm on the page, waiting to be used. She leaned over, breathed a word on them and shut her eyes. Above the faint yells as more and more regiments raced towards the city, each soldier full of the desperate need to kill anyone in their way, came a great rushing sound followed by a hollow boom.

Licio cheered and clapped his hands, and even the under-stated Orgull gasped. She opened her eyes and looked out over the city. In particular towards the guild, whose imposing battlements were just visible above the city walls. A great gaping hole had appeared in those battlements. Orgull gave her a sidelong look as though reassessing her. Sabates had never done anything half so impressive, at least not anything Orgull knew about.

"Have you got more of those?"

"Only Sabates' blood will work for this spell. But perhaps a dozen more."

"And blood for the soldiers?"

"Oh, any blood will do for that."

"Excellent." Orgull nodded to one of the life-warriors standing beside him, who promptly took three steps forward and slit Licio's throat. "Get a bowl for that, someone, would you? The lady here needs blood."

Licio dropped to his knees, fruitlessly scrabbling at his throat as he tried to breathe. Blood coursed down his fine tunic and into the grass before one of the signallers, ashen faced and shaking, got a bowl under the wound while the life-warrior held the rapidly weakening king. Finally, with a last despairing gasp and a twitching kick, Licio died.

"Not a moment too soon," Orgull said. "He was beginning to get on my nerves. Now, is that enough blood for you?"

A message. No one was so important they couldn't die if Orgull willed it.

Alicia and the king stared at each other, neither willing to break first, but a twitch of her hand on the parchment, a nod of her head to the chaos behind her in Reyes, and he looked away. There would be a battle of wills later, but for now they would take the city and leave that for after-wards.

"Certainly," she said. "What would you like me to target first?"

An uncertain smile form Orgull. "I never liked the palace. Wait, no. That stupid Clockwork God of theirs. Start there."

That suited her very well.

She dipped the paintbrush into the bowl of blood and began.

Kass turned back from the window and what was happening outside. A huge section of the arch over the gates had fallen, leaving rubble and dust and injured guildsmen scattered over the courtyard. Beyond, she could hear the faint yells and gunshots of a furious encounter down by the main city gate.

What greeted her when she turned was little better: Eneko, only he wasn't Eneko any more. Or not exactly. She should have felt something about that, some grim satisfaction that he'd got no more than he deserved, but while there might have been a twinge, it was overshadowed by too much else. Besides, she'd wanted to skewer the bastard and watch him bleed to death.

Dom and Voch had strapped him to the chair, and he'd lost the pale green shade across his skin, but there was still something . . . odd about him, and not just because it looked like Esti's eyes were peering out of his face, or that his fingers still looped and writhed like vines. The voice too, as he tried to reason with them, was odd. Eneko's rough accent and Esti's smoother Ikaran-tinted tones mixed together.

The fingers twisted in ways no one's ever should, and then the straps were open, and Eneko stood, swaying slightly. "You can't hold me," s/he said. "But I can help you."

Dom and Voch both drew their swords, and Kass had a hand on hers, but it stayed in its scabbard, for now.

"You keep saying that," she said. "But what help have you actually been? You took off Voch's tattoo but left him hooked on your jollop or in pain. Poisoned him with it."

"Not poisoned," s/he said. "It was the only way to deal with the remnants of the tattoo. Dom told you that, didn't he? He wanted that antidote, to give to Eneko. You've more reason to distrust him than me."

Kass glanced at Dom.

"Never trust anyone, Kass," Dom said. "Not even me. We all have our own dreams and desires, and Eneko had – has – what I want. I had no intention of it hurting you or Voch, if that's any consolation, and that jollop might well have been poison. How many people have you poisoned now, Esti? Twelve? Fourteen?"

"Three. Under duress from Sabates. I gave you the antidote, and it would have worked too. I only wanted Sabates to stop forcing me to work for him, to get back at Alicia."

Kass spared a look at Voch, who just shrugged like he had no idea what the hells was going on. She knew that feeling. It felt like the whole world was a rug that had been pulled from under her.

"Maybe that's true, and maybe it isn't, and it doesn't matter for now. Let's start with what we can see, what we need to know," Kass said in the end. "Esti, you start with what the hells you've done to Eneko. Truthfully this time."

S/he laughed at that, and Kass couldn't hear either of them in it. "No time now. Not if you want Reyes to survive. You need me."

Outside, another resounding crash, a series of screams, the grinding sound of metal under stress. She didn't need to look to know where it came from – the Clockwork God.

Further away, the sounds of fighting grew louder, the shouts in Ikaran more distinct.

"She's using magic," Esti said. "Making farmers into warriors. Sabates wanted the destruction of Bakar for his own revenge, but Alicia is far worse. She's got a husband to kill and a child to find and then Eneko to kill too. Her daughter, that's what she wants most, as no doubt Dom has told you. This body here − Eneko − he's the only one who knows where that child is. Part of why she made me . . . Alicia's coming and she'll kill anyone in her way. Unless you let me help. Actually . . ." Eneko began to vibrate, fingers twisting over one another, eyes rolling. An arm shot out, longer than a horse for a few seconds, and smacked Kass to the ground before it withdrew. "Actually I think you've done me a favour, Dom. I didn't realise how strong it would be if I was too close . . . Stronger than Alicia. I also think you'll find you can't stop me."

With that, vines shot out from all over Eneko's body, knocking them all breathless to the stone floor, and scrambled out of the window.

"What the everloving . . ." Vocho mumbled as he climbed to his feet.

"I don't know," Kass said. "But I think if we're ever to call ourselves Reyens again, we need to get down to the main gate."

Outside the shattered guild gates the streets were a maelstrom of panic, so that movement was impossible. They found Cospel lurking before they took to the rooftops, where it was at least quiet if not empty. Guildsmen flitted to and fro ahead and behind, all moving with purpose according to whatever Eneko's plan had been.

Whatever that plan had been, it was likely up in smoke

now. As they neared the main gate, panic became outright terror. Reyens flung down their weapons and ran, or more sensibly kept hold of them and ran. The shouts and yells had grown steadily louder until now they were deafening. Men poured through the gate – wild eyed, snarling – shouting in Ikaran that Kass could barely understand. Only one word stood out – blood. They'd come for blood. They were finding plenty too.

A phalanx of guildsmen stood between them and that blood lust, protecting the city. A few of the hardier citizens stood with them: one man armed with a blacksmith's hammer that dripped with the blood of the men who lay at his feet in crumpled, broken heaps, a woman with more than a dozen guns, a younger one next to her frantically reloading, winding, as her sister took shot after shot.

The Ikarans were dying by the score, but they didn't seem to care. If it had been only between soldiers, Kass thought, men and women who knew what warfare was about, Reyes would have had the upper hand. Ikaras had its life-warriors, but not many. Maybe only four dozen, for all they were fearsome. Reyes had its guildsmen, maybe half a thousand in total. The farmers, merchants, weavers, clockers on both sides, who knew nothing of fighting, of taking a man's life, didn't count for much more than sheer weight of numbers. It was the trained men and women, those who'd fought before and knew whether they had the mettle for it, knew they could do what needed to be done, who would tell.

Or would have done, if not for the transformation of the Ikarans from an ineffective rabble into a shrieking mass of would-be murderers and cut-throats. They poured through the gate with none of the hesitation Kacha would have expected, with no pause between seeing a Reyen and flying at them with savage strokes of their swords, wild

shots from their guns. The man with the blacksmith's
hammer fell to a bullet in the head; a guildsman fell gurgling
blood from a sword wound to the throat, a random thrust
from the baying mob that surrounded him.

No matter how untrained they were, with enough of
them Reyes would fall.

Kacha was just about to jump down anyway when Eneko
came striding along the street towards the gates. A long
thin tendril sneaked out of one sleeve and dipped itself in
the copious amounts of blood that splashed the flagstones.
He grinned in an entirely un-Eneko way and flicked his
hands up.

For all Reyes was a city of clockwork, of steel and stone,
there were plants everywhere: trees shading narrow alleys,
planters outside doors with bright flowers, blades of grass
between flagstones, weeds and even small bushes growing
on roofs or from cracks in walls. Now these plants rose up
like soldiers themselves. A great tree bent down and swept
a cohort of screaming Ikarans into the sky, for them to fall
like bleeding rain among the roofs. Grass twisted up, grabbing ankles, bringing down more attackers, to be finished
off by surprised guildsmen who nonetheless knew an
opportunity when they saw one. A flowering vine on a
wall grew and twisted and grew some more until it was
ten times the size and tendrils swept up to choke Ikarans'
screams from their throats.

"I'm still pissed at her about the whole tattoo thing, but
holy hells!" Vocho said.

Kass looked over towards the gates. "We're not in the
clear yet. And she's got to want something for this."

"Let's worry about that later," Dom said. "She's helping,
that's the important bit. Now, how about we try to save
this city?"

Kass shook her head, not to refuse but because that wasn't the only reason she was here. But killing Eneko – if he still was Eneko – was going to have to wait. "Over by the gates," she said.

"Just what I was thinking," Dom replied and they were off, darting along secret paths, ducking behind chimneys. An Ikaran came screaming for them, mouth foaming with blood, but Vocho put a shoulder to him and turfed him over the side.

Then they were in the thick of it with no time to think, no time to see anything but the enemy in front of them, behind, everywhere. The Ikarans didn't fight like people, but like clockwork that bled and they were mindless, heedless of any danger to themselves, wanting only to hack and slash and kill.

Kass dropped onto a wall where six guildsmen were under attack from dozens of Ikarans. One guildsman looked up at her, surprised as he recognised her perhaps, but a brief nod told her that while she might be exiled, might be under threat of execution, no one was bothered right this second. She waded in but was soon engulfed, and was glad of Vocho at her back.

After that time became a blur of swords, of sweat and blood and sharp words called in warning or hatred. Her arms grew numb with weariness, her face and back slicked with sweat, her sword and dagger cloaked in blood, and still the Ikarans came on.

Some unknown time later she had a moment to catch her breath and she and Vocho were leaning against each other's backs. She swiped sweat from her face and looked out over the city wall.

"What the fuck?" Voch echoed her thoughts.

Hordes of Ikarans still blackened the plain, though they

were fewer now. That wasn't what caught their attention. Eneko, or what passed for him, stood in a wide, clear circle. One arm, longer and more pliable than any man's should be, sought about for blood. In front of him . . . She didn't know what was in front of him. Great green pods, they looked like, with gaping slits along one side. It was only when one shot forward and snapped at some hapless Ikaran who got too close, cutting him in half, that she began to understand. So did the Ikarans — some still ran towards Eneko like mindless automatons, screaming for blood, but more hung back.

Further away, on a hill, stood a number of tents that looked familiar. The Ikaran king, Licio no doubt and Alicia. A blast of wind howled down from the hill, tore across the plain in front of the city, not caring that it blasted Ikaran soldiers from their feet, and threw them up to scatter like petals across the dusty plain before it reached Eneko, staggering him.

"Do you know," Voch said in a voice beyond tired, "I never thought I'd be in a battle between two magicians. Can't say I'm enjoying it very much. Maybe we could just leave them to it and have a beer or something until they've finished."

"Voch," she began but was struck dumb as another pod leaped at some Ikarans, caught them in its jaws but was then swept away by the wind. Blood and greenish sap splattered into the dust. This was not the sort of battle she was used to either. "Yeah, I wish."

Dom staggered up, Cospel in tow, and Kass wondered just how smug Voch would be at the sight of him — not pristine now. Dust and blood spattered his fine tunic, and there was a rip in one sleeve. He'd lost his hat and the ribbon in his hair, which now danced around him in sweaty tangles. Kass thought she'd never seen him look finer as he slumped against the wall.

"What the fuck?"

"That's what I said," Vocho muttered.

"At least we might get a breather," Kass said. "No Ikarans are getting past him. Her. Whatever."

It looked like they might get that breather too. Everyone had stilled to watch the two magicians – waiting to see who would come out ahead, no doubt. No one was trying to kill her at the moment, and that was about all Kass cared about. So when Cospel dug out a water bottle they all took the chance to drink. The guildsmen alongside them did the same – practical to a man. In a fight you took what you could because you never knew when you might get any more. There were one or two odd looks, a few whispers, but none of the duellists said a word to Vocho or Kass and only looked curiously at Dom. That might change later, but they'd all have to survive first.

Dom swilled water around his mouth, spat and then swallowed the next mouthful. "It seems to me that in a battle like this our talents are wasted. We can't defend against Cee – I mean Alicia – they can't attack against whatever Eneko is now. It's down to those two."

Kass took a swallow of water and poured some over her head. "So what do you suggest?"

"I think a nice rest is just what we need," Vocho said. He was sweatier than the fighting warranted, and his face seemed pinched. He was hardly likely to admit it, but things were starting to tell on him. "When it all kicks off again, we'll be fresh as daisies. Which one do you think will win?"

Dom shrugged and frowned out towards the hill where Alicia stood, faint in the distance but unmistakable. "I have no idea. But whichever it is, Reyes isn't safe."

Kacha leaned forward. The same thought had occurred to her. "So?"

"I'm not sure, really. Only . . . only we need to be careful. What do we want the outcome to be?"

"Still alive at the end of it seems sensible," Vocho said.

"Reyes in one piece," was Kass's effort.

A smile from Dom. "Both of those seem admirable. But if either of those two wins, we're still in trouble. Alicia wants – hells, I have no idea – but getting Eneko would be top of the list. He has information she wants. That I want too, as it happens. He said he didn't know but . . . And once she's got it, do we think she'll just let Reyes off the hook? Esti, what do we think she wants?"

"Alicia?"

"I think it likely. Reyes is just a means to an end for her, for both of them. We are disposable. And whatever Eneko's plan was doesn't seem to have been put into effect. So what do we do?"

Kass looked over at the guildsmen. "I think . . ." she said slowly, working it out as she spoke. "I think that Reyes will turn on Eneko, whether he wins down there or not. He's a magician, at least he is now. Reyes fought a bloody revolution to be rid of magicians and their puppet king. They aren't going to take kindly to having one in charge, no matter what Eneko said before Esti got to him. But I think you're wrong on one point. Esti gave us that antidote to give to Bakar, not Eneko. She intended to do this to him. Why?"

"I have no idea. I agree though that she'll be less than welcome in Reyes, no matter whose body she's wearing. And Reyes killed magicians before. It can do it again."

Kass stood up and looked behind her, to the square behind the gates, further along the streets. "Reyes needs someone to follow, some*thing* perhaps, which is what Eneko used. He had the guild as his edge. Bakar had one of the first guns, and that tipped his hand before. That, and people *wanted* to follow him. A way with words, and people."

"When he was sane, you mean?"

She waved a hand dismissively. "Of course when he was sane. We need something like that gun, and I think we need him, with his mind back. Someone familiar to lead, that's what Reyes will want, at least for now."

Dom stood up. "What are you thinking?"

"I'm thinking that Eneko had a plan, and it was probably a good one. Why else would he have left the gates open? To draw the Ikarans in for . . . something. He had smiths and clockers working all hours down in Soot Town. He's got something down there, something he planned to use once the Ikarans got inside, something we can use."

"And Bakar? We've no antidote."

"No, but Esti said the poison only works if he's in prolonged contact with it. Wherever they've put him, and I'm betting the Shrive, he hasn't been getting his daily dose, so perhaps it's starting to wear off. She said something else too. Sugar. Something about sugar being a cure. I know she was lying about a lot of things, but I think there was truth mixed up in there, which is why it all seemed so plausible."

Dom leaned against the wall, and Kass watched him as thoughts ran behind his eyes like cogs spinning.

Finally he cocked an eyebrow her way. "We'll need to split up. We can't do it all in time otherwise."

"Do what?" Vocho said. "I mean, whatever it is, I'm happy to help because it beats sitting here watching two magicians slug it out, but I like to know what I'm getting into."

"Winning, Voch," Dom said. "That's what we're doing. That's what we always like to do, isn't it?"

It seemed to take for ever before they had it hammered out, and Vocho was starting to wish he'd never listened. His bones ached, his back felt like it was going to explode, and all the magic out on the plain was making his teeth itch. He would rather have died than admit it though.

In the end they had a plan, of sorts. Dom had even roped in the guildsmen, who kept on giving Kass and Voch the evil eye. Cospel and Kass would go down to Soot Town, to where Cospel had seen all the smiths and clockworkers taken before. Dom and Vocho were going to find some sugar and try to break into the Shrive. Because that's what you did, wasn't it, when confronted with a couple of magicians trying to blow each other up and you had a price on your head? You broke into the prison they'd put you in if they caught you.

"Oh, good," Vocho had said when they decided this part. "For a minute there I thought you were going to get me to do something stupid." He paused. "Are you out of your tiny little minds?"

"Got any better ideas?"

No, he hadn't.

However, being the first person ever to break *into* the Shrive, well, that had an appeal.

Dom was deep in conversation with the guildsmen, giving them a brief and not especially truthful outline of what was going on and enlisting their help. They were to try to keep this area secure so that the others had somewhere to aim for if they survived. Meanwhile, out on the plain Alicia had knocked Eneko flat and was now lifting him up in a whirlwind, only to drop him, and . . . and he was gone. Ikarans ran to and fro, looking for him, but he was nowhere. Biding his time, no doubt, but it left Alicia free to concentrate on the city again.

Cospel checked his pack and looked pretty woeful. Kass just looked pensive. Vocho caught her staring wistfully towards the palace. Her hand crept inside her tunic, and Vocho had a sudden pang for her, and what Dom had whispered to him quickly when she couldn't hear, about who Eneko had been torturing, killing, in that cog's awful room. Vocho might loathe the very name of Petri Egimont, but he didn't want the bastard dead. Well, mostly. For Kass's sake.

"He might be alive," he said now. "Probably is, even."

Kass started and shot him a look. "You think so?"

"Even I have to admit he's a tough bastard, Kass. I think so."

"Voch, your left eye is twitching." The smile was wan and strained. "But thanks anyway."

"Time to go," he said to that. "Meet us back here as soon as you can, and try not to die, OK?"

This smile was better. "I'll do my best. You too. And stay out of trouble!"

"Yes, Kass."

There was a whole host of other things he could have said, wanted to say even, but now, in front of everyone, wasn't the time. Then Dom was prodding him on, and they dropped over a parapet and onto one of the secret pathways, and Kass was lost to view.

"Where are we going to get sugar?" Vocho asked after a while, because they seemed to be heading for King's Row. Not known for its grocer's shops. "I mean, lack of sugar was one of the reasons everyone was getting so antsy before we left. And it's not like it grows on trees. Not here at any rate."

Dom paused halfway around a cupola.

"I'm still thinking about that. Bakar first, because I suspect he'll prove trickier."

Vocho slipped on a roof tile and just about caught himself on a chimney before he slid off into the void. One last turn around a circular roof, and the Shrive came into view. They dropped down onto the street.

"So, Dom, just as a matter of interest, how are you planning to break into the Shrive? I mean it's not like it's easy to break out of, is it? And don't suggest getting arrested. I think the guards have other things on their minds today."

"Something will come to me, I'm sure."

"Very reassuring."

They lurked at the edge of the square in front of the Shrive and watched. Behind them the sounds of fighting drifted over the rooftops, an eerie counterpoint to the silence within the city, only broken by the peal of chimes as all the clocks struck the hour. A half-dozen guards came out and climbed some stairs set into a wall beside the square, then shaded their eyes as they strained to see what was happening outside the city. They were close enough, the city quiet enough once the chimes died down, that Vocho could hear snatches of their conversation.

"And I say screw the inmates. We leg it down to the docks. There's still a few ships there. We can blag our way onto one, if we're quick, because mark my words we won't be the only ones thinking of it."

"Aye, and the Ikarans will have thought of it too, be sure of that. Got ships all over, lurking, so I heard in the pub last night. Not fired a shot yet, but they will. I'd rather take my chances here. Can't swim, see. Rather be shot than drown."

"I'd rather take my chances drowning than see magicians

in the city again," one of the older guards said. "I remember what they was like from afore. People going missing, all so as they can have their blood, and thrown away like yesterday's news when they were done. People having their heads chopped off for saying anything about it. Bakar was mad, right enough, but even then he weren't as bad as the magicians. Not by the longest shot there is. Now here's Eneko becoming a magician without so much as a by your leave."

The conversation went on, but it was clear the guards were in two camps – stay or run. The runners seemed to be more numerous. Then a blast of something, the Clockwork God only knew what exactly, rocked their feet under them as the whole city shook. Drops splattered on Vocho's hand, making him wonder how it could rain from a clear sky, before he saw what the drops were. Not just drops now, a deluge. Blood ran over the cobbles like rivers, seeped between cracks, made lakes in the square and bubbled in gratings. Then, almost as soon as it had started, the bloody rain stopped.

Not before the screams rang out, along with the shouts, the exhortations to run, the sounds of men and women gagging. Vocho very nearly lost his meagre lunch himself. The guards fled from the wall, drenched in blood, and not all of them headed for the safety of the Shrive. At least half made for the docks and the lure of the sea.

In the chaos no one remembered to close the door of the Shrive.

Vocho needed absolutely no encouragement to leave the bloody square. He and Dom headed for the open door. They only just made it before the sizzling started. The blood on his hands grew warm, then hot. He frantically tried to wipe it off with a sleeve that was itself soaked with blood, before he gave up and ripped the tunic off. It steamed where it landed and then burst into flames.

The pair of them stamped on their tunics to put out the flames and gave each other a look.

"We need to be quick," Dom said. "Come on."

Guards ran to and fro inside, some clearly panicked, some more stoical. Many of the guards lived inside the Shrive with their spouses and children. More than one was packing his family up to take them to the docks. No one paid them the least attention.

"Where?" Vocho asked.

"Could be anywhere! But Eneko has a twisted sense of humour. I know where we'll look first – the cell Bakar escaped from before."

"You know where it is?"

"I've an inkling."

They sped down corridors crowded with people and on into others that were echoingly empty apart from the cries of the prisoners trapped behind their cell doors.

Chapter Twenty-five

Petri woke to a gentle shake and sat bolt upright, bringing a lance of pain to his eye socket that dragged a groan from between clenched teeth. He blinked hard and tried to make sense of his surroundings, work out where he was. Who he was.

Dark again, but not so dark he couldn't see anything. A faint light outlined a room far larger than he'd been used to. The air didn't feel right for him to be back in his last cell. Besides, someone had shaken his shoulder.

"Petri?" A gentle voice, one he'd known well for many years until it had twisted into madness. "Petri, is that you?"

He lay back down again and shut his eye, trying not to imagine Eneko's delight at this final torment.

"Petri, it is you, isn't it? I always said I'd know you with my eyes shut," Bakar said. "Or maybe you're part of this odd dream. Yes, maybe. So strange, but the colours are very pretty. I dreamed I went quite insane, you know. Or maybe I'm dreaming that I'm not. It's all so hard to tell. Petri?" Bakar's voice broke on that last. "Petri, please say something so I know I'm not imagining you."

He thought of saying nothing — what could he say to the man he'd betrayed as surely as with a blade in the back? But there was a glimmer there of the man he'd once known, before madness had eaten away at him. Before madness had eaten them both perhaps, because Petri couldn't be sure he was still sane.

"You're not imagining me." He struggled to sit up and was rewarded with a shaft of pain so fierce it robbed him of breath.

"Clockwork God be praised!"

And that was enough to snap the slender thread that kept this Petri linked to the old one, who'd dreamed of being noble and good. "Fuck the Clockwork God!"

A shocked silence followed, but Petri was past caring — about Bakar, treason, the Clockwork God and what was good for Reyes. Even Kass. He didn't care about any of them or what they thought of him, because caring would hurt worse than his ruined hand.

"Petri, I—"

"Shut up!" A strip of light bled under the door and down its hinge. Petri moved across it, and Bakar flinched back at the sight, trembling. The sour stench of sweat filled the cell. Petri wondered if Bakar was still mad, took a look into the watery eyes that darted everywhere, and knew the answer was yes. "The Clockwork fucking God had me end up like this. The only comfort is truth, you say. Well here's some truth for you. I plotted your downfall because I wanted, very badly, to be out of that palace, away from the rails you and your god put me on. Everything mapped out, my whole life, and why? Because you said so, no more. Well, I wanted to be alive, not clacking along like an automaton. I wanted what you promised and never gave, that's all, and then I ended up like this. I never wanted you harmed before, but I do now. Right now I would happily kill you."

In the dim light he could just make out the pale blur of Bakar's face, the trembling hands raised to his slack mouth, the shock and disgust and pity there. That would be how everyone looked at him now. Even Kass . . . Even Kass. He was a ruin and wanted to take it out on whoever came to hand.

"I only ever wanted this city to be fair, equal," Bakar whispered. "You know that, Petri."

A brief pang at that, soon squashed. "Fair? You call this fair? You call all you've done in this city, all you've done to make the poor poorer, taxing them into starvation while the clockers have ended up richer and more debauched than the old nobles ever were. Giving them an imaginary god to believe in, reading their prayers. You call that fair, Bakar? How about keeping me chained to your side, never letting me even breathe? Eneko was right about one thing: life isn't fair. And your precious clockwork universe is a crock of shit."

"How dare you! Guards!"

"Your guards won't save you now. Don't you know where we are? Do you think we're still in your palace? We're in the place you spent all that time before, the place you said would never be used again, until it was, until you started sending people here to die. The Shrive, Bakar. That's where you are. You got out before, but you had your sanity then. I'd be surprised if you could find your way out of your own shirt now."

Bakar scrabbled about on the floor, digging his fingers in between the flagstones, sending tufts of rotten straw every which way. He muttered under his breath and every few seconds looked up at Petri with his mad watery gaze before he went back to scrabbling.

Petri got as comfortable as he could against the wall and shut his eye. The muttering grew louder, and stranger. Petticoats and periwinkles, flags and taxes. Bakar suddenly stopped and Petri opened his eye. For a brief second Bakar looked utterly sane, then the mouth slackened again, and he launched himself at Petri, his hands surprisingly strong as they reached his throat.

Petri had been strong once, but not any more, not after what Eneko had done to him. It took all he had for his one hand to wrench Bakar from him and smack him soundly across the mouth.

Bakar shuffled away, blood on his lip, muttering about murder and betrayal.

"Believe me," Petri said. "I will kill you if I can for this. For all of it. The Clockwork God can spin me into cogs and gears if he likes, but I will kill you."

Bakar subsided into a corner, still muttering. Petri settled back against the wall. There would be no sleeping now, not chained up with a madman. Not until someone came to let them out, if they ever did. Instead he kept his eye open and his head full of whirling red-tinged thoughts.

She hadn't come. She'd abandoned him to this. They all had, everyone.

He had nothing left except what he could claw back for himself, and that clawing would be the sweetest satisfaction of all.

He started humming in the dark.

Kacha, trailed by Cospel, made it to Soot Town easily enough. Away from the gates everywhere was quiet, waiting. Usually the factories and smiths would be full of bustle and noise, the air choking with the smoke that gave the area its name. Today the furnaces were cold, the hammers still. A few faces poked out of doorways as they passed, quickly withdrawn into shadowed whisperings. Cospel nodded in the direction of one of the smaller factories, a place which specialised in bespoke clockwork goods for a hefty price. Alone in the silence, it hummed with activity.

"They weren't letting no one in or out, miss. Course, they might now that things have gone tits up."

The gate was locked, but the two of them scrambled over in moments. No one stopped them. The other side was a courtyard full of heaps of scrap, a tangled pile of rusting cogs, a large metal bin full of contraptions that had failed in the casting process, a graveyard of bent gun barrels and twisted winches. Behind that was an open door and noise.

A head poked around the door, caught sight of them and disappeared, slamming the door behind it. No amount of rattling or thumping would open it, so finally Kacha beat on the door and shouted, "Open up in the name of the guild!" Cospel gave her a look but she shrugged. "Well we are. Sort of."

The door cracked open and an eye peered out. "Guild's already here, so bugger off."

She didn't have the time or patience for this, so she shouldered open the door, ignoring the pained squeak of whoever she'd just squashed behind it, and strode into the room beyond.

"Room" didn't do it justice. Her step faltered for just a second before she recovered herself. A vast expanse greeted her, full of the heat of furnaces, ringing with the noise of clockwork hammers and the shouts of the men working them, overflowing with the scents of sweat and hot metal. Smoke obscured the far end of the room, but what she could see was enough. Eneko had had a plan, sure enough, and here was where it was being born.

Black-smudged faces turned to look at her, but she gathered all the arrogance a duellist could muster and ignored
them, striding towards a man dressed in a guild tabard
over lace cuffs and breeches that no doubt had once been
white but were now sullied with streaks of soot. He turned
towards her with a frown, and she was surprised to note
she didn't know him – she thought she knew everyone in
the guild. A tickle of apprehension flickered in her gut.

Someone whispered in his ear, and his eyebrows rose
for a moment before he walked towards her. No hand on
sword yet, but the threat of it was there in the way he
moved. He was a swordsman right enough.

"Yes?" he asked when they met in the middle of the
room. A tall man, older than her by some way, but he
looked like age had hardened him to a point rather than
softened his edges as it did some people. His face was like
a slab of blackened oak that had weathered centuries, and
his eyes were chips of grey flint. "Kacha, I'm given to
understand. You must excuse me; I've been working elsewhere for quite a time. I am also told that I should execute
you. Some matter over a priest?"

She raised an eyebrow of her own. "You are aware of
what's going on outside?"

"Eneko is defending the city, as any good guildsman
should."

"Technically, yes. Specifically, no, because he's not Eneko
any more. Now there are two magicians trying to blow the
crap out of the city, one of whom is Eneko. Sort of.
Whichever one wins, we get a magician in charge. You
look old enough to remember what that was like. Fancy
seeing it happen again?"

She was gratified to see that hard face blanch. He whipped
round and called into the general gloom and fug. Two

more guildsmen sauntered up with a sneer for her and a grudging nod for him. She knew these ones all right.

"Shouldn't we kill her?" one of them said to the older guildsman. "Eneko said—"

"Maybe later." The older man twitched with impatience. "You two, go take a look at what's happening at the gates and report back. Go on. What are you waiting for – the end of the world?"

They turned to go, but not without more sneers her way. One leaned in and whispered to her, "Your bloke, he screams ever so pretty. But he doesn't look so pretty now."

The sight in Eneko's rooms flashed in front of her mind, of Petri's blood-soaked hair, the knife and the brazier. Made sense Eneko hadn't been alone. Secretive yes, but Eneko liked an audience – adoring guildsmen to look up to him, to keep secrets with him. Liked to use those secrets to bind them to him. Petri's blood all over, and a hot knife . . .

Her sword slashed a line across the guildsman's face, chin to brow. Bone showed under the sudden blood and the man howled as he put a hand to it, tried to gingerly press the flap of his cheek back into place.

"Neither are you," she said. A glance at his friend, who'd drawn his own sword. "I'll kill you later, if you like. Be my pleasure, because it's been a trying day and I'm just itching to take it out on someone. But first do as the man says."

They glanced behind her and evidently got a signal to leave, right now, and they went, trailing blood and curses. She looked about, saw a few more duellists with drawn swords. She'd have to watch her back later, but for now a growl behind her settled them.

"Just as I was beginning to despair of the youth of today," the older man said with a snort. "Pair of little shits, those two. Like to boast they're Eneko's favourites. Like a few other things a bit too much as well. Sadistic bastards, the pair of them. You just leave it between them, as a good duellist should."

That last was aimed at the other duellists in the shadows as she turned to face him.

"My name's Esmuss," he said. "I used to run the border guards between Reyes and Ikaras until Eneko recalled me for some reason. Do I look like I'm old enough to retire? Don't answer that. I could have held a fucking army at the Neck, but no, he gives the post to some spotty little oik who promptly lost half the guard to Ikaras, and here we are, facing an army with fancy bastards like that on our side." His gaze slid to the still ansty-looking duellists. "That goes for you lot too. Swords *down*, thank you, or you'll have me to answer to, and I still have enough in me to slice you all to fucking ribbons."

Swords went down. The duellists shuffled back into the shadows. A brief reprieve from retribution perhaps.

Esmuss looked her up and down and nodded.

"I've been away a while, and life's hard up in the mountains, where we don't practise our manners much, but if you're anything to go by maybe you city guildsmen aren't all soft as this sorry lot. Now, how about you tell me what's going on, and then we can see what to do? Because something's going on I don't know about, and I'll be buggered before I let a magician run this city again."

Half an hour later they were sitting in an office commandeered as Esmuss's base of operations. Invoices, blueprints and rubber stamps sat in a sad heap in one corner, and a map of Reyes had taken their place on the desk, held down with a pair of evil-looking daggers.

Esmuss shook his head over it and what she'd just told him.

"Knew he was up to something when he called me back from the border. Crafty bastard, Eneko always was. Cheated when he sparred, I know that. But sometimes devious is what you need in a leader, and the guild did well under him. He sent me to the border because we, huh, didn't get along." He fingered a scar on his neck. "Not at all. But I ran that border well; he couldn't deny that. So why call me back just when I'm really needed? Then dump me here overseeing a damned factory when there's a war going on?"

"What are you making here? He'll have had a plan, we're counting on that."

He looked up at her from under beetling brows. "Plan? Oh yes, he has a plan. Stupidest thing I ever heard. Here, I'll show you."

He led Kacha and Cospel back into the vast room. Twisted skeins of metal spun into new shapes loomed out of the smoke as they passed, but it was what lay at the end that stopped Kacha in her tracks.

Against the far wall were a number of Clockwork Gods. Exactly like the one outside the guild, down to the last rivet.

"What the . . ."

"We're to wait for his signal from down by the gates – you noticed he turned the towers off, left the gates open? To draw the Ikarans into a nice confined space, the square behind the towers. I don't suppose we'll get a signal now though. Maybe we should just set them going anyway. "

"Set them going? What do they do?"

Esmuss grinned at her and nodded to a man fiddling with one of the gods with a spanner. He touched something at the rear, and the god came to life, whirring and clanking forward, its arms swinging like giant clubs, its eyes utterly dead. It unnerved her more than she could say.

"A regiment of these and an opposing army's going to have a tough time, especially when Eneko meant to shut the gates behind the Ikarans and leave them trapped with this lot. They're far in advance of anything we've ever made before. Eneko must have been working on them secretly for weeks, months, years maybe. In a little dive down by the river, they were, all nice and hidden until he got us to bring them up here. And that makes me wonder. Bakar would never allow them, would he? Blasphemous to make an image of the Clockwork God. So Eneko knew, or hoped, Bakar would be deposed. Expected an invasion when Reyes hasn't been at war for, what? Centuries? This is all part of his plan. I just don't know why exactly."

Kacha thought she might, but that wasn't the worry right now.

"Are they ready? And what makes them go?"

"Ready as they'll ever be. We were just waiting for the signal. And actually I don't know what it is that makes them go — neither do any of the men working here — except it's some sort of clockwork heart with something else in there powering it. Magic, if I'm any judge, and no one seems able to work out if that makes the automatons really alive or just very complicated. I know what the new parts look like though. Here."

He handed over what looked very like a clockwork heart. She'd seen one before, hadn't she? Once for real, a clockwork heart belonging to a madwoman, and then the plans they'd found in Sabates' safe.

"You're right, you won't be getting a signal now," she said. "I say we set these things going. We let them flatten the Ikarans and we concentrate on the magicians. Worry about the rest later."

"Funny. Just what I was thinking."

Vocho was out of breath long before they made it to the cell they were heading for.

"How is it," he panted, "that you know your way around the Shrive so well?"

Dom was looking none too fresh himself, Vocho thought smugly. "If you recall, I was locked up here with your sister. And Bakar told me quite a lot about the place. I've got a good memory for those sorts of things. I'm pretty sure it's this level, but it could be either one of these corridors."

The stairs led out into a small antechamber which looked like it would usually hold a guard or two – a table, two chairs, an abandoned game of cards. Two corridors led from it, both looking as dark, dank and desperate as the other.

"Let's take one each." Vocho headed left. A small oil lamp hung from a hook. He took it and held it up to the grille of each cell. Behind him he could hear Dom calling Bakar's name softly. The stench was indescribable. Vocho held his spare hand over his nose, though that did little to help. Neither did what he saw through the grilles. If he'd had the time, he would have had these people out – he'd always been good with locks so the lack of keys wouldn't hinder him much.

A soft hand, pale and skeletal, touched his through the bars, but it wasn't Bakar. "Please," a voice said. "Please." A face to match loomed up, scarred and bruised, and Vocho had to swallow hard. Bakar had put too many down here who didn't deserve it, but there were plenty who did too. Still . . .

"Later," he said. "I'll come back."

"Please, please." The word followed him down the corridor like a ghost to haunt him. The last grille produced no flapping hand, no begging. He held the lamp up. Someone in there all the same, a small huddled figure against the far wall. It raised its head.

Bakar. At last. He found a hook for the lamp and set to work on the lock. Every time he glanced through the grille, Bakar would look at him, blank faced, slack jawed. God's cogs. He'd seen Bakar many times, and the man had always seemed so alive and vital, full of self-assurance. Now he looked like a gleam-eyed wraith. Were they really going to try to save Reyes with him?

Finally the door opened. Vocho pushed it open and took a step inside. "Bakar—"

He got no further before something hit him on the back of the head, staggering him. He whipped round, eyes blurred, knees threatening to give way, and screamed at the face in front of him.

It was half in light, half in shadow, and all Vocho could see was a gaping hole where an eye used to be surrounded by mangled ropes of pink weeping flesh. The thing – he couldn't think of it as a man – snarled and lunged at him before he could gather his wits enough to drag his sword from his scabbard. A hand found his throat and squeezed, banging his head on the stone floor as it did so. Another lamp appeared at the doorway to light the other half of the face, and suddenly Vocho could see who it was.

Petri? God's cogs, what had Eneko done to Petri?

Whatever it was seemed to have sent him mad, and no wonder.

Dom yanked Petri off Vocho and held him, struggling viciously, as Vocho regained his feet. Even Dom couldn't hold him for long, though it was clear that only one of Petri's hands was working – the other was a replica of his face, with mangled, weeping flesh. The fingers, what was left of them, dangled uselessly.

Petri wriggled out of Dom's grip and leaned, breathing heavily, against one wall.

"Say it," he growled. Vocho couldn't link the voice with the Petri he'd known, who was all smooth upper-class drawl, so self-assured. "Just say it, and get it over with."

Vocho shook his head. He'd have cheerfully strangled Petri fucking Egimont a dozen times in the years he'd known him, but even he couldn't bring himself to say what he might have once.

Half of Petri's face broke into a smile. The other half writhed, making Vocho's stomach turn. "You always were a coward. Come on then. Come through me."

"Sabates is dead," Dom said, and Petri twitched at that but said nothing. "Alicia murdered him, I'm pretty sure. Now she's outside the gates, and Eneko . . ."

The single eye bored into Dom's with an intensity that rattled even his imperturbability. "Eneko what?"

"Eneko is dead, I think, to all intents and purposes, though his body's still moving. Bakar's the only chance we have of keeping some order in the city."

"He's a lunatic!" Petri lurched forward but stopped when Vocho raised his sword. "Why do you think I was working with Sabates? Not for the fun of it. Because Bakar's mad, and he'll take down Reyes."

"He's mad because Sabates made him so," Dom said quietly. "And we think we can unmake him."

That seemed to hit Petri like a gut punch.

"Sabates made him mad?" Petri whispered, and then laughed, such a jagged desperate sound Vocho wanted to cover his ears. "All for nothing then, or for lies. All of it. Even this." He waved his working hand at his face, where Vocho was surprised to see tears. "Take him then," Petri said. "Take him. Do what you want. I won't stand in your way. Save Reyes like the hero you always thought you were."

He slid down the wall and sat slumped at its base. Vocho and Dom shared a look. Dom shrugged helplessly then went to Bakar and helped him up. Vocho kept a wary eye on Petri, but he just sat there.

Vocho wanted to say something, but what? They'd loathed each other and hadn't been shy about letting the other know. Maybe Vocho was finally growing a conscience, but he couldn't leave without saying . . . What? He turned at the door and searched for something – anything – to say, and came up blank. What do you say to a man who's just lost half his face?

Petri saved him trying. "Do me one favour, Vocho."

"If I can. For Kass's sake if nothing else."

"Tell her I'm dead. I . . . She . . . I can't. Tell her that. It'll be kinder on all of us. It's not a lie in any case. Petri Egimont is dead."

Half an hour later Vocho was half dragging, half carrying the prelate of Reyes across town, while Dom was trying to find a herbalist or healer who might be able to help. Sugar, that was the only clue they had, mixed with goats-foot trefoil, if they could find it. And where was the one place almost guaranteed to have some sugar? A brewery, at least one too cheap to use proper malted grain, so that's where he was going. Dom would meet him. With any luck Vocho could have a free sample while they tried to get Bakar back to something approaching sanity, because, god's cogs, he really felt like he needed a drink at the moment.

Bakar muttered something as they passed the shattered remains of the Clockwork God, minus its head.

"What?"

"Petri – was that Petri in the cell with me? What happened to him?"

The prelate seemed almost lucid and attempted a few steps on his own, so Vocho let him because lumping a fully grown man around was doing his back absolutely no favours at all.

"Eneko happened. That's all I know."

Bakar frowned and just for a second seemed normal. "Eneko, yes. I recall . . . something about Eneko. Last night? Night before? It's hard to recall. My clock . . . The bones talk to me, you know."

Vocho worked hard to keep his sarcasm in check. "Do they? That's nice."

"They tell me things, those bones. Petri . . . Petri betrayed me? No, that can't be right. Only Eneko said, the bones said . . . Everyone betrays me. All of them!"

"How about you just try not to think, and we'll get where we're going, OK?"

Bakar subsided into a silence that Vocho might have termed thoughtful if there was any chance there were any coherent thoughts available. Luckily the streets were empty, though Vocho noted a few people peering round doors as they approached and muttering once they'd passed. He wasn't sorry when the facade of his chosen brewery loomed up ahead. Banging on the door had no effect – everyone was probably hiding under their beds awaiting the coming invasion – so he took the liberty of propping Bakar against a wall and picking the lock.

Inside it smelt malty and delicious, but Vocho did his

best to ignore that. Leaving the door open for Dom, he dragged Bakar into the brewing room and plonked him on a seat while he had a look around.

A small doorway at the back led him to where he needed to go – a series of great bins where all the ingredients were kept. All of them were full – grains, hops, a smaller one for dried yeast, but one was virtually empty. The sugar one, naturally. Vocho recalled that a shortage of sugar had been one of the grievances in Reyes not all that far back, and the war with their one supplier, Ikaras, wouldn't have improved matters.

There were a few cupfuls, not much use to the brewer but maybe enough for his purposes. He found a bowl, got as much into it as he could and went back to Bakar.

The prelate was sitting bolt upright on the seat and looking around him with interest.

Clockwork God, please do your best with your greatest servant. Not me, obviously. Him. A tall order, I know, but otherwise you're as dead as we are.

"They destroyed the Clockwork God, the one outside the guild," Bakar said when Vocho came back. "And Eneko put me in the Shrive. I think."

"Oh, he definitely did." Vocho considered the best way to get as much sugar into the man as possible, found water and a jug and added a cupful. "Here, drink this."

Bakar peered into it. "What is it? You try some first. People have been trying to kill me, you see. The bones told me. Pays to be careful. Oh yes, they're all out to kill me."

"It's sugar, look." Vocho took a swig and almost gagged at the sweetness. *Any time now would be good, if it pleases your Clockiness.* "Now get it down you."

Bakar sniffed, pulled a face and did as he was told.

"Keep going."

"How much?"

"Until you seem sane. Could be quite a lot because I've known almond groves with less nuts."

Bakar was still drinking, between weak protests that he was going to be sick, when Dom turned up.

"Well?" Vocho asked because Bakar was still paranoid to his eyeballs.

"Not a lot of luck. I found a herbalist and described the poison. She thinks she knows what it is, but apart from what we're already doing or finding goatsfoot trefoil, which she hasn't got, we're out of luck. How is he?"

"See for yourself."

Bakar had muttered under his breath about bones, which was a good sign. He still thought his clocks talked to him, which was less good.

Dom shook his head. "She said it can take days to wear off, if we can't do something."

"In the meantime he's not going to be running anything. Let alone look like a sensible figurehead. One mention of talking clocks, and there'll be bloody chaos. What about the councillors?"

"What about them?"

"Could we get one of them to . . ."

Dom laughed bitterly. "No, not really. You pick one, the others will want him dead on the instant. Half of them have tried employing me to kill the other half. Bakar only barely managed to keep them from each other's throats by playing one against the other and never showing any favouritism. Of course, since he went very visibly insane, they've been jockeying for position anyway. Eneko has most of them in his pocket, or did. The rest are petrified of him. Which way they jump is going to prove very interesting when they find out what he is, isn't it?"

"This whole bloody day is going to be far more interesting than I care to imagine. Bakar can walk a bit better
now anyway. Let's find Kass and see what she's got."

And hope his Clockiness has found us a miracle.

"You've got what?" Vocho gaped at Kass.

"About two dozen replicas of the Clockwork God, fully
operational and able to walk. And fight. They're inside."

She seemed to be just about holding it together, but his
sister could never keep her feelings inside for long, and
they were there for anyone to see. Violence simmering
under her too-still face, a hitch in her calm voice, a palpable
need to use the sword and dagger that jigged in her hands.
Vocho shared a glance with Dom and got a tiny shake of
the head in return, even though, this one time, lying to
her – even by just not telling her that she was wrong
about Petri being dead – felt wrong. Even the possibility
of Petri being out of Vocho's life for good couldn't shake
that feeling, but for now he chewed on the inside of his
cheek and kept his mouth shut about him, about what was
left of his face and what he was now. Petri had asked, and
Vocho understood why and had given his word as a
guildsman. That had never stopped him before, but he was
starting to see things a bit differently.

"Looks like the god answered my prayers then," he said
instead. "What are we going to do with them?"

A hard-faced man came up and looked Vocho up and
down with a tiny frown that cleared when he saw Dom.
"God's cogs, if it isn't Jokin. I remember you. Couldn't
forget the way you fight. Heard you got thrown out or
somesuch but didn't believe that bullshit Eneko came out
with about it. Come on. I'll show you what we've got
planned." He peered behind Vocho. "Is that Bakar?"

The prelate stood, juddering from the effects of all the sugar they'd managed to get into him. His eyes jumped about in their sockets, and his hands trembled so hard they blurred, but he'd stopped telling them how his clocks talked to him, so Vocho was taking that as an improvement.

The older man turned away, clearly expecting them to follow. Vocho cocked an eyebrow at Kass.

"Esmuss. Used to run the border guards until Eneko brought him back for what he says were trumped-up reasons, leaving someone greener than grass to lose half the guards. Esmuss and Eneko don't get on."

Dom muttered something under his breath about understatements, and they followed Esmuss into his office. The guildsman pointed to the map.

"Right, here's the city as it stands now. The plan, as I understand it, was to lure the Ikarans into that first square behind the tower traps, shut the gates behind them and then unleash the gods on them while they were pinned down. That's not going to work now because they're already that far in and working their way further. And I don't know what he was going to do about the magicians."

"One less now," Dom said. "Alicia killed Sabates."

"Did she? Well that helps, perhaps. I'm sure there'll be others, not as strong perhaps but still tricky."

"Got to get them quick, take them unawares." They all turned to look at Bakar. He'd stopped juddering and his eyes looked clear enough, though there was still a little jump to them, a rhythmic twitch to his hands. "That's how we managed last time. Distract them and then get in quick before they know what you're about. They die just as easily from a shot to the head as anyone else."

Vocho sneaked a look at Dom, whose face had suddenly become as grim and set as Kacha's, and wondered what it was like to have people discussing how best to murder your wife. Or to have your wife trying to destroy the city you were in, and probably you with it.

"I know what will stop her," Dom said quietly. "I know what she wants. Eneko. Information only Eneko has. Give her that—"

"She'll have to beat me to him," Kass said in a tone of voice that suggested the sentence could have easily ended with "because I want to slice his face off."

"That won't stop the Ikarans, will it?" Esmuss poked at the cup he was using to mark the position of the Ikaran king.

"Without magic Reyes can beat that army," Bakar said, and he was sounding more and more sane. "We've weapons stockpiled against just such a thing, traps galore, and the Reyen people will fight for their city. I know they will. They did before. I will fight for my city too."

Esmuss glanced at him. "Not to put too fine a point on it, you've been a raving lunatic for quite some time now. The city's fed up. Worse – was on the point of revolt. They welcomed Eneko with open arms, that's how bad it was. They want someone to lead them but someone they can trust. Then, yes, then perhaps we'd have a chance. If we take out the magician."

Bakar stared out over the factory floor, and when he smiled he had the look of an angel. "What if their spiritual leader gave them a miracle, straight from their god?"

Kass watched as the sun set over a bruised and bloody Reyes. The streets by the gate were full of Ikarans, who seemed to be running on sheer willpower and whatever spell Alicia had cast on them. Bodies piled up against the walls of houses, blood soaking the stone and gurgling along gutters and into drains. And yet more Ikarans came, mad on magic, while Reyens cowered in their houses from the periodic showers of blood or hurried to the docks. More than one family had come to grief on a makeshift raft in the harbour. The city was rudderless, with as yet no one to take the place of Eneko. Instead of a coherent defence, little bands did their best to keep their streets their own, with varying success. At least the two magicians were no longer battling it out. The plain had descended into silence.

Kass, Vocho and Dom lurked on the roof of a house that overlooked the wall and peered out into dusk.

"Are we sure about this?" Vocho asked.

"Yes." Kass checked her blades again, for something to do with her hands, with her brain.

Dom nodded grimly in the gathering dark, and Kass put a hand on his arm, as much for herself as for him.

A blast of trumpets split the quiet, a ragged fanfare blown by clockers more used to spanners and hammers than musical instruments. Starting in Soot Town, the trumpets moved along the main avenue to where the dented, decapitated but still upright – just – Clockwork God stood on his plinth, gathering a few curious souls as they went, and then headed towards the main gate. Kass shut her eyes and it seemed to her she could hear the city come alive, hear every door opening as what followed the ragged trumpeters passed. Hear the gasps, feel the hope.

Bakar, resplendent in some white robes they had cobbled together, strode tall and proud and above all reasonably sane at the head of two dozen gods marching in time. His voice, almost back to its deep, compelling best, echoed along the streets.

"Your god has saved you, has sent these warriors in his image. He will not allow the heathen Ikarans to take this

city, not while Reyens defend it! Take comfort in the truth
of him, take comfort in knowing he has given me back to
myself after a long trial to prepare me, sent me back to lead
you out of this shadow. The clockwork is clear, for those
who can read it. While you stand with your god, he will
not abandon you, and Reyes will not fall!"

Kass caught glimpses of Bakar as he moved along the
streets, trailing men and women in his wake now, hesitant
at first but growing braver as more gathered, and more,
until the street was thronged. Behind him Esmuss and more
clockers were handing out guns and bullets to anyone who
would take them.

"Time to go," Dom murmured.

They swung down from the roof, over the city wall and
into the gloom beyond. It was easy enough to move across
the plain – the Ikarans seemed oblivious to anything that
wasn't inside Reyes, and so they moved from shadow to
shadow with barely a pause. Kass felt as tightly wound as
a clock. Twice she missed Vocho's signal, and Dom had to
give her a nudge. The second time he took hold of her arm
and breathed in her ear, "We'll find him, and you can get
what you want. He's screwed too many lives, yours and
mine and Petri's. Not after today, I promise you that, no
matter what."

She looked into eyes so bright she was surprised they
didn't glow and nodded, still too tightly wound to speak.
She followed Dom as he led the way past abandoned farmhouses, across deserted tracks and flattened fields. Get
what she wanted . . . If it was only that simple. If only
she knew what it was she did want.

Her old life back? She'd wanted that once but now she
wasn't so sure. And she'd wanted Petri back, and then not,
and now she had no choice. No chance. That was what

was missing from her aching chest — the chance to ask him why he'd written that letter. Had it all been true or all a lie? She'd wanted to ask him and see the look on his face when he answered because that look would *be* her answer. Now she'd never know. And Eneko had robbed her of that — and more besides, just as surely as Sabates had. He'd be up on that hill, Dom had said. Because Esti would head for Alicia, for whatever reason, and where Esti went Eneko had to go. He'd be there, and she could show him just how bloody perfect she was at killing people, and maybe that too was part of the ache. She'd lost the man who'd been her da for good, and she was going to be the one to kill him.

Vocho stopped halfway up the hill, in a stand of trees that hid them from Alicia's tents. He leaned against a tree for a second, catching his breath, but straightened up quickly when Dom and Kass looked his way.

The pair of them had been twitchy the whole way here, Dom silent and thoughtful, Kass tighter than a drum. He wanted, badly, to tell her the truth, a notion so strange to him he almost gave himself a slap. He wanted something worse than that though, wanted it so badly his hands shook at the thought. It had been something of a godsend meeting Esti out on the road with no Kass around. It hadn't taken her long to brew him up a nice new batch of jollop. She hadn't told him the whole truth by a long shot, but it hadn't all been lies either. Damn it, he wanted that jollop so badly he could taste it. It had some side effects, he knew, like he couldn't stop wanting it. He didn't care; he only cared about having another taste, just a bit, to feel the wave of numbness, the light-headedness that made the world retreat for a while, made it easier to move, to breathe, to be bloody great.

He waited until Kass and Dom were intent on spying out the layout of the camp before he slid a hand inside his tunic. Just a little nip for now. Because the trek up the hill had tired him more than he cared to admit, because his back was paining him, because . . . because his hand shook when he didn't take a nip of Esti's jollop.

A quick slug, the green taste of it satisfying on his tongue, and then the little flask went back into his tunic. Just enough to take the edge off. Perfect.

He crept forward to crouch next to Dom. A cluster of tents, two massive ones at the centre, one slightly smaller to one side, lots of little satellite shelters. Most were dark and quiet, but the two bigger tents were lit up like a new sun. Men milled around, gathered in little knots talking in murmurs. A flap opened, and there she was: Alicia, at a desk, dipping her brush in a pot. Dom shifted next to him but said nothing.

Kass moved up from behind, where she'd been watching the gates of Reyes. "Any minute now." A look passed between her and Dom, and a slice of hurt cut into Vocho's stomach, soon lost in other thoughts.

The sound of discordant trumpets came from the gates. The fanfare started off well but tailed off to a tattered parping as men unused to playing lost their wind. Never mind. It had the desired effect.

Three men jumped up from where they'd been sitting by the biggest tent and went to look before hurrying back. The tent flap was raised and left open. Alicia looked up, frowning as they fractured her concentration. Lots of arm-waving and shouting. A man dressed in richer clothes than Vocho had ever seen in his life – a man he instantly hated – imperiously moved a lazy arm, but Alicia stopped him with a shake of the head. Orgull? Probably. At Alicia's nod, four life-warriors strode off down the hill. More men rushed after them at a quiet command, before she rose and went with Orgull to the edge of the hill. Two guards followed.

Dom and Kass moved off together, silently, like oiled silk. Wasn't that Vocho's place? Wasn't that always his place, at her side, watching her flank as she watched his?

A movement half seen from the corner of his eye brought him up short, leaving them to go on. Not like they needed him, really, especially as he was. There, in a deeper shadow behind Alicia's tent. A movement, another, someone unfolding like a pocket knife. Someone bringing out a heavy *palla* that could chop a man in two. Someone who, when he turned his face, had only a nub of a nose left amid ritual scars. Vocho had a very powerful need for another nip right now.

A glance told him the worst. Kass and Dom hadn't seen the life-warrior and were too far away for him to call without being overheard, without sending the whole plan, sketchy as it was, to shit.

OK, now come on. You're Vocho the Great, remember? Vocho the wonderful, the unbeatable, who thrashes everyone he fights with style and panache, who drips glory. You always tell everyone.

Yes, but I was lying. I'm good, I'm great, but this might be a step too far.

The life-warrior's gaze locked on his, flicked back to Kass and Dom and back again with the tiniest shrug of his shoulders. The heavy blade hummed as he twirled it.

Think of the glory, Voch.

Fuck the glory. I want to live!

Then there was no time. The warrior was on him with a leap and a growl, the heavy blade battering his, numbing his arm and sending him sprawling. Vocho rolled with the

movement and popped back up again, doubly wary, ready
for anything despite the ache of his back through the numb
of the jollop.

Icthian style was the only way to beat this bastard.
Vocho kept his sword up, his feet ready, eyes on the warrior
as he moved to one side. Icthian was always better if you
had something in the other hand. He groped around and
came up with nothing, then had to duck the blade coming
round at head height. A quick thrust was all he had time
for before the warrior was gone again, out of reach. And
the man had a lot of reach, far more than Vocho.

He came again, and Vocho darted away – if that blade
caught his one too many times, he wouldn't have a sword
left. He scrabbled around with his other hand. Still nothing,
only the slippery wall of a tent. Away behind him came a
sudden uproar, a scream, the sound of two blades clashing,
the smell of cooking blood. All the glory was happening
over there, not here in the dark between two tents. This
time he wasn't fighting for a bit of adulation, this time he
was fighting just to live.

A crashing elbow arrowed for his face the same time as
the blade came for his side. He slashed at the elbow, felt
the sword bite into skin and a warm splash of blood, but
caught the edge of the *palla* on his hip and was knocked
back into the tent.

The warrior dipped back into the dark, blade humming
as he considered his next move. Vocho put a hand to his
hip – it came away bloody and a stabbing throb worked
its way out from the bone – and wondered what the hells
he was going to do when the bastard came again.

Kass moved forward with Dom to the edge of the light.
The trumpets down on the plain had stopped, replaced

with the clanking whirr of two dozen gods marching in time.

Orgull and Alicia stared down, he in a fit of rage, she with cool detachment.

"What's happening?" Orgull demanded. "You there, signals. I want to know—"

"Flags don't work in the dark, you idiot," Alicia snapped. "Here, let's shed a little light on the matter."

Her pot and brush came out. A quick dart of her fingers, the slash of blood on paper and a murmured word. A light brighter than the sun flashed out over the plain, searing Kass's eyes so she had to look away before it faded to bearable.

"What in—" Orgull began.

"Clockwork hearts, he said." Alicia snapped her brush in two. "Clockwork hearts for clockwork gods."

Down on the plain the gods were clearly visible, moving through the Ikarans serenely if fatally. Men ran at them, hacked at them, beat on them with their fists, but the automatons were impassive, impervious. Behind them came the men and women of Reyes. The crack of bullets echoed up to the hill.

Kass glanced over at Dom, to find he wasn't there. She cast around wildly. Orgull and Alicia's guards had disappeared. Then she spotted a pair of feet sticking out from behind a tent and Dom oiled back round it, dusting his cuffs. He caught her eye, inclined his head in a "Shall we?" and drew his sword.

Orgull and Alicia seemed oblivious to the loss of their guards, still arguing over what was happening down on the plain and what to do about it. Then Alicia's scalpel flashed, and the king fell with a comically surprised look, scrabbling at his throat.

"Your mistake," Alicia said softly, "was thinking I ever cared about what you wanted, or taking over Reyes." She bent down, dipped her broken paintbrush into the blood that soaked his rich robes and smiled sadly at him. "But you did very well, if that helps. Eneko can't fail to give me what I want with his precious city at my mercy, and that will be just as soon as I deal with these automatons."

She brushed blood over Orgull's face, tenderly almost, and said a word. The Ikaran king's still-twitching body flew up into the air, twirled like a ballerina and flew towards where Dom hid in the shadows. He went down in a tangle of limbs and blood.

"And your mistake," Alicia said, "was thinking I wouldn't know you were there. And the lovely Kass, if I'm not mistaken? Ah yes, I thought so. Where is your ridiculous brother?" She cocked her head. "I see. Gerlar is playing with him. Come on then, Narcis, Jokin, Dom, whatever you like to call yourself now. Out of the shadows and into the light. You too, Kass. And make no mistake, I have plenty of blood at my disposal, should I need it."

Dom disentangled himself from the body of Orgull and stood up, adjusting a crease in his bloodstained tunic as though at a picnic. He carefully avoided looking at either Kass or Alicia.

"I can get what you want," he said. "The same thing I want, have been trying to get." He looked up finally, and the look in his eyes gave Kass the shivers. Deadly serious, more serious than she'd ever seen him. Yet his face was crumpled, vulnerable. "I never gave up trying. We can get her, find her. If you stop this now. Please, Cee. I want the same thing you do. I always did."

The change in Alicia was instant, from ice cool to spitting feathers. The hand with the brush came up, and she flicked blood at Dom, droplets splattering on his face and bringing a hiss of pain. "Lies. You always lied. You're lying now, aren't you, like you lied to dear Kass here? I'd bet my blood on it. I listened to you before, and look where it got me – childless, alone, hated, ostracised. Until I met Sabates. He did that for me at least. Though maybe I should thank you because without you I'd never have discovered I can do this."

The scalpel appeared in her other hand, a flash in the light, and she threw it. Dom ducked, but the scalpel followed, swerving in mid-air, drops of Orgull's blood flying from it.

Kass hesitated no longer. Her sword was out, the knife in her other hand as she went for Alicia's back. Not a killing blow, not yet, for Dom's sake. Even now she could hear him, warning her to leave Alicia, leave her. But Kass was beyond reason, tied up with grief and rage and hate, and this woman, she'd been part of it, part of everything that had been done to Petri, to Voch, to Dom, to herself.

The hilt of her knife took Alicia in the base of the neck, sending her sprawling to the ground, but she was quicker than she had any right to be, was up and going for Kass in the blink of an eye. Not with any weapon, but with blood on her hands, which was more terrifying than any sword.

Shut her up, got to shut her up, was all Kass could think. The smell of cooking blood overpowered everything else as it splashed over her face, blinding her. She lashed out with the sword at where Alicia should be, where she could hear her. The blade connected with thin air, and the blood on her face tightened, moving into her nose, her mouth, stopping her breath, making her gag with the stench.

"Stupid woman," Alicia hissed. "Don't you want Eneko

dead too? Leave me to it, and you'll have your revenge for poor Petri. Eneko will be a hundred pieces of meat when I've finished with him, just as soon as he tells me what I need to know."

Another word, and needles of pain lanced into Kacha, skewered her eyes, her lips, her cheeks, dropping her to her knees. A last desperate slash with the sword connected with nothing. Couldn't breathe, couldn't breathe.

Vocho peered out from the slash he'd made in the tent wall. The bastard was still out there, somewhere. He could hear the hum of the blade as the life-warrior swung it but was never quite sure which direction the sound was coming from. A hiss was his only warning when the *palla* came through the fabric a scant inch from Vocho's head.

This had stopped being funny, if it ever was.

The cocky bastard was playing him, he was sure of it. Mainly because it was the sort of thing he'd do, given the chance and a sufficiently crap opponent. That stung him into action. Vocho a crap opponent!

The blade withdrew, but Vocho was already moving, smashing one shoulder into the tent wall where the life-warrior had to be. A whooshing grunt and the feel of heavy flesh was his reward. He didn't stop to crow about it, for once, but ripped at the slash and widened it, launched himself through, leading with the sword, and caught the bugger a good one right in the sword shoulder.

It didn't slow the warrior down much, if it all. Blood ran from the shoulder, the wound serious enough to at least make using the weapon difficult. Except the man gave a hideous grin that warped the nub of his nose and flipped the *palla* into his other hand, immediately bringing it down overarm in a blow that would have split Vocho in two if he had been there to meet it.

He only barely wasn't. He was losing this fight, and he knew it. Vocho jumped back through the slash in the tent and landed in a sprawling mess, pain shooting through the wound in his hip. He tried to stand up and fell back down. Nope, that leg wasn't going to work.

OK, your Clockiness, now would be a really good time for a miracle. One of those extra gods down on the plain perhaps? I'm sure you can spare one.

The rip widened as the life warrior bulled through and grinned down at him. The palla gleamed dully as he twirled it, and Vocho scrabbled backwards, trying to find something, anything that would help. He held on to his sword, trying his best at a defensive posture from his arse. Like that would help when this bastard put all his weight behind his blade. Wind whipped through the tent, sending the ripped wall into billowing waves, a tang to it of green things, growing things, and blood. A glimpse of a face in the gap. Oh crap, that was all he needed.

The life-warrior had finished playing, it seemed. A last whirl of the blade, his eyes hardened, and he drew his arm back for the next blow, possibly the last one he'd need.

The green smell grew stronger until Vocho thought it might crush his head. A vine as thick as his leg burst through the rip in the tent fabric and smacked the blade from the life-warrior's stunned hand. Another vine, as thick as the first, snapped around his waist and yanked him back through the gap. There followed some vicious cursing, the rustle of leaves and a series of thumps before silence and then a familiar face that was at the same time alien.

"Help me," Esti said through Eneko's mouth. "Help me, Vocho, for the gods' sakes."

Chapter Twenty-six

Kass blinked hard to clear the blood. It had run from her mouth and nose as quickly as it had come, leaving her heaving for breath on her knees. Not a good place to be with a magician about to . . .

She looked up, hand questing for her sword without conscious thought.

Alicia stood as if frozen, looking down at the sword that poked out of her ribs, at all the blood that gushed from the wound. Her lips flapped, once, twice, trying to say a word, and then she slid silently off the blade and into the grass. Dom stared after her, a quizzical look on his brows as he watched her blood drip from his sword.

"Get in quick while they're distracted," he said in a faint voice. His sword was quivering in his hand. "Bakar knew his stuff all right."

Kass levered herself to her feet. "Dom?"

He gave her a blank look, dropped his sword as though it was hot and sat down abruptly. Down on the plain a series of howls caught her attention. Without Alicia to drive them on, the Ikarans fled every which way, to wherever there wasn't a god to pulverise them. Bakar, resplendent in his white robes, which gleamed in the light Alicia had made, strode at the head of a wedge of Reyens.

Seemed they'd won.

Kass looked back at Alicia on the grass, at Dom where he sat and stared at his hands, opening and closing, opening and closing. A flash of memory, of Petri's blood-soaked hair on a chair. They'd won, but there was still work to do, rage to slake in someone's blood. Afterwards she thought she might look like Dom, but for now rage kept her going, fizzed through her like wine. If she let it go, she might sit down and never get back up.

Eneko, Esti rather, or maybe it was both of them, they were here somewhere. She was going to find him, kill him, and then perhaps she'd come back and sit next to Dom and they could be shattered together.

Vocho hesitated, gripped his sword all the harder. Maybe Esti had just saved him, but she'd possibly poisoned him too, lied to him, and by the Clockwork God's cogs and gears, he wanted a damn hit of that jollop. Once he thought of it, the craving wouldn't go away. Just a taste. A nip, that's all. His hand slid inside his tunic and found the flask.

"Help me," s/he said again.

"I would," he said. "But you know I'm not sure I want to."

S/he climbed inside the tent, all jerky like a puppet on strings. Eneko's hair, Eneko's face . . . but her voice.

"I can make you more. Lots more. You'll never run out."

"You might kill me too, I hear."

"Vocho, please." S/he ripped at the front of Eneko's guild tabard. Something brown and pulsing sat on her/his chest.

"A leech. Alicia . . . It's her version of the tattoo. After you left Ikaras, she found me, she made me . . . It was only moving into Eneko that made it so that I could stop."

A flash passed across his/her features so that, just for a moment, they were hers alone. Vocho saw something in them that echoed inside him, a dark remembrance of the day he'd killed a priest – hadn't wanted to, barely even recalled it, but he had. Thanks to the tattoo, the tattoo that Esti had taken off the best she could. No matter what else, she'd done that.

"Can't you just pull it off?"

"Don't you think I would have, if I could?"

"What do you need me to do?"

She pulled a scalpel from a sleeve. "We need Alicia's blood. And then you need to cut it out. Then I can make myself be me again."

"What about Eneko?"

A shrug, a twitch of the lips. "Do you care?"

"Help me up."

Between the two of them they got him on his feet and out of the tent. Something was different. He could see down across the plain, even if only dimly because Alicia's light was fading fast, but there was definitely something. The Ikarans were retreating. Not just retreating; they were running like the hounds of hell were after them. Vocho could make out half a dozen gods following them, picking up stragglers and banging them together before dropping them. Clockwork couldn't do that, could it? He recalled the heart that Esmuss had showed them, recalled too where he'd seen that before.

"You helped them, helped Eneko?"

"Sabates made me. He planned to use Eneko then kill him. And Alicia hated me because Sabates favoured me.

Why do you think she wanted me dead so badly? When she found me, she figured she could use me instead."

Then it hit him like a wall. "Where's Kass? And Alicia and Dom and . . ."

"There."

Esti pointed over to one side. Someone dead or doing a good impression. A figure slumped nearby. Another getting grimly to her feet with sword in hand. He knew that posture even if he couldn't see her face.

"Kass."

Kass saw them, and then she was on Esti/Eneko, her knife arrowing for the throat, what seemed like every vile curse she could think of dripping out of her mouth. She stayed her hand at the last second, to savour the moment if the look on her face was anything to go by. Vocho grabbed for her wrist but she shook him off, almost flattening him again.

"I'm going to kill this bastard if it's the last thing I do. And you aren't stopping me, Voch." She looked down at Eneko's face and her lips twisted. "And Esti's no better, is she?"

"Wait! Just wait a second, Kass. Look," Esti pulled aside her shirt, and the leech pulsed, glistening on her skin. "It's like Voch's tattoo."

"So?"

"So she just saved my life, Kass," Vocho said. "And she took the tattoo off."

"She got you hooked on that bloody syrup too, lied through her teeth. And what about the antidote?"

"It really would have worked, if Bakar had taken it," Esti said. "Later. I'll tell you later, but you have to help me first. I wanted Alicia and Sabates dead. So did you, and so I wanted to help you. Do the means of her dying matter? If you help me take this off, get me back in my own body, you can have Eneko. If it helps, it'll be exceptionally painful for him."

Kass shook herself away from the pair of them. Vocho didn't have a clue what she was going to do — he'd never seen her even halfway approaching this angry. It was what lay behind that anger that shifted something inside him. He'd never felt sorry for her either, not once, but he did now.

He shuffled over to her, put out a placating hand but dropped it when he caught the glare. "We won, Kass. Look down there. Bakar's striding about like he owns the place, and he does. Owns the people again too. They'll trust him, for a while. Ikaras is retreating."

"Ikaras has no king either," she said.

"Even better. They'll probably spend months arguing over who gets to be the next one. Reyes is safe. You did what you said you were going to do. You did what seemed good, right?"

Her face cracked at that, but she soon had it under control, gripping her sword and knife like they were the only things keeping her upright or sane. "Didn't save Petri though, did I? And you were right, and that's why I came."

"I know, Kass. And I thought you were stupid, and I still came with you. You *couldn't* save Petri." That at least wasn't a lie. "I think it was too late for him a long time ago. What Eneko did . . ."

She twitched at that, and he shut up about it.

"Esti helped us, in the end. In the beginning too." He caught sight of Dom slumped on the ground, staring at his hands as they opened and closed. "And maybe she can help him too. Look, Bakar's going to want to put Eneko on trial. Let everyone know that he was poisoned, that he wasn't really mad. That's for the good of Reyes too, right? And you can watch his head bounce across the cobbles. Because you told me you were sick of killing. I don't think doing this will make you less sick of it, or any less angry. And it's not the good thing, is it? You swore to that. You didn't unswear later."

She glanced over at Dom and her breath hitched before she nodded.

Vocho let out a breath. He hadn't been sure she wouldn't try to get to Eneko, and the state he was in a small puppy could have got past him. "Good. Now get some of Alicia's blood and help me cut this damned leech off."

Chapter Twenty-seven

The room made Vocho's stomach churn for many reasons. The first reason being he'd seen what had happened to Petri. Dom stood next to him as they looked down at the bloodied chair in a long silence.

"Do we know . . ." Vocho began and hesitated.

"He got out of the Shrive, we know that. Pretty much everyone did, as far as I can make out. Other than that, no. No idea where he is."

Vocho picked up the knife on top of the brazier. Kass's stiletto. An extra twist just to grind it into Petri, and grind it into her too perhaps. Eneko thought she'd betrayed him somehow, and this had been some twisted sort of revenge. Maybe. They'd probably never know the truth of it because there wasn't much left of the mind of the guild master. Esti had been as good as her word there, which was why Vocho and Dom were looking to see what they could find in his rooms. It wasn't making for a pleasant experience, but by unspoken agreement they'd decided not to tell Kass they were here. She'd have insisted on coming too, and even Vocho had enough empathy not to put her through that.

Besides there were a few questions he wanted to ask Dom, and he felt easier doing it without Kass butting in every two seconds. They left the room, much to Vocho's relief, and found a stairway going down. Dom led the way, Vocho hobbling along behind, his still-mending hip a constant pain that made his back feel fine. It was easier asking the questions of Dom's back than having to see his face. "Alicia," was all he needed to say. Dom stopped on the stairs, one hand braced on the wall, the other doing that odd opening and closing, opening and closing.

"What about her?" he said in the end.

"Her and Esti and why do you keep popping up? Not that I'm not grateful or anything, only, well . . ."

A funny little laugh under his breath, and Dom started down the stairs again. "Lots of reasons really, but mostly me and Alicia wanted the same thing. We wanted information from Eneko, and he's a canny bastard who gives away nothing for free. Me and Alicia, we just went about it in different ways."

They reached the bottom of the stairs and Dom groped around until he found a torch and the means to light it.

"Cogs, looks like his own personal Shrive down here."

Dom wasn't wrong. They were in a short corridor with four doors along it. The stench of no sanitation, the grim feeling of inevitability. Vocho shivered. The door at the end was open, and Dom headed for it.

"The thing is," Dom said as they stared into a space that was hardly large enough for a man to lie down. The floor was a mess of rotting straw and human waste. "The thing is, up to a point I was working for Eneko. In return for said information. I'd tried everything else, you see. So, when we first met I was keeping an eye on you two for him."

"Spying on us? We seem to have been popular."

"Spying, yes, I suppose so. Then everything got complicated, and I found I was enjoying myself. Remembering what it was like to be a guildsman. And he kept saying just one more thing and then I'll give you what you want, and I'd do the one thing, and it would be just one more thing. So I stopped telling him everything. Just the bits I wanted to. When Eneko found out about Bakar being poisoned, about the antidote, he sent me to Ikaras to get it – one more job before he'd tell me what I needed to know. I thought I knew Esti, you see. I knew a lot *about* her anyway. As it turns out, quite a lot of it was wrong. I think that antidote would have worked on Bakar much better than what we managed to cobble together, would certainly have been quicker."

While Bakar had managed to pull himself together for the defence of Reyes, there were still lingering after-effects. Every time he saw a clock he screamed, and he still had a tendency to mutter about periwinkles, but he was getting there. Esti had offered to help, but he'd seemed happy to let things take their course. Even if it meant destroying all the clocks in the palace so he could sleep at night.

Dom turned a faded smile on Vocho and answered his next question before he could ask it. "I had a long talk with Esti after she separated from Eneko. Alicia found out about the antidote when she caught Esti. Found some magic to make it all go wrong, only it went wrong with Eneko instead of Bakar. A bit of luck that, I think, and the truth as Esti knows it. I found a herbalist to take a look at that jollop she gave you too. I was wrong. Nothing in there that would kill you. But Alicia was always a very determined individual. She murdered Sabates for his position to get what she wanted, tried to sabotage us curing Bakar, but it all went wrong. I got it in the end, what we both wanted, the last known whereabouts of my, our, daughter. Or rather Esti got it for me. She had rather intimate access to Eneko's mind for a while."

A long silence followed. Dom had what he wanted, and Vocho had a pardon, and Kass – what did Kass have? Vocho stared down at the reeking straw where it seemed Petri had been kept for some time.

"Do you think we ought to tell Kass about Petri?"

"No," Dom said at last. "No, I don't think so. How would it help? Either of them? Besides he asked you not to, and you gave your word."

"That's never bothered me much before."

"But it does this time?"

Vocho looked down and tried to still the roiling in his gut. A small square of paper, half hidden in the straw. He ignored the painful twanging in his hip as he bent to pick it up. Kass's name was on it, very faint. "Yes," he said. "Yes, this time it bothers me. When are you leaving?"

"As soon as we're finished here. What I told you – about working for Eneko – would you not tell her that too? I'd prefer she didn't think too badly of me."

"If you like." Vocho left the tiny space. What had gone through Petri's head in here, in the room above? What was going through his head now? Vocho was pretty glad he didn't know. "What's one more lie to add to all the rest, eh?"

Kacha sat on the wall of the guild and looked down over the harbour, as she'd spent so much time doing in her days in the guild. It didn't look much different. Boats still crammed every jetty; the god-buoy still rang out in the harbour; longshoremen hurried to and fro loading and unloading, though mostly today they were unloading people who had fled the city and were now returning.

It didn't look much different, but it felt it. Or rather she did. She'd barely seen Vocho for days, hadn't sparred for as long and couldn't work up the effort to care much. Instead she sat and watched and wondered, too tired to stir. She was unable, or unwilling, to sleep for what she found in her head. She looked over at the Shrive, hulking on the other side of the guild. Half the city had turned out for Eneko's trial, so they'd had to conduct it in the main square. The truth had come out, at least mostly. Bakar was restored. The councillors had cheered outwardly and no doubt cursed inwardly.

A bustle down there in the square today. Setting up the guillotine. The man she'd looked on as her father was going to die this morning, and she still didn't know why he'd done all the things he had.

The scuff of limping feet on the stairs. She looked around, and there was Vocho. He looked different as well, she thought. Less swagger. He hobbled over – the surgeon had done her best with the hip but it was still early days – and plumped down next to her.

"Though I'd find you lurking up here. What are we looking at?"

"Does it look any different to you?"

He gave her an odd look and a sly grin. "Yeah. Looks peaceful."

"That's not what I meant."

"I know. Got something for you. Couple of somethings actually. Firstly there's this."

He handed over an important-looking paper, all smooth with an embossed Reyes crest at the top: "*The council* requests the presence of Kacha of the Duellists' Guild to be rewarded for services rendered."

"I got one too," Vocho was saying. "Going to get a special title or something to go with the pardon."

The smug look on his face made her smile for the first time in what felt like weeks. Typical Voch. "Vocho the Great?"

"Well, why not? We did save the city, didn't we? Deserve a little something for it, I say."

"What about Dom? Doesn't he get one?"

Vocho shifted guiltily. "If he was here. Gone again. Full of surprises, that Dom, wouldn't you say?" An edge to that, and Kacha took a good look at him. He gazed out over the docks as though he didn't care what her answer was, which was his normal way of showing that actually he cared quite a lot.

"Full of them," she said. "But you can never depend on him being there when you need him."

The slightest relaxation of his shoulders.

"Good point. Oh yes. The other thing."

This paper was nowhere near as impressive. A scruffy scrap, ragged at the edges, much folded.

"Down under Eneko's rooms . . ." he began, then hesitated, gauging the way she was looking at him. When she didn't say anything he went on in a rush, ". . . there was a little room. Looked like, er, someone had lived there a while. Sort of lived anyway. Um, and I found this. I thought you might want it."

He studiously looked the other way as she took it and read it: "*Kass. Regret nothing, remember everything. Petri.*"

She stared at it while the words blurred and came true again.

"Voch . . ." she started, but she couldn't finish the

sentence. He put an arm around her shoulders and squeezed, and she thought maybe he did love her sometimes, when he remembered. If nothing else, she always had Voch, even when she didn't want him.

After a minute or two he pulled away awkwardly and cleared his throat. "So, uh, they're going to elect a new guild master later."

"And?"

That sly grin again. "Fight you for it? Found your blades in Eneko's rooms too. But I'm still going to beat your behind. Because I can."

That grin, always in the background of her life, always taunting her, always lightening her whether she wanted it or not. She'd missed that grin and was glad it was back, found a tentative one in return on her own lips.

"God's cogs, Voch, if you become guild master the city'll fall to bits in a week."

"So you want the job then? Oh, but you'd have to beat me, and you're out of shape with all this sulking about up here. Tell you what, I'll let you have a point on account. At least give you half a chance."

A full-blown smile then, a brief lifting of the ache. It'd be back later, but for now that was enough. If nothing else, she had Voch. "Bloody well will not. Besides, you're still not right on that leg. I should give you a point. Bet you I can have you on your arse in under a minute. Bet you a bull. If only to save the city from you. For the good of Reyes and all that."

"Now *that* is the sister I know."

Chapter Twenty-eight

Petri sat back in the surgeon's chair and gripped the arm with the one hand that still worked. A knife came towards him and he flinched back – he had no good memories of knives. Fever sweat slicked him head to toe, and pain pulsed through his face, or what was left of it.

"Keep still," the surgeon said, and tried again.

The surgeon's hands shook, with drink perhaps, or age. He stank too, of piss and blood and rum. But Petri had no choice, no money, no nothing but the clothes he stood up in and a face that had been stripped of skin down one side, thick now with the infection that surged through him, made him hot and cold and sick with it. He had nothing to pay with but a good pair of boots and the buttons on his tunic. All he could get for that was a surgeon who reeked of piss, and nothing for the pain.

"Keep still," the surgeon said again, and came for his face with the knife to cut away the infected skin and muscle. Cut away his life, kill Petri Egimont stone dead and leave someone else in his place.

You are weakness.

Petri may have been, but this new man knew nothing of that. All he knew was pain and hatred and the sweet temptation of revenge on everyone who had wronged him. Petri was dead, but this new man wasn't weak, and he wasn't good and noble either because that had brought him nothing but pain. And he was going to make everyone pay for that pain.

He clamped his teeth shut on the scream as the knife came again.

extras

www.orbitbooks.net

about the author

Julia Knight is married with two children, and lives with the world's daftest dog that is shamelessly ruled by the writer's obligatory three cats. She lives in Sussex, UK and when not writing she likes motorbikes, watching wrestling or rugby, killing pixels in MMOs and is incapable of being serious for more than five minutes in a row.

Find out more about Julia Knight and other Orbit authors by registering for the free monthly newsletter at www.orbitbooks.net.

if you enjoyed

LEGENDS AND LIARS

look out for

WARLORDS AND WASTRELS

The Duellists: Book Three

also by

Julia Knight

The freezing rain driving into his face made Petri Egimont's empty eye socket burn behind the sodden mask that hid it, but that was the least of his worries. Night came early as autumn span on into winter, and with it came a blazing cold that threatened every bit of him that was exposed. If he wasn't careful, an eye and the use of a hand weren't all he'd be without.

The road drowned in freezing mud, ankle-deep and more, dragging at bones that were so weary they felt made of glass. His cloak, such as it was, was no real protection against the rain that found every crevice and wriggled its bitter way onto his skin. He barely even knew why he was on this particular road, except that it felt like he'd tried every other, and had yet to find a place where he was welcome. He'd traded every fine thing he'd had on him when he escaped the city, every trinket, every polished button, even his boots, until all he had left was a shirt, his breeches, the holed shoes he'd traded for the boots and a threadbare cloak that was no match for his old one. Traded them all for a bite to eat, a place to stay. For a disreputable surgeon who was so far gone on rum his hands wouldn't stay still, the only surgeon he'd been able to afford, to cut out the infection that had settled into the wounds on Petri's face, and a mask to cover what was left when he was done. Even with that mask, there was no hiding the ruin of it, or hiding from the reaction it got, which meant sleeping under a lot of hedgerows, in a lot of stables. Weeks spent reeking of mud and horse piss, and grinding his teeth.

Reyes mountains in the coming winter were no place for a man with nothing, not even a pot to piss in. But the plains were full of people, villages, farms, fields and hedges that people owned and didn't want *him* in. Not a man whose face scared the horses, whose right hand was now useless, who was still learning to use his left, who couldn't do much of work to pay his way. A man who dare not say his name because he'd betrayed the prelate, sent him mad, helped plunge the whole country into war. Who was dead, so the newssheets said, and was in any case dead inside.

The mountains were all that were left to him, no matter the stories of robbers and cutthroats and highwaymen, and even that thought brought a sharp pain to his chest.

Two ponies trudged past, heads down against the weather, a man bundled up in furs on one, a woman on the other. Petri's heart gave a lurch, but it wasn't her. Not Kass. Couldn't be. Besides, her horse was a deadlier beast than either of those two ponies and doubtless would have taken a chunk out of his leg on the way past. If it had been her, what would he have done? Slunk off into the shadows like the coward he used to be, or taken out his newly forged rage on her? The old Petri was dead, but he hadn't discovered who the new one was yet, except he seemed to boil with anger, and that hadn't helped him much down on the plains either.

The ponies passing him and taking a tiny side-track that wound around a sharp fold in the land did show him one thing. If he squinted with his one eye through the rain, past a stand of trees, there was a light. Several lights in fact. What might be a village and maybe, if he was lucky, an inn. One or two innkeepers had taken pity on him down on the plains, mistaking him for a man wounded in the battle with Ikaras in the summer, whispering with their patrons at his scars, at the accent that marked him. Not pity for long, or for much, but they'd let him sleep in a clean bed, had given him the few jobs they had that he could do to repay them rather than take their charity. Other payments once or twice that he shuddered to recall, dark and sweating and furtive, giving the last, only thing he had to give, leaving him shamed and shameful, torn and tearful, but alive to know it.

But an inn was a good bet — and was out of this freezing rain, where he'd die if he stayed much longer. He'd find something to trade, find some job he could do in return for something to eat, a dry place to sleep. Even the stables would be better than this. Maybe up here in the mountains, things would be different.

He turned his numb feet in the holed shoes towards the lights and lurched through the mud after the ponies, hoping only for a warm place.

Light and warmth and the glorious, half-forgotten smell of cooking food, of the meaty smell of stew, the yeast of new bread, stopped Petri dead as he stumbled in the inn door. He stood there, dripping freezing rain from his sodden cloak, and savoured it for half a heartbeat.

All he was allowed. The room didn't go silent, but it did fall to sudden whispers punctuated by the loud laugh of a drunkard in the corner who hadn't seen him yet. He gritted his teeth against the stares, shook out his cloak one-handed – that action grew a whole new set of whispers as they saw what was left of the other hand – shook the rain from his hair that was now just growing back, long enough for it to be curled over his shoulder in the way that would mark him as a man of means. Long enough, but he left it wild because he was a man of means no more. The soaked mask had slipped and he hurried to get it back into place, but the fabric was ruined and with a pang he ripped it off.

In his head, he strode serenely towards the bar, ignoring the muttered comments of "poor bastard" and "God's cogs, that's ugly" and "I feel sick" and "should be ashamed to be out in public". But numb feet betrayed him, made him stagger his way, and the need to tell them all to go fuck themselves burned behind clenched teeth.

He curled what was left of a lip at the nearest, a heavyset man dressed in a thick smock and loose breeches above mud-caked boots, who flinched back and fell into his chair. Petri didn't blame him – he'd looked in a mirror once down on the plains, and had no wish to look again. His old face was dead, like the old him.

The lump of a man behind the makeshift bar gave him an appraising look from under a heavy brow, but shrugged. "As long as you've got coin I don't give a crap about your face," the shrug said, which was an improvement on the whispers behind Petri.

"Battle of the Red Brook," someone said in voice loud enough to carry and was soon shushed. Red Brook, or as it had been before so many were slaughtered in it, the Smith Brook that fed the Soot Town waterwheels. That battle had been hard fought not two months ago during the war for Reyes as a regiment of clockwork gods had fought off the Ikarans at the front gate of the city. Yet there had still been other battles to fight, and people to fight them. Ikarans had assaulted the brook hoping to breech the walls by Soot Town and Reyen guards and duellists had defended, even as red-hot blood had fallen from the sky, burning skin and hair and eyes of Reyens and Ikarans alike. Many had died on both sides so that even the ground was stained red now, so they said, and most of those that survived had scars like Petri's.

He'd been nowhere near Red Brook, though at times he thought it had to have been better than where he had been. Most of the survivors had been Ikaran; almost all the Reyens who'd lived had been deserters, and that was where he came unstuck. But up here, so close to the border, where families were Ikaran or Reyen almost by accident, maybe he'd get away with the pretence if he kept his mouth shut, kept his accent behind clenched teeth. He'd always thought more than he spoke, but that had changed, along with a lot else. Down on the plains talk was looser, and angrier, and no matter how he told himself to keep quiet, someone would say some bullshit about Eneko, or Bakar, or Kass even, and his once even temper would explode, for all the good that did him. But up here on the edges of the mountains that had so lately been a bone of contention between Reyes and Ikaras, where laws were something you kept to if you felt like it, things were kept closer to the chest. Maybe he'd get away with it.

Until – "Petri? Petri Egimont, is that you?" from behind him.

"Of course it's him, Berrie, you idiot. Petri? Petri!"

They approached on his good side, from a corner where they'd been drunkenly oblivious to his entrance. Now they moved towards him in a flurry of powder and faded silks, hair curled over their shoulders like they were still nobles and ruled Reyes. The whispers about Petri stopped, to be replaced by other words.

"Fucking nobles, *ex*-nobles more like," a man said. "More money than brains, and less use than a custard truss. Came up here because they was too scared to fight for Reyes, and now they're stuck. I'd give 'em coin to bugger off, if I had any."

Berrie didn't hear, or maybe pretended not to – he'd always had a talent for that. He swooped down on Petri like a pigeon after scraps, with Flashy close behind. Petri caught a whiff of fear about their movements. Too sharp, too jerky for these two, who'd raised indolence to an art form. Stuck, the man had said, and it was certain they didn't fit here in this rough inn in the middle of nowhere, with no one of their own imaginary stature. Maybe they'd run out of people to borrow money from.

"Petri, old boy, how the hell are—?"

Petri turned to face him with what passed for a smile on his ruined mouth. Berrie blanched and staggered backwards with a very uncharacteristic word. Flashy waved a handkerchief in front of suddenly white lips and swallowed hard.

Nothing for it now. No hope of escaping without talking, revealing what he was, that these scars were not the scars of a hero but more likely that of a Reyen deserter. He could protest he'd been nowhere near the brook, but he'd tried that down on the plain and no one had believed him. So he cranked the smile up a notch and felt the ropes of scar tissue that ended where bare bone began bend and twist.

"About as well as could be expected," he said. "Under the circumstances."

A hiss of indrawn breath from behind; a startled curse from further off. Petri had tried, but couldn't get rid of the accent that gave away who he was, or rather what he had once been. Rich, noble, privileged. Hated by all the men and women who'd risen up against the king and his favoured few two decades ago. Time changed many things, but not hatred, Petri was beginning to understand. Battle of Red Brook or not — and with this accent it would be quite clear not — he was noble and up here in the mountains things were different. *Very* different.

A glass smashed behind him, and another. Something metal clonged heavily against wood. Flashy keeled over backwards before anyone had even made a move towards him, while Berrie clutched his clinking but skinny money purse to him.

"Them tosspots been up here a while," the voice behind said slowly. "Throwing around their cash like confetti, acting like they was still lord of the manor, giving people all the more reason to hate 'em. Didn't peg you for one of them though, not in that getup. So are you?"

Petri shrugged. "Does it matter?"

"And the Battle of Red Brook?"

Another shrug.

"Here, isn't Petri the name of that bloke in the newspapers? Didn't he poison the prelate?"

With that, a bottle flew end over end and smashed on the unconscious form of Flashy. Something shiny slashed at Petri's good side but he managed to dodge, barely. It wasn't going to stay that easy, not with only half his vision and half his hands working. He whipped around and got his back to a wall – at least he cut off one avenue of attack that way. Berrie screamed like a child as a rugged set of fists slammed into his face.

"Petri," he gasped when he could. "Petri, help me."

Petri grabbed up a bowl of hot soup and flung it in the face of the nearest man. Berrie would have to fight his own battles, because Petri had his hands full with his own.

The evening descended, as it so often did when they saw what was left of his face, heard his voice, into fists and chaos. It was a miracle he wasn't dead already, but while people down on the plains seemed eager for him to bugger off out of their nice village, they drew the line at killing him. He sometimes wished they'd get over their morals and do it.

It looked like he might get that wish here, in mountains known for their scant regard for the finer points of law. This wasn't just bar-room brawling, not just thrown pint pots and brass knuckles and the cracked ribs that seemed to follow him wherever he went across the plains. This was the mountains, and the people in this inn were as hard as the rock underneath them, and had knives and swords and even a clockwork gun or two.

Down on the plains, Petri hadn't fought back. What could he do against men and women burly from farming, and brave from numbers? Not much, except give way, live and loathe himself for doing it. He hadn't fought anyone since he lost the use of his right hand, not drawn a sword he no longer had or thrown a punch with a left hand he was still unsure of using. Now the swords came out, the knives glinted under tables, guns clicked as they were wound and it was fight or die.

He tried to punch the burly man advancing on him with a knife in each hand, but his left hand was too slow, the punch erratic and weak. Someone else's hand grabbed his useless right wrist, squeezed hard enough to make him gasp, then twisted so that Petri ended on his knees with nothing to look forward to but the knives advancing on him. An image flashed in his mind of a hot knife coming for his eye, of a voice telling him he was *weak, Petri Egimont, weaker than bad steel, softer than lead* before the blade had taken his eye.

That voice, that memory, had him lunging forward, trying to break free of the hold on him, trying to escape that knife coming for his face. All it got him was a cracking sound in his wrist and a boot in the back that sent him sprawling, leaving him open to the knife that glittered above him.

Weakness. You are weakness, Petri Egimont.

It was true, and he wanted — more than he wanted his eye back, or his face back, more than he wanted to hold a sword again in a good hand, or to see Kacha just one more time — he wanted that not to be true.

He kicked out, got the man a good one on the knee that staggered him and then Petri was up off the floor, back to the wall, wrestling for one of the knives. A knee to the man's gut and he had one, wobbling in a weak hand, but he had a knife and no compunctions whatsoever about using it. Let them all come, every last one, and he'd show them what was pent up in his head, let them taste it through the knife.

He stabbed forwards with it just as a blow connected with his cheek, leaving him reeling, with a dying man falling off the end of the knife and another ready to kill him.

A sudden silence rippled out from the doorway and the man set on killing him backed away. Petri, unable to see what had caused the cease of fighting, took the opportunity to shove the dead man off the long knife and grip it harder, keeping himself ready in a modified duelling stance. Sod Ruffelo's gentleperson's rules for duelling, now it was kill or die, and with his back to the wall it became suddenly clear in his head – he had no intention of dying, not here, not like this. If he had to, he'd kill every last one in the place before he died.

Slow clicking boots across the flagstone floor from Petri's blindside, a general shuffling backwards and lowering of weapons from the mob, Berrie quietly sobbing somewhere. He turned towards the steps so that his one eye could see and came face to face with the woman whose entrance had caused such a stir.

She was tall, half a hand taller than Petri, with corded muscles showing at cuffs and collar. Her fingers were criss-crossed with old scars, perhaps from the long knife that sat easily at her hip, or the sword, no duellist's blade but solid nonetheless, at the other side. She looked Petri up and down, cocked her head at the mess of his eye and cheek, and never even flinched. Maybe she'd never flinched in her whole life – he'd believe it of that face, with its thin sharp nose and jutting chin, a face like a hatchet ready to split wood, with its own puckered scar that ran from lip through to hairline.

He let out a breath when her glance went to Berrie where he sobbed under a table, one hand to a nose that was leaking blood all over his fine clothes, the other hand clutching his now empty purse.

"Well now," the woman said in a cracked, husky voice like morning crows. "It looks like we've got a problem, doesn't it? These two," one hand lazily indicated the sobbing Berrie and the prostrate Flashy, who appeared to have lost his boots, "are the ones I've come for. I told you to leave them be until I got here and then we could all have a share. That's the deal."

Everyone looked to the lump of a man behind the bar, who still had a large chunk of wood in one hand, which he hastily put away when the woman looked his way with a questioning eyebrow.

Given the man looked like he could bend steel with his teeth, the contrite "Yes, m'm" he came out with was the last thing Petri expected. "Well, not the one with no face, m'm."

The woman looked Petri's way again, and a cold shiver itched across his back at the appraising nature of her gaze, as though assessing the value of everything he wore, and him too. She turned back, dismissing him from her thoughts, and speared the barman with a look.

"Sorry, m'm." His lips twisted and he shuffled his feet like a five-year-old caught stealing sweets before he whacked the gawping potboy next to him into pulling Berrie out from under the table while another propped Flashy up in a chair.

Berrie resisted half-heartedly as they made him face the woman. Whatever she'd been after him for — and given the general lawlessness of the region coupled with Berrie's habit of flashing his money about, it wasn't hard to guess — he wasn't looking a very nice prospect, what with all the blood and tears and torn clothes, not to mention the empty purse.

The woman tutted under her breath and a small shower of coins that had, presumably, recently belonged to Berrie cascaded onto the floor at her feet.

"Better," she said and two men who'd been lurking, unseen by Petri, behind her went to pick up the money while delivering menacing looks to all and sundry. "And don't forget, you and this miserable inn are here under my sufferance. We have an agreement and I expect you to stick to it."

She turned away from the barman and his muttered "Yes, m'm, sorry, m'm," and back to Petri. He gripped the knife and tried to figure his best way out. The door was on his blindside though, and any chance of being subtle had been lost with that eye.

"And who is this wretched little shit?" she asked the crowd.

They fell over themselves to tell her he was Petri Egimont, you know, that bloke what poisoned the prelate, it was in the papers from Reyes.

Her interest perked up. "Really? Isn't he supposed to be dead? Doesn't seem to have worked out so well for him anyway." Then to him, "Is it true? Are you this Petri? A man trained in the duellist's guild, if I recall. Did you poison the prelate?"

He screwed his courage into the knife in his hand, screwed all that pent up rage and fear too. If he failed here, there was nowhere else to go. If he failed here . . . he was sick of failing, sick of being a coward, of people looking at him like a freak. "Maybe," he said and she raised another eyebrow at the accent. "Who the hells are you and why should I care?"

Unexpectedly she laughed at that. "I am what you might call lady of this manor. In a manner of speaking. Valentian, at your service. And why should you care? You look like you need a job, someone to feed you, clothe you. I might be that person. In return, I get a duellist in my pay, someone with a guild education. My lads and lasses," she indicated the men collecting Berrie's money, "they're good boys and girls, and we do well enough in our own small way. But with a duellist to teach them we could be so much more. We could live, rather than merely exist."

"Highwaymen?"

"Oh, not so high class as all that. More sort of free-booters. My boys and girls need feeding is all. We don't take too much, and nothing that'll be much missed. A sheep here, some coin there. A couple of places, like here, we have a little arrangement that keeps these fine upstanding if drunken gentlemen from being dragged to the Shrive, in return for letting us know about likely-looking donors to our cause. We keep our heads down and don't cause enough trouble for the guards to bother with as a rule. Safer that way." She looked him up and down again, and nodded to herself. "You look like shit, your sword hand is useless and your left is weak, but there's something under that layer of crap. I can see by how you hold that knife, the way you stand, that you know what you're about. We'd never get someone guild-trained else, not without kidnap, and how would we manage to kidnap a duellist without the guild coming down on our heads? Now here you are, guild-trained, supposedly dead, and in dire need of a job, and a bath. Barman! Quick as you can, or quicker. Give this man a good meal and as much beer as he wants."

Petri shook his head. "I can't pay."

The calculated smile that answered brought his stomach into his mouth. "Oh, but you will. One way or another. Sit down, unless you have somewhere else to be?"

A bowl of thick beef soup landed on the table next to him, with a plate of hot bread swimming in butter, a pint of foaming ale. His mind was dizzy with hunger and his stomach told him to agree to any damned thing just to eat. His pride tried to say something but his bloody pride had got him into this mess in the first place.

He sat and shovelled in the soup as fast as he could with his left hand before anyone could take it away, only half listening to what she said. His priorities had changed somewhat over the last months. He'd wanted to be free, but not free to starve to death, to be run out of every town and village and inn for the way his face looked, the way his voice sounded. Not free to be hated everywhere.

"So, Petri," she said as he mopped up the last of the soup. "What would you rather? A job with me, or freezing to death out there, if this lot don't kill you first?"

He watched her face, the stillness of it, the intensity – and the seeming honesty in the offer.

"Come with me and they'll never dare touch you," she said as he hesitated. "Teach my lads and lasses how to fight properly. All the soup you can eat, and no one will ever dare lay a hand on you again. Because I bet they have, with that face, haven't they?"

Heat rushed to what was left of his face, shame for it, that he'd let them too, not fought back. "Yes," was all he said.

"Of course they did. I know, you see, because they

used to for the scar on my face — people fear it, I find, fear disfigurement and those that show it, and people attack what they fear. But I found my place, and a use for that fear, how to make it work for me. Maybe you can find your place, a use for their fear of you. You could have a chance to get back at all those pathetic peasants who wouldn't take you in, who ran you out, who hated you, abandoned you. A place among my little band of outcasts."

He stopped shovelling and stared at the soup. Oh, he was going to pay for this, one way or another, as she said. But there was nowhere else, no one else and a chance to get some semblance of a life back, maybe even get his revenge, yes, that was tempting. Eneko was dead, but others weren't. Kass — the word came unbidden, boiled up on the top of a fountain of rage. She'd abandoned him to this, this face, this hand, this fate, of being feared wherever he went, of being tolerated at best, beaten more often. The old Petri had been weak and soft. Maybe the new one could be strong, given half a chance.

He gave Valentian — Scar she said later, call me Scar — a terse nod that seemed all he could manage, and set to the soup again, trying not to think about how he'd fallen so low a bowl of it was the price of his soul.